2/23

DOUBLE EXPOSURE

ALSO BY AVA BARRY

Windhall

DOUBLE EXPOSURE

AVA BARRY

PEGASUS CRIME
NEW YORK LONDON

DOUBLE EXPOSURE

Pegasus Crime is an imprint of
Pegasus Books, Ltd.
148 West 37th Street, 13th Floor
New York, NY 10018

ISBN: 978-1-63936-224-0

10 9 8 7 6 5 4 3 2 1

Printed in the United States of America
Distributed by Simon & Schuster
www.pegasusbooks.com

For Tilda and Huon, with love and admiration.

PROLOGUE

⸺◦⸜⸝◦⸺

Melia leaned back in the bathtub and gazed out the window. She hadn't removed her earrings, and as she sank down into the water, the diamonds glistened. The bathroom afforded one of the best views of the city: pine trees and chaparral clung to the sides of the canyon above Los Feliz, which was violet and gray at this time of day. As evening descended, all the houses along the ridgeline lit up like tiny lanterns. Beyond the canyon lay downtown Los Angeles, with its hopeless spires and blocky silhouettes, a dull cemetery. From this distance, none of it seemed real.

"On days like this, I'm almost glad they're dead." Melia sighed. "Almost."

"Don't joke about that," I murmured.

"Oh, Rainey, you know I'm kidding." Melia turned and gave me a bored smile. "It's nice being alone here with you, that's all. Without distractions. Nobody to bother us. Isn't this nice?"

I rested my head on my knee and studied Melia's profile from across the room. The heat of the bathwater flushed her skin pink, and the contours of the scar on her chest glowed white. It was the only ugly thing about her body, that scar: sometimes it appeared to me like the jagged edge of a puzzle piece, or else a water fissure through sandstone. A line drawn parallel to her clavicle, then split at the middle to form a flagging J, a souvenir of the knife wound that had nearly ended her life. Melia was all long limbs, wide eyes, and slender wrists; the scar was jarring but did nothing to diminish the beauty of her other features.

I had borrowed a robe from Melia's closet, the same one I had been wearing all week. The robe was indigo silk, handprinted in India, and it was so light it felt like I was wearing nothing at all. Melia's mother had bought the robe from a tiny boutique in Iceland years before but had never worn it; the price tag was still on it when Melia offered it to me. I had blanched at the cost.

"I can't wear this," I had said, handing it back. "It's too valuable."

"The color suits your eyes," Melia replied. "Besides, my mother's dead. *Someone* should wear her things."

For the last four years, Slant House had sat empty, waiting—waiting for someone to come along, perhaps, or else simply waiting for Melia to return. For all those years the rooms and hallways had been quiet, protected from dust and intruders by the ministrations of the housekeeper. A small stack of library books sat on the nightstand next to where Melia's mother had once slept—years overdue now, but no one had ever thought to return them. Their laminated covers were swiped clean twice a week, along with the rest of the house. I confess that on one quiet afternoon I had gone through the stack of books, checking their spines and riffling through the pages, looking for flecks of blood.

In rare moments of introspection, when I was alone—or upon passing a mirror and catching my own reflection, feral with reckless beauty, hair pinned upon the crown of my head—I could see what living at Slant House had done to us. We had absconded from society, shrugged off the leaden cloak of collective expectation. The ease with which I had taken to this new life hinted at something about my true nature, some latent, unknown longing for privacy. For comfort.

I was an unlikely candidate for invisibility. I came from a family of performers and artists with household names, and as soon as I was old enough to lift a violin to my chin, I started lessons, began training to perform. I'd been all around the world and couldn't tell you anything about most cities beyond what the airports and hotel lobbies looked like. When I finally quit music, I told myself I was done traveling as well. No more jet lag and unfamiliar radio stations. No more horizons dwindling into two dimensions from an airplane window.

Melia had never wanted to be famous either, and whenever I felt unlucky I had to remind myself of all the things she'd lost. On those quiet evenings when it felt like the sun would never drop from the sky, when I felt hopeless and cornered, I tried to remember how very lucky we were to be there. To be alive.

When I was touring the world's stages, playing violin for one dark audience after another, one critic had written that my performance was wooden, rote—that the mantle of performance had been draped across my shoulders against my will, a fact made evident by the dull glint in my eye. "Spoiled, with little discernible talent," he had gone on. "If her father weren't a famous composer, she would just be any other little girl at home, playing with her dolls." That critic had been castigated by the music community, hunted by my fans and my father's famous friends. His byline disappeared from the newspaper column, and his comments gradually faded away, forgotten. Years later, after I stopped playing and my family fell apart, I still thought of that man and his appraisal of my performance. *From an audience of millions*, I thought, *you were the only one who actually saw me.*

If Melia and I had met all those years ago, I doubt we would have become friends despite common themes. We were each sheltered in our own right. We both came from wealth, old families with all the scandal and weighty lore that accompanies lineage. In the last decade, both of our families had dwindled down to spindly dregs—my mother had disappeared, while Melia's mother had been murdered. I was an only child, while Melia's brother was missing. "Hunted," she sometimes said, with a sadistic gleam in her eye. "But he's very good at hiding."

It was something about Melia that had shocked me at first—her light-hearted jibes about her dead parents and missing brother.

"Gallows humor, darling," she told me. "A survival mechanism."

Something else we had in common: the ability to slip from a room unnoticed, to wear a mask, to fade into the background. It's how a horned lizard survives in a desert prowled by wild dogs. *Lie still, close your eyes, don't breathe. Vanish.*

Melia flicked a spray of water toward me, startling me from my thoughts.

"Don't *do* that, Melia."

"Look at you," she said. "So deep in thought. I never know what you're thinking about. Where do you go?"

"I'm just tired," I said, evading the question. "Nothing to worry about."

"I'm ready to get out," she announced. "Hand me a towel?"

I stood and retrieved a pale blue Turkish peshtemal from a hook on the wall. Melia emerged from the water, dripping, then stepped forward to examine her face in the mirror. She pressed the tips of her fingers to the shadows below her eyes. She hadn't been sleeping well lately, and it showed.

I draped the towel around her shoulders, startling her out of her thoughts.

"You need to rest," I said.

"You know I can't."

"Try."

"If you insist," she said, giving me a faint smile. "Good night, Rainey. See you in the morning."

We had spent the night before in bed together, her body curled tight around mine. Now I was being punished for something, relegated to the spare bedroom (*Jasper's bedroom,* I thought, before pushing it aside). On days when Melia was particularly nasty, I forced myself to remember the eighteen-year-old girl who had been removed from Slant House by police, catatonic with shock and blood loss.

Melia had only been stabbed once (the knife missed her heart by mere centimeters), unlike her mother, whose body was pocked with damage. The key difference in wounds was not only the number, but the depth and the clarity of intention. Abigail had been toyed with, tormented, and by comparison, Melia's resulting scar seemed a small mercy. In another part of the city, in a neighborhood where the houses were closer together, someone might have heard the screams. The police would have been called right away, perhaps; Abigail's life might have been saved.

If Melia still acted like a spoiled child, raging against every injustice, it wasn't entirely her fault: before the murders, the outside world had been kept at bay. Life inside the house was a controlled, safe environment, and the van Aust children were cosseted and protected from anything unpleasant. Los Angeles—all the grit, the murder, the chaos—existed only as a flat image visible from the western-facing windows in the house. Melia had once let a comment slip about her mother's lingering fear of immigrants, of unknown foreign diseases, and though the remark was disguised as idle chatter, it colored everything else I knew about the cold, haughty woman I had only seen in photographs.

I had studied the crime scene photos again and again since moving into Slant House, because there was a ghastly beauty at play. The bodies of Melia's parents were found tucked in amongst Abigail's furs and silk dresses, the designer pieces worth thousands of dollars. Abigail's blond curls flat with blood, her slashed silk robe, the dull eyes. Abigail had not been raped. Nothing, Melia would later verify, had been stolen. And nobody was ever caught for the murders.

———

Melia and I had fallen into the habit of evening discourses after supper, and more often than not, these conversations took place in the bathroom. Melia didn't like to bathe alone; it stemmed from nearly drowning when she was a very young girl. Whenever Melia revealed something that felt too vulnerable, she would laugh, shade her eyes, and quickly change the subject. Sometimes, later, she would claim exaggeration. The small truth in the statement was that Melia didn't like being by herself, not for any stretch of time.

It had been a rough week, and most mornings Melia was too depressed to get out of bed. It fell to me to bring her a bowl of coffee and some toast, then sit at the end of the bed and make sure she sat up to finish every last bite. She was by turns sweet and cajoling, then nasty and impatient. Restless. For what, I could not say. Certain mannerisms or affectations would have been unforgivable on anyone else, anyone with a normal childhood. Each time she spoke to me sharply, though, she would come around later and ask me to comb her hair or read her a chapter from whatever book we were sharing. It wasn't an apology—Melia never apologized—but it was her own way of reaching out.

I could only imagine that our near solitude was jarring for her: for the last four years Melia had been surrounded by people. Many of them remained nameless as far as she was concerned; she had trained herself to see only uniforms, not faces or personalities, all the small identifying features that made a person a person.

"The nurses never lasted long," she explained. "Nobody with any sense works in a rehab clinic for more than six months."

While the routine of our day might have varied, mornings were consistent: a walk in the rambling garden behind Slant House, now in a state of lush neglect. Melia had dismissed the caretaker and his wife, who had tended the plants for the last twenty years or so. We would sit at a table overlooking the canyon, and Melia would smoke in silence until the midmorning heat forced us back inside. More often than not we would head straight for the library, sifting through stacks of books, looking for something we hadn't already devoured. No television, no internet, no movies: Melia wanted peace. And so we read.

Melia was not fond of venturing outside Slant House, especially outings that required her to mingle with large crowds of people. She was always concerned that she would be recognized, pointed at, assessed. She wasn't always wrong about this—I had noticed the lingering stares when we were out, no matter how hard Melia worked to blend in. Once, a young woman in a flowing peasant dress and glossy hair had approached.

"Excuse me, aren't you . . . ?"

Even in Los Angeles, where celebrity was graciously ignored or spectated upon from afar, Melia was not left alone. She was too emblematic with her coal-black hair against that pale skin, and each time Melia wore so much as a T-shirt, the jagged scar was on display for anyone to see. Enough time had passed that the specificities of the van Aust family murders had mostly faded away, but thanks to a couple of bad TV movies and a character in a recent crime show that paid homage to Melia herself, the memory of the murders hadn't completely disappeared.

When we were first acquainted, Melia only made trips of necessity: to the lawyer's office, because her lawyer insisted on face-to-face appointments, and occasional trips to the doctor, as mandated by some obscure clause in her parents' will. At first, Melia was obliging about these errands, but as the weeks passed and her inheritance and the future of the family estate lay suspended, she grew restless.

"They're trying to cheat me out of everything," she would rant, returning from a visit to the lawyer. "That philistine had the nerve to bring up Jasper! I'll find a new lawyer, see if I don't!"

And then there would be half-hearted forays into the world of Guaranteed Win litigation, with calls to the types of attorneys featured on billboards and bus stop bench signs. In the end, nothing changed: Paul Karnak did not represent Melia, but rather the van Aust family, both present and past, all six hundred years of it. Melia couldn't undo staggering familial wealth and history with a tantrum. Each obstacle served to underscore one sad, simple truth, which was that she had never learned to take care of herself. Her future was dependent upon the whims of the people around her.

Trying to get Melia to see reason was futile, I had learned long before. She could be stubborn, bullishly so, even when it was to her detriment. My job had evolved over the course of our time together: occasional therapist and sounding board, abiding confidante, occasional enabler of bad behavior. At times like this I was glad no one else was around to see how we interacted, because I wouldn't have been able to justify it. My relationship with Melia was entirely contextual, and no outside influence interfered.

In most of our conversations, the unspoken name was the central theme: Jasper. He entered all our daily interactions, regardless of how we might attempt to evade his presence. Jasper's things still lay around the house, untouched; his room was exactly as it had been on that fateful night four years ago, with the exception of fresh sheets and a new bedspread. Jasper was the reason for Melia's latest sulk—for almost *all* her sulks, really—and one of the main reasons she had withdrawn from the world. He was partially responsible for her sense of isolation and helplessness.

———

After Melia disappeared to her bedroom and I retreated to my own quarters with a book (I was working through the van Aust collection of Theodore Dreiser), I lay back on the covers and listened for footsteps. No noise throughout the house. When I was sure Melia wouldn't pop in and surprise me, I went to Jasper's bookshelf and pulled my phone out from its hiding place.

There weren't many places to hide things in Slant House, owing to its minimalist mid-century design. Melia was given to dangerous moods when she felt she had been betrayed, and I knew that contact with the outside world would constitute treachery. I muted the volume and turned my phone on, waiting for my notifications to load.

Slant House was positioned in just such a way in the canyon that reception wasn't great. Privacy and solitude came at the cost of modern communication, which hadn't been even a remote consideration when the house was built in 1952. There was a chance that Melia could reconsider her desire for solitude and come to find me at any moment. I willed my phone to load faster.

Three notifications as new messages came in. I hadn't had a chance to turn on the phone since the previous morning, and I knew Lola must have started to get worried because she hadn't heard from me.

Lola (3:19 P.M.): Got a list of potential new clients. Meet at the office? Call me.

Lola (7:22 P.M.): Possible Jasper sighting DTLA. Has Melia told you anything else?

Lola: (11:12 A.M.): What the fuck, R. At least send up a smoke signal to prove you're still alive. FFS.

I started to compose a text when I heard a noise from somewhere in the house. It was shortly past nine o'clock. Melia often fell asleep immediately after baths and woke later to wander around the house. Footsteps came padding down the hall, and I turned off my phone, then put it back on Jasper's bookshelf. Slant House adhered to an unusual design: the house might appear spacious and discreet, with plenty of rooms and hidden nooks, but you could hear everything. Secrets were not possible here. The only safe room was Jasper's bedroom, because Melia refused to cross the threshold.

Melia knocked on the door. She popped her head into the room, looking sheepish and rumpled.

"I can't sleep," she said.

I sighed and patted the mattress beside me. Melia shook her head.

"Not here," she said. "I hate this room."

"I thought you wanted to be alone," I countered.

"Changed my mind."

As I followed Melia through the dim house, my thoughts strayed to Lola. Lola was even-keeled and could stay calm even in the face of conflict, but she didn't like to be ignored. I had agreed to keep her informed of everything that happened with Melia, no matter how trite it might seem at the time. Lo and I were a good match because we saw things differently. She had always been good at seeing the big picture, while I was better at getting my hands dirty.

In the last week, though, I had started breaking my promises to Lola. First, her text messages went unanswered or else I deflected her questions with half-truths. *Has Melia told you what happened with her aunt? Any more threatening letters?*

I hid behind the digital smokescreen, texting rather than calling. Lola would have detected a lie in my voice in ten seconds flat. The moment I called her, she would insist that we cancel the whole thing, shut down the operation, and move on.

Do you still feel safe, Rainey?

This was the last of her messages I had responded to, and it had taken a good two hours for me to work up the courage to send the lie to Lola, my best friend, the person I trusted most in the world, someone who knew me better than I knew myself.

Yes.

ONE

⸻⸎⸻

ONE MONTH EARLIER

I pressed my forehead against the bottom of the fish tank and willed the African dwarf frog to move. Last week he had been perfectly fine, swimming around and coming to the surface for air. For the past few days, though, healthy activity had been replaced with lethargy. Guppies, swordtails, and firemouth cichlids glided through the water above, content. I could only focus on the frog.

I gently tapped the glass.

"Come on, Dart," I whispered. "Swim."

"You named him?" Lola appeared beside me and peered into the tank. She wore a bright floral dress she had gotten on her latest family reunion in Mexico. Silver bangles shone against her brown skin. Lo could be irritating and assertive, but she had a knack for distracting me at just the right moment. "Dart?"

"One of my books suggested it," I said, not taking my eyes off the frog. "Supposedly it helps build rapport."

"Rapport!" she exclaimed. "Ladies and gentlemen of the jury, may I present Rainey Hall: onetime violin prodigy, now spends her days caring for sick frogs."

1

I turned to her, anxious. "You really think he's sick?"

"They should do one of those 'Where Are They Now?' features about you," Lola said. "From humble roots to the dizzying heights of fame . . . to frogs."

I poked her arm. "My roots aren't humble."

She picked up a book from a stack next to the aquarium and read the title. "*The Beginner's Guide to Tropical Aquariums.* Oh, Jesus."

"What?" I said, defensive.

"Books, Rainey? When did you have time to get all these?"

"I had a chance to go downtown yesterday," I said. "The Last Bookstore has a great section on aquarium maintenance."

I already knew what Lola was going to say: I was replacing one obsession with another. For the last three weeks, I had spent all my waking hours looking for a missing teenage girl. Every day that passed meant a greater likelihood that she was dead, that I was looking for a corpse. My colleagues had been just as diligent in the pursuit of the girl, but somehow, they always managed to keep a healthy degree of separation between work and their personal lives.

"I'm going to recalibrate the pH," I announced, turning back to the aquarium. "Maybe that'll help."

"Rainey."

"What?"

"Rainey," Lola said again, putting her hands on my shoulders. "I love you, but consider this a reminder to come back to the real world. Forget the fish for a few hours. Do some work."

I opened my mouth to fight with her, but to my surprise, Lola leaned in and gave me a hug.

"Let it go for the moment, Rai," she said. "We've done everything we can to find this girl. Just focus on something else."

Domenica was our first teenage runaway case, which was part of the reason I was having trouble letting her go. Our team was a small operation, and although we had experience with child endangerment, those cases mostly involved violent husbands and unsafe living situations. The bulk of our investigative work was standard PI fare: cheating spouses, insurance claims, unfair dismissals.

Nine times out of ten, the cases were cut-and-dried; the spouses *were* cheating, the bosses *were* corrupt, the injuries *were* exaggerated, and we'd get our man. Sometimes our clients gave us a generous bonus for our hard work and discretion. The aquarium had been an unexpected gift from our last client, whose husband had not only been cheating, but also working for a black-market business that smuggled priceless artifacts out of Mexico and sold them to wealthy private collectors.

After my team discovered the smuggling operation, our client turned her husband in to the police. The aquarium had been an afterthought.

"I don't have any use for the fish," she said. "They'll die if someone doesn't take them."

I claimed the aquarium for my office, and there it had sat for the last week, occupying whatever was left of my attention after trying to find Domenica.

There was a reason why we didn't deal with teenage runaways. We weren't the police, and teenage runaways should be pursued by the proper authorities. Domenica's parents had done everything right, though, and it hadn't helped. Javier and Mercedes were Honduran immigrants who had been professors in their home country before enduring a grueling immigration to Los Angeles. Javier had found work as a truck driver and was gone forty-eight weeks of the year, while Mercedes cleaned houses. Javier had filed a police report as soon as he realized his daughter was missing. The police had taken a cursory look at the text messages that Domenica exchanged with a predatory white rapper in his thirties—Brendan Bole, alias B-Bo—and decided Domenica had disappeared of her own volition and there was nothing more to be done. She was fifteen years old.

"Most teenage runaways come back on day three," the police told Javier, who had taken a leave of absence from work to look for his daughter.

Their case struck a chord with me—on top of the child endangerment issue, I knew what it felt like to have a family member vanish—and I agreed to represent them pro bono. Blake, Lola, and I had all contributed sixty hours a week to finding this girl, and so far, we had turned up nothing. I was almost embarrassed to look at the facts on paper: me, a privileged little shit who had barely finished high school, offering charity to two tenured professors who had five degrees between them and now worked blue-collar jobs to support a family they never had time to see. The irony was not lost on me, not for even a single minute, which is why I had refused to stop looking, even as my business started to slip into the red and we turned down other cases.

The phone rang. Lola went over and picked it up.

"Left City Consultants," she said. Then, after a pause, "Go ahead."

It had been one of Lola's many brilliant ideas to anonymize our business so we were harder to find. A person wouldn't find us online, not under any review site or business listing: we were strictly under the radar. As soon as we changed our name and slipped into the shadows, our business exploded with new clients. "People want cachet, they want something no one else has," Lola pointed out. "A referral-based PI firm is intriguing, to say the least."

I returned to my desk and flipped through my paperwork. It was midsummer in Los Angeles, a time of year when almost everything died; fruit dried up on the branches of trees and farmers abandoned their crops. Native Angelenos like myself found the heat a familiar irritant, nothing more. We retreated to the cool dim interiors of our offices and our cars, then waited to emerge until sundown, when the heat finally began to dissipate. Summertime was when newcomers and visitors fled back to Ohio, Nebraska, North Dakota, or whatever tiny little burb had spat them out.

We had air-conditioning in the office, but it was mostly a nominal feature. A desk fan labored along jerky parabolas and did little to dissipate the heat. Lola had always seemed impervious to the suffocating Los Angeles summers, claiming they were nothing compared to the heat she endured every time she visited her grandparents in Mexico. True to form, she was barely breaking a sweat, while my silk top had been damp since nine that morning. My long hair was tucked up in a bun, but tendrils kept falling down around my face.

I was so lost in my thoughts that I didn't notice Lola standing right in front of me until she snapped her fingers. I jerked to attention.

"Rainey," she said. "Holy shit. You'll *never* guess who just called."

I perked up. "Did we get a tip?"

"It's not about Domenica," she said. "Does the name Melia van Aust mean anything to you?"

Melia van Aust. The name conjured a blurry image, something dark that danced at the edge of my mind and then quickly disappeared.

"It rings a bell. Who is she?"

Lola took out her phone and typed something in. A moment later, she held it up to show me. It was a *Cue* article from four years ago. The main image was a pale young woman with jet-black hair. The girl looked dazed, maybe even drugged, as she leaned on the arm of a policewoman. A car sat in the foreground, surrounded by paparazzi and journalists with notepads and cameras. Behind the girl, a house was set into the hillside, all clean glass and right angles.

I leaned in and examined the photo. "She looks familiar."

"Holy shit." Lola was practically vibrating with excitement. "She's back. She's back in Los Angeles."

I had seen this girl somewhere, but I couldn't remember where.

"I know that house," I said. "I almost feel like I've been there."

"You would have seen hundreds of photographs around the time of the murders." Lola watched my face. "Four years ago. The hills above Los Feliz. Ringing any bells?"

I rubbed my eyes. "I can't remember all the details."

"Stop me when it starts to sound familiar. Weird family—super rich, the dad was a German aristocrat or something. Melia's parents were brutally murdered, and Melia was stabbed too, but the police arrived in time to get her to the hospital."

"Melia was the one who called the cops," I said slowly. "Right? That recording—*Cue LA* broke the story, didn't they?"

"That's right!"

"And wasn't there something about a brother?"

"Jasper," Lola confirmed, looking pleased. "That's exactly right. He was supposed to be at boarding school the night the murders took place, but get this: he had disappeared from school the day before. A lot of people think he killed his parents."

I felt chills go down my arms. "That's right, I do remember this. Shit."

Lola typed something else into her phone, then held it up again. The image of a pale, unsmiling boy with dark hair and wide, unblinking eyes stared out at me. I had seen that type of face before: it was a blank page, an emotionless void.

"Where's Jasper now?"

"The million-dollar question," Lola said. "Gone. Nobody's seen him since the murders. There are a lot of theories about what happened, like maybe Jasper was murdered at the same time as his parents, but that the killer hid the body, or that Jasper killed his parents and disappeared to Mexico, blah-blah-blah."

"What do *you* think happened?"

"Oh, it was definitely the brother. Those eyes are dead."

"You just got off the phone with her?" In spite of everything, I couldn't help feeling excited.

"She wants to hire us, Rainey."

"Did she say why?"

Lola's eyes sparkled. "She has a stalker."

TWO

⸺⸰⸺

Later that afternoon, I sat in my car across the road from Slant House. Willow Glen Lane was a dead-end street lined with weeping willows, and at this time of day, everything drowsed in the heat. The neighborhood was an architectural cross-section representative of the city's crazed whimsy, lacking an adherence to a single palette or style. Slant House sat like a skull against the mountain.

For the most part, the other houses on the street seemed unoccupied, with only a few cars parked along the curb. I noted a vintage Mercedes, two nondescript sedans, and a vintage Alfa Romeo. As I sat there, a white BMW with mud splatters across the hood pulled into the street behind me and parked in front of a neighbor's house.

The house where the van Austs had been murdered was a mid-century modern gem, two stories of wood, glass, and geometric lines. I had wanted to delay the meeting with Melia until I had more time to research the particulars of the case, but Lola had insisted we take the meeting as soon as possible.

"First of all, she could be in real danger," she said. "Second, this is a chance for us to make some real money. We're pretty close to broke, Rai. Wait too long and she might call someone else."

The research I had done in the hours leading up to my meeting with Melia was cursory at best. This part of the job was unpaid, so there was nothing I owed to the client until the case officially began. We also didn't do much research before a case because there was usually nothing to find online yet, and we preferred to hear the client's version of events.

Still, I had read enough online to paint a portrait of what I was getting myself into. I had read old articles and studied the photographs of the inside of Slant House shortly after the murders—the minimalist kitchen with its chrome and pale wood, the spacious living room, and the unfinished jigsaw puzzle: a haunting detail the public had clung to in the aftermath of the crime.

The story behind the construction of Slant House was almost as interesting as the murders that had taken place within. Finished in 1952, Slant House was the final creation of famed architect Tule Windsor, once the darling of all those old movie star types with their dark rooms, hidden bars, and underground tunnels.

Tule (pronounced *too-lee*, like the elk) had slowly succumbed to madness as she designed the house, and she didn't live long enough to see its completion. History has always been unkind to those afflicted with mental illness, particularly women: while men who profit from their neuroses are heralded as geniuses, women are altogether too often dismissed as deranged, erratic, or unhinged.

Today Tule might have been assessed as schizophrenic, a condition certainly unaided by her ritual drug use. I had unearthed images of her during my research: Tule's twisted body on the path leading from the house to her garden; her wide eyes and beatific smile, unchanged in death. Shortly before her death, Tule had written a letter to her sister claiming she had learned the secret to flight. The letter was seized by police and later used by her husband as evidence of madness. "Slant House" was actually the derogatory name her estranged husband had bestowed upon the undertaking. According to all accounts, he had been a bitter man who was upset that his wife was more well-known than he was, and that she stayed out until all hours of the morning with a coterie of famous friends.

The house had been featured in *Architectural Digest*, the *New York Times*, and *Town & Country*. None of the photos indicated a creator's lack of control, at least not to me: I saw raw beauty on display, perhaps even a vulnerability in the open design of the home. It was full of spacious rooms tucked within a geometric frame, each room unfolding into the next like a set of origami pieces.

Left City had helped clients like Melia before. It was almost shamefully easy money: nobody was as paranoid as someone with too much wealth, and ninety percent of these cases solved themselves. Angry voicemails were from ex-husbands who were scared off with legal documents drafted by Lo; missing items were less often stolen by maids than by adult children with drug habits and no day jobs; and *Yes, ma'am, I'm sorry to report that your fiancé is sleeping with his colleague.*

I returned to the image of the jigsaw puzzle on my phone. The puzzle appeared to be of a quiet woodland scene. The edges were completed, but the top half lay unfinished. A story came back to me then, the kind of urban folklore that was always told second- or thirdhand: according to everyone brave enough to set foot on the property and peer through the windows, in the weeks, months, years after the murders, when Slant House lay vacant, the jigsaw puzzle lay exactly as it had on the day of the crime. The house had remained a sort of time capsule of that last, fateful May. Nothing had changed within.

A sharp rap at my window jerked me from my reverie. The woman outside my window had smooth skin and wide, unblinking eyes. A fist of blond curls sat atop her head, and a dewlap hung beneath her chin. Fat smoothed her features and obscured her age—she could have been anywhere from mid twenties to late thirties.

"This is a private street," she said, her voice muted through the window. "You can't park here."

I turned on the engine so I could roll down the window a crack, then frowned. "What do you mean, 'private street'?"

"Do you know what the words *private* and *street* mean?" she snapped. "Move along before I call the police."

"I wasn't questioning the etymology," I replied, keeping my tone even. "You might be interested to know that there *are* a few privately owned streets in Los Angeles, but this isn't one of them. And you can call the police if you think you'd feel more comfortable, but I wouldn't recommend it."

Her sneer expanded to something almost cartoonish. "And why's that?"

"Your son just got out on parole. Isn't that right, Mrs. Flack? I have nothing but respect for our brothers in blue, but I bet Zac could use a break from law enforcement for a while."

It was a cheap shot, but it worked. The woman tried to look brave, but her expression faltered. In addition to researching Melia and the history behind Slant House, my team and I had done a quick bit of internet reconnaissance on the neighbors, both present and former, to see whether Melia's most recent problem might be local. It had taken Blake less than an hour to come across information on Zac Flack—evidently his parents found no fault with a rhyming moniker—erstwhile jailbird.

Almost all the residents of Willow Glen had something they wanted to keep secret, from the trivial to the potentially dangerous. I hadn't planned to use any of the information, but fortune favors the well prepared. Zac had been arrested the first time for petty larceny when he was still a teen, then again on a breaking and entering charge, committed when he was still on parole. His most recent stretch in jail had been a little over three years. The mugshot Blake had shown me was of a sullen young man with dark blond hair and a thin mustache. He was only twenty-two and had been released on good behavior about a month before.

"Who are you?" Janine Flack asked quietly. "Who do you work for?"

"I'm a private investigator," I replied. "And I work for myself."

Cruelty was not a tactic I favored, and I couldn't blame the woman for being on edge: ever since the van Aust family murders—according to multiple articles I had seen online—Willow Glen Lane had become a magnet for true crime fanatics and trophy hunters. Still, self-appointed authority had always been a pet hate of mine, and I didn't want this woman harassing me.

"Look," I said, stepping out of my car. She retreated to the path leading up to her house and watched me with trepidation. "I'm not here for your son. My business doesn't concern you at all, actually."

Janine's head jerked up suddenly to look across the street, and I followed her gaze. The front door of Slant House was open, and a young woman stood on the threshold. Even from this distance I could see it was Melia: I recognized the fine bone structure and long limbs, the blue-black hair. She leaned against the doorway and shaded her eyes with one hand.

"Is that . . ." Janine seemed almost at a loss for words. "Is Melia back? Is that why you're here?"

"I can't say."

"Tell me who you are," she pressed.

"I'm nobody, really," I said. "Have a nice day, Mrs. Flack."

Every time I went to meet a new client, I got nervous. The feeling was oddly similar to how I used to feel when I stepped offstage after a big concert. A common belief around performance anxiety is that it only occurs in the hours preceding a show, but that's not true—or at least it wasn't true for me. The only time my anxiety ebbed was when I held the bow to strings, felt the wood thrum against my chin. Nerves before a show came from girding oneself against an onslaught of emotion; they came from the fear of fucking up. After-show nerves were about vulnerability. Once you stepped off that stage, you were immediately vulnerable. It's when everyone came rushing back in. When they told you what they thought.

That's how meeting new clients felt to me, but I would be hard-pressed to explain why. Something about having a stranger crack themselves open and share their dirtiest, most shameful pieces with me put my teeth on edge. I was a good listener, though, and I doubted anyone could tell I was focusing on calming my nerves as they told their stories.

I felt a combination of nerves and excitement as I walked up the path toward Slant House. I couldn't deny being curious about the famous dwelling: as much as I tried to be professional, I was still a true crime junkie, and in terms of Los Angeles murder lore, Slant House was the holy grail.

The foyer was sparse and sunlit, but it felt like it had been cleaned recently. Light filtered through the windows and shone on the parquet floor. All the photos I had seen of the house showed an abundance of such windows, from every angle. No wonder the van Austs hadn't succeeded in their quest for privacy.

Melia leaned against the doorjamb and smiled. She wore black silk pants and an oversized white T-shirt. On her feet were understated leather loafers that probably cost at least three thousand dollars. Her black hair was pinned in a messy knot at the back of her head, and as she moved toward me, I saw the top of her scar peeking out of her shirt. I blushed when I realized I was looking at it, but Melia didn't seem to notice.

"Rainey," she said, extending her hand for a shake. "I'm Melia."

Her grip was surprisingly strong, but just as cold as I had imagined. There was something chilling about her, beautiful and crooked, something you didn't seek but couldn't help noticing. She wasn't wearing makeup, but her skin glowed anyway, milky white and almost translucent. A pale flush of violet lingered under her eyes, and I wondered if she ever ventured outdoors, exposed her skin to sunlight. I was stunned by her unexpected beauty. None of the photos I had seen had done her justice, or at least, they hadn't revealed enough to make a proper evaluation. It was startling to find myself face-to-face with her, now.

"I see you met Janine," Melia went on, rolling her eyes. "She's appointed herself guardian of the neighborhood. Did she tell you why she's home in the middle of the day? She got laid off a few months ago."

"It's a tough economy," I said.

"I wouldn't know. Everyone in Los Angeles reeks of desperation to me anyway."

I refrained from commenting, but the remark stunned me. All the stories I had read indicated that Melia's had been a sheltered existence, but her dismissive comment belied a casual narcissism. *Think of where she's been*, I reminded myself.

"Well, come on, then," Melia called behind her.

She moved gracefully through the house, at one point shucking her loafers and then stretching her arms above her head. Seeing her walk barefoot through her house felt strangely intimate.

As I followed Melia into the living room, I noticed the way the light filtered through the windows, illuminating the wooden floorboards and walls in a way that made them seem to glow from within. There was a smell I couldn't quite place. I appraised my surroundings, trying to match the room to the images I had seen of Slant House. Melia was watching me.

"I put the puzzle away," she said.

"Sorry?"

"Don't worry, I've read all the stories about my family. Ninety percent bullshit. A tragic story sells papers though—or ad space, now, I guess," she said. "Nobody reads physical papers anymore, do they?"

She had stopped walking and stood facing one of the windows that looked out over Los Angeles. Downtown was visible in the distance, little spires that twinkled in the sunlight. The hills beneath Willow Glen Lane rose one behind another, clad in dense foliage and the spindles of pine trees.

Pine-Sol, I realized. The house's strangely familiar smell was cleaning fluids and nonhabitation.

Melia turned back to look at me. "Wasn't always easy to get access to those stories, of course. They wouldn't let us use computers at Aggie unless we were well-behaved. It was so draconian. There were ways to get online, though, if you bribed the right person."

Melia dropped onto a gold velvet couch, and I sat down opposite her. I hadn't expected her to be so talkative, and I was having trouble keeping up with everything. I tucked a strand of hair behind my ear and parsed together what she had said: *stories, jigsaw, Aggie*.

"Um," I said, trying to get my bearings. "Sorry—what's Aggie?"

She laughed then, and the sound was so innocent and charming that I almost laughed too.

"I'm sorry," she said. "I'm so nervous, you can probably tell. I've only been back a week, and already someone wants me dead. You wouldn't *believe* the horrible letter I got yesterday evening . . . I keep waiting for you to tell me the whole thing is my fault."

I saw a flash of something in Melia's face—it was vulnerability, but not the angry, shameful kind I tended to see in clients. People who hired Left City often seemed like they were drowning, and I was the only life raft for miles of open water. In Melia, I saw something else. It looked more like an invitation to communion. *She wants me to like her*, I thought.

"You don't need to be nervous," I said, giving her a smile. "Really. We don't judge or make assumptions about fault. I'm here to help."

She took a deep breath and released it. I watched some of the tension disappear from her shoulders. "Thank you."

"That's okay," I said. "Really."

"I'm glad you're here," she said. "I spent all morning calling around, trying to find an agency who would take my case. I called Eclipse, and they said no—then I tried QT Investigators, and there's a week-long wait, which doesn't work. Slewfoot wasn't taking on new clients, and the Agency said they'd have to do a background check—on me! Unbelievable."

I ran a hand through my hair and nodded. I was familiar with those firms and all their various practices and sometimes unsavory ways of handling clients.

"How did you find Left City?"

Melia raised an eyebrow. "You were a dark horse," she said. "Unlisted. I liked that. Referral only—is that right?"

I smiled. "That was my colleague's idea. It's not always the case anymore, but for the most part, referral only."

"I called Double Check, and when they explained how you operated—all women, no background checks—I decided to give you a call."

"And who did you talk to there?"

"Howie."

"Ah." The small PI world of Los Angeles. Although there was a healthy degree of competition and sometimes outright nastiness between agencies, common practice—and common decency—was to refer cases on if a particular client didn't suit one agency. Howie and I weren't friends—if anything, he was a distant acquaintance—but it made sense that he would refer Melia to us.

"Let's get back to your case," I said, taking out a small notepad and pen. I had tried to take notes on my phone before, but I always reverted to analog. "You mentioned something called Aggie?"

"Right. St. Agnes. It's the . . . well, it's where I went to rehab."

I paused, giving myself a moment to compose a neutral expression. *Rehab.* Another piece of the puzzle. It wasn't the first time I had been surprised to learn that a client had been to rehab, but I had learned to hide my surprise.

"Go on, then," Melia said, poking my arm. "Pretend to be shocked. *You? Rehab? Why, I never!*"

I felt myself blush. "I've been doing this long enough that not many things surprise me."

"I dallied with drugs when I was at school, but that wasn't the main problem." She looked bored, as though reciting a catalog of rote misdeeds. "*Melia's real problem is her inability or unwillingness to engage in a normal human relationship.* Or so the psychiatrist said when they had me tested."

"Verbatim? You memorized it?"

15

"Of course I did." Melia picked at her nails. "I broke into my doctor's office at Aggie and read it the first chance I got. It went on and on about how I can't get close to someone unless I'm the one in control."

I set my pen and notepad aside. Melia looked exhausted, and sad, maybe, too.

"It doesn't sound like you've had a lot of control over your life," I offered.

She bent over her fingernails again, a strand of dark hair slicing across her face. I was struck once again by how vulnerable she looked. I'd never had trouble finding common ground with most of my clients—if anything, I felt it more difficult to maintain a sense of distance. It struck me now how similar my own story was to Melia's, if only in a superficial sense.

"I know how that feels," I went on. "My family had a lot of expectations of me as well."

She looked up and gave me a small smile. "*You've* never been to rehab though—have you? You don't seem the type."

"I don't think there is a type." I could almost hear the clink of bottles tumbling into my recycling bin on a Tuesday morning, the one weekday morning when everyone was out of the house, when I could hide my misadventures and keep my mask firmly in place. That wasn't a part of my life I was going to share with Melia though.

"I have to say I'm surprised it's still secret," I said. "You've been under some form of media scrutiny for a very long time, yet I didn't come across your rehab stint in my research."

"I have a very expensive lawyer," Melia said, folding her feet up underneath her. "Mummy Dearest used to rely on him to hush up all the scandals."

I paused, wondering if I should enquire further. Melia's thoughts seemed to scatter like sparrows with each new line of inquiry, so I decided to hold off for the moment.

"Lawyer's name?"

"Paul Karnak." She said the name with distaste.

I glanced up. "You're not a fan."

She scoffed. "He's been with the family for as long as I can remember. Doesn't mean we have a relationship though."

I was about to respond when she cut me off.

"Karnak is your typical old white dude who thinks women under the age of thirty-five still need chaperones, and anyone unmarried above that age is of retirement age, should be shuffled offstage, and quietly shot."

"Wow."

"Yes. The man still treats me like a child, even though I'm technically head of the family now." She crouched at the edge of her seat. "You know he won't even agree to see me? Since I've been back, it's all kinds of phone tag—leave-a-message and see-you-later."

"Has it always been like that?"

She leaned back and thought. "He was polite to me when my parents were alive," she said.

"So when was the last time you actually saw him?"

"Well, now, let's think. I didn't have a lot of cause to see him when my family was still alive—he's one of those lawyers who runs everything behind the scenes, so you don't meet up unless things are real bad. I saw him once or twice before I got shipped off to Georgia. Other than that, I've probably only met the man once or twice in my life. Probably wouldn't even recognize me to say hello on the street if my pictures weren't already everywhere."

It pained and angered me to hear what Melia had to say about her situation. The world would have been shocked to know she was so helpless, while at the same time the sole beneficiary for such a vast fortune. I picked up my notepad again and scratched away at it, writing quick notes that I would refer to later with my team.

"You look pissed off," Melia noted.

"Yeah. Well, I guess it's not my fight, right? Your lawyer sounds like a prick."

Melia looked delighted and surprised. "He is. Thank you for saying that."

"I won't patronize you by asking if you've tried to fire him yet."

Melia gave one sharp laugh. "Oh, honey. I have threatened to fire that man using just about every bad word you can think of. Unfortunately, until I gain control of my own estate, it's sort of a legal quagmire. I can't fire him. My parents appointed him, and until I take the helm, I'm stuck with him."

I played with my pen for a moment, mulling this over. "I'll talk to Lola," I said. "My colleague. She's our legal expert—she might have some thoughts. Do you mind if I ask you a bit more about rehab?"

"Go ahead." Her face had gone distant, blank.

"Whose idea was rehab? This was after your parents . . . after your parents died."

"That's right. I have Karnak to thank for the rehab—he petitioned a judge to have me sent away for emotional distress and drug counseling. Claimed it was for my own good. That's what every woman needs—a man looking out for her interests."

I wrote all this down.

"How long were you there?"

"Three months the first time," she said. "Then six, when that didn't work."

"Six months!" I exclaimed. "Is that normal?"

"Probably not." Melia gave me a rueful smile. "I did try to kill myself once I was there though. The nuns didn't like that."

I looked up. "Melia, I'm sorry," I said. "I'm sorry to hear that."

"That was years ago. I'm fine now."

"Where was this rehab?"

"Outside Savannah." Melia's face had gone distant. "I went three times in four years. I had frequent-flier status."

Three times in four years. I tried to mask my surprise at the number. "So in and out a few times," I said, trying to stay casual. "When you weren't at rehab, where were you?"

"I lived with my Aunt Belinda," Melia said, adopting an exaggerated Southern accent. "My god, the stories I could tell. She's a dipsomaniac with misanthropic tendencies. I swear to god, when I was a kid, she drove over someone in her car and complained about spilling her drink."

I coughed back a laugh. "Were you close?"

"I can't stand the bitch."

"Then . . . why live with her?"

Melia toyed with a strand of her hair and seemed to consider something. "I know what people think of me," she said. "That I'm a sheltered little shit who doesn't know a thing about the real world. Hate to tell you, Rainey, but it's partly true. I've tried my hand at day jobs—I worked at a pharmacy in Savannah for a little while, but one of the clerks tried to feel me up, and I stabbed him with a ballpoint pen. Living with my aunt was easier."

I frowned, trying to connect the dots. Something was missing.

"I don't mean to be crass, but didn't you inherit a lot of money when your parents died?"

She gave me a catlike smile. "You're good," she said. "You get right to the crux of the issue. That's the other reason I lived with Belinda—until I turn twenty-five, she controls everything. *E-ver-y* dime."

"Is she the executor of the estate?"

"Wow," Melia said. "How'd you know that?"

"I've had other clients with similar issues," I said. "So you had to go to your aunt every time you wanted money?"

"That's right."

There was a moment of silence, filled only with the sound of my pen on the paper.

"And you don't get along with her," I said, looking up.

"She blacks out drunk almost every night," Melia said. "Screams at the staff, goes around breaking things in a drunken rage, then sobers up and blames other people for the mess. *Bitch*," she added softly. "She ran out of her own money long ago, I might add. I don't have access to the paperwork for my trust since she controls it, but I can guaran-goddamn-tee that she's been skimming off the top."

I stared at her. "Is that—is that something you'd like us to look into? I can have a word with my colleagues."

She looked surprised. "Could you?"

"I'll talk to Lola," I said, making a note of it. "One more thing, Melia. Can I ask why you're back in Los Angeles after living in Georgia this whole time?"

Melia looked uncomfortable. I watched her squirm in her seat, then glance around, as if she wanted to make sure nobody was listening.

"I'm twenty-two," she said. "Three years until I get control of my trust and all the money that's coming to me from my inheritance."

"Right."

"But the way things are going—with my aunt and her spending—it might be gone before then. I came back to Los Angeles to petition the courts to give me control of my family estate. I got a doctor's note and everything. Clean bill of health, no drug problems or self-harming."

She looked so sincere that I felt my heart surge for her. There was something very charming about her, about the way she offered up information and then seemed to retreat, shy away from her own admissions.

"Good for you," I said, smiling. "That's really great. I hope you get it."

"Thanks," she said, her face breaking into a tentative smile.

I put the pen and notepad away. "Before we go any further, let's get some official business out of the way."

"Sure."

"Let's start with the letter," I said. "Do you mind if I see it?"

"Of course, sorry," she said, flustered. "I should have shown it to you as soon as you got here."

She hopped up to retrieve the letter from the next room, and I waited for a moment for her return. She came back and held out the slip of paper with shaking hands.

Since I had anticipated the letter, I had brought a pair of latex gloves, which I retrieved from my pocket. I slipped them on and then opened the plastic bag containing the letter. Melia watched as I unfolded it.

imagine imagine me
peeling away
layers of your face
will you bleed like she did?
will you scream?

she did.

I could feel the blood draining out of my face, and when I glanced up at Melia, I could tell the fear on my face was visible. Thick bands of sunlight came streaming in through the windows, but the daylight felt incongruous against this kind of violence. I felt vulnerable, susceptible, and I could only imagine how Melia must be feeling.

"So you see," Melia said softly.

"Sorry," I said, and set the letter down with shaking hands. "I just—*damn*. I wasn't expecting it to be quite so . . ."

"It's fucked," Melia said, her voice quiet.

"Yeah." A cold thrill went down my spine, and I suddenly felt as though I were being watched. "It's very . . . well, it feels very personal. Almost specific. Do you have any idea who might have written it?"

Her face had gone white, and she was having trouble making eye contact with me. Her gaze stayed on the letter.

"I don't . . ." she started, then shook her head. "No. No, I don't."

It seemed like she wasn't being completely honest, but I could also sense she was fragile. It wasn't hard to understand why.

"You don't have to tell me," I said gently. "But you can."

She was quiet for a very long time, still watching the letter. "It looks like my brother's handwriting. Jasper's."

"Oh, wow," I said. "Okay."

She picked at her fingernails so hard that one of them began to bleed. "Shit," she muttered. "I'm sorry. I don't know that Jasper *wrote* it—I mean,

I don't think—I don't know what to think. I haven't seen him in *years*, obviously. I can't—" She stopped talking, then stuck her bleeding finger in her mouth.

"Okay," I said, trying to sound calm. "If this is really from your brother, I think you should contact the police."

"I already did," she said, looking up. "I went into the station and everything. They took my statement, but I could tell they were just trying to get rid of me. It's been four years, Rainey. I don't think my case is a priority for them."

"Did you tell them that it looks like Jasper's handwriting?"

"Of course I did," she snapped, then immediately looked regretful. "I'm sorry. I know you have to ask these questions. It's just . . . the police were dismissive. The detective I spoke to said that if Jasper tried to make contact, I should call them. I don't *want* him to make contact, Rainey. There has to be a reason why he's been hiding for the last four years."

I cleared my throat, then tried to think of a delicate way to phrase my next question. "I'm sorry to ask, but do you think he had anything to do with what happened . . . with your parents' murder?"

She was quiet, studying her hands. "I didn't, not for a long time," she said quietly. "Jas was so sweet when he was young. I didn't think he was capable . . . but then he vanished and stayed in hiding all this time. What innocent person does that?"

"Melia, have you considered staying at a hotel? Just for a few days? You might feel safer . . ."

"No hotels," she said flatly. "Slant House is my home, and I've already been forced to leave it once. Nobody's going to make me leave again."

"Okay." I picked up the letter one more time and analyzed it. I took out my phone and took a photo, then slipped the phone back into my pocket. When I looked up at Melia, I was surprised to see tears running down her face. She looked angry and frightened in equal measure. She hiccuped a sob, then wiped her tears away with an angry brush of her hand. "I hate this," she said in a low voice. "I hate feeling so vulnerable, so helpless—I was starting to get better, Rainey. Back in Georgia, I mean. I really was."

I guided her into the dining room and helped her sit at the table overlooking the canyon.

She swiped at her eyes and looked out the window. "Nobody believes I can live on my own. My aunt called me a goddamn fool for coming back here . . . back to this house, back to Los Angeles . . ."

"Deep breaths," I said, miming inhaling and exhaling.

Melia finally took a few breaths, and it seemed to calm her down a bit.

"This isn't your fault," I said. "You survived one of the most traumatizing experiences anyone can go through—but you did survive. You're still here, Melia."

She nodded. "I'm still here."

Something else occurred to me. "Did this letter come in the mail?"

"No," she said. Her face was pale. She drummed her fingers on the table. "I found it in the foyer."

"Where exactly?"

"It was on the floor." Her face had gone distant again, her eyes dreamy. "Almost to the entrance of the dining room."

"So someone was in the house? Jasper or someone else?"

She sank her face into her hands. "I don't know, I don't know. I've mapped it out in my head, and if they pushed it under the front door hard enough, I guess it could've slid across the hardwood floor . . . I just don't know, Rainey."

"Anyone else have keys to the house?"

She sighed. "Well, the locks were changed after the murder," she said. "The only people who have keys are the Endos. Jas doesn't have keys anymore, obviously; they were changed after he disappeared."

"The Endos?"

"The caretakers," Melia said, rubbing her arm. "They lived in the bachelor quarters out back, behind the pool. They lived here for as long as I can remember, actually. They stayed here, taking care of things while I was in Georgia."

I tapped my notebook. "They don't live here now?"

She tucked a strand of hair behind her ear. "I let them go when I came back," she said. "They didn't do anything wrong, of course. I just needed space to be by myself. I've never been alone, you know. Ever since I was a kid, someone has been standing over my shoulder, watching me."

I paused. "I'm sure this has already occurred to you, but is there any chance that one of the Endos might have written the letter? Were they angry when you let them go?"

"They'd never do that. They're like family."

"Okay." I glanced over what I had written down. "Let's set Jasper aside for a moment. Did you make any friends in Georgia who might have been upset that you were leaving? Someone who might have followed you back here?"

Melia shook her head and bit her thumb, looking embarrassed. "No," she said softly. "No one there gave a shit about me."

"You were there for four years?"

A nod.

"And you didn't make any friends?"

"I made some friends at Aggie, but we didn't keep in touch. I needed a fresh start."

I slipped off the gloves. "Let's get a few other things out of the way," I said. "What do you think Left City can do for you?"

She blinked. "If the police aren't going to look into this, I need to find someone who will," she said. "That's where you come in."

"So you want us to confirm that Jasper wrote the letter?"

She thought for a moment, then nodded. "That's a start."

"Do you have any handwriting samples we could compare?"

Melia looked stumped. "Nothing comes to mind. I think most of his things got thrown away after . . . after."

"That makes it harder," I said, nodding. "We can't exactly ask him for a fingerprint sample. Then again, you could check his room to see if you missed anything. A grocery list—well, not that, specifically, but something a teenage boy would write. A love letter. A poem. I don't know Jasper well enough to speculate what that might be."

Melia shuddered. It was small, barely perceptible, but I noticed the way her shoulders tensed, the way her forearms closed in around her midsection. Like she was protecting herself.

"Can you find out where he is?" Melia asked, her voice cautious. "The police weren't able to, but if I pay you . . ."

"We could certainly try. That's one of the things my agency does."

She mulled this over, then nodded.

"Before we agree to move forward, we need to discuss our agency fees," I said. "If we accept your case, we charge eighty-five an hour. That covers a range of expenses, from the salary of my colleagues to general costs, but it also goes toward future pro bono cases."

Melia was frowning.

"It might seem like a lot, but our agency is highly qualified, and you'll actually end up paying less than you would with a cheaper but less experienced agency."

"What do you mean by *if* you accept my case? I thought I already hired you."

I nodded. "I can understand the confusion. We don't take cases lightly, Melia. If we think something is impossible, for instance, we don't want to waste your time. Or ours."

A thin line had appeared between Melia's eyebrows. I wondered how often people turned her down.

"I need to discuss this with my entire team before we agree to represent you," I said.

"Okay," she said finally. "But let me know as soon as possible, so I can hire someone else if I need to."

"Of course."

Melia studied me. "I looked into you, you know," she said finally. "I watched all your old videos online. At first I thought there must be two of you with the same name, but I can see it now. The resemblance."

"To my younger self?" I smiled.

"Your dad's Charlie Hall," she said, marveling. "I can't believe it. My dad was a huge fan. I can't tell you how many times I had to hear his music blasting through the walls."

I never knew how to respond when people mentioned my father.

"I mean, the music was beautiful," she said quickly. "But pretty fucking dark."

"I tend to agree."

"You were incredible," she went on. "Do you still play the violin?"

"Thank you, but no. I don't. I gave it up a long time ago."

The videos Melia referred to were undoubtedly the performances I had done from ages eight to fifteen, first as a gawky young girl holding an instrument that was almost too big for her small hands and then ultimately a fearsome virtuoso. I didn't mind admitting that the girl in those videos was some kind of genius, because I had no more claim to her. That girl was a stranger to me, which was part of the reason I stopped playing. There were nights when I would come home after a concert and not recognize myself in a mirror. It may have sounded cliché, but it was absolutely true, no hyperbole necessary. I hadn't touched a violin since I was fifteen.

"I don't understand how you could give something like that up," Melia remarked. "Why become a PI?"

"It's complicated and boring at the same time."

Melia leaned over and reached out to touch my hair. "You're so pretty," she said. "I didn't expect you to be *pretty*."

I laughed. "Now I'm uncomfortable."

"Look, I've never hired a PI before, but I thought they were all men in slouchy suits with alimony payments and glamorous addiction problems."

"I see you're caught up on Raymond Chandler," I said. "Yeah, no. The reality is a lot more mundane—lots and lots of paperwork. And, sure, it's a male-dominated industry, but there are a lot of incredible female investigators."

"Yeah, I picked that up real quick. Spent all day on the phone trying to hire one of them."

I hesitated before responding. "Look, I have to ask one more time. Are you sure it's a good idea to live here again? This house must be worth a fortune, given its location. Have you thought about selling it and starting over somewhere new?"

Melia nodded. "Sure, I thought about it. I spoke to my lawyer as well, and he said that given the dark history, it would probably sell at a loss. I don't have a job or any immediate plans, and the thought of selling the house and starting over is just way too fucking stressful."

"Fair enough." I tapped my notepad, thinking. There was a delicate question, one I was almost afraid to ask.

"Is this the first time Jasper has tried to contact you?"

She looked confused. "What do you mean?"

"It's been four years," I said. "I know that you were at . . . well, that you went to rehab, and maybe you were more protected there, but Jasper has to know where your aunt's house is—right?"

"Yes—and?"

"He never tried to contact you in all that time?"

"No, never." A thin line appeared between Melia's eyebrows. "What are you suggesting?"

"Do you think there's a reason why he waited? Why he's reaching out now?"

There was a long silence as Melia contemplated my words, and I could see by the look of fear and understanding that she had arrived at the same conclusion I had been afraid to mention.

"There's only one possible explanation," Melia said, visibly shaken. "It's the first time I've been alone in four years."

THREE

After I left Slant House, I headed back toward the office in Culver City, turning off the radio to coast in silence. I pulled up to a stoplight and glanced in my rearview mirror. A white BMW sedan sat behind me. I studied the car for a moment, glanced at the spatters of mud across the hood, and realized it was the same car that had been sitting down the street from Melia's house. I'd picked up certain skills and instincts by spending all my time studying people and tracking them, and one of them was clocking every car within a five-hundred-foot radius when I went to visit clients.

Still, sometimes things were a matter of coincidence. I cruised through the intersection and took a side street through a suburban neighborhood. The BMW slowed down but continued to follow me. Curiouser and curiouser. Someone affiliated with Melia? Press, perhaps?

I hooked a right at the green light and continued down Franklin Avenue, merging into the steady stream of afternoon traffic. The BMW was now a few cars behind me, but I heard an engine rev, then saw the white car speed up and dodge between lanes, pulling up behind me. Sunlight glanced off the windshield, making it impossible to see the driver.

Relax, I told myself. *You're being paranoid.*

I had been followed away from clients' houses before, which is why the BMW made me uneasy. The ugly side of PI work included digging through sometimes literal garbage, turning over stones, and looking for bodies.

I had been harassed, stalked, name-called, and threatened more times than I cared to admit. Once, an angry ex-wife had surprised me behind my house and attacked me with a broken vodka bottle she had found in my neighbor's recycling.

That was the early days of Left City. The incident left me with a three-inch scar on my left arm, a heightened sense of paranoia, and a much stronger sense of what it took to protect myself. I moved from my house into an apartment building, and once my stitches had healed, paid for self-defense training for me and my team.

There was nothing to indicate that the driver of the BMW was following me, but I was still on high alert. Melia wasn't even my client yet, so I wasn't exactly in danger from a connection with her; but the contents of the letter and the details of the van Aust murders, still fresh in my mind, made me extra wary. As unlikely as it was, the thought crossed my mind that whoever had written the letter to Melia might now be following me. Just to be safe, I deviated from my plan to head to the office and instead headed toward Hollywood.

The four or five blocks that comprise the epicenter of Hollywood are a morass of advertisements, hot pavement, homeless encampments, anonymous office buildings with graffiti slung across their faces, and overpriced parking lots. Weekday afternoons in Hollywood belong to patchy mascots and drunk Charlie Chaplin impersonators trawling for autographs. Everywhere you look, there are confused tourists who come to Los Angeles expecting to see the film industry of yesteryear—the sweeping pepper trees, quaint studios, and beaming doyennes kneeling to press their hands into fresh cement outside Grauman's Chinese Theatre. Modern Hollywood is hell, and driving through it is a chore I avoid at all costs.

Still, the neighborhood had its use as a veritable rabbit warren of one-way streets and dead ends that could disorient all but the most seasoned of Los Angeles drivers. I drove down Sunset, passing the Fonda Theatre and the Pantages, then entered the thicket of Hollywood Stars and the clusters of tourists posing next to them. Glancing both ways, I zipped down a side street and then immediately cut left, heading down a street parallel to Sunset. The street behind me was clear: no sign of the BMW.

I cruised through the lower level of a parking structure and breathed a sigh of relief, reassuring myself that I had just been paranoid about the car. As soon as I emerged back into the sunlight, however, the BMW swooped up behind me.

"Shit!"

I pulled over in front of a drugstore and watched as the BMW pulled over half a block behind me. It was the middle of the afternoon, and we were surrounded by people, so I wasn't worried about being attacked. The driver wore a baseball hat with the brim pulled down low; I couldn't even tell if it was a man or a woman.

I took out my phone and called the office.

"Left City Consultants," came Blake's laconic drawl. Blake was our IT specialist, the third part of our team.

"It's Rainey," I told Blake. "I just left Los Feliz, and I'm being followed."

"Gotcha. Need me to call in reinforcements?"

"Not yet. Can you get me an ID on a plate?"

"Fire away."

The BMW had stalled half a street back, but I could still make out the license plate. I read it off to Blake.

"Stand by, sugar tits."

"Blake, come on. This is serious."

"Relax, relax."

Looking up someone's license plate in California was alarmingly easy. There were plenty of websites any moron could use, but I liked to have Blake do all my research because she rarely made mistakes. It was comforting to hear her voice on the other end while I watched the car stall behind me.

"Shit," Blake muttered.

"What is it?" I asked, alarmed.

"Where are you?"

"In Hollywood," I replied. "By the Walk of Fame."

"So you're surrounded by people?"

"Blake, you're freaking me out."

"It's Calvin," she said. "The car is registered to Calvin."

My stomach clenched, and I gripped the steering wheel. "I thought he was still in Montana."

"Sorry, Rai. Want me to call the police?"

I thought for a moment. "No," I said. "I think I can lose him."

"Keep me posted."

I put my phone away and glanced up at Calvin's car again. It was a different car than the last one I had seen him driving, which is why my senses hadn't been on high alert. Seeing Calvin in any capacity was bad, but knowing he had followed me from Melia's place was much worse. If he knew I had spoken to Melia, then my personal and professional lives were about to collide in a big way.

Most of the last year had been consumed in one Calvin-filled nightmare. For the last month, though, I hadn't seen him, and when Blake did a little digging online, we found that Calvin was working on a dude ranch in Montana, ostensibly doing some soul-searching. Now, apparently, he was back.

Calvin represented the biggest lapse in judgment of my professional career, and probably the biggest misstep in my personal life as well. I knew he was bad news long before we got involved because Calvin's family had hired me to dig up information on him. They were suing him for fraud and embezzlement—his own family. And somehow, even after I had gone through his figurative (and sometimes literal) garbage, I wound up falling for his bullshit.

I might not have gotten involved with Calvin if my own personal life hadn't been a mess, if my family had been anything like normal, if I wasn't at a point in my career where I was questioning my trajectory. The day before Calvin and I first spent time together, I ran into an old ex, the only person in my life who had been really, really good to me. I had broken up with her in a very bad way because I'm a shitty person, and right before I saw Calvin at a party in Santa Monica, I saw my ex with her new girlfriend. Running into her forced me to remember a very dark time in my life—a time I still wanted to punish myself for. When Calvin tapped my shoulder and I turned around to see his shit-eating grin, he seemed like just the right punishment.

"Hey, I know you," he said. "I caught you going through my trash once."

"For a con artist, your trash is pretty boring," I said, turning away.

"Hey, hey," he said. "I appreciate everything you did, really. It might sound like a line, but at the end of the day, I still care about my family. I'm glad they had you to look out for them."

"Right." I tried to walk away.

"Wait," he said. "Can I buy you a drink?"

"I don't drink."

"Can I buy you an ice cream?"

I surprised myself by saying yes, maybe in part because nobody had ever given me that line before. Maybe also in part because his sister, who had hired me, had never been nice to me, not even as I was doing her dirty work. We sat and talked for three hours. Calvin was a good listener—a really good listener. I ended up telling him about Emily, and about running into her the day before.

"Was she the first person you fell in love with?"

"She's the only person I've ever loved," I said. "In that way, I mean. I haven't gotten serious with anyone since then."

"You're telling me you haven't put yourself out there since *high school*?" He gave me wide eyes and shook his head. "Stop beating yourself up, Rainey. Everyone's shitty in high school."

"I bet you were *really* shitty."

"I was," he said, then leaned in and kissed me.

That I was able to ignore all the evidence and talk myself into feeling safe with Calvin speaks to how good of a con artist he really was. He would give me shoulder massages and make me food, listen to me talk about my day. We saw each other every night for two weeks straight, and the only reason we didn't sleep together is evidence that a very small, insistent part of my brain was screaming, *This is dumb, this is so fucking dumb, stop this.* Almost every day he would call his mom and check in on her. I couldn't hide my shock at these daily phone calls.

"Aren't they suing you?" I asked. "Do you think it's a good idea to keep talking to them?"

"It's not *them*, it's just my mom," he said. "She's trying to patch things up with the rest of the family. My mom's the only one who believes I didn't gamble away the money. I really was just trying to invest it so I could help them out with their retirement fund."

I hadn't spoken to my dad in over a month, but neither one of us had come out and acknowledged the rift. I was hardly one, therefore, to lecture someone on a healthy relationship with parents.

"That sounds sweet," I tried.

"The only way you can make money from an investment is to take a risk," he said. "I guess I've always been lucky in the past."

A month passed, then two. For that entire time I was able to set aside my reservations and sink into the private world that Calvin and I built together. As long as we weren't fucking, I could convince myself that I hadn't lost all my professional credibility, even as I began to sleep at his house more than I slept at my own. Then one afternoon, I ran into Calvin's sister, Lacey, at Trader Joe's. I would have ducked and hid down another aisle, but it was too late; we had already made eye contact.

"Hi, Lacey," I said. "How have you been?"

She sneered. "I'm surprised you have the nerve to ask."

"I'm sorry . . . ?"

"Doesn't it violate some ethics code? It should be illegal, actually, but you'd probably know more about that than I do."

"I'm lost."

"Calvin," she said. "You're involved with Calvin."

"Yes," I said, looking at my feet. "I am. I can understand why that would make you angry."

"He *bankrupted my parents*," she hissed. "They'll never be able to retire now. Why on earth are you sleeping with him?"

People nearby were staring.

"We're not," I whispered, knowing she wouldn't believe me, knowing my protestations were almost entirely beside the point; she was still right about me.

"Sure, sweetheart."

"He's trying to make things right," I said.

She barked a laugh.

"Talk to your mom," I said desperately. "They speak every day. She knows that he's doing better."

She gave me such a look of pity that I finally realized what was going on.

"Oh my god," I whispered.

"I'm going to do you a favor," she said. "Lord knows why. Get out, Rainey. Before he gets your bank details."

The fake phone calls to Calvin's mom should have been incentive enough for me to end things, but they weren't. I was so goddamned lonely that every time Calvin looked at me, every time he wrapped his arms around me and said, "It's okay, baby, it's okay," that small human gesture was enough to pull me back in. If Calvin was broken, then so was I, and it was nice to be with someone who didn't judge me for being a damaged thing.

And then one day I showed up at my office and found Blake and Lola waiting for me. They told me Calvin had put a private investigator on both of them. He knew where they lived, who they saw, how much time they spent at the office. It hadn't occurred to him that Blake would discover the betrayal almost instantly—or that Lola would lead the private eye on a wild-goose chase and send him home with pages of erroneous reports.

Blake and Lola didn't force me to choose, for which I was grateful. Laying out the facts was enough to shake me loose. I ended things with Calvin the next day.

Calvin was someone I had allowed myself to forget, not out of naïveté but more sheer exhaustion. For five out of the last six months I had triple-checked the locks on my house before I went anywhere, because on three separate occasions, I had come home to find Calvin waiting for me.

"Please just let me explain," he would beg.

But there was nothing to explain. I couldn't even take on a new client without fearing that Calvin would interfere. I had broken it off as nicely as possible but was still punished for my lapse of judgment. His stalking, calls from blocked numbers, and weird emails from fake accounts persisted. Sometimes the emails were mild (Calvin would pretend to represent my credit card company, saying that after some suspicious activity on my account, they were recommending I cancel my cards), but other times the emails bordered on violent. He'd once written from a fake account claiming to have nude footage of me from the time in my life when I spent every night getting blackout drunk. This email sent me into a panic spiral in a way none of the others had; it was something I had been secretly fearing for ages. This was also the point when I had to admit to Blake and Lola that Calvin was still haunting my life, much to my chagrin. Blake was very chill about the whole thing, and after less than an hour on her computer, revealed that all the damaging emails had come from the same IP address, which was linked to Calvin's address.

I was never tempted to get the police involved. There was a chance that Calvin would make our messy affair public, most likely to his fifty thousand Instagram followers. Irony of ironies, Calvin ran a financial advice website which is where—and here I could only speculate—he sniffed out potential victims. He had cultivated a lot of fans with his images of the "Good

Life," thousands of photos of him paddleboarding in Hawaii, cliff-diving in Tahiti, sampling raw fish on a tiny Japanese island, doing yoga beside his Malibu infinity pool.

Occasionally Calvin would post a "real talk" video in which he discussed some minor problem he was working through, and his fans ate that shit up. He never mentioned the trouble with his family or the impending lawsuit—surprise, surprise—but he had delved into relationship woes in the past. Since his fan base was primarily composed of incels with chin implants, his popularity seemed to surge every time he admitted he had problems with women. That our own unfortunate saga had escaped his page thus far was nothing short of a miracle: if I were ever outed in that way, I knew my business would take a serious hit, which would be nothing compared with the online stalking and ire I would face from tens of thousands of scrawny losers with hentai posters nailed all over their walls.

When the stalking abruptly stopped, I thought Calvin had finally moved on, but now I saw I had been naïve. I turned off my car and opened the door, then got out. No movement from the BMW. I walked quickly toward the car and saw Calvin sitting with his hands on the steering wheel. His eyes went wide as he registered my approach. I was close enough that I could almost open his passenger door, but suddenly he put the car in gear and screeched away from the curb.

"Fuck!" I clenched my fists, adrenaline coursing through my bloodstream. As I walked back toward my car, I forced myself to take deep, calming breaths. Calvin was the last thing I needed today. Leave it to my crazy ex to surface now, right as I was looking to take on a very challenging case.

Focus, Rainey, I thought. *Focus.*

I hadn't decided whether I was going to take Melia on as a client. If my hunch was right and Melia was just the recipient of another creepy stalker letter, there wasn't much I could do for her other than recommend she get new locks and a better security system. A part of me thought it would be easy to bilk her for money, and throwing money at a PI might ease her worries. As much as we could use the income, though, I couldn't stomach the immorality of the thing.

There was something else that lingered at the back of my mind. It was nothing more than a premonition, an odd sense in the pit of my stomach—but those instincts had served me well in the past, and I didn't want to ignore the feeling. I resolved to mention it to Blake and Lola when I saw them at the office.

It was early evening by the time I got back to Culver City. Even though I had watched Calvin drive away from me in Hollywood, I still felt spooked by his unexpected presence. I wanted to make sure he didn't follow me back to the office, so I had spent forty minutes deviating, taking side routes, and sitting in my car until I was really sure he was gone.

After Calvin had left Los Angeles, I moved into a new apartment. I had also insisted that Left City move to a different office, one where he couldn't track us down. Our previous office had been conveniently located in Mid-City, but I found a place for rent in Culver City, and a week after I went to inspect it, we moved in.

In some ways, Calvin's antics had been a blessing, at least insofar as our new office was concerned. The bungalow was one of six near-identical cottages built by a set designer who worked for the Culver Studios. The cottages, which had been built in the 1920s to house studio staff, had fallen into disrepair before being recently snapped up and refurbished by a developer who now leased them to small businesses.

I had always loved Culver City, and it was an ideal place for a film nerd like myself to work. We were within walking distance of the Culver Studios, which was set up in 1918 by Thomas Ince, one of the pioneers of silent cinema. Six years after the studio was founded, Thomas Ince died under mysterious circumstances, and his unsolved death drew so much speculation that in some ways it overshadowed his illustrious career. *King Kong*, the original *A Star Is Born*, and *Citizen Kane* were all filmed there, as was *Gone with the Wind*.

I parked in front of our office bungalow. Before getting out of my car, I glanced around to see if the white BMW was anywhere in sight and was relieved to see it wasn't.

Our office looks like an old-timey sleuthing agency, complete with a wooden door with a frosted half-panel window and black lettering spelling out the name: LEFT CITY CONSULTANTS. Even though we try to keep a low profile, the decoration was my only concession to the true nature of our business. I stepped inside and saw Blake sitting at the front desk, typing away. She looked up and winked.

"Guess you shook Calvin," she said, stretching her arms above her head.

"Yeah, well, he drove away. Coward."

"Want me to find out what he's doing back in the city? I could use a fun distraction."

"Don't waste your time. I've spent too many hours of my life on that loser."

Left City probably wouldn't have existed without Blake. She was a genius with computers and online crowdsourcing for information about cold cases. A few years ago, she used her amateur sleuthing skills to bring down a wealthy religious cult that had been eluding arrest for years. The cult, Kindred Folk, drew lonely rich people into its folds, then brainwashed them into handing over all their worldly possessions. Many of the members who were able to defect were stalked and harassed by the cult, some to the point of suicide.

Blake didn't even have to break the law to bring them down. Kindred Folk was run by a husband-and-wife team, and Blake had gone digging into the husband's past. It turned out he had changed his name, and his former persona was still legally married to three other women. The police were able to bring him in on polygamy charges after Blake published all her findings on *Slate*. The article made a big name for Blake, who had gone by the gender-neutral handle BlakeOwnsYou on the popular web-sleuthing platform Spyber. It also stoked the ire of the predominantly male populace on Spyber, who weren't thrilled to discover that a popular case had been cracked by a young Black woman in a wheelchair. She then found herself the subject of hatred and death and rape threats.

When I heard about the story, I scooped her up to help me and Lola, and our business had been on fire ever since. Blake was the most laid-back person I knew, her philosophical attitude at odds with a twisted sense of humor. She had a mane of loose curls, a spray of freckles across her nose, and large, dark eyes behind round glasses. The bags of Cheetos, Oreos, and Milky Ways were thanks to Blake: she may not have been a typical tech genius, but she had the predilections of one, taste wise.

I came over and leaned against her desk. "Have you talked to Lola today?"

"Yeah, she was here a few hours ago. She said something about Melia van Aust?"

"Yep," I said. "I just met with her."

"That is some psycho shit right there," Blake said with wonder. "I still remember when those murders went down."

"Right," I said, and for some reason, I felt chills go down my arms. I hadn't had time to process what had happened with Melia, especially after being followed by Calvin. I felt unsteady on my legs, exhausted from the adrenaline coursing through my system. I walked over to my desk and collapsed into the chair.

"Whoa, you okay?" Blake looked alarmed.

"It's been a weird day." I rubbed my face and took two deep breaths. "Look, I was hoping to talk to you and Lola together, but I guess I can fill her in later."

"Shoot."

"It's about Melia," I said, leaning against my desk.

Blake's face was impassive as I filled her in on Melia's history—the rehab stints, Aunt Belinda's mismanagement of the inheritance, and the decision to return to Los Angeles. When I mentioned the threatening letter and the potential ties to Jasper, she let out a low whistle.

"That reminds me," I said, taking out my phone. "I took a picture of the letter. I'll text it to you."

Blake opened up her phone as the text came through, and I waited while she studied it.

"You really think Jasper would write her a letter?" she said finally. "After successfully hiding out this whole time and evading the police, you think he'd risk getting caught *now*?"

"I haven't drawn any conclusions yet." I shrugged. "I agree that it seems like a risky move, but either way, she seems scared of him. Let's say the letter came from someone else—I can still understand why Melia would be scared of Jasper."

"Why?" Blake was watching me.

"She thinks he might have had something to do with the murders. Whoever did it had a good knowledge of how the house worked, when the housekeepers would be away . . ."

Blake typed something into her computer.

"What are you doing?"

"Nothing," she said. "I'm just making notes."

I waited while she continued typing, and then she turned back to me.

"What does she want from Left City?"

"She wants us to find Jasper," I said. "And she wants to make sure he stays away from her, and from Slant House."

Blake nodded. "Let's talk about it when Lo's here."

"I was hoping you could do me a favor in the meantime," I continued.

"Hit me."

"Dig around a little online," I said, then consulted the quick notes I had taken in my meeting with Melia. "Her rehab place was called St. Agnes, just outside Savannah."

Blake started typing.

"Also, I don't know how much you can find on the aunt, but Melia plans to petition the courts for control of her own estate. Belinda Harris, that's her name. She's the executor of the estate and has access to all the money, so she can dole out small amounts to Melia at various intervals."

I went over to the fish tank and knelt to look at Dart. He glanced at me, then scuttled off toward the other side of the tank.

"Do you know anything about frogs?"

Blake laughed. "Man, not at all. I don't trust myself around anything requiring that kind of maintenance and attention."

"I'm starting to feel inadequate myself."

Blake gave me a look. "Lola said you're replacing one obsession with another."

"Speaking of, have you found anything on Domenica?" I dreaded the answer.

Blake shook her head. "It's fucked," she said. "Pedophiles are scum, man."

"Yeah." I cleared my throat and looked away, hoping she wouldn't see the despair that I felt.

"I hacked into Domenica's email accounts and checked the location data, but she hasn't logged into any of them."

"Thanks, Blake."

I had barely made it back to my desk before the front door banged open. Lola stood there, grinning.

"Guess what," she said. She looked winded, as though she had run to the office. I hadn't had the chance to catch up with her since the morning.

"What?"

"I've got good news," she said. "Go on, guess!"

Blake and I exchanged a glance.

"You taught yourself how to juggle," I suggested. Lola picked up random hobbies every other week, and last month she mentioned she had found some juggling videos online that promised instant results.

41

"What?" she looked confused. "Oh, no. Definitely not. Gave that up ages ago."

"So . . ." Blake prompted.

"Just tell us, Lo."

"I got her," Lola said, giving us a radiant smile. "I found out where Domenica Avila is."

FOUR

—◦◦◦◦◦—

Lola looked triumphant, but her words didn't land with me straightaway. We had already had so many false leads, near misses, and dashed hopes.

"How?" I asked finally. "What makes you so sure this time?"

"Let's go," Lola said. "I'll explain in the car. I want to get there before this creep has the chance to vanish."

"Wait—what's the plan? Where are they?"

"Brendan's in Benedict Canyon. I have the address and everything. We'll get there and suss the place out, and if we're sure Bole's there, you can call Maya."

Without waiting another minute, I grabbed my things and followed Lola out to her car.

Private investigators had a limited range of powers; for the most part, they did exactly what the name suggested. Take notes, track, observe from a distance. My team and I specialized in drawing together a narrative where other people might've seen only disconnected pieces. We couldn't, however, arrest people, and as any good PI would, we had connections with the police department. The LAPD was sprawling and convoluted, so it wasn't as if every cop in the system would recognize me. But I didn't need every cop: I had Maya Pearce.

Maya was a twenty-year veteran detective who had more solves than many of her male colleagues. She was a strong Black woman—two minorities in law enforcement—who wasn't intimidated by her male colleagues or the rampant misogyny and racism within her department. She specialized in missing persons, particularly kidnapped children. I had met her a few years before, when my family had its own crisis, and while the police never found anything, Maya and I had stayed in touch. I had been a kid back then, and although Maya was tough, she also had a maternal side.

Even though the LAPD had declined to pursue Domenica's case, we had one small thing working in our favor. Brendan Bole had been wanted for questioning in connection to a child pornography case they had investigated the previous year, but when they tried to bring him in, he had mysteriously vanished. His connection to the case—for which a close friend was ultimately arrested and charged—was enough to put a warrant out for Brendan's arrest.

Detectives didn't get to choose where they devoted their energy—ultimately, the chief of police decided which detective worked which case—and finding Brendan was low on the LAPD's list of priorities. When Blake discovered Brendan's open arrest warrant, though, we brought all our information to Maya. If we found Brendan, she said, she would make the arrest happen.

"Okay," I said, once we were in Lola's car. "I'm impressed. How'd you find Domenica?"

"Don't get mad." She put on her turn signal and screeched out into traffic, cutting across three lanes in a slightly illegal maneuver.

"Bad start."

She coughed. "I used Araceli as bait."

"*What?*"

"It's all good, girl. She's safe."

"What the fuck, Lo? What were you *thinking*? How . . . ? I don't even know where to start with you!"

We pulled up to a red light, and Lola held up a hand. "It's fine, she gave consent. I even made her sign something saying she understood what she was doing."

"A seventeen-year-old *cannot give consent.*"

"Well, it worked, so let's not get caught up in details."

"Lola!"

The light was still red. Lola finally glanced over at me.

"She didn't meet him or anything like that," she said. "I used her Instagram page to send him a message. That's it, Rai. Just a message. He wrote back real quick. Said he loved her photos."

Domenica's parents had told us that Brendan found Domenica through Instagram, so it only made sense we would track him down using the same site. We had tried nearly everything so far: Blake hacked into Brendan's Facebook page and Instagram accounts, an exercise which showed he had been exchanging unsavory messages with hundreds of underage girls over the last few years. We couldn't exactly present our findings to the police—hacking is obviously illegal, though I never said we didn't occasionally stoop to conquer—but I knew Maya wouldn't ask too many questions if I delivered Brendan.

It hadn't occurred to me, though, to just send him a message. Lola had been out twelve hours a day talking to people, chasing leads, hustling information. We'd hardly crossed paths lately, so I figured she must have something good. It had never crossed my mind that she might be dangling her younger sister as bait.

I wasn't ready to congratulate her yet.

"You know that's not even half-legal, right? Using a child as bait? Your dad would kill you—and then he'd kill *me*—if he ever found out."

Lola coasted through the intersection as the light turned green. She wasn't looking at me. "Are we going to pretend that most of what we do is legal?"

"Lo. *This is different.* You gave a pedophile access to your baby sister, for fuck's sake!"

"One—she's seventeen. Eighteen next month. Two—have you *seen* Ari's Instagram? It's public, she's half-naked in most of the shots, and

45

she's already got eight thousand followers. I mean—you know what types of human fungus exist in dark corners of the internet. Lastly, Ari thought the whole thing was fun."

I scoffed. "Let's table the morality issue for a minute. You said you had something good. How do you know where Brendan is?"

"I've been exchanging messages with him for the last week. I didn't want to tell you until I was actually sure he'd fall for it."

"And?"

She smirked. "There's a party tomorrow night at some mansion in Benedict Canyon, so that's where we're going. Little old me got an invite. Brendan's been camping out at a friend's place for the last month."

I held my breath. "Is Domenica there?"

"Well, I couldn't exactly ask him, could I? 'Hi, I'm a teenage girl interested in the music industry, and I'll do pretty much anything to get my big break. By the way, do you have any other underage girls stashed away at your pad?'"

"Good point."

"Thank you. Anything else?"

"We can table the discussion."

"I know you and I do things differently," she said, glancing over and giving me a wink. "But that's why the team works. We need all three of us."

I didn't need to be reminded where I would be without Blake and Lola. Left City started as a hobby after I realized that I spent all my spare time reading about unsolved crimes and reports of missing people around Los Angeles, looking for answers. I had enough connections through my boss, Marcus, to start doing it professionally, first tracking down missing and stolen pets, then moving my way up to finding items that had been taken in home invasions. Without Lola, I would still be operating out of the guest room where I had lived after moving out of my childhood home.

We reached the foot of Benedict Canyon, one of the wealthiest neighborhoods in Los Angeles. My mother had taken me out to this part of LA once. The canyon was where some of the old movie stars from the wild twenties had built elaborate palaces, full of hidden rooms and winding staircases. My mother used to tell me stories about the silent movie stars that she had watched as a kid, on nostalgia nights at the local theater. She knew everything about the world of Old Hollywood, it seemed, and most of it wasn't very pretty.

Benedict Canyon was a sleepy patchwork quilt of scrub brush and leafy canopies. The sunlight was dappled and strange, as slats of jade light fell on the road in pretty patterns. The road wound through some of the most secretive properties in Los Angeles, and some of the most storied: Sharon Tate was killed in this canyon, on Cielo Drive, but that house was torn down years ago. Rudolph Valentino's Falcon Lair was built here, back when Los Angeles was just miles and miles of orange grove and sun-wrinkled farmers. Not so very long ago, these hills were the dominion of coyotes and wild deer, wild-eyed things that went stalking through the night, and actors who played cowboy on the weekends.

"This is the last place I would have gone looking for Brendan," Lola muttered. "You never expect monsters to live in pretty houses."

The canyon was mostly silent at this time of day, with houses spaced apart at intervals. The driveways were crooked, bent to the whims of the mountain, and the houses were hidden behind trees. Now and then I caught a glimpse of a turret or a balcony buried in the growth, but no signs of human life.

Something felt oddly familiar about the neighborhood, and not just because I had visited it with my mother.

"Oh, my god," I murmured as Lola parked across the street from a large gated mansion. The gate was twenty feet high, decorated with elaborate scrollwork, and the walls on either side were covered in ivy.

"What?"

"I've been here before," I said slowly. "I've been in this house."

Lola frowned and double-checked the address on her phone. "You sure? You think Blake got the wrong place?"

It was an old Italian Renaissance mansion built in the early years of Hollywood. When I worked for Marcus, he had asked me to run an errand for him: to pick up a remastered score of an old Chaplin movie that needed to be added to an updated archive. The man who owned this house was a brilliant sound engineer, the kind who won Oscars and traveled half the year. From what I heard, he let friends live in his house when he wasn't in Los Angeles, and they threw the kinds of parties where people went missing.

I filled Lola in on my visit and the man who owned it.

"Marcus?" Lola stared at me. "You don't think he has any connection to Brendan, do you?"

"Definitely not. The guy who owns the place probably has no idea either. He's gone half the time. You'd be surprised how small the music scene in Los Angeles is though. Everyone knows everyone."

For the last month, I had pictured Domenica holed up in some near-derelict house, a mansion gone ragged with coyotes and rainwater, deer stalking through the empty living room. This was somehow so much worse.

Lola took out her monocular and peered through it. "Movement in the upstairs window."

These were the moments I lived for, the reason why I could never do anything else. There's an odd feeling I got when close to a solve. A combination of thrill and relief. A tingling in the fingertips.

"That's him," Lola murmured. "Brendan."

Our car was far enough away from the house that we wouldn't draw attention, but I still felt a chill when I saw Brendan Bole step onto an upstairs balcony and light a cigarette. He was rangy and pale, with a shaggy mane of dark hair around his shoulders. His body was decorated with an inky scrimshaw of tattoos, a dark net visible even from this distance.

I had studied Brendan obsessively for the last month and felt like I knew almost everything about him. I had studied his purported reading habits; the man loved to post photos of himself reading Kant, Hume, and Descartes—whether he actually absorbed anything is anyone's guess. His predilections for underage girls, even his dietary habits, were also always on display. I had realized years before that if I learned how someone operated as a consumer, it became easier to track their movements. To those who doubt: billion-dollar industries like Google and Amazon were founded on these basic principles. How we shop, we live.

"Piece of shit," Lola said. "It's taking everything in me not to run over there and cockpunch him."

Brendan scratched his balls and yawned, then pulled out his phone. He leaned against the balcony railing and smoked while he studied his screen.

"Where's the camera?" I asked Lo, not taking my eyes off Brendan.

"Back seat. What's wrong with your phone?"

"He's too far. I want a better zoom."

I reached back and found the camera bag, then pulled out the hefty camera and removed the lens cap. I trained the zoom on Brendan, then snapped a few quick photos. Just in case anything happened, in case he got away, I wanted something concrete to give Maya to help track him down.

"I'll text her right now," Lola said, taking out her phone. She tapped away at her phone before setting it on the dashboard. There was a ping as a message came in, and Lola checked it. "Sweet, she's not too far away."

"Already? Are you serious?"

Lola grinned. "I reached out to her this morning and let her know I might have something."

⁂

Thirty minutes later, Maya finally appeared. A black SUV pulled up in front of the property, blocking the gate. The driver and passenger doors of the

SUV popped open, and Maya hopped out, followed by her partner. They both held guns down by their sides and moved efficiently toward the house.

"Here we go," I said.

The SUV partially blocked our view of the house, but we were close enough to hear Maya bang on the front door. When there was no response, she banged again.

"Police," she called. "Brendan Bole, we have a warrant for your arrest. Open the door."

Impatient, I climbed out of the car and glanced both ways, then darted across the street and crouched behind Maya's SUV. Lola's door opened as well, and a moment later, she knelt beside me. I could make out the front door of the mansion, where Maya and her partner stood tense, ready to move. Maya nodded to her partner, he nodded back, and then Maya lifted her foot and kicked in the door. Both detectives disappeared into the house.

For a moment after that, the neighborhood was quiet. Then, an upstairs window opened, and a skinny leg poked out.

"This should be good," Lola muttered.

We watched in silence as Brendan retracted his leg and stuck his head out to gauge the distance to the ground. His head disappeared, followed shortly by both his arms. The window was too small for him to squeeze through. He tried a leg again, and it looked like he had almost positioned himself for success when his body was violently jerked back into the house.

"Gotcha," I whispered.

The perp walk was amazing. Maya frog-marched Brendan out of the house, his hands cuffed behind him. Hanks of dirty hair swung around his face. In the light of day, helpless and blinking, Brendan looked like a genetic permutation of something that shouldn't have survived evolution.

I glanced over at Lola and was surprised to see that she looked exhausted.

"You okay?"

"It's been a long fucking month."

"Let's go see if we can find Domenica," I said, squeezing her arm.

We stood up as Maya reached the SUV, her hand on Brendan's shoulder. He didn't seem to register our presence as Maya opened the back door and shoved him inside, then closed the door behind him.

"Thanks for that, Rainey," Maya said. "I'm not going to ask how you found him."

"Lola gets all the credit." I glanced at the house behind her. "How many people are in there?"

"No sign of anyone else, but we found this asshole pretty quickly."

"Come on," I told Lola. "Let's see for ourselves."

The inside of the house was cavernous, filled with light. The marble floors gleamed, and the smell of fresh flowers permeated the space.

Lola and I exchanged a glance.

"You take downstairs, I'll go up," I said.

"Done."

A sweeping marble staircase led to the upper part of the house. When I had come here before, I had only entered the foyer to grab the music from Marcus's associate. I wondered where he was now, if he knew what was happening at his house.

Upstairs was a long hallway lined with closed doors.

"Domenica?" I called. "Are you up here? I don't want to scare you. My name is Rainey. I'm friends with your parents."

I opened the first door. It was a sparsely decorated guest bedroom, with light furniture and thick drapes. The next room was a bathroom, and then a room full of recording equipment. At the end of the hallway was a window that looked out over a garden. Then—the sound of muffled weeping.

"Domenica?"

I took each step quietly. There was another room across from the recording studio, where the weeping seemed to come from. Slowly, slowly, I opened the door.

Domenica was crumpled up against the wall. She wore a long white T-shirt and a small pair of underwear. Even though she was fifteen, she was the size of a twelve-year-old, with coltish legs and small feet tucked underneath her.

"Hey," I whispered.

She gave me a blank look.

"Are you hurt? Do you know what's going on?"

"I said I was sorry," Domenica mumbled. Her voice was slow, stumbling, as though she were struggling to get the words out. "I got scared, that's all."

"Scared of what?"

She was high. Her eyes were too bright and unblinking, and her skin looked clammy. In spite of everything, she almost seemed tuned out to what was going on around her. I had spent enough time around people on drugs—both the kind you swallowed and the kind you smoked—to know what it looked like. I knelt down and took her into my arms. She smelled like young skin and unwashed hair and was surprisingly hot to the touch. I lifted her to her feet and found that she weighed very little. Behind me, I heard Lola's footsteps on the stairs.

"Yikes," Lola said. "I'll go get the car."

Domenica was asleep by the time we pulled off the freeway into South Pasadena. With traffic, the drive took an hour, which was a small mercy. I had always loved the movie set quality of South Pasadena, with its quaint streets tucked beneath intersecting canopies of jacaranda trees, its little Craftsman houses behind manicured lawns, but coming here on this kind of errand made the neighborhood feel tainted.

Domenica's house was a tidy Mission-style home behind a stucco wall lined with various cacti.

"Stay here with her," I told Lola as she put the car in park. "I'm going to talk to her parents."

The front door flew open before I had the chance to cross the front yard, and Mercedes and Javier came tumbling out into the darkness, their hands outstretched. I had called Domenica's parents to let them know we were coming, and now they ran down the path toward me, desperation etched into their features. I had spent hours with the family, watching as they transformed from a beautiful couple with radiant faces into little more than gaunt skeletons. Mercedes was a curvy woman with long black hair, which now fell around her face in a wild mane; Javier was tall and already prone to thinness, but this tragedy had rendered him an angular shadow.

"Rainey! Rainey! How can we ever thank you?" Javier exclaimed, while at the same time Mercedes made a half-lunge toward the car, screaming, "Nica!"

"Wait!" I said, taking her arm. "I want to talk to you first. Please."

Mercedes's eyes darted to the car.

"She's fine," I said. "I promise. But I have to warn you, I think she might be on drugs. I'm not sure what he gave her."

Mercedes let out a strangled cry.

"She's fine, Mercedes, I *promise*." I sighed. "All the same, I think you should take her straight to the hospital. They might have something to counteract the drugs. And you should get her checked out—she looks like she needs protein and vitamins."

Mercedes was still staring at the car.

"Okay, that's all I wanted to say. Go get your girl."

Mercedes ran toward the car, but Javier lingered for a moment. "Rainey, I want to pay you."

"My colleagues did most of the work, and we're not going to take your money."

He looked disappointed.

"It was our pleasure, really," I added. "Anyone who harms children should be locked away forever."

"Rainey, if you ever need anything—*anything*—I want you to come to me. Please."

I laughed. "Thank you."

He took my hand. "I'm serious, Rainey. You saved my family, and that is a debt I will never forget. Please."

"Okay. I'll remember that. Thank you."

───

It was past eleven by the time we headed back to Culver City. We never held regular work hours, being in the office at odd hours to meet clients or else to do research. Since I didn't have a healthy division between work and home life—and, like most good PIs, I struggled with helpless rage–induced insomnia—I spent more time in Culver City than at my house.

The lights were still on when we reached the door, which meant Blake was still there. She rubbed her eyes when we walked in. A mug of coffee sat at her elbow.

"Well done, mates. Time to celebrate."

As soon as Domenica was in the back seat of the car, I texted Blake. We had planned to celebrate at one of the restaurants in Culver City when we reached the office, but now that we were here, Lola and I were both too tired to do anything else.

"I think I might actually go home and get some sleep," I said. "It's been a really long time."

"Right. Well, I finished looking into your girl Melia. You want me to email it to you or print it out?"

"Hit me with the highlight reel."

"St. Agnes checks out," she said, slipping her glasses on. "It's an expensive rehab facility outside of Savannah, and not one of your New Age treatment places where they focus on the well-being and growth of the individual. It's a real Old Testament kind of place. They believe in addiction as the manifestation of the devil, blah-blah-blah, and since they're run by a branch of the Catholic Church, there's not a lot of government oversight. I found a few articles written about ten years ago—someone tried to do an exposé, but it was shut down real quick."

Lola glanced at me.

"It looks like they've ramped up their security on-site, but the website's old-school," Blake went on. "As is their medical database. It took me about half an hour to find Melia's records."

"And?"

"She was there four times," Blake said. She rubbed her eyes and sighed, then sat back in her chair. "The first time was for three months, right after the murders."

"Yeah, Melia mentioned that."

Blake tapped her fingers on her desk. She looked like she was mulling something over.

"What is it?" Lola asked.

"It was something I saw in Melia's records," Blake said slowly. "It looks like she tried to break out a few times, but they always caught her, and the punishments were brutal. Like being locked in a dark room for three days without any food."

"Shit," Lola whispered. "Is that even legal?"

Blake gave an expansive shrug. "If Melia's lawyer arranged for her to be in there, and they made the family sign some kind of waiver, then yeah, I'd say it's legal."

I sat down across from Blake's desk. "Speaking of the family, did you find anything about the aunt?"

"Belinda Harris. We're talking *old* money. Slaves, sugar, and cotton. Racist fucks," she added. "They've even got their own family cemetery plot on the property—you know, so they don't have to be buried with the commoners."

Lola and I exchanged a look.

"Where did the van Aust family money come from?"

"Both sides. Mom was from the South; Dad was from Germany. That's where *van Aust* comes from—and *they* were loaded as well. A big old wealthy German family that goes all the way back to when the country was run by Goths and Vikings."

"What about Jasper?" Lola interjected. "You have any idea where he's been this whole time?"

"I hate to admit defeat, but I couldn't find anything. He must have changed his name somehow. Either that, or he could have left the country at some point. When you come from that kind of money, anything's possible. Again, it doesn't make sense to me that he would risk everything to write her a letter now."

"Does anyone else in Melia's past stand out to you?" I asked. "Any potential stalkers who might have written the letter?"

"Gee, between the ancestors who treated human lives as a commodity and the wealthy German heritage—dare I say collaborators . . . ?—I can't think of anyone who might want to see Melia dead."

"Irony duly noted," I said. "Her family history hasn't aged well, got it. Anything personal to Melia though? Was she maybe the original target on the night her parents were murdered?"

Blake hit a few keys. "I'm emailing you the dossier. Then I'm going home."

"Wait—are you upset about something?"

She pushed her glasses up on her nose. "This family sounds rotten to the core. I'm not surprised someone killed the parents. If she's anything like them—based on what I've found—she'll be an entitled, racist piece of shit."

"What if she's a victim too?" I said quietly. "We haven't given her a fair chance to present her side of things."

Lola cleared her throat. "I think we should take the case," she said.

Blake looked indignant. "Here we go."

Lola ticked the reasons off her fingers. "We haven't taken many new cases this month because of Domenica. We're going to fall behind on rent if we don't take something soon, as well as other bills. This is our model, after all: we represent wealthy clients we don't like so we can continue to serve the community."

"There's something weird about this family," Blake said. "*Someone* had a reason for killing them."

"They tried to kill Melia too," I said. "I don't want to play the shitty relative card, but you can't choose your family. You shouldn't be blamed for their mistakes either. You and I know that better than anyone, Blake."

"You asshole," Blake said, pointing at me. "You had to go there."

"Maybe you should meet Melia," I suggested. "You might change your mind about her."

Blake looked like she was considering it. "I don't think so."

Lola was watching us, but she remained silent.

"Let me point out that her aunt may or may not be skimming from her trust fund," I added. "The family has a rotten history, but Melia isn't exactly profiting from that."

"Fine. *Fine.* We can take the case," Blake said. "But I'm not going to meet with her, and we're not going to bond, and you make *sure* she pays her bills on time. This country has enough rich white people who see themselves as victims."

"Thanks, Blake," I said.

"Yeah, yeah. I'm going home so I can clear my head."

"Let me give you a lift, at least," I said.

"Lon's picking me up. He's almost here. I'll see you tomorrow."

She maneuvered her wheelchair toward the door, waving me away when I went to open it. She was pissed, but Blake didn't hold grudges, and I knew we could revisit the conversation the next day.

When I was sure she was gone, I turned to Lola. "If Jasper really did write the letter," I said, "do you think we can track him down and put a stop to this? He's managed to hide from the police this whole time."

"The police have more money and resources, but we have fewer demands on our time," Lola pointed out. "And Jasper doesn't know about us, so he doesn't know he should be hiding from us."

"And if Jasper *didn't* write the letter? If it's from someone else?"

Lola stifled a yawn. "So Melia's got a stalker. She's a helpless rich kid with first world problems; we've both seen plenty of those. What could she possibly throw at us that we haven't already seen?"

FIVE

———✺———

She disappeared a week before my sixteenth birthday. Everything else about that summer spelled domestic simplicity—fog rolling in every morning to obscure the folds and peaks of the mountain; June Gloom; my father's unpredictable schedule; the baskets of laundry my mother insisted on hanging from the clothesline in the garden so that each slip and pair of socks came in smelling like earth, like rosemary.

The week of her disappearance marked nearly four months since I had told my parents that I was quitting music. Summers had never belonged to me, not for as long as I could remember: while the school year was given over to rigorous rehearsal schedules, training, and the occasional performance, summers were reserved for touring abroad. By the time I was twelve, I had already played with orchestras in Copenhagen and Prague, my spidery hands and small stature belying a skill beyond my years. Music had always taken precedence over standardized education, and I was homeschooled by a procession of tutors, each with their own flaws and eccentricities. I didn't even set foot in a traditional school until my freshman year of high school.

The fact that my mother disappeared four months after I quit music altogether meant the events would be forever linked in my mind. In the third week of my first summer of independence, of long, untethered days spent smoking pot in my best friend's garden and going to see old movies at the New Beverly, I came home to an empty house. The door leading to the garden was open, swaying back and forth in the faint breeze. She hadn't packed a bag, and later, when the police came and combed through the house for clues, I helped out by going through her wardrobe. Not a single pair of shoes was missing.

"Someone must have taken her," I kept saying. "How could she have left like that? How could she leave the house barefoot?"

"Maybe," one of the detectives told me, not unkindly, "maybe there were parts of her life you didn't know about."

Even then I knew my father's clout translated to an unusual amount of help from the police. If anyone else had come home to find their wife missing, the searches would have been perfunctory, and the police would have handed over a list of numbers to call for emotional support. *These things happen, you know.* Instead, a pair of detectives was sent to the house, and for the next week we answered questions about my mother's daily habits and the type of people she came into contact with.

Was she unhappy?

Did she have a phone we didn't know about?

Did she take her passport?

Given our family history, was there anyone who might have wished us harm? An obsessed stalker, perhaps?

The questions were baffling, exposing an ignorance of how very abnormal my family was. My mother's passport was found tucked between medical documents and old ticket stubs from a trip my family had taken to the South of France five years before. She hadn't taken any money, any mementos, nothing.

The police left eventually because there was nothing more they could do. We had no leads, no answers. They never determined if she was taken or if she really did just leave of her own volition. I combed through the house in the days, weeks, months after she went missing, trying to find some kind of clue. There was nothing, nothing at all. When six months went by and she still hadn't used her credit cards or even tried to access her bank accounts, something in my father changed.

For the first year after my mother vanished, I struggled with the phrasing of the thing; since the police never determined what had happened, I never knew what to tell people. A disappearance could be construed as just that: ceasing to be visible. Eventually I realized it was easier not to talk about her at all.

The symphonies that my father wrote during this time hinted at something dark, something troubled hiding beneath the surface. He performed one of them—only one—with the Vienna Philharmonic, and after that, the rest of them remained locked away in a box within his office. He wouldn't discuss that time, wouldn't entertain theories or bold conjectures, and eventually, the house seemed to swallow the evidence of my mother altogether.

The early years were magical, a gilded life. My family lived in a rambling Spanish mansion off Mulholland, with views of Los Angeles on one side and the San Gabriel Mountains on the other. Our house had belonged to one of the old silent film stars from the 1920s, an actor who was huge at the time but faded away as sound came to films. I didn't even know his name until I was going through some old boxes and found it on a document. *Cade Hart.* We still had boxes of his ancient film reels, disintegrating in their tins. Sometimes I found mementos in our wild, tangled garden: costume jewelry and animal bones, glass jars and dolls' eyes.

Cade Hart killed himself in the thirties, destitute and alone, and the house sat in disrepair for forty years, until a screenwriter moved in with his underage lover. They lived in a state of splendid squalor for two years, nearly setting the place on fire when one of their parties went awry, and then the girl developed a drug problem, tried to rob a post office, and ultimately got shipped back to Idaho to live with her parents.

Dune House sat empty on and off for the next twenty years, occasionally occupied by teen runaways or wild animals. The origins of the house's name were never confirmed, but I heard it was an ironic title because Cade Hart had always wanted a beach house in Malibu. By the time my parents came to Los Angeles and visited Dune House with a real estate agent, a family of coyotes was living in the kitchen, and rats had eaten their way through the walls. The repairs would cost more than the selling price. My mother, barefoot, walked through the house, trailing her fingers along the walls.

"We'll take it," she said. "Yes, this is the house."

They stripped out the old walnut floors and replaced them with ash. Workers came in to replace the copper wiring, most of which had been torn out by thieves over the years. The foundations were cracked, but they were restored, along with damaged faucets. The roof was patched up, the terra-cotta tiles and structural beams replaced. The windows were given new seals, the kitchen a fresh coat of paint, and my parents moved in.

Our neighborhood was always artistic, and in that way, my parents were a perfect fit for the new house. To the right of us was the summer home of an opera singer from Portugal, while on the left was the tidy modernist home of a disgraced royal from Scandinavia. Sometimes my friends and I would see him when we did midnight laps in my pool. He would stand on his balcony, looking out over Los Angeles, smoking three or four cigarettes before retreating back inside. The opera singer was gone most of the year, but during the day, gardeners and men came to clean the pool and tend the plants.

I was too young to see that domestic life had done something to diminish my mother, but after she disappeared and I started trying to understand her, the contrast between the woman I had known and the woman she had been before Dune House was clear. Family life must have consumed and dismantled her, replacing a vibrant soul with a husk of a woman.

She was an installation artist, and at one time, she had international clout. Before meeting my father, her pieces had filled the cavernous halls of abandoned train stations, ruined mansions, and rural playgrounds. She was the one who taught me that art was a tool.

"Art should mean something," she said. "It should disturb you. Beauty has the power to destroy."

Her art wasn't designed to sit in an air-conditioned room where bored schoolchildren could pass it on a field trip, where housewives might stare at it in the hours between cleaning the house and fixing supper. Her art was explosive. She used it as a weapon.

She started painting when she was still in high school, living with her family at the edge of Topanga Canyon. The pieces were impassioned statements about cultural numbness and capitalistic expansion. By the time she finished high school, her works had grown from angry paintings to installation art, pieces that took up public space. She found empty warehouses and swept the floors, set up orbs made of found objects: broken twigs and birds' nests filled with the dead bodies of birds contaminated by unregulated pesticides.

After warehouses came empty houses, the cottages and bungalows that had popped up in the post–World War II optimism, only to be vacated in the first wave of unemployment that hit Los Angeles. She climbed through the windows of these vacant houses and rewired the electricity, filling the windows with a collection of lamps she had salvaged from dumpsters and other abandoned houses.

Not all of her artwork was angry, however. Her most playful piece—and my favorite of her installations—was built between two apartment buildings in an impoverished part of Los Angeles. The buildings were occupied by families, and there were a lot of small children around. Even though the area was poor, it was a happy community, and my mother had been saddened that the buildings were slated for destruction.

In an act of civic defiance, she had collected a number of fallen tree trunks and erected them between the buildings. When the tree trunks were securely in place, she had covered them with ferns, lichens, and moss, creating the appearance of a thriving forest. After the plants took hold, she began construction on tree houses, pathways, and swaying bridges that extended from the windows of one apartment building across to the other.

Looking back, I could see a pattern. Even during her best years there was a sense that my mother was fading away, stepping back from the limelight as soon as she had occupied it. She didn't like the public scrutiny that came with fame, and it seemed she was always running from something. The more successful she became, the more she tried to outrun her own ambition, eager to reach for silence, anonymity, a back door she could slip through to escape her own larger-than-life image.

The summer before my mother disappeared, my parents rented a house in Malibu. It was an aristocrat's home with a path to the beach and too many bedrooms, but there were holes in the walls. I could see why they had picked it. No music, no pictures, nothing but wide-open windows that looked out upon a sweeping blue-green ocean. There was nothing to remember, nothing to forget. Later, I would look back on that time and wonder if that was the point where my mother realized she wanted to slip her skin, step into a different life, but back then, I had seen it only as a welcome break from the stilted chaos of Dune House and my touring schedule.

That summer, my parents hosted a troupe of artists: sculptors, acrylic dabblers, mosaic creators, ceramic crafters, miniaturists. The artists sifted through our house and left pieces of themselves in the rooms they occupied. Broken combs, gummy with unwashed hair. Palettes unrinsed of color. A scalpel and curved knife in the room of a sculptor, the wood floors chalky with dried clay. Popped foil of birth control packets, stained underwear, stiff sheets, and the smell of body funk.

For a while, my mother made do with family life and contented herself with smaller works of art. I came home to the beach house one day to find she had removed all the furniture from the living room. She had painted the walls dark green, a forest tableau with pale birches winking in the artificial moonlight. Deer and bears stalked through the two-dimensional woods, and an owl surveyed the room from its spot above the bookshelf. And in the corner, beneath a crooked elm, the body of a girl in a white dress. Whether she was dead or asleep, my mother wouldn't say.

The works became more intrusive. She sketched piles of bones on the walls of our bathroom. I soaped up in the tub, staring at crooked mandibles, disjointed femurs. In the kitchen the next morning were Troilus and Cressida, a dagger clasped in a slender white hand.

The walls of her studio were covered in skeletons half-cloaked in muscle and skin, their crooked tibias misaligned with vertebral columns. The floor was littered with charcoal sketches of triceps, scapulae, iliac crests, strange appendages, slitted eyes, dislocated joints. Broken limbs, skin peeled back over the knuckles.

Sometimes we didn't see her for days at a time, and then she would turn up at breakfast, slicing oranges in the facsimile of a perfect mother. She moved her bed to a downstairs studio and bleached the curtains, then filled clay urns with the bones of creatures who had washed ashore.

Finally, I cornered my father.

"Is something wrong with her?"

"She's an artist," he said, ducking the question. "Artists can only confront the same canvas so many times before they start going a little mad."

When I think back on that time, I remember a five-color palette: green, gray, brown, milky blue, and the off-white color that everything became, no matter how many times my mother boiled the sheets or scrubbed the walls.

Green was outside; it seemed to be everything beyond the perimeter of the house. Most plants refused to grow on the salty lawn of our rented house, but the front of our property was fringed with ice plant and pickleweed. At some point an artist gathered up driftwood and pieces of abalone, then lined them up along the edges of the garden. The neighbor's ivy crept along the broken tines of our shared fence, and a tribe of stray cats came to shit in the green morass outside the front door. Brown for cat shit, brown for decay. Gray for morning mist and the unending fog, for the flat slate of the ocean without sunlight. Brown for the fruit flies and the soft, rotting produce that nobody but the watercolor artist ate. Milky blue for the Malibu skyline.

As the days slipped away, I let myself believe we would never return to Dune House. My parents seemed happy for once, not segregated by their opposing mediums. He didn't talk about music, and I didn't wander into the kitchen in the morning to find music scribbled on any willing surface. We were tourists; for once the curious gaze belonged to us. In the evenings, we ate in the garden, or listened to old records we found stored in the attic of the villa.

The vacation couldn't last forever, as much as I wanted it to. It had come back while we were away, the darkness that he had been running from. It had slipped in unnoticed between the door and the floorboards, made itself cozy in front of the hearth. As soon as we had allowed the villa to feel like home, it knew where to find us.

On the days I was convinced that my mother had left of her own volition, it was easy to speculate why. As powerful and independent as she had always been, there was a stronger legacy that dominated our household, one she couldn't possibly hope to compete with. That legacy belonged to my grandmother.

My father had been born into Hollywood royalty. His mother, Kay Taylor, was one of the most sought-after actresses in the forties and early fifties, starring alongside all the old greats, like Clark Gable, Fred Astaire, and Bette Davis. My father had been born as that world was beginning to fade away, but in many ways, he was still a product of that time, a quiet, stoic artist who lingered in the background and never seemed quite at ease with all the fame surrounding him.

All the photos of Kay showed a life of refinement and grace—in one, Kay stepped out of a limousine, one hand extended to grasp the arm of her handsome escort; in another, she glanced down at a sweeping gown stitched with silk roses. Each gesture was gracious, yet unselfconscious. I tried to imagine my father growing up in the middle of all that, but I could never see him there, in a world of flickering black and white, shadows in his eyes.

The way we lived our lives was quietly counterbalanced against her legacy, and for years, I lived in her shadow without knowing it. Her story was one of decadence and ruined luxury, of diamonds swirling in a storm drain. In pictures she was tragic, beautiful, always with an element of something secretive in her light eyes. She had the same features as my father, the same half-concealed smile.

She had been born in Germany, out in the countryside. The first few years of her life were spent in a crumbling castle covered in ivy; the family had been rich. Her childhood was divided between Bavarian country and villas in Spain. I pictured jacaranda, winding cobblestone streets, magnolias and marigolds, fables about royal children who lived in glass castles. In the mid-1930s, however, the family was savvy to the threat of war on the horizon, and her parents fled to California. Warmer weather beckoned.

By the time they came to America her parents were penniless, but she had grown up accustomed to wealth and all its trappings, and her parents pushed her to restore the family name. She had to succeed, had to claw back to what they had lost; failure was never an option.

For most of my life, the film industry was little more than a dark fairytale, a polished stone rubbed between my fingers so many times it had started to lose its luster. Whenever I tried to imagine the world of my father's childhood, I always pictured it in black and white, flickering softly out of focus, a world of diamonds and thin golden bracelets. The men were stoic and handsome, with slender suits and tragic smiles, while the women were goddesses, untouchable, unreal. When my father was willing to talk about the world of his mother's childhood, all the stories were cast in shadow.

He told me tales about William Randolph Hearst, who had his gardeners work only at nighttime, lacing the roots of poisonous flowers into the desert earth, their progress illuminated by violet lights. I pictured night gardens filled with dark fruit, leaves pale in the starlight. If you cut the fruits open, they would smell like flowers, honey sweet with white flesh. The fruit would drink up the bitter moonlight, growing fat on the silky night air.

Back then, my father told me, the early pioneers thought they could turn Los Angeles into a jungle. There had been acres of farmland, but the land was stubborn, refusing to perform under pressure. A German immigrant came to California intent on growing tropical plants, which flourished in the California climate. He planted date palms, cherimoya, coffee beans, papaya, avocados, pineapples. There were far too many tropical fruits for people in Los Angeles to eat, however, and the German man finally returned to his homeland.

I liked the thought of overflowing tropical gardens, papaya and mangoes dropping to the ground and splitting open in the endless sunshine. I liked to imagine early Hollywood as the pioneers dreamed of developing it: a dense forest filled with the rich smells of turning fruit, animals gorging themselves on bananas, cherimoya, things America had never seen before.

Most of the time, though, he didn't want to talk about the past, and he avoided questions about Kay. He described Hollywood to me once as a hollow wilderness, but he was just as vague when I asked him what he meant.

"Los Angeles is a place of dead poetry," he said quietly. "Plastic castles and movie stars gone mad. Nothing can survive here."

There were stories about actresses who had swallowed cyanide pills when they found their lovers cheating on them, stories about unsolved murders, and stories of corrupt politicians bought off by the studios.

Another time, he said there was a dark brand of magic at work, visible in the pink glow that settled upon the city's shoulders at sunset. Maybe there were witches. Some days he talked about the city like it might eat him alive.

In the beach house that summer, he was at peace. Evenings found him collapsed in a chair by the window, lost in his thoughts, a book trapped beneath his long fingers. It was rare to find silence in our house with its cool white walls and dark wooden floors; something was always howling at the windows, begging to be let in. I never dreamed that someday it would get inside, that someday the silence would be replaced by the one kind of separation I couldn't handle.

Even when things appeared perfect at home, some element of my father seemed to be looking for a way out. He took me to Europe one summer, when I was first starting out, and we visited all the capitals. I was enchanted by the aging old hotels, the bankrupt grandes dames with their moth-eaten furs and their inherited gems, and the sleight-of-hand artists escorting young ingenues through the hotel corridors. Everything in Europe seemed stately, eternal, and beautiful without effort. Los Angeles, by contrast, was parched, starving for water.

We were not an ordinary family; I knew that even from a young age. A normal family might have encouraged me to have more friends my own age. Instead, I spent all night lingering on staircases after I was supposed to be in bed, listening to parties dwindle into idle chatter. In photographs from this period I was almost always alone: even when there were other people, I was apart from them. Me sitting on the edge of a sailboat, my small frame drowning in one of my father's oxford shirts, then languishing in the shallows of a swimming pool—a vacation or work trip, impossible to say. There were other photos of me practicing the violin, face closed off and unrecognizable, even to myself. On a stage, illuminated while the audience hid, hushed in shadow. All the photos followed a similar pattern of aloneness, except the ones when I was very young, four or five. In those photos my mother was always with me, holding my hands, wrapping her arms around me, her face blissful. That was before I picked up a violin for the first time, began to perform, and she lost me to music. To public acclaim.

One night we went to a party thrown by one of my father's composer friends. The house was near the coast of Normandy, and all the doors were thrown open to the night. There were glass bowls filled with candles and calla lilies, roses piled on countertops, music cascading through the hallways. Dark hedges glowed with tiny lights, and white flowers stung the air.

As the night wore on, the women swayed down the garden paths, their laughter bright as sugar. They ran their hands along the piano keys, down the banisters, stared into the mirrors in the hallway, and then danced away, frightened by their own pale beauty. My father watched the party from a distance, his eyes dark with starlight and champagne.

In the early evening, I wandered off and fell asleep in one of the guest bedrooms. When I woke up, I wandered down to the garden and found it empty. All the party guests had gone down to the water to see the host's boat.

Something winked up from the grass, and I knelt to pick it up. It was a diamond necklace that had slipped from someone's neck and gotten caught among the stones. I admired it for a moment before brushing it off and draping it across my collarbone.

My father came out to find me a few minutes later. He took the necklace from me, then leaned down and looked into my eyes.

"There is something rotten behind every beautiful thing," he said. "We are not like them."

I was fifteen when I found out the truth about my grandmother. Not some doe-eyed vixen, but a drug addict who had once tied my father to a chair in the living room because he had wet his bed. My father's childhood was filled with moonlit soirees and diamonds, yacht parties and gifts from visiting royalty, but it was also filled with *her*—with Kay—a larger-than-life presence he could never climb out from under. It was her face that stared down from the pictures on the walls of Dune House. When I was young, before I knew anything about her, I imagined her as some beautiful friend of the family who lived in every room, smiling at me while I combed my hair, practiced the violin.

The truth emerged one night after a concert, when a reporter cornered me near the bar.

"Do you think your father finally managed to outlive her legacy?" the woman asked, eyes glinting. "All that fame and money, she should have been so happy."

It didn't take much convincing to get the rest of the story from my father. It was alcohol in the early years, when she was still young enough to be considered America's sweetheart, drugs by the time my father was born. She fell asleep at the breakfast table and slipped tiny blue pills under her tongue to dissolve while she drove him to school. The circumstances surrounding his volatile upbringing and the tragedy of her death at sixty-four were cushioned, repackaged as Hollywood folklore. Nobody ever knew the truth, except for my mother and a few family friends. There were rumors, of course, but none of them were substantiated.

"Enough money and a powerful lawyer mean you can write your own legacy," my father told me. That was when he thought he could keep her a secret, that we could escape, live our lives in some semblance of privacy.

A year before my mother disappeared, however, a crew of documentary filmmakers put together a story about my grandmother, unearthing long-lost letters and old transcripts from her psychologist, and I knew then we would never have that kind of privacy.

The documentary was an assassination of an American dynasty. They showed clips of my father composing and performing music, then contrasted these against snatches of testimony from anonymous staff who had worked for my grandmother. My father declined to be interviewed or participate in any way with the production of the documentary—"a hack job," he called it—but he was so public that his participation wasn't necessary for a complete autopsy. They glossed over his successes and triumphs with evidence of a childhood spent in the shadow of an unstable mother. The silk gowns and awards ceremonies were only one fraction of an incomplete picture, and when the documentary was released to great acclaim, the world came rushing in.

They had heard about the diamonds drifting to the bottom of our dark, secret pools, about the silver bangles caught on tree limbs. There were stories about golden rings tossed into fires, flames burning blue and violet. *Everything was true, nothing was real.* There were images of Kay's last movie premiere, the ravenous crowds surging against the theater doors, Kay's throat choked with emeralds and pearls.

My father couldn't go out for lunch without drawing a small crowd, and dozens of photographs popped up in minor publications each day. My father buying bread from the local bakery. My father standing in the wings of an empty concert hall, his face half-cast in shadow. He had always craved privacy, but success demanded recognition, and tragedy guaranteed it.

If my father was the victim of unwanted recognition, however, my mother had it worse. She became a pariah, a mother who had neglected familial duties to pursue a questionable career in the arts. *Just like Kay.*

The most famous image of my father was a picture of him looking out a window, gazing down at a crowd near the Champs-Élysées. His hand was raised close to his face, but whether it was to wave to someone or to deflect the photographer was unclear. Either way, he looked completely isolated and untouchable. It was the image that would appear on the cover of every newspaper in California after my mother disappeared, only a few months after the documentary was released.

The reporters never completely vanished, but my father was decent toward them as long as they didn't interrupt our lives. Interview requests were granted with resistance, or else ignored and then forgotten. My father believed that all things must rise and fall; sharp dives would be followed by smooth crescendos. Fame did not concern him. He was modest and didn't like attention, and reporters never knew what to write about him.

Sometimes I wondered that he had let me perform music at all, that he had encouraged me to play. Some days I thought if I hadn't gone on to perform, we might have ultimately faded from public life, but I knew that was never going to be possible; there would always be people waiting for him to explain, to offer himself up. Perhaps my musical accomplishments were meant to override or quash the existing legacy. Sometimes I felt this was the only explanation for why I had been introduced to music—to performance—at such a young age; I hated my father a little bit more for tipping the balance onto my young, defenseless shoulders. And then I would hate myself for feeling that way, for blaming a man who had once been a child with a mother who demanded so much of him.

"Tell us about your childhood, Charlie," they would say, or, "Tell us about Kay." It always came back to her eventually. His past was always lingering in the next room, down a dark corridor, beneath a sweet breeze on a quiet night. It was the reason why he didn't want to be famous, why he was content to lose himself in the rhythm of a concerto. He wore his music like a dark cloak; he wanted to forget where he came from, but the reporters wouldn't let him. He rarely gave them the answers they wanted, but that didn't stop them from badgering him for more. After all their damage was done, they were left with nothing but the sound of the hot Los Angeles wind ripping through the grass.

Kay was the reason he didn't linger after concerts, waiting to hear the mounting avalanche of applause. On the rare occasions when he came onstage, he would bow and vanish before the applause stopped, leaving the audience to wonder where he had gone, why he couldn't accept their gratitude. His image in the public eye was of a face half-hidden in shadow, turning away from the camera, deflecting the photographer, or shielding his eyes from the light. It was never possible to tell.

After my mother disappeared and I had given up hope that she might come back, I kept waiting for the grief to wash over me, to arrive in a suffocating catharsis. I couldn't help thinking how stupid the trappings of modern loss were, however—how all the quiet murmurs and glances in my direction were really just chutes and funnels to contain my sorrow. If I did break down, a thousand hands would be upon me, shushing me and soothing me, trying to diminish the pain.

For years I jumped out of bed each time I heard the phone ringing, hoping that Matilda was calling to let me know where she had gone. I sought insight in strangers' faces and wondered if she still looked the same. Her hair had been wild and long that last summer, frequently pinned in a messy bun with a pair of chopsticks. I tried to picture her with a sleek bob, a tight perm, a shaved head. I had dreams of men with black eyes, of mountains that melted into the sea.

My father and I had gone through her room together after the police left and found nothing but a slip of paper that had gotten caught behind the bed frame. It looked like a print from a woodblock carving, something roughly drawn, carved, and then stamped. The image was a nude woman in profile, seated, her face contorted in pain or contemplation; it wasn't clear which one.

My father crumpled it up and threw it away; later, I salvaged it from the bin and smoothed it out, then tucked it away between the pages of a book.

He never talked about my mother, and he never made me feel responsible for what had happened to her. The house gradually accumulated the evidence of a quiet life: books, glass animals, sheets of music, stones. Pictures of my mother hung around the house like guiding eyes, and sometimes I tried to imagine her cool hands resting on my shoulders, comforting me when I couldn't sleep. Three bottles of perfume remained in the bedroom she had shared with my father, barometers for an eternally brisk fall, unseen clouds knitting together in the east.

Two years after that early summer afternoon, we stopped guessing, and we stopped looking. We came to an unspoken agreement: *Matilda doesn't live here anymore.*

If my mother hadn't disappeared—if I hadn't spent years searching for her—I'm not sure I would have ever become a private investigator. I can't remember when people started paying me, because at first I was just doing it to fill the hours between working for Marcus and sleeping. At some point, though, it was taking up so much of my time that Marcus insisted—kindly— that if I didn't make it my full-time job, he was going to fire me.

"You can still live with us," he added. "But this is clearly what you're meant to be doing with your life."

Starting Left City was the first time I had felt something like hope in a very long time. I had stopped drinking throughout the day when I first moved in with Marcus, and a month later, I gave up alcohol altogether. It wasn't an easy habit to break; for the four years before I moved in, I couldn't remember being sober for more than forty-eight hours at a stretch.

Either way, both the booze habit and the idle sleuthing had their merits. In the years I spent careening from dive bar to dive bar, picking up friends in low places, I did manage to make some contacts that stuck. I befriended drug dealers, both practicing and reformed, junkies, inebriates and dabblers, sex workers, thieves, and bouncers. I couldn't count the amount of times I got carried out of bars, my hair a dark curtain over one of the bouncer's shoulders. I started going to the same three bars, got to know all the bouncers who worked there, and I could thank those tall, burly men for making sure I didn't get killed.

If Marcus hadn't finally put a stop to all of it, I might have never gotten my life together. Marcus had always been like family to me—he and my dad were colleagues who became good friends, and our families grew up alongside each other. He saw some long-forgotten potential in me, and within a week of moving in with him and his family, I was working as his assistant at the film studio where he composed scores for movies. I had loved that job something fierce, but Marcus was right: being a private investigator was a stronger calling.

I didn't do it in any official capacity at first; in order to be a private investigator in California, you had to meet certain requirements. You had to be over eighteen and a United States citizen, and you couldn't have criminal convictions. You had to undergo police checks and file an official application with a government bureau, among other things, like passing an exam and working in a paid capacity for a few years. Gone were the days of Sam Spade drinking martinis for breakfast and scoping out schoolgirls—you couldn't run a PI firm if you didn't have your shit together. I somehow scraped all the necessary documents together and registered with the city of Los Angeles. Even though I had stopped working for Marcus, I was still living with his family, and that was eventually how I met Lola.

Lola and Diego, Marcus's son, had been friends for five years, but somehow I had never met her. Lola had heard that I worked as a private investigator, and she spent the afternoon plying me with questions. At the time I thought she was just talkative, but a week later she came back to the Loew household and said she was going to work for me.

At first I thought she was joking. She was a few years older than me, a Stanford Law School graduate, and a public relations savant. I had only been officially operating as a private investigator for five months, and I didn't have enough money to pay an employee. Even when I realized she was serious, I tried to convince her that working for me would be a step in the wrong direction. Lola listened to all my reasons for not hiring her, then calmly explained that she earned way too much money doing a soul-sucking job for a faceless law firm, that she didn't find the work fulfilling, and that if she didn't quit now, she would end up a three-time divorcée with no family, no life, and a job that had taken everything.

She laughed when I said I couldn't pay her a living wage, and explained that with her help, my client base was about to get much bigger. She had made a lot of wealthy friends through her job, and she had absolutely no qualms about taking those connections with her.

"I don't know how to sleuth," she explained. "But if you can cover that, then leave the rest to me."

A month later, we had almost too many jobs to handle, and we started making so much money that we set up shop in an office space in Mid-City. It was Lola's idea to still take on the occasional catch-my-cheating-husband case from aging gold-diggers looking to get a massive divorce settlement. We quickly developed a "two for them, one for us" style of operating: we'd accept the occasional rich client in order to fund our work helping impoverished immigrants and low-income families. Lola was a good asset physically as well: she was six feet two, all generous curves—"fat, Rainey, I'm *fat*"—and she had started martial arts training in high school after a classmate made a crack about how big girls couldn't defend themselves. Lola was gorgeous and proud of her size, and her training made me feel safe whenever we found ourselves in a dodgy situation.

When we finally brought Blake on board, we had everything we needed, and by the time we moved into the Culver City office, we had struck a comfortable balance. I had started the company, but it was clear that we didn't function without each other.

SIX

The day after we found Domenica, I woke up with a heavy feeling in my body. It was another perfect summer morning, the promise of heat already seeping in through the window. I could hear laughter and voices outside my window as people in my neighborhood got a start on their day. Nothing was worse for depression than sunshine and the illusion that everyone else carried on with their lives unaffected.

I often felt depleted after a big case ended, even if we had a positive outcome. On mornings like this I felt like I was standing on the edge of the ocean as wave after wave nearly took me under. Even if I survived this one, there would always be another one right after it: whatever small impact or good my team managed to do made no real difference in the long run. Evil always won.

I opened my email and saw a message from Lola.

> *Finished Melia's contract. Just need signatures and the deposit.*
> *L*

I didn't have a printer at my apartment, so I uploaded the attachment to a USB stick and got dressed, then brushed my teeth and ran a hand through my hair.

Instead of driving, I opted to walk the few blocks to the nearby copy shop. Los Feliz village was bustling: Bourgeois Pig was doing a hefty trade in takeaway coffees, and through the window I could see a dozen would-be screenwriters hunched over their laptops. Even Counterpoint was busy. Most of the time the dusty old record and used book shop was limited to two or three customers at a time.

Fresh Prints was two blocks away from the tall, glowing building that housed the Scientology headquarters. The sunlit print shop was filled with students, all rumpled hair and wrinkled clothing, laptops tucked under their arms. I handed my USB stick to the young woman behind the counter and waited while she printed out Melia's contract.

On the way back to my apartment, I sent Melia a text letting her know I was on my way over. Slant House was near Griffith Park, at the edge of Los Feliz—in Los Angeles terms, therefore, Melia and I were almost neighbors. It was only a ten-minute drive from my apartment to her front doorstep, which was a rare proximity in Southern California, where neighborhoods sprawled for miles and most people commuted an hour to work.

I hadn't considered the distance between our houses before, and thinking about it now made me slightly anxious. I had never lived so close to a client, which wasn't entirely on accident: even though work sometimes took over my life, it was important for me to maintain physical distance between myself and my work, especially after getting attacked by a client's ex-wife.

When I reached Willow Glen Lane, I was alarmed to see a police cruiser parked in front of Slant House. I sat in my car and watched the property until I saw a pair of police officers emerge from the house. They were conversing quietly, heads close together.

For the most part, I had nothing against cops or the LAPD. I knew from experience that tracking people down and putting the pieces of a crime together could be difficult—if not downright impossible—and I had a wary respect for the people who had to do it every single day. That respect, however, didn't always go both ways, and my team and I had found ourselves the targets of more than one officer's ire when we showed up at a victim's house and started asking questions. Left City stayed away from active investigations because we didn't want to obstruct or interfere with police work, but we had still met a fair few cops who seemed to consider us nothing more than vultures, picking at leftovers.

The cops walked down the steps in front of Slant House, then got into their cruiser and drove away. I waited until they were gone to climb out of my car and glance both ways. I started when I realized I wasn't alone—someone was standing outside of Janine's house, smoking a cigarette and watching Slant House with interest.

Zac. I recognized him from the mug shot Blake had pulled for me. His dark blond hair had been trimmed on the sides but left to grow long on top. Zac had a nervous, caged look, and the type of honed physique that indicated malnutrition paired with physical activity. He was lanky and tall in an ungainly way—as though the top part of his body had spontaneously sprouted, leaving the lower half behind. His odd clothing only emphasized his body's odd proportions: an oversized T-shirt and tiny, ripped shorts which revealed long, pale, hairless legs.

Zac finished the cigarette and tossed it into the bushes behind him, then turned and saw me watching him. In the house behind him, a window screeched open, and Janine poked her head out.

"Zac? Zac!"

She saw me standing there and frowned.

"Come inside, Zac."

Zac ignored her and continued watching me. I finally broke eye contact and walked across the street, then climbed the steps leading up to Slant House. Almost as soon as I had knocked, the front door flew open. Melia stood inside, wan and fearful, blinking against the onslaught of sunlight.

"Rainey," she whispered. "Come in, come in. Quick."

I crossed the threshold, wary, and Melia immediately shut the door and locked it.

"Oh my god," she said, then leaned against the wall and closed her eyes. "I'm so glad you're here."

Something out of the corner of my eye caught my attention, and I glanced down at Melia's dress. A dark stain.

"Melia—oh, god, is that blood? What happened?" I exclaimed, stepping forward. "Are you okay? Did someone—"

"I'm fine," she said, cutting me off. Her eyes fluttered open, and she ran her hands through her hair. "Look, something happened. I don't want you to be alarmed, but it's . . . well, it's rather violent."

"Where did that blood come from?" I reached out and almost touched her shoulder, but then thought better of it and let my hand drop to my side. There was something about Melia's wide eyes and sweet nature that made me want to gently put an arm around her shoulder and insist that everything was going to be okay.

Melia didn't seem to notice my stunted gesture, though. She motioned vaguely toward the back of the house. "There's so much wild space up here," she said. "We used to get all kinds of animals stalking through the backyard. Quail, coyotes, deer . . . I heard a crash early this morning, and when I woke up . . . well . . . it was an animal. A coyote, or a feral dog. I couldn't tell. It was all cut up."

"Where?" I narrowed my eyes, trying to parse meaning from the story. "Melia, what happened?"

She hesitated. "At first I thought it had fallen through the window of the library, and got cut up in the process. But, of course, that wasn't possible—those windows are so *thick*—"

"Show me."

I followed Melia through the house and was struck once more by the feeling that it was an elaborate stage, a viewing platform accessible from a hundred points. Shafts of light angled through the living room, illuminating the recessed floor, the fireplace, the velvet couches. Last time I was here, I had only been in the living room, the dining area, and the kitchen, but as we moved through the house I recognized many of the details I had seen in the photographs of Slant House.

The house had a minimalistic, open floor plan with furniture and pieces of art staged at intervals. I had been in some very luxurious houses, both from working as a PI and from my work with Marcus, but Slant House was one of the most beautiful homes I had ever seen. Part of the elegance lay in the balance between lavish and austere: the spare nature of both the architecture and the interior design precluded a shift toward excess. Each room contained just enough—a wooden stool from Scandinavia, an antique birdhouse, woven baskets from Japan, a low-slung side table—and not a whit more. For the most part, walls and barriers between rooms had been foregone in favor of a space that flowed seamlessly from one room to the next like a folding house, a life-sized piece of origami.

The library was at the back of the house. Three walls were lined with floor-to-ceiling bookshelves, while a fourth wall was a large window that looked out onto the garden and tennis court behind Slant House. The lower half of the window was shattered, and shards of glass lay across the floor. In the middle of the chaos was a dark swipe of blood, a stain the size of a dog. A smear amidst the shards indicated a hasty cleanup job.

"Jesus," I whispered, willing myself not to look away. I was okay with blood in a theoretical sense—gore and violence were tangential and inevitable facets of private investigation—but there was something raw about the tableau in front of me. I could imagine Melia blinking awake to the sound of glass breaking, stumbling blearily through the empty corridors of the house, and finding . . . this.

"What happened to the animal's body?" I almost gagged on the salty, rich smell of iron. A baby grand piano sat in the corner, and beneath it lay a green Persian rug. The coyote blood had stained the edge of the carpet, and I knew it would never come out—that no matter how hard Melia scrubbed at the damaged filaments, she would never be able to erase this.

"One of the cops . . . he threw it away for me. In the garbage out back," Melia said, rubbing her arms as if cold. She looked dazed, as though she might still be in shock. "They said they'd look into it, but I think they were just saying that to calm me down."

"Do you think Jasper did this as well?" I held my breath, dreading the answer.

"I don't know." Melia's voice was quiet, emotionless. "After that letter . . . I just don't know. I spent several hours going over everything with the cops, and I realized that I just don't know him anymore. He's a stranger to me."

"Did you tell them your suspicions about Jasper?"

"Of course I did." She closed her eyes and pinched the bridge of her nose. "I don't mean to sound dismissive, but it's been a long morning."

"And what did they say?"

She opened her eyes and fixed me with her gaze. "They didn't believe me. They said the same thing you did. Why would he make contact after all this time? Why would he risk his safety? Blah-blah-blah."

I closed my eyes and thought. "What time did you hear the crash?"

"Six? I was still half-asleep. I don't normally get up until nine or ten."

"And was there a rock or something on the floor? Do you have any idea how the window was broken?"

Melia shook her head. She looked like she was having trouble summoning the words. "I don't . . . I didn't see anything. Maybe a shovel or something they took with them. The cops looked around the yard, but they didn't see anything."

I glanced around the room, noting how open and vulnerable the space was. Three large windows. Slant House hadn't been designed with the modern world in mind, with all its dangers and prying eyes.

I couldn't keep looking at the stained carpet or the bloody spot on the floor, so I cast my gaze around, finally looking at the piano. In all the chaos I hadn't even noticed it, but looking now, I saw it was an antique Wurlitzer, a rare and highly coveted instrument. It must have cost a small fortune.

I felt a wild urge to touch the keys, strike a chord, but I refrained, knowing it would have been completely inappropriate to the situation. I had some casual piano training, nothing more than amateur status. Then I was struck by a sudden fear that Melia would ask me to play something; I hated it when people asked me to perform on the spur of the moment. Fortunately, though, Melia's thoughts seemed to be elsewhere.

"I'll clean that up later," she said, gesturing to the glass. "I had to show the cops. I suppose it was only a matter of time before it happened; the whole house is made of glass."

I noted the contrast between the library and the other rooms of the house. Here, simplicity had been discarded in favor of a sort of gleeful clutter. In one corner of the room sat a clear Lucite chair, stacked high with books. An antique desk stood in front of one wall of bookshelves, and a large globe sat next to it. A stack of art prints leaned up against the desk.

"Can we go somewhere else?" Melia said, her eyes seeking mine. "I need to get out of this room."

"Of course."

I followed her back through the house, into the kitchen. Melia started banging open cupboards, looking for something. "Damn it. Lived here my whole life and suddenly nothing's where it's supposed to be."

I glanced out the kitchen window, toward the Flack house across the street. From this distance I couldn't see anything—no movement in the windows, no other signs of life—but I was still thinking about Zac and the way he had watched Slant House.

Melia produced a small machine resembling a spaceship, then turned it over, looking baffled. "Damn it," she muttered. "I wanted to make you coffee."

"Melia," I said, wondering how I should broach the question. I had more than enough experience with anxiety, and thanks to a top violin teacher and performance coach, I knew how to defuse it. Melia's stints at rehab hadn't seemed to give her many coping strategies, or at least, nothing that could help her self-soothe. If Blake was right—if the administration had seen weakness and addiction as a manifestation of the devil—Melia would have seemed like a problem child, something to be whipped and broken into shape. I wondered how much information and dark conjecture I could give her without causing her to shatter, fall apart.

She reached up and started rooting through the cupboards again until she found a jar of coffee grounds. It slipped out of her hands and scattered across the counter.

"Damn it!"

She turned, and again I saw the bloodstain from the coyote smeared across the front of her dress. The dress, like everything else I had seen Melia wear, looked expensive, and she hadn't even bothered to change. Perhaps she wasn't as naïve and frightened as I had initially thought. My pity was replaced with a sort of admiration for Melia and everything she had endured. She was a survivor.

"Here," I said. "Forget that rig. Let's see if there's anything else in this kitchen."

Melia swept a pile of coffee grounds into her hand and dumped them into the sink. "I don't know how anything works in this house," she said. "I'll be honest, Rainey—the kitchen was Caroline's domain, and my parents didn't let us do anything in here. Not that I was home most of the time. I was at school during the week."

I went through the cupboards until I found a Chemex with a wooden handle. Melia stared at it when I held it out.

"What's that?"

"It's for pour-overs. Do you have filters?"

Melia gave me a helpless look.

"Right," I said, looking into the cupboard again. The Chemex filters were on the shelf where the coffee grounds had been. I had escaped working in a café, unlike most of my friends, but I was familiar with various methods of coffee and tea preparation from working at the studio with Marcus. Every composer he had worked with seemed to prefer a different hot drink, from black coffee to authentic matcha from Japan.

I put the kettle on the stove to boil, then turned to face Melia.

"We need to talk about your neighbor," I said. "Zac Flack."

Melia looked confused for a moment, then laughed. "The dirtbag who lives across the street with his mother?"

"Do you know him?" I asked seriously.

"Do I *know* him?" Melia gave me an incredulous look, then laughed. "Yuck, pass. It might sound harsh, Rainey, but I've spent the last four years in the deep and dirty South—I think I'm done with snaggletoothed white boys."

I watched her without saying anything.

"What?" she snapped.

I sighed. "This is part of my job. I have to ask you about all the suspicious characters in your radius. Someone who lives across the street and recently got out of prison ranks high on that list—especially if you just found a dead animal on the floor of your library."

I pointed at the blood on her dress, and Melia looked down.

"I take something like that very seriously, Melia."

She looked abashed, then, and blinked. "I'm sorry," she said, her voice quiet.

"Thank you."

The kettle screamed as the water boiled. I scooped coffee grounds into the Chemex and slowly poured the water over the grounds. Melia watched as the first drops began to percolate through the filter and drop into the glass bowl on the bottom.

"So, I have to ask you again," I said. "How well do you know Zac Flack?"

Melia rubbed her arm, hard, and looked out the window. "Like, not at all."

"Not at all? You were never friends with him, even as kids?"

"I boarded during the week," she said. "And I think he went to one of those remedial schools for troubled kids. Even when I was here, it's not like I spent all my free time getting to know the neighbors."

"Do you happen to know which school Zac went to?"

"No," she said, her voice short. "No idea. My parents didn't like the Flacks, and we tended to stay away from them."

I drummed my fingers on the counter. "Do you know if Zac has any violent tendencies? Violent, as in psychopathic. He just got out of jail for breaking and entering."

Melia stalled for a moment, thinking. "No. I don't think so. I mean, I don't know."

"Okay, I'll look into him some more," I said. "Let me know if you remember anything else."

Melia nodded and wrapped her arms around her body. She looked like she had disengaged for a moment, retreated inside herself.

"Let's get some business out of the way," I said. "We'd like to work with you, obviously, which is why I'm here. If you still want to hire us, of course—I mean, I know you called the police about the coyote, so maybe you want to turn things over to them."

"No!" she exclaimed, reaching across the table to grab my hand. I jerked my hand away, surprised by the sudden unexpected contact, then felt bad when I saw Melia blush.

She dropped her gaze, and when she spoke, her voice was quiet but insistent. "Rainey, you have to help me. There's a chance the police won't *do* anything. They bungled the entire case last time."

"We're happy to help you in any way that we can," I said, trying to re-establish a sense of camaraderie with the warmth of my tone. I could see how desperate Melia was to connect with someone—with anyone—and I worried I had embarrassed her by jerking my hand away. "I spoke to my colleagues, and we've agreed to take the case."

She nodded, seeking my eyes before glancing out the window again. "I'm sorry," she said. "I really hate being this emotional. It's just . . . the last four years have made it hard for me to trust people."

"I understand," I said softly. "I can only imagine what this time has been like for you."

The coffee was done percolating. Melia had already set out two cups, and I poured the coffee into both. Melia dosed hers with milk and sugar, then held the milk carton out to me.

"I take mine black, thanks."

Melia watched me as she sipped her coffee. I glanced involuntarily at the bloodstain on her dress, and she followed my gaze down, then started when she saw the blood.

"Shit," she whispered. "With everything that happened, I just sort of forgot—here, I'm going to go change. Be right back."

She scampered out of the room, and I listened as her footsteps receded into the house.

I glanced around the kitchen, waiting for Melia to return. There was a curious dichotomy at play inside Slant House: while all the glass and sunlight made the home feel incredibly exposed, there was an insular element about the architecture and design that hushed the outside world. I closed my eyes and listened to the sounds of the house: the tinny whir of the old Northstar fridge, which dipped occasionally into a reluctant, guttural chatter; a branch dusting against the side of the wall outside the kitchen; the *plip-plip* of water from the kitchen tap. And then I heard something else, coming from deep within the house.

It came through the halls as a low whistle, a snatch of sound, and then a slashed *oooOOoooh!* I left the kitchen and followed the sound as it faded away, then grew in volume once more. The sound led me through the living room and down the hall, dappled with shade and light from the dancing trees outside. I emerged in the library. A slice of wind tossed the trees, and suddenly I knew what I had heard: nothing more than the resistance of broken glass against the growing gale. I felt a sudden throb of horror as I looked at the animal blood on the floor, the jagged web of broken glass—and realized, once again, how very unsafe Melia was here, all alone.

"What are you doing?"

I jumped, shocked out of my thoughts, then spun around to see Melia standing in the doorway. Her hair was damp, and she had changed out of the stained dress. She wore a pair of thick, high-waisted cream trousers and a camisole made of mint-green silk. The camisole revealed the top of her scar, which was a shiny pink against her pale skin. Melia wasn't wearing a bra, and I could see her nipples through the fabric of her top. As soon as I noticed this, I glanced away, blushing furiously, then hating myself for it.

To my surprise, Melia laughed out loud. "You're blushing."

"No, no, it's fine. I'm not."

"You *are*. What happened?"

"God, I'm so embarrassed," I muttered, putting my hands over my face. "I've never been very good at hiding my emotions."

Melia looked down at her chest. "Whoops," she said. "I stopped wearing a bra years ago. I hope that doesn't bother you."

I glanced up to see a playful smile on her lips. Her hair was pulled away from her face, and I was struck once more by how stunning she was. If things had been different, she could have been a model, or perhaps an actress.

"You okay?" she pressed.

"Sorry—you just caught me off guard, that's all—I was thinking about your security, actually. We need to get your window fixed. Today."

"I already called someone about that," Melia said. "They'll be by this afternoon."

"What kind of security do you have? Is there a system installed in the house?"

She sighed. "We have a system in place, but the police said I should upgrade it."

"Good," I said. "Yes, that's very important."

"So what happens now?" Melia said, folding her arms across her chest.

I took out my notebook and a pen. "Left City charges eighty-five dollars an hour," I said. "I believe I mentioned that already. That's per associate, so if we're all working on it at the same time—"

"Eighty-five per person, per hour," Melia interrupted. "That's fine."

I raised an eyebrow. "These cases can add up quickly," I said. "Especially if we don't find Jasper straightaway. We'll also look into other people who might have motive to hurt you, in case Jasper didn't write the letter—but all of this takes time."

"This is important to me."

I set the notepad down and faced Melia. "We've had stalker cases before," I said. "One of them cost the client fifteen thousand dollars, and she was able to recoup some of that through a civil suit, because the stalker turned out to be her boss. If you're not planning on taking this to court, you'll never get that money back."

"But I'll have peace of mind," Melia countered. "Can't put a price on that."

"And we'll require a retainer of five thousand dollars," I said. "Before we begin. It's standard practice."

Melia went to a desk against the wall. She produced an envelope from a drawer, then pulled out a wad of bills.

"I'm not trying to patronize you, but are you sure you want to keep that kind of cash around? Especially now, with people breaking windows."

"I've always kept cash on me," Melia said. "Cash is freedom, Rainey. Nobody can track you that way."

I watched her count off a section of bills.

"I'm sorry," I interrupted. "I should have explained—the deposit needs to be a check."

"Why?"

"For a variety of reasons, but first and foremost because we need to establish a paper trail." I spread my hands. "I'm sorry to make it complicated. It's just the way we've always done things."

Melia drummed her fingertips on the desk. "I hope you won't laugh at me," she said, her voice quiet. "But I don't have any checks."

"That's fine. You can just sign the paperwork today and mail a check later, once you stop by your bank."

"No," she said, her face flushed. "I mean, I don't *have* any checks. I don't even have my own bank account."

She looked embarrassed, unable to make eye contact. I was stumped, unsure what to say.

"This is what I meant," she said desperately. "They've always treated me like a child. I've *never* had my own bank account, not even when my parents were alive. As soon as I turned eighteen, I wanted to open one, but my parents insisted that someone was liable to take advantage of me. Everything's always been managed for me, Rainey, you don't understand."

"Now, hold on—"

"And then they were killed, and I was shuffled away to Georgia."

Melia wilted into the desk chair. She looked perilously close to tears.

"Look," I said. "It's not really a big deal. I guess we could make an exception, as long as you sign the paperwork."

She sniffled. "No, I don't want you to do that. You shouldn't give me special treatment."

I did a quick mental calculation of how far the cash would go toward smoothing out Left City's deficit problem. We needed a new case, one that would pay well, and thinking about it now, the rule about taking checks seemed almost arbitrary.

"It's not really special treatment," I reasoned. "You'd still officially be a client, and all that. We try to be flexible when we can. You do have some unusual circumstances."

"Thank you." Her voice was faint. "I didn't think it would be so hard to come back to LA. I thought I'd be free once I finally left Georgia, but that was a joke."

I handed Melia the contract, and she grabbed a pen.

"Read it before you sign," I said. "I'll wait."

A lull fell over the room as Melia flipped through the contract, reading it. I heard the scritch of a pen as she signed her name, and then came over and handed it back to me.

"Melia," I said carefully. "Feel free to tell me this is none of my business, but don't you think you'd feel safer if you moved out of Slant House? Is there anyone you could stay with?"

"I don't have any friends." Her face was unreadable. "I used to, I guess, but I haven't spoken to anyone from Los Angeles since . . . well, I've been away for a long time."

"There must be somewhere else." I glanced at the shards of glass on the floor. "Have you considered staying at a hotel?"

"Where?" Her voice was hard. "I don't have my own bank account, so it's only a matter of time before I'm destitute. And if I moved into an apartment, the landlord would have the keys. I don't trust anyone right now."

"Do you have any skills?"

She pondered my meaning for a moment, then gave a harsh laugh. "You're suggesting I get a job."

"I'm sorry," I said, flushing. "I don't mean to interfere in any way, but if your lawyer controls all your money and you don't have access to your bank accounts, it might make you feel more empowered."

"I *will* get a job," she said, still an edge to her voice. "Believe me, that's my plan once I sort all this stuff out. Even if I could afford to move out of Slant House, though, I wouldn't. This is *my* house. Nobody's going to force me to leave."

"Fair enough. Point taken."

"Look, I know you're just trying to help," she said, softening. "And I appreciate it. I'm tired of feeling scared all the time, and I'm ready to live my own life. That's all."

"I understand."

"So," she said, rubbing her hands together. "What's the first step?"

"This is the part where it gets uncomfortable," I said. "I need you to tell me the names of everyone who dislikes you. We have to cross everyone off the list, not just Jasper."

She chewed a fingernail. "Like, minor dislikes or long-standing grudges?"

"Unfortunately, we need to go through all of them. If you're serious about finding out who broke into your house and left the letter, that is."

She mulled it over for a minute. "Do you want me to think about it and email you? It could take a while for me to go through my whole life."

"Give me a few names off the top of your head. I can start looking into those while you come up with the others."

"There was this bitch named Gretchen at Aggie," she said. "That girl would always report me for the smallest infractions. Oh! My aunt's maid, Laura? Fucking hate that girl. She's this uptight French chick. I swear she used to read my journal. I *know* she went through my things. I caught her doing it once."

"Last name?"

"Something French . . . ? No idea, sorry."

"Okay, well, if she's still in Georgia, I think we can rule out the possibility that she's in Los Angeles, leaving you notes."

"Fair."

"Anyone here waiting for you to come back?"

"You already met the neighborhood welcoming committee," Melia said. "Janine. Ugh. She's the most obvious choice, right?"

I wrote down the name, even though Janine had already crossed my mind.

"Okay. Anyone else?"

To my surprise, Melia burst into laughter. "Oh my god," she said. "I almost forgot. Kitty Curley."

"Are those *C*s or *K*s?"

She spelled it out for me.

"Kitty fucking Curley," she said, leaning back in her chair and looking at the ceiling. "Now there's a social climber for you. My parents used to be friends with her husband, back in the nineties, and even before that, I think. Count von Faber. So along comes Kitty, this dumb college dropout from Long Beach, marries him and changes her name."

"Do you know her name now?"

"I think it's like . . . well, it's *Countess* something. Her husband's dead now, but she kept the name and title. Countess Katrina. No! Catalina! Her name is Catalina von Faber."

I wrote that down.

"Why does Catalina have a grudge against you?"

"The grudge was against my parents," she said. "They cut her off because she started a reality show, and she filmed every part of her day. She kept name-dropping them on the show, and then she'd mention something confidential . . . yeah, she was really angry when they cut her off. I wouldn't be surprised if she still held a grudge against me."

"Can I be honest?"

"Always," she said.

"That seems like a stretch."

"No!" she said, eyes wide. "She has it out for me, believe me. I heard from my lawyer a few days ago—she's writing a tell-all, and apparently there's a lot of stuff about my family. He threatened to sue, but we haven't heard anything back."

I tapped my notepad. "When was all that?"

"About a week ago, I think."

"Do you think she's the type of person to throw a dead animal through your window?"

To my surprise, Melia gave me a pale smile. "I wouldn't put it past her."

Once I was back at my apartment, I booted up my computer and looked up Kitty Curley. It didn't take long to find a wealth of information: she was not only extremely popular on social media, but she had produced three different reality shows, all of which centered around her social life.

On her website I found the generic email address for Kitty's production team, then composed a quick email describing my relationship to Melia and asking if Kitty had any availability in the next week.

I went into my bathroom and splashed water on my face, then drank straight from the tap, feeling overheated. There was a ping from my computer in the next room.

I went back to my desk and sat down. The email address was not one I recognized, but the subject line read "URGENT: Catalina von Faber." I opened the email.

> *Hi Rainey,*
>
> *I'm Catalina's producer. Catalina is most eager to speak with you as soon as possible. She believes she has some information she can impart about the van Aust family.*
>
> *How's tomorrow at noon in Calabasas?*
>
> *Love and light,*
>
> *Mackenzie*

SEVEN

At the office the next morning, I told Blake and Lola about my visit with Melia. They were both quiet as I described the imprint of the coyote on the library floor, the blood that had spilled onto the Persian rug, the glass shards, the wine-colored stain on Melia's dress. Blake, normally circumspect, looked spooked as I shared everything that had happened.

"Wow," Lola murmured when I finished. She looked stunned, and I could see her processing everything I had mentioned. "Does Melia think Jasper killed the coyote too? Or was that someone else?"

"We didn't spend a lot of time discussing it, but yes," I said. "I got the impression she still thinks of Jasper as the main candidate for all of this."

"I've never even *seen* a coyote," Blake said. "How does someone catch and kill one? Where do you even find a coyote?"

"You've never seen one?" Lola frowned. "There are tons of them in the LA mountains. They're nocturnal. Just like you, Blake."

"Thanks, David Attenborough," Blake said, rolling her eyes. "I know what a coyote *is*—I've just never *seen* one."

"Slant House is at the edge of some scrubland," I pointed out. "Lots of chaparral and wild grasses. And it's near Griffith Park."

"Where is Melia staying tonight?" Lola asked. "Surely she's not going to stick around at Slant House, not while all this is going on."

I sighed. "You're thinking like a rational person," I said. "Unfortunately, Melia is not in a rational frame of mind."

Lola stared at me. "You're joking. Really?"

"Really."

"Her funeral," Blake muttered.

"She seemed kind of pissed that I suggested a hotel room." I glanced at my watch. "Before I forget—I want to look further into one of Melia's neighbors. He lives across the street from Melia, and he's out on parole for a B and E charge."

Blake snapped her fingers, frowning. "The kid. I looked him up with the other neighbors."

"Zac Flack."

"Zac muthafuckin' Flack!" Blake crowed. "That's right. As soon as I heard that name, I knew that I was going to write a song about him. It sounds like something a cartoon duck would say: *Zac-Flack, Zac-Flack, Zac-Flack—*"

"You think he might be a threat?" Lola asked, cutting Blake off. "What's his motive, if he's out on parole?"

"Don't know if there is one," I replied. "I just think we need to be thorough. I want to make sure he's not the kind of sicko who'd kill an animal and throw it through a neighbor's window. Or write a threatening letter to scare a woman living on her own."

"I'll do some digging online," Blake said, flexing her fingers.

"Thanks." I grabbed my phone and slipped it into my pocket.

"And where are you off to?" Lola asked.

"Calabasas," I said. "I'm meeting up with someone who used to be friends with Melia's family. Her name's Kitty Curley, also known as Catalina von Faber."

"Oh my god," Lola said, sinking her head into her hands. "Say it ain't so."

I glanced at her, surprised. "You know her?"

"Araceli spends all day watching her show, so of course I know her," Lola groaned. "She's a vapid social climber."

"What do you think this Kitty person will be able to tell you?" Blake asked.

I shrugged. "I'm not sure yet, but she was friends with the van Austs for a long time, and then things ended badly. I'm not sure why, or even if she'll tell me what happened. Either way, she might give some indication of who's out to get Melia."

There were two ways to get from Culver City to Calabasas, and either would take about an hour, depending on traffic. Even though I'd lived in Los Angeles my entire life, I'd only visited Calabasas two or three times, with good reason: it was out of the way and populated entirely by reclusive celebrities who didn't want to mingle with the hoi polloi. There was no real reason to visit that neighborhood, either, unless you lived there; it was comprised of sprawling compounds and gated communities blocked off to the general public.

"Private worlds, my friend," Lola once told me. "You don't get to see inside these houses unless you're the dealer, the doctor, or the divorce attorney."

I decided to avoid driving through the concrete basin of Encino and Tarzana and take the coastal route, which wound along a dazzling strip of bone-colored sand that fringed the Pacific. There were still bits of Old Hollywood out here: I had gone for picnics with Marcus and his family at multimillion-dollar vacation bungalows that had been built as ramshackle cabins to suit the whims of Norma Desmond types back in the 1920s. Most people don't realize that the intersection of Sunset Boulevard and the PCH was once the location of one of the very first film studios, way back in the 1910s.

The sun glanced off my windshield as I turned up Topanga Canyon, and suddenly everything was hushed in shadow. Along the winding canyon roads, traffic took on a different feel; it was easy to identify locals because they careened around curves and whipped past cars that adhered to the speed limit. I had driven this road hundreds of times, knew its ins and outs, but my steadfast old car—a 1970 Datsun coupe—muttered to herself and growled a bit as I shifted gears. In addition to all her other problems, the radio wasn't great, and as soon as the trees knit together over the road, static purred in through the speakers. I snapped the radio off.

Pamela was my car, through and through. I had saved up for a car working hospitality jobs in high school, and then, when I worked for Marcus, finally bought the old girl off a sound engineer who was moving to Japan. Marcus took me aside and counseled against it.

"I know it's flashy, but the blue book value on this kind of car is in the negative," he said. "You'll spend your whole paycheck on parts and labor. Let's go out this weekend and visit some used car dealers, find something practical."

But I didn't want something practical. As soon as I saw the grainy photograph the sound engineer handed over, telling me that he needed to clean shop and sell everything, I knew I was looking at my car. She was worth the steep mechanic's bills and the stifled laughter from Marcus and Diego—each time I came to visit, one of them would stand in the driveway, arms extended like an air traffic controller, guiding me toward the garage. It had been almost six years since I had bought her, though, and other than a few mechanical hiccups, she had never let me down.

I reached the end of Topanga Canyon and abruptly emerged into the manicured concrete and scrub of Calabasas. Here, whatever nature remained had been whipped into submission; the rocks, earth, and chaparral all looked like they had been staged for effect.

It wasn't long before I reached the imposing sandstone gatehouse and iron fence of Palmetto, the gated community where Kitty lived. The guard came out and eyed my car, then took out an iPad.

"Name?"

I told him and waited as he checked something. He took out a walkie-talkie and muttered into it, then nodded and disappeared back into his hut. A moment later, the gate opened, and I drove through.

As I drove, I took stock of the neighborhood. The quiet street stretched on for about sixty feet before it reached a gentle curve and tapered out of sight. All the mansions on the street clung to the same basic color palette: peach, beige, brown. In the distance, a squat range of mountains sat on the horizon, obscured by a thin haze in the air. They looked like they had been etched in the sky with chalk and might be washed away with a swift, clean rain.

The address I had directed me to a gaudy Italianate mansion, the biggest one on the street. Two big vans sat in front of the property, and a camera crew loaded gear into the sides of the vans. I parked across the street from Kitty's mansion, then gathered up my things and made sure my phone had enough battery to last the meeting.

The rippling emerald lawn stretching toward Kitty's house was so jewel-toned that I couldn't help looking for flaws. I walked up the path to the enormous front door, but before I could knock, the door swung open.

A woman with an unnatural tan and bronze curls stood before me, holding a clipboard. She let out a little "Oh!" of surprise. Before I could introduce myself, she sprang forward.

"You must be Rainey!" she exclaimed, her curls bouncing up and down. "I'm Mackenzie, one of the producers for Three L."

"Three L?"

"Catalina's show—*Love and Lust in Los Angeles*? Fans call it Three L."

I followed behind her, confused. "Reality shows have directors?"

She gave a loud chuckle, and I noticed how large her teeth were. "Even reality needs a bit of tweaking now and then," she said. "I'm mostly a continuity expert. It's all *real*, you know . . . but sometimes the camera doesn't catch it, and we need Catalina to repeat it louder, with less cursing."

We had hardly stepped into the house before another woman came swooping in. She didn't even look at me before pressing a clipboard and pen into my hands.

"Standard release and consent. Sign, initial, and date the highlighted sections."

I blinked. "Sorry—what is this?"

"It's a release form," Mackenzie chimed in.

I laughed, embarrassed. "No, of course—sorry, I know what a release form is—"

"All you have to do is sign."

"But I'm not going to be on camera."

The second woman scoffed. "Mackenzie, I don't have time for this. Deal with her."

"As soon as you set foot in Catalina's house, you've basically already agreed to be filmed," Mackenzie said, her smile failing to hide the irritation in her voice. "Someone should have explained that to you."

I could feel them pressing closer, and the foyer rapidly felt more and more claustrophobic. "I'm here on a private matter," I explained. "Nothing to do with Kitty, or the show—"

"You're here about Melia van Aust," the second woman snapped. "And don't *ever* refer to Catalina as Kitty, if you know what's good for you."

I glanced at the walkie-talkie on her waist. A white label across the top read ROSIE H. Rosie had olive skin and black eyes, and she looked like she might punch me if I told her no one more time. I almost consented, just to get her out of my face.

"Right," I tried again. "I'm a private investigator, and this is a *private* matter. Really—we can't put this on television."

I watched Mackenzie's Botox-smooth forehead nobly attempt a frown. She cleared her throat. "It would make excellent television, you know. And you're gorgeous—our audience would love you!"

"I really must insist."

"Everyone already knows what happened to the van Austs!" Mackenzie protested. She gave another sharp laugh, but I could sense the irritation behind the façade. "Come on, Melia was on *Cue* this morning."

"Rainey, *darling!*"

I turned and saw Catalina walking toward me. In person, she was magnetic, radiant, and she almost floated barefoot across the room. As she walked, everyone's gaze followed her.

She came over and took my shoulders, then gave me a kiss on each cheek.

"You beautiful girl," she said, leaning in. "I knew your father. Charlie probably never mentioned me though—different worlds."

The crowd of people pressed in around us.

"You knew my dad?" I shouldn't have been surprised—I was always meeting people who knew my father in one capacity or another, but it was hard to imagine him mixing socially with Catalina.

"I've actually met you too," she said, still holding onto me. "You wouldn't remember. You were so young back then. Such a beauty, even as a child—it was right after one of your concerts. You played with the Chicago Phil. I was back East visiting family."

"I don't remember, I'm sorry," I said.

"That's okay, darling," she purred. "I heard you quit music years ago. And your poor mother—I should have reached out. Life has a funny way of throwing things at you."

At the mention of my mother, I started to feel claustrophobic again. I wished Catalina would release my shoulders.

"And now you're a private investigator! I could hardly believe it when Mackenzie told me you were coming. My goodness. Investigating Melia van Aust and the tragedy around her murdered family. *Butchered* family. The family was butchered. Shit."

She hit her forehead and turned. "Sorry, guys," she said. "Can we go again?"

I blinked, stunned.

"That was good, Catalina." A young woman with glasses and purple hair brushed toward us. "I had everything up until 'now you're a private investigator.' The audio wasn't great after that—we'll run a check on your audio pack. And we need to get Rainey miked up."

I stared in disbelief as the woman came toward me with an audio pack and a small clip-on microphone. She didn't even make eye contact as she started lifting up my shirt to attach the equipment.

"Hey, hold on! What do you think you're doing?" I pushed her away and stepped backward, back into the sunlight.

The woman followed, still holding out the equipment. "It's a microphone? So we can hear what you're saying?"

"I know what a microphone is," I said, exasperated. "Who gave you permission to touch me? No, you know what? This is over. We're done here."

I shuddered as I hurried back down the path. I could hear confusion and then indignation as Catalina's crew all started talking at once. *Fuck those guys.*

I reached my car and glanced up to see someone watching me. A car sat across the street. Beat-up and nondescript, there was nothing noteworthy about it except for the man behind the wheel. He had the type of bulk that indicated muscle gone to flab. He wore cheap sunglasses; even from across the street I could see that his clothing—beige polo, cheap knockoff shades—didn't fit in with the neighborhood. Thinning red hair stood up from his scalp.

He was staring straight at me and didn't look away when I met and held his gaze. I was so distracted by the man in his cheap car—a dust-colored Acura—that I didn't hear anyone on the path behind me.

"Rainey! Rainey, wait!"

The Acura suddenly screeched off, tearing away from the curb and careening around the curve in the street too quickly for me to register the license plate. I turned and saw Catalina picking her way down the path in bare feet.

"My pedicurist is going . . . to . . . kill me!" She gasped, then burst into laughter. "Always running around in bare feet."

Catalina reached me, then blew her hair out of her face and put her hands together.

"I'm sorry," she said. "Filming can be chaotic."

"Yeah," I said, failing to hide the irritation in my voice. "Don't worry about it. Thanks anyway."

"Look," she said, her face going serious. "I meant what I said. I remember Charlie. He probably didn't think much of me, at least not at first. I think I won him over in the end."

I glanced behind her and saw the entire crew watching us.

"Right."

"I'm serious."

"Is this being filmed? Is someone hiding behind one of those bushes?"

"Oh, Rainey, don't be paranoid! Filming doesn't work like that."

I squinted against the sunlight glancing off the windows behind her. "I worked at a film studio for three years. I do have some idea of how filming works."

"Okay." She bowed her head, and I saw a little of the bounce go out of her posture. "I hear you. Your feelings and your concerns are totally valid. I really just want to talk, though, and I promise we won't film any of it."

I hesitated.

"And I won't sit down and discuss it with my friends at brunch next Saturday when we film a reunion episode," she added. "Oldest trick in the book, hon. If someone refuses to be on camera, you just quote them in a later episode and get the information across that way."

I almost laughed at the unexpected candor.

"You still don't trust me?"

To my shock, Catalina unzipped her dress and pulled it down around her waist, exposing everything to the entire neighborhood. As I watched in stunned disbelief, she removed her audio equipment and tossed it on the grass behind her with a little flourish.

"Don't look so scandalized," she said. "I've paid enough for this body, so I might as well show it off. Come on, let's talk by the pool."

I followed her around the side of the house. We emerged into the backyard, which melted into the golden hills beyond the property. There was a turquoise infinity pool surrounded by beige stones. Catalina walked over to the edge of the pool, plonked down next to it, and dipped her feet in the water.

"Join me," she said. "It's so hot."

"All right," I said after a pause. I slipped off my shoes and sat next to her, then lowered my feet into the pool. The water felt nice on my ankles.

"You're quite pretty, you know," Catalina said, studying my face.

"That's what counts in Los Angeles, right?" I tried not to roll my eyes.

Her face went serious. "Yes, it does."

I gave a surprised laugh. "You're not going to give me some platitude about how girls can become anything they want, as long as they work hard?"

"Do I seem like the type to give bullshit platitudes?"

"Maybe not."

Catalina stuck a hand in the water and shook it. "I got into Stanford as a junior in high school," she said. "A junior. Me. I wanted to study psychology and make a *difference*." She spoke the last bit ironically. "Halfway through my third year, my little sister got sick, so I came home. Finished my courses at the local community college because we lived out in the middle of nowhere. Before the internet, you know?"

She had transformed from the camera-ready clown into someone more introspective.

"The world was different back then, but some things haven't changed," she said. "When my sister died, I moved to New York. I didn't want what I had before, and in some ways, I think I wanted to destroy myself. Started doing prescription pills, alcohol, yada yada. And then I met the count."

"Was that your fairytale ending?"

"Nah," Catalina said, shaking a finger. "The count was broke. *I* brought us back from the brink. *I'm* the one who consolidated our debts, set up an investment plan, started thinking about the future. He was a complete fraud in the end—coasting on some old family title—but really, he was completely lost until he met me. Everyone gives him credit for discovering me. What bullshit. It was all me, sweetheart."

She flicked a hand through the water.

"Nobody sees past a pretty face. If they're going to reduce you to *pretty*, at least find a way to use it to your advantage."

To my surprise, I found myself respecting Catalina.

She stared out over the canyon behind the house. "Believe it or not, I got myself on this path because I was sick of all the lying. How ironic, huh? I had learned so much in those two years watching my sister die, I couldn't go back to some Ivy League school and listen to an old white dude lecture me on the 'real world.' I wasn't going to climb someone else's ladder, not anymore. They wanted me to start from scratch, prove myself to them—instead, I built my own ladder."

"Reality TV?"

"Honey," she said. "Everyone is lying. Everyone has an agenda. If your agenda can make you ten million dollars a year, *earn that money.* This is just a fun diversion. Believe it or not, studying psychology taught me everything I need to know about working in entertainment. I know what people want. I can take someone's dream and package it up, then sell it back to them for a tidy profit."

I heard a *snick* and a *whoosh* as the patio door opened behind us. Catalina and I both turned to look as Mackenzie stuck her head out the door.

"Hey, Cat," she called. "We're on a schedule here. Can you wrap it up?"

"Give me five minutes," Catalina said, turning back to look at me. Once Mackenzie had disappeared inside, she shook her head at me.

"*Cat,*" she said, with venom. "I can't fucking stand her."

"Who—Mackenzie?"

"She's a studio lackey who thinks she'll make studio head one day," Catalina said. "My name is not *Cat*, but no matter how many times I tell her that, she keeps chopping the rest of the syllables off."

"Doesn't she work for you? I mean, it's your show."

"Ha! Try telling her that. One of the downsides of working in this industry is that you have to put up with people like Mackenzie. They think they're smarter than you, even as they fail to advance beyond even the lowest of the bottom rungs. She works for Bravo." Catalina sighed and looked at her phone. "You didn't come all this way to talk about reality television, and if I'm not inside within five minutes, Mackenzie will be back. So—shoot your questions."

"Well, Melia hired my team because someone wrote her a threatening letter," I said. I decided not to mention the coyote or the shattered window. "I know that you used to be friends with the van Austs, but you cut ties a long time ago."

"And you're wondering if I'm the new pen pal?" Catalina's eyes twinkled.

"Not at all," I said honestly. "But you were friends for a long time, right? Any idea who might have a grudge against Melia?"

Catalina gave a bitter laugh. "Where to even begin? Fucked up doesn't begin to describe that family. The van Austs were toxic, and if I knew you any better, I'd tell you to stay away from the whole mess."

I must have looked surprised because Catalina patted my arm. "How much do you know about their history?"

"I know all the stuff that was printed in the papers," I said. "But I only met Melia two days ago. We haven't had much time to dig into the particulars."

"The first thing you should know about the van Austs," she said, leaning in, "is that they were bullshit artists, just like my husband."

"How so?"

Catalina sighed and ran a hand through her hair. She glanced behind her, toward the kitchen. "You sure I can't convince you to do five minutes for the show?"

I shook my head and smiled. "Not a chance."

Catalina nodded. "Fair enough," she said. "Well, Lem was good friends with my husband. I probably knew them better than anyone before they were killed."

"Lem?"

"Wilhelm's nickname," she explained. "He was very tight-lipped on some matters, but they would go off sometimes for a weekend in the mountains, and when Anton would come back, he'd talk about how Lem was scared of losing everything. Lem always thought someone was after him."

"After him?" I echoed. "Do you know who it was?"

"Debtors, I'm guessing." Catalina shrugged. "This is the thing with nobility: it's outdated, we've evolved past it. Once you don't have three thousand peasants paying tithes to your estate, you actually have to work for a living. And when you're very, very old money, there's a certain shame around having to work. Lem had debt in spades, sweetheart. I think he made some bad investments and people were after him."

"I know the murders were never solved, but do you have an opinion on who might have killed Wilhelm and Abigail?"

Catalina leaned in. "This isn't conclusive, of course, but there was something off about Jasper," she said. "When you spend all day studying faces and how to best convey emotion to an audience, you can see when someone doesn't have emotions. Or feelings. There was something black in those eyes."

My heart started pounding, and despite the heat of the day, I felt cold all over. I thought again of Melia and how vulnerable she was, how vulnerable she had always been. I knew it was unlikely that Jasper would come back for Melia in broad daylight, but then again, Melia's neighborhood was secluded, and if Jasper *did* return that afternoon, Melia might be in real danger.

"Jasper," I repeated, trying to keep the panic out of my voice. "I've heard rumors that he was involved, but you actually knew him—and you really think he could have murdered his whole family?"

Catalina spread her hands and shrugged. "You know they sent him away to boarding school, right? And this wasn't Choate, either—they sent him to a disciplinary school, one of those awful Élan places. They were trying to rewrite his personality."

The door opened behind us, and Mackenzie stuck her head out again. The plastic smile was gone. "Catalina, we need to get rolling."

Catalina nodded and turned to me. "Well," she said, "thanks for coming by. I hope I was able to give you something."

"You did," I said, and meant it.

"Oh! My memoir's coming out soon, I almost forgot to mention it. We're putting the finishing touches on it now."

"Right," I said, remembering. "Melia actually mentioned that."

Catalina gave me a coy smile. "What'd she say?"

I decided not to lie. "She mentioned her lawyer wants to stop publication."

"Ha! Wouldn't be a proper memoir without at least one lawsuit. I'll have book galleys to send out soon. I'd love to send you a copy."

"That would be great," I said. I reached into my bag and found a business card, then handed it to her. "My phone number and the address of my office are here."

She gave me one last appraising look. "You're smart, I can tell," she said. "Not just another pretty face. Look out for yourself, Rainey. The van Austs have a way of eating people alive."

EIGHT

As soon as I left the gated community, I called Melia. She picked up after two rings, and I could almost hear her smiling into the phone.

"Well, hello, Rainey. Didn't think I'd hear from you so soon."

"Hi," I said, immediately reassured by hearing her voice. "I just wanted to check up on you."

"You're sweet," she said softly. "I'm fine—I spent the morning clearing out the library, but I think I got most of the blood."

"And what about the window?"

"There are some men here now, fixing the glass. Did you know that someone who fixes windows is called a glazier?"

I laughed. "I didn't know that."

"Sometimes I'm in awe of all the things I don't know," she said. "Brave new world."

"I'm heading back to the office," I said. "I'll be in touch soon, but call me if anything happens."

It was three o'clock, a deep summer afternoon. One of the best things about setting my own schedule in Los Angeles was the ability to drive in non-peak traffic. Believe it or not, sometimes the freeways were like glorious, unclogged arteries, smooth silver ribbons linking various parts of the city together. On a clear day, when I was listening to a great soundtrack and could drive a hundred miles per hour and not have to tap my brakes a single time, the city made me believe anything was possible.

My conversation with Catalina had given me a lot to think about. One of the most interesting facets of being a private investigator was how the span of a few hours could change my entire outlook on not only a person, but an entire industry. Since I had never been a big fan of reality television, it had never occurred to me that most of it might be scripted, rehearsed, and coddled into perfection. It seemed so blatantly obvious that I felt stupid I hadn't realized it until now.

An image of the Acura flashed into my mind. If the man had been sitting in a Range Rover or a Porsche, he might not have stuck out to me. Then again, if he hadn't been staring straight at me—or if he hadn't driven away as Catalina came to talk to me—he might not have been suspicious either.

I tried to shake off the image of the man—red hair, squat nose, eczema—as I walked into the office. I was so distracted that I nearly collided with someone who was standing just inside the door.

"You have a guest," Blake called, unnecessarily.

The man was compact and nondescript. He was somewhere in his late fifties, shorter than me, with thinning dark hair and an olive complexion. He held a manila envelope in his hands, which he handed to me.

"Paul Karnak," he said. "I represent the van Aust family estate. You must be Rainey Hall."

He didn't extend his hand for a shake.

"Pleasure's all mine," I said, after a momentary pause.

"I'll skip the pleasantries, Miss Hall. We appreciate your time, but your assistance of Melia van Aust is unnecessary."

I glanced down at the envelope. Blake was watching the visitor with interest.

"What's in the envelope?"

"A cease-and-desist order," he said.

"Well, Mr. Karnak," I said, raising an eyebrow. "Thanks for stopping by, but as Melia is legally an adult and therefore entitled to hire whomever she chooses, you're not entitled to terminate our contract."

He heaved a sigh, as though he were already impatient with me. "Are you aware that Melia was declared a threat to her own well-being and ordered to complete inpatient treatment at a facility in Georgia?"

I nodded thoughtfully. "That was four years ago, right?"

A line appeared in his forehead. "Melia has been deemed unfit to manage her own finances, and as the lawyer managing her estate, I can tell you right now that you will not be paid for your work. Do I make myself clear, Miss Hall? It's a waste of your time, money, and efforts, not to mention a potential legal liability."

I grinned, then glanced at Blake. "Wouldn't be the first time a client couldn't pony up the cash. Lucky we don't have a big overhead."

"I'm here as a courtesy," he said with another sigh. His lack of emotion told me I was nothing more than a speed bump to him, an obstacle he felt confident in overcoming. "I could have easily sent this by courier, but I wanted to make sure that you got it immediately. That you didn't waste any time on research or investigating . . . or whatever it is you do here."

"I'd be interested to know how you found out about me," I said.

"I decline to answer that."

"Phone surveillance," Blake called from her computer. "They probably have cameras on the house as well. Maybe someone watching the street for visitors. Is that too old-fashioned? No," she concluded, giving Karnak a once-over. "Dude's old-fashioned."

Karnak slowly turned to look at Blake and seemed to notice her for the first time. "This is cute," he said. "Girl power. You have anyone over eighteen working here?"

Blake gave Karnak a Cheshire cat grin and leaned back in her wheelchair. "You gonna quote the Spice Girls and tell me you're not a retrograde chauvinist who has a single book by Germaine Greer on your bookshelf that you take out every Thanksgiving to assuage the temper of your angry feminist daughter when she comes home from college?"

Karnak blinked.

"Never mind, Grandpa," Blake said, flexing her fingers and turning her attention back to the keyboard. She slipped on a pair of headphones and started drumming out a beat on her desk.

Karnak looked dazed.

"I'd tell you to fuck off on behalf of my colleague, but I think she just did it for me," I told him kindly.

"Miss Hall, you were alarmingly easy to find," Karnak said with a condescending smile. "It took me less than an *hour* to locate your office. I know your name, your history . . . a young woman like you should really be more careful. There are a lot of dangerous men out there."

"An hour?" I replied. "I'm surprised it took you that long, Mr. Karnak. While we do not advertise, we make it easy for the determined customer to find us. Make no mistake, we want to be found. Since you already had our phone number—from surveilling Slant House, I might add—you had a massive head start. Might I suggest updating your internet browser?"

Karnak gave me a pale smile. "I'm not here to argue with you, Miss Hall," he said. "Because there's nothing to argue about. You can accept this missive and move on to a different case, or you can face litigation."

The front door opened, and Lola stepped in. She was glancing down at a piece of paper and nearly collided with Karnak.

"Sorry, excuse me," she said, deftly stepping aside. She frowned at Karnak, then glanced at me. "What's going on?"

Karnak's eyes slid toward Lola. "It's a real *Charlie's Angels* setup in here, isn't it? Gal gang?"

Lola opened her mouth and looked like she might give him a piece of her mind, but I beat her to it.

"You need to update your references. They're about ten years out of date," I told Karnak. "And now, you need to leave because my own legal counsel has just arrived."

Karnak slowly turned to assess Lola. "Her?"

"Yes, *her*," Lola said in a mocking tone. "*Her* went to law school and everything."

"Goodbye, Mr. Karnak. I assume your phone number is somewhere in this document? Never mind answering that; my colleagues and I *do* know how to use the internet. Have a nice day."

⸺

I didn't realize how exhausted I was until I sat down at my desk and rested my head on my arms. The last two days had depleted me, and I was starting to understand how trapped Melia must've felt.

When I raised my head again, Blake was watching me with a look of trepidation.

"What's up?" I said.

"Jasper."

I sat up, revived at the mention of Jasper's name. Blake was the best hacker I knew, and if anyone could track down a missing person who had recently surfaced, it was Blake.

"What did you find?"

"Nothing," Blake said, shaking her head. "*Nothing.* At least, nothing in the last four years. I found plenty of stuff about his history, all the things that happened before his family was killed."

"But . . . what does that mean? He's *that* good at hiding?"

"Not necessarily," Blake said, glancing at her computer. "I seriously doubt that a sixteen-year-old kid would have the foresight and planning to disappear for four years when everyone was looking for him. Anyone can disappear; that's easy. You get on a bus and go somewhere unexpected, use cash instead of cards, toss your phone. The hard part—the almost *impossible* part—is staying hidden. You'd have to plan years ahead to pull off that kind of vanishing act."

"Maybe he's been dead this whole time," Lola mused, glancing between us. "Wow, I just gave myself chills."

"So that leaves the question: Who really killed the van Austs?" I asked. "And where is Jasper's body—if Lola's right?"

"And who's leaving these messages for Melia?" Blake added.

The room fell quiet as we all glanced at each other.

"What else did you find on Jasper?" Lola asked Blake. "You said you looked into his history?"

Blake adjusted her glasses. "Yeah. He went to Harvard-Westlake until tenth grade, and then halfway through tenth grade he was abruptly removed and sent to this school in Utah. Summit Ridge."

"Why does that name sound familiar?" Lola frowned.

"Because there was a class action lawsuit last year brought by former students." The light glanced off Blake's glasses. "It's a reform school where parents pay a shit ton of money to have their kids broken into shape. Apparently there's a lot of abuse."

Her words echoed in my head, reminding me of something. Before I could remember what it was, Lola spoke.

"Sounds like Melia and Jasper both went through something similar," she said. "Like the place Melia went to in Georgia."

"Yeah," Blake said. "Well, I think we all know that the most fucked up kids come from the wealthiest families."

"Do you know why Jasper was sent to Summit?" I asked.

"The records were sealed online," Blake said, then grinned. "But what's a seal to a hacker? Jasper was on the lacrosse team, and from everything I read, he was a pretty decent student who didn't do anything wrong . . . until he beat the shit out of one of his teammates and put him in the hospital. Induced coma."

"Holy shit," Lola whispered. "So he was a violent teen. Mark one in the 'Jasper killed his parents' column."

"Was it a one-off incident?" I pressed. "The attack on the teammate?"

"From everything I read, yes," Blake said. "I found the school psychologist's report as well. When they asked Jasper why he snapped, he said the teammate had made a remark about his sister."

The room fell silent once more. Blake glanced down at her notebook.

"Side note," she said. "The neighbor, Zac Flack?"

"Yeah?" I looked over at her, hopeful.

"He was at Berkeley Hall until junior year, when he was kicked out for selling drugs. Transferred to . . ." She flipped through her notes. "Well, it looks like he just dropped out, because shortly after that, he went away on B and E charges."

I frowned. "Berkeley Hall. Isn't that a really good school?"

"Yeah. Top-tier." Blake looked up at me. "Why?"

"Melia said he went to some reform school."

Blake looked through her notes. "I didn't see that."

"Blake," Lo said. "It's six thirty."

"Shoot," Blake said, glancing at her watch. "It's later than I thought. We'll have to come back to this tomorrow. You guys cool if I jet?"

"Go, we'll see you there." Lola had picked up the envelope and was weighing it in her hands.

"See you?" I looked between them, confused.

Lola glanced at me and gave one sharp shake of the head.

"It's fine," I said, catching on. "Go on, we'll finish up here."

Once Blake had left, I looked up at Lo.

"You asshole," she said, rounding on me.

"Please remind me."

"If you weren't so busy feeding your stupid frog, you might have time to pay attention to your friends."

"My fish!" I jumped up and ran over to the tank. "I haven't even checked on them today. Have you been keeping an eye on them? Everything look okay?"

Lola looked exasperated. "Shade Riot. Tonight at the White Monster. Were you seriously going to bail?"

I hastily shook some flakes into the tank and watched as the fish rippled toward the surface and began eating. Dart lingered at the bottom of the tank, but when he saw the fish moving to the surface, he swam upward. "Thank god. He's moving. He's okay! See, the books worked!"

"Rainey!"

"I'm sorry, I'm sorry," I said. "Of course I'm coming. It's been a long day, that's all. I wouldn't miss Blake's show for the world."

"Don't do this again," Lola warned. She looked irritated, arms folded across her chest.

"Do what?"

"Forget us," she said. "Don't do it again."

NINE

The White Monster was a rambling mansion in the hills above Silver Lake. The hulking Victorian with Gothic spires and gingerbread trim had belonged to a doctor and his wife nearly a hundred years before. The elegant façade belied a gruesome history: Dr. Ness had performed illegal abortions on young women who were desperate and often didn't have the money to pay him for the procedure. The good doctor and his wife performed abortions for years before the couple began murdering the girls and stealing their belongings.

After Dr. Ness was finally caught, at least a dozen girls were unearthed from the garden. Half of them were never properly identified. The house had gone through a few owners and transformations since then, but the current owner also owned a music studio. He used the White Monster as an event space and occasionally let friends throw parties in the backyard, which had been cleared of human remains decades before.

I stopped at my apartment before the show. I quickly pulled on a silk and lace slip that reminded me of Rodarte, swiped on some lipstick, then hopped back in my car and headed toward Silver Lake.

Like myself, Blake was a classically trained musician: she was proficient in piano and could make sense of a violin, but her real specialty was the cello. Like me, she had been a talented young performer on track to keep climbing the somewhat arbitrary ranks of stardom, feeling more and more claustrophobic and out of touch with reality as the years passed. We had both experienced crises that spun us off course: Blake's came in the form of a car crash in her last year of high school, which meant she would spend the rest of her life in a wheelchair.

After six months of grueling physical therapy, Blake told her parents she was done with classical music, and she started taking drum lessons. She was barely on speaking terms with her parents when she started Shade Riot with her boyfriend, Lon. I never would have connected classical music with heavy metal, but for Blake, the transition came naturally.

I parked down the street and ran a hand through my hair, then started walking toward the White Monster. I could already hear muffled laughter and muted conversations.

Diego was smoking a joint outside the house when I arrived. He was in a tuxedo, but the bow tie hung undone around his neck. He coughed and looked up through a cloud of smoke, then grinned at me.

"Pal!" he said, bounding over and throwing his arms around me. "Welcome to the party."

Cars lined the driveway and spilled out onto the street. I could hear the smoky tones of a saxophone drifting out of the backyard, and the quiet babble of voices rose up and over the hedges. A pair of caterers lingered at the edge of the drive, sharing a cigarette.

Introducing Blake and Diego had been lucky happenstance. I knew first-hand how tragedy and suffering can cause people to distance themselves; my friends in high school had abandoned me en masse when my mother disappeared, and the grief morphed me into someone else. Ever since that betrayal, it had been hard for me to trust people, and as a result I tended to compartmentalize different parts of my life. Even though Diego and Lola were already friends, I tended to hang out with all of them separately, trying to keep my friendships separate. When Marcus and Jac announced a huge party to celebrate their thirtieth wedding anniversary, though, the Loews insisted I bring my colleagues around to celebrate. That's when I finally introduced Diego to Blake.

Shade Riot had needed a new guitarist because theirs had just moved back to Spain. As the son of a composer and musician, Diego was well-versed in multiple instruments, including guitar, and although he had never played metal before, he fit in so well with the members of Shade Riot that he soon stepped in to fill the vacancy full-time.

I followed Diego up a garden path made of flagstones. Low lights in cups lit our way, and I trailed my fingers against the plants along the path. The air smelled like milky sweet jasmine. I paused to bury my nose in an orange blossom.

Backstage was a converted dining room that opened out onto the garden, where the bands were performing. Blake sat in the corner, hair done and glasses off, painting thin lines of kohl around her eyes. She looked up and winked at me in the mirror before going back to her makeup.

Shade Riot had put out two albums and been courted by several record labels, but so far, all the band members still held down normal day jobs. Diego was an audio technician, Blake kicked ass at Left City, Lon—Alonso, Blake's boyfriend—worked at a film studio, and Tabitha bounced between jobs because she was easily bored.

Before every show, the members of Shade Riot held a little something they called Rant Sesh. Friends of the band were invited backstage as they got ready, and everyone sat around in a circle to talk about the worst parts of their day. Not along the lines of traffic or missing keys either; we really got into it. More often than not, Diego set the gripes to music.

Tabitha was in the middle of her rant when I sat down. She was sitting on a couch, her ankles tucked up beneath her. She wore an old tennis dress, with long white sleeves and a pleated skirt, and her skin looked almost translucent against the fabric. Her dark hair was tucked up under white ribbons.

"I like the café, don't get me wrong," she said. "But I wish I never got promoted."

Diego picked up his guitar.

"I work with a bunch of party animals," Tabitha went on. "Nobody ever cleans shit, people are always turning up late, and people call in sick when they're hungover. Anyway, I realized I was the only one doing any work around there, so I talked to the manager and told her she had to promote me."

Diego strummed a chord.

"I thought you didn't want a promotion," Lon said.

"I don't! I didn't! But nobody else does any work, so I might as well get paid for it, right? Anyway, check this shit out: the manager gets paid eighty grand a year."

Lon let out a low whistle.

"Lord knows why. The owner's a drunk, he's never there, but as soon as the manager promoted me to second-in-command, she started jagging off work, showing up late, calling in sick, going on vacation."

"How much are you getting paid?" Blake asked.

"Um, she didn't give me a raise."

The entire band crowed their disbelief.

"She sounds like a bitch," Lon said.

"That's the thing," Tabitha said. "I thought we were friends. We *were* friends, and then she promoted me, so basically she's getting paid for the job that I'm actually doing."

"Cunt," Blake muttered.

"So she goes on vacation, right," Tabitha continues. "Five weeks. Five weeks of paid vacation. Tells me, 'Don't worry about a thing, Tabitha. I've organized all the deliveries, all the schedules, etcetera. Call me whenever you need.' And then she leaves, of course, and I have to run the entire place by myself, and the bitch doesn't pick up her phone once."

The band groaned as one.

"So I quit today," Tabitha said. Everyone started clapping, but she held up a hand to stop them. "It wasn't as victorious as all that though. My manager comes back from this solo vacation—the old gal doesn't have any friends, go figure—and I tell her I want a raise. I've been doing all the scheduling, all the ordering, covering people's shifts when they're sick. Anyway, I ask for a raise, and you know what she does? The bitch has a meltdown in the middle of the café. Starts screaming at me in front of customers, in front of staff. Her face was the color of strawberry jam. It was frightening, man."

Everyone was quiet.

"She told me to go home. Get out of her face."

Blake hissed her disapproval.

"So I start to leave, right," Tabitha continued. "And the fat bitch chases me out the door. 'Tabitha. Tabitha. Tabitha. TABITHA! DON'T YOU FUCKING IGNORE ME, TABITHA!' Literally chases me down the street! Thank god she's out of shape and all that. I finally outran her. I didn't say, 'Fuck off, you bitch,' but I'm never going back, so I guess that's quitting."

Everyone was quiet for a moment, then Diego started to play.

"You're a little bit awful," he sang. "No, more than just a little bit, I think you're really full of shit awful. You always tell me what to do, you think I'm not as smart as you—awful I used to think we could be friends—but wait, no, you don't have any friends because—"

"You're awful," everyone else chimed in.

"Awful," Diego continued. "You stamp and shout and lose control, you're nothing but a big asshole, you're—"

"Awful."

"You're—"

"Awful."

"Just—"

"Awful."

Diego finished the song by quickly strumming the guitar and then swinging it in the air. Everyone shouted and cheered, and with their energy up high, they left backstage and went to go set up.

I went outside to find Lola standing by the drinks table. She looked perfectly comfortable there alone, swaying slightly to the music. It was one of the things I admired most about Lola: she was happy by herself at a party and could be present in the moment without even taking out her phone for distraction.

I went up behind her and slipped my arms around her. She tensed, startled.

"Guess *I'm* not the asshole who's late to her friend's party."

She turned around and squeezed me. "Apologies, my queen."

"You look nice." I held her at arm's length to take in her outfit. She was wearing a cream-colored silk jumpsuit with long sleeves and bell bottoms. "I'm going to steal this."

"We're not the same size."

"Oh, fuck off."

I also loved how Lola was always completely comfortable in her own skin. She did nothing to hide the ample shape of her body, and as a six-foot-two woman, she already attracted enough attention. When I was going through puberty, I shot straight upward, leaving the rest of my body behind. I was all out of proportion and hated being tall, but Lola embodied it with grace.

On top of being tall, Lola had the most beautiful, generous curves, and she exuded health. I had never once known her to be on a diet to lose weight, and she openly embraced her love of food. In a city—nay, in a world—where women were constantly being told to be smaller, to diminish themselves, to *fit in*, Lola was a welcome punch in the face.

"Did you just get here?" I asked.

"Yeah, I lost track of time. *Sorry.*"

"They're setting up now. You didn't miss anything except Rant Sesh."

"Damn it. I would have loved to tell them about Melia." She caught my wide-eyed look. "Kidding! I can respect confidentiality agreements."

"What do you think about that whole mess anyway?"

Lola shook her head. "She's got a dick for a lawyer, for a start," she said. "I can't remember ever having a client where the lawyer swooped in and told us not to get involved. That's a bad sign, Rai—the family's clearly hiding something. Or they were, anyway, before they got killed."

"But do you think the letter is the reason Karnak doesn't want us getting involved?"

"I haven't had enough time to think about it." She took a sip of her drink. "I'm guessing it's something bigger."

I chewed a fingernail. "Do you really think he'll sue if we keep her as a client?"

"Good luck with that, buddy. She has a right to hire her own counsel. If he pulled out the old 'she was under a psychiatric hold, she doesn't know what she's doing' card—well, I'd say that's nothing more than a bluff. The hold was four years ago, and if anything, she has a right to another evaluation. No 5150 would hold up after all this time."

I frowned. "Why does he even *care* though? The parents are dead, right? So doesn't that mean Karnak's obligations to the van Austs are done? Melia's in charge of everything—or at least she should be."

Lola sucked her teeth and grimaced. "I'm no expert at estate law," she said. "So take my knowledge with a grain of salt. The same thought occurred to me the other day, though, and I did a little bit of digging. Karnak doesn't represent the parents—he represents the estate. There would be money set aside from the estate's dividends or interest or some such—if the van Austs were worth as much as I think, he'd still be getting paid."

"And Melia can't fire him?"

"Not until she inherits the estate. The executor could fire him, or at least I think she could. That's the aunt, right?"

"Yeah. I'm not too hopeful on that count," I replied.

"I hope Blake can find out how much that family is worth," Lola went on. "Think about it: you've got this staggering wealth and a lineage that goes back hundreds of years and it's always been in the hands of powerful men. But now, Melia's the only one left. Suddenly this vast fortune is in the hands of a mentally shaky young woman."

Her words gave me chills.

"It doesn't really matter how much they're worth in the end," Lola mused. "When you've been *that* rich for *that* long, money stops being real. You know what I mean? It doesn't exist in the real world, you can't touch it—it's just a theoretical amount of power you have over everyone else."

A woman with a partially shaved head took the stage. She wore an elaborate leather corset over a vintage ball gown.

"It is my absolute pleasure to introduce our next group," she said. "Please welcome to the stage . . . Shade Riot!"

"Come on, then," Lola said. "Let's find a spot closer to the front."

In the corner, a man dressed like Cleopatra smoked two cigarettes. Lola and I slipped past tall, slender women, their necks like swans, glassy-eyed and beautiful, roses blooming on their cheeks. Conversations flowed around us in quiet streams, broken occasionally by the sound of laughter. The smells of a Los Angeles summer night saturated the garden, jasmine and leather. Candles sat in glass jars around the garden, behind waxy flowers and goddess statuettes. Everything was so *nice*. I leaned my head against Lola's shoulder and slipped my arm through the crook of her elbow.

I looked up and saw Diego standing on the stage, grinning down at me. He was wearing lipstick now, and he blew me a kiss. I waved back at him.

Shade Riot began to play, and I watched as my friends transformed onstage. There was a lick of guitar music, a surge of bass from Tabitha, and then Lon stepped forward and grabbed the mike as Blake threw her hands out and started whipping out a tempo on the drums. I was always amazed when this shift happened, when my smart, nerdy friends turned into metalheads, anger and power distorting their faces. I could feel the thrum of the music through my body, and the crowd surged toward the stage. All at once I felt suffocated, pressed against an amp, separated from Lola.

"Hey!"

Someone pushed past me, and I was nearly shoved to the ground. I righted myself and looked up to see someone facing me, turned away from the stage.

He was wearing a baseball cap, so it took me a moment to place him. He broke eye contact and moved away. Then I caught a flash of red hair. My heart started pounding. I could feel my lungs restrict as I realized who it was: the man I had seen earlier that day in front of Catalina's house.

"Hey!" I cried, struggling through the crowd. I extricated myself from a surging mass of people who jumped up and down, throwing their fists in the air. Shade Riot was so loud I couldn't make myself heard above the din.

By the time I finally got some space from the roiling mass, the man had vanished.

TEN

It was after midnight by the time I finally got back to El Palacio, my apartment in Los Feliz. I was exhausted—I normally went to bed around ten—but I had a happy buzz from seeing my friends and watching Shade Riot perform.

My building was a Spanish-style apartment block with wrought-iron balconies and stucco, complete with old letters dripping off the façade like something you might see in a Billy Wilder movie. It was an authentic piece of Hollywood history: Cecil B. DeMille had once rented out the top four floors to house his entire production crew for a film he was shooting in Echo Park.

El Palacio was rumored to be haunted. There were occasional sightings of weeping women in the staircase who disappeared when the lights were on, or an old jazz-era man in a boating hat and white suit who lingered around the broken elevator. I liked to think the place was full of friendly ghosts. I had lived there for a little over two years, and despite the landlords and the occasional lengthy power outage, I loved my home.

I parked in the lot behind my building and gathered my things, then entered through the back, taking care not to make too much noise. The night smelled like jasmine and car exhaust. The trees formed a lush canopy around the parking lot, and I felt a strange fondness toward my city.

Any good feelings I had evaporated as I passed through the lobby.

"Hall! Come here, right *now*."

I remained at the bottom of the stairs and gradually heard Robbie's labored breathing as he emerged from his office. I always thought the myth of the scumbag landlord was just that—a myth—until I met Robbie Grundle. Somewhere in his forties, he had the incipient health problems of someone who donated his living corpse to the scientific community and said, "God Bless. Experiment away." Robbie shuffled everywhere, wincing and clutching a hand to his lower back. His teeth sprouted out of his skull with the gleeful abandon of convicts escaping from a prison bus, and I learned long ago to stand at least two yards away from Robbie when he talked because apparently floss and toothpaste violated some basic tenet of his homegrown belief system.

"I said," Robbie growled when he finally reached the lobby, "come here!"

"What do you want, Robbie?" I sighed. We had long ago reached a stalemate of sorts: Robbie knew he couldn't evict me (I had rights as a tenant, but more importantly, I had Lola), and I knew he was going to make things as unpleasant as possible for me so long as I lived in El Palacio.

As much as I disliked Robbie, though, I reserved my true disdain for his wife.

Paulina was a Russian (or so Robbie claimed) who spoke no English (or so Robbie claimed). There was a rumor going around El Palacio that she was, in fact, from Van Nuys, and was a failed artist who came up with the idea of reinventing herself as an exotic émigré with a dark past. While Robbie might huff and rail against the tenants he didn't like, Paulina was the one who sat in his office fifteen hours a day, glued to the small bank of security monitors that covered most of the public areas of El Palacio, snacking on cheese and writing down any perceived infractions that took place.

When Robbie came to relieve her, she would stick out her little fist and give him the list of wrongs, which Robbie would then follow up on by terrorizing the offending clients.

I had tried to talk to Paulina a few times in the month or two after she first started working with Robbie. When I approached her and attempted conversation, she blinked at me with dull eyes and gave no sign that she understood anything I said. ("How do you like Los Angeles? How long have you been here?") I didn't take her silence as malice, not then, but when I discovered she was watching me on a video monitor and writing down every single visitor who came to see me, I soured on her.

"Where you coming from, Hall?" Robbie asked, leaning against the door of his office.

"It's been a long day, Robbie," I said, turning toward the stairs. I was used to Robbie's bullying tactics: for a very long time, he insisted that as my landlord, he could question me about anything he wanted, night or day. For a while I had given in, trying to avoid the inevitable confrontation, but as Robbie's questions got more and more personal, I realized I could just walk away.

I was almost at the next floor when Robbie called after me. "Someone came to your apartment while you were gone."

"I have a job, Robbie," I said, pausing on the top step. "I don't spend all day in my apartment."

"He was asking me about you," Robbie said casually, examining his fingernails.

"Great. Good night."

"He seemed pretty dodgy. That's all I'll say," Robbie said.

I gritted my teeth, hating myself for playing Robbie's game. "What's your idea of dodgy, Robbie?"

"Seemed to want a lot of information. I think he even tried to break into your apartment."

I turned around and walked toward the office. "Do you have footage of this?"

"Well, unfortunately, no," Robbie said. "Paulina accidentally deleted it."

"Why did you even tell me this, Robbie?" I asked, exasperated. "What do you want from me?"

He gave me a smug little smile. "Thought I was doing you a favor," he said. "Next time I won't warn you when someone dodgy comes stalking around."

———

Robbie and Paulina made me feel small almost every day. I only had a vague idea of why Paulina resented me, but I had a feeling I knew why Robbie disliked me. He had been very friendly when I first moved in, going so far as to help me move my things up to the third floor. He had refused any kind of payment, and although I had insisted three or four times that I wanted to pay him, he had shrugged off the gesture with a smile and said that's what friends were for. After a few months of living there, I noticed Robbie always seemed to pop out of his office or do repairs on my floor around the time I was coming home from work, or he happened to be taking a cigarette break in the parking lot when I was on my way to do errands.

I was nice to him at first, spending the time to go grab a coffee with him at one of the cheesy cafés on Franklin. He'd had a girlfriend when we first met, and I didn't even remotely get the vibe that he was interested in me romantically. He had just seemed like another lonely person in Los Angeles. I knew all too well how the city could make you feel invisible.

"You're the only tenant who's nice to me, Rainey," he'd told me repeatedly. "The rest of those snobs think they're too good to talk to me."

Things started to feel weird around the three-month mark. If I walked by his office, he would conveniently have a box of chocolates or a pizza that someone had delivered to the wrong address. Would I like to have it? When he found out I had connections in the film industry, he begged me to give him thoughts on his script, and even though I told him I was hopeless at analyzing stories, he looked so pathetic and hopeful that I finally agreed.

The story was about a janitor who works in a palace and falls in love with a series of princesses, each more beautiful than the last. The most beautiful princess of all—and this was when Lola told me to move out—was called Sunny.

"Sunny!" Lola groaned, reading the script. "Why not Stormy or Cloudy? Or—wait—why not Rainey?"

"Please be quiet."

"You sure this dude hasn't broken into your apartment and gone through your underwear drawer yet?"

"Fuck. You had to say that, didn't you?"

Lola checked out my rights as a tenant and found that based on the type of outdated doorjambs (and the periodic break-ins that happened in Los Feliz), I would be well within my rights to have new locks installed.

"I'd recommend getting hidden security cameras too," Lo suggested.

"Do I have to tell Robbie that I'm changing the locks?"

"Don't worry about that. If he tries to retaliate, you can say you heard about neighborhood robberies."

As it turned out, however, I never had the chance to let Robbie know about my plan. He found out almost as soon as I had a contractor come and look at my apartment. When I lied and told him it was just because I didn't feel safe in El Palacio, Robbie screamed at me for over an hour, yelling that I was a fucking child, that I was "just like the rest of the uptight bitches in Los Angeles who think they're better than everyone else," and how dare I go behind his back and make changes to my apartment?

Undeterred by Robbie's tantrum, I continued looking for a locksmith to Robbie-proof my apartment, changing all the keys and installing heavy-duty bolts, when Lola—my brilliant Lo, legal counsel extraordinaire—came bearing bad news. In further researching the legality of the situation, she'd found that in California, landlords needed access to all apartments in case of an emergency. So even if I changed the locks, I would have to give Robbie a key. In the end, the headache wasn't worth it.

Afterward Marcus counseled—nay, insisted—that I move out. He suggested I move back in with him and his family if I wanted, but that wasn't what I wanted. Robbie and Paulina aside, I loved El Palacio, loved my weird creative neighbors. I loved the history and the neighborhood, loved how I felt every morning when I woke up and saw sunlight slanting in to illuminate the green and cream tiles in my bathroom. I had a tiny wrought-iron balcony that looked out over Franklin Avenue, and I wasn't going to uproot my entire life because Robbie was a creep who maybe—definitely—broke into my apartment once or twice.

Paulina appeared on the scene shortly after Robbie started giving me the silent treatment. I heard it secondhand that Robbie had married her sometime the year before, which hadn't stopped him from putting the moves on me and a few other women who lived in the apartment building. I figured this probably had something to do with why Paulina hated me, even though she had never come out and accused me of anything. To do that, I knew, would probably mean admitting that she spoke English, among other things.

When I got back to my apartment that night, I sat down at my desk and forced myself to do deep breathing exercises for a full minute. It had been three years since I stopped numbing myself with alcohol every time difficult emotions rose to the surface. There were still some days when I felt like I was going to peel my own skin off just to distract my brain, to avoid the claustrophobic feeling setting in. Sometimes I felt small fireworks going off inside my rib cage, small stabbing sensations nobody else could hear or feel, but I had gotten better at calming myself down with breathing exercises I found on the internet.

When I felt calm, I opened my eyes and found a notebook, then started to make some notes.

I wrote down what Robbie had said about the man who had come to visit me (not much). I didn't believe in coincidences, not since becoming a private investigator: I had already been surveilled by a strange man, first outside Catalina's house, and then at the Shade Riot show. My strongest suspicion was that he worked for Karnak's office, and the lawyer had hired him to track down any information I might have on Melia. If the man had come to my apartment building, though, that crossed professional boundaries, and Karnak was going to hear from me.

I wrote down nearby surveillance cameras in the neighborhood that could have caught this man's face. It was a habit of mine to learn surveillance routes surrounding any area I was investigating, so it went without saying that I applied the same protections to my own residence.

Other than that, the list of people who might have come looking for me was short. Although I had stuck a pole into a few rattler's nests and poked around, there were few lingering possibilities for anyone who might still be pissed at me for upending their lives. Part of the job description of being a PI meant revealing some dark secrets and bringing ugly truths to light. I'd been threatened on more than a few occasions by angry ex-husbands whose wives were able to leave them because of my team's hard work.

I'd never been the type of woman to curl up in fear and wait for a threat to pass. When threatened or bullied, something would churn behind my rib cage, and all my muscles would tense, as though preparing to physically fight. My friends and colleagues bemoaned and sometimes championed the fact that I would brawl and scrap if someone came after me, even if it meant getting punched in the face. I wasn't going to let Karnak bully me, and I definitely wasn't going to drop Melia's case.

I set aside the possibility that I had a tail for the moment and focused on the next step of Melia's case. The people who knew Slant House the best—better, even, than Melia—were the former caretakers. The Endos, Melia had called them. I didn't have a first name for either of them, but I opened my computer and went to an internet browser to see what I could find.

Even though the van Aust murders were four years old, my search returned an immediate wealth of information.

The first and second articles were from the *New York Times*, but neither of them had anything on the caretakers. The third article was from a small funky online magazine called the *LA Lens*, and the story featured not only the death of the family but what had gone on with the property in Melia's absence.

The story featured an old photograph of a tall man in work attire holding a rake. He was squinting as though the sun was directly in his eyes.

"Katsumi Endo has been tending the garden and grounds of Slant House since the early eighties," stated the article. "He and his wife, Caroline, maintain the upkeep of the property and the interior of the house. Katsumi studied architecture and is uniquely qualified to make design-appropriate repairs."

I wrote down the names on the pad by my elbow, Katsumi and Caroline Endo, and then remembered that Melia had mentioned Caroline's dominion in the Slant House kitchen. There was no photo of Caroline in the article. Even though Melia had let them go before she got the threatening letter, there was still a chance they knew something. The Los Angeles Public Library had an enormous database of white and yellow page directories, and fortunately the name *Endo* was fairly uncommon in Los Angeles. I only had to dig through a few pages of results before I found what I was looking for.

K. and Caroline Endo, 37a Arroyo Pinion Drive, Atwater Village.

Bingo.

ELEVEN

⸺ oⷠⷡⷢ ⸺

Atwater Village lay on the other side of the 5 Freeway from Griffith Park—a backward J-shaped afterthought sandwiched between the Los Angeles River and Glendale, and small enough to often be overlooked even by people who'd lived in Los Angeles for most of their lives. Whenever I thought of Atwater, I pictured tall warehouses with misty glass windows, water slowly coursing across concrete riverbeds, skeletal transmission towers framing the sky in bony metal, and now, in the last five years, overpriced coffee and desserts. Nowhere in Los Angeles was safe from gentrification.

Tucked behind the warehouses and hipster coffee joints were streets lined with modest prewar bungalows and weathered A-frames. The address I had found for the Endo residence led me to a Spanish hacienda. The property was hidden behind a lush green hedge and a tidy wooden gate. After hesitating for a moment, I opened the gate and stepped through.

The property was small, but it was clear someone had invested great care in the grounds. A path of flagstones led through a plush green lawn, and cacti bordered the edge of the property. The front windows of the house were hidden behind an ambitious bird-of-paradise plant. Banana plants flanked the drive.

I followed the flagstone path to the door and knocked. There was a long pause, and I thought I heard movement, but nobody answered the door. I checked the notes I had scribbled down and found the phone number for the landline at the house. I punched the number into my cell phone and waited, then heard the corresponding *ring-ring* inside the house. Nobody was home—or at least nobody who wanted to come to the door.

I walked back down the path and stepped through the gate. I could feel someone watching me and turned around to see that the woman next door was watering her sparse garden. Compared to the Endos' botanic display, her yard was scrappy and wild. *Unfettered,* I thought.

Her eyes didn't leave my face as I walked down the sidewalk toward my car. When I glanced back, she was still watching me, one hand on her hip. The hose lay forgotten at her feet, percolating a thin stream of water along the sidewalk.

I glanced at the tree above her head. "Is that an avocado?"

She looked up at the knotty tree with its thick, glossy leaves. "Might be," she said, poking the trunk. "Never gives me any fruit though. Just hard little green nuts."

I lingered by the car.

"Avocados are temperamental," I said. "You can't water them too much or they sulk."

She looked down at the hose by her feet.

"And it might sound weird, but the young trees can get sunburn," I said, moving a bit closer. "You have to protect them from the sun."

She squinted. "Sunburn?"

"My dad used to wrap the young trees in gauze. Some people paint them with whitewash."

She picked up the hose and looked uncertain about what to do with it.

"You should ask the Endos for advice," I said. "They're gardeners."

"The people who live there?" She glanced at the hedge. "I don't know them."

"How long have you lived here?"

"About fifteen years," she said. "The house sat empty for such a long time I thought it might be abandoned. Then, about four years ago, someone started taking care of the garden. Never saw them though."

Four years ago. That was when the van Austs had been killed.

"Have you seen anyone coming and going?"

She glanced down at her feet and realized that her shoes were getting wet from the hose. Without a word, she hustled toward the wall with the spigot and turned it off, then dusted her hands off and walked back to rejoin me.

"Well, let me try and remember," she said. Her voice was full of gossip. "There's a lot more activity lately, but they seem to like their privacy. I've seen a white woman come and go a few times, and then a Chinese man."

Katsumi was Japanese, but I was pretty sure she was talking about the Endos.

"The one who's there most, though, is the son. I'd guess he's the son, anyway, but I've never met him. He's very loud. Comes back late at night, plays his music real loud. His name is Alex. That's what I heard his friends calling him."

A son. I hadn't come across mention of a son when I was researching the Endos. "Any idea how old the son is?"

She gave me a wide-eyed shrug. "Twenty? Thirty? Never talked to him, just seen him from a distance."

I thought it was slightly odd that Melia hadn't mentioned the Endos having a son, especially if he was an adult. The Endos had worked for the van Aust family for two decades, which meant their son would have lived with them at Slant House.

The woman glanced up and down and gave me a conspiratorial look. "I called the police on the house a few times."

I started. "Why?"

"Oh, that awful music. It's like he has no concept of other people."

Some of my best information came from nosy neighbors. The woman had given me more than she realized.

"Thank you," I said, turning to go.

"You a friend?"

"Sorry?"

"Saw you knocking on the door and all," she said. "Oh, unless! They're past due on a bill or something?"

"Friend of a friend," I said, smiling and turning back to my car. "Have a nice day."

⁂

I sat in my car for at least an hour, waiting for something to happen. The time crawled by—first the neighbor disappeared into her house, having fulfilled her lackluster watering duties, and then a group of mothers with strollers ambled by, laughing and chattering.

Finally, a beat-up red Chevy sedan rolled up in front of the Endo house. There was a quiet moment before a man with dark hair climbed out of the driver's side door and quickly disappeared through the front gate.

There was always a moment before I approached an unsuspecting stranger when my breath would halt, when my heart rate would quicken. I had to talk myself into the approach every single time, because no matter how many times I performed when I was young, I still got a tremendous case of stage fright. I always envisioned the worst, no matter the context, and in a case that was rapidly progressing beyond the realm of what was familiar to me, every potential lead could wind up in chaos.

I steeled my nerves and got out of my car, then crossed the street and entered the gate of the Endo residence. Before my nerves took over, I knocked on the front door.

A few moments passed before I heard footsteps inside. The door swung open, and a young man stood before me. He was around twenty, with jet-black hair and high cheekbones. Small patches of stubble and acne dotted his chin.

"Yeah?" He frowned.

"Are you Alex Endo?"

He hesitated. "Who are you?"

"Rainey Hall," I said, producing a business card. "I'm looking for either Katsumi or Caroline Endo—this is their house, right?"

He took it and stared at the writing. "What do you want?"

"I'm a private investigator working for Melia van Aust."

At Melia's name, the man's face closed off. For a moment I thought he might shut the door in my face.

"We're not in touch."

"Okay, that's fine," I said.

"I don't know anything either."

I tried to stay neutral. "Know anything about what?"

"We've been through all this," Alex said angrily. "The police questioned my parents for months. They questioned me too, but I wasn't even there that night."

"So you used to live at Slant House?"

"Who are you, again?"

"I'm a private investigator," I repeated calmly. "I'm not with the police, and I don't work for law enforcement. I'm not here to make any arrests, or to haul anyone in for questioning. The most important thing I can tell you is that I'm hoping I never have to see you again."

"What?"

"I'd really like to cross you off my list," I said. "You answer a few questions for me, I'm satisfied you're a dead end, we never see each other again."

Alex slouched against the doorjamb, studying me. "Huh," he said. "How do you become a private investigator anyway?"

"It's one step up from an internet troll."

This earned me my first laugh. "Pay well?"

"After you deduct expenses and pay the bills, you'd be better off waiting tables at a decent restaurant," I admitted. "But I don't know how to do anything else."

"You hiring?"

"Wow, I didn't exactly consider that a rousing speech," I said. "Not hiring at the moment, but you've got my card."

Alex tucked it in his pocket.

"You'd be doing me a huge favor if you just answered a few questions," I said. "I promise I'll leave when we're done."

"Yeah, shoot."

"When was the last time you saw Melia?"

He scratched his chin. "Like, a week before her parents were killed. Four years ago—yeah, that's it."

"That long?"

"She was only home on weekends," he said. "She went to some fancy boarding school on the Westside."

I had already heard this from Melia.

"And were you close?"

"Sometimes? She could be really hot and cold though. I was tight with Jasper when we were kids, but he went off to some school in Utah when I was like fifteen. We were the same age."

"Any idea why?"

"Nah. He was just gone one day. I mean, I had my own friends then, so . . . we stopped hanging out when I was like thirteen. He left a couple years after that."

"Do you think he had anything to do with the murders of his parents? Do you think he might hurt Melia?"

Alex suddenly looked very sad, and I realized I had pushed him too far.

"I really don't know, man," he said, and his voice was very soft. "They asked me all this back then. I just don't know."

"Just a few more questions, Alex," I said. "When did your parents move here?"

"This house?" He thought for a moment. "So my dad bought it four years ago, back when all that stuff happened with Melia's parents. He didn't want our family around that, just wanted a fresh start. But the lawyer offered them a lot of money to stay and keep an eye on the property. He just never sold this place. They've been renting it out until recently."

"Do you know if your parents still have the keys to Slant House?"

"Yeah, man, I don't know. Sorry."

There was movement above us, and I glanced up. A curtain in an upstairs window had moved, just slightly. Alex followed my gaze.

"I have to go," he said suddenly.

"Alex, wait," I said. "I have more questions for you."

"I shouldn't even be talking to you," he said. "If you knew the van Aust family lawyer, you'd be scared too."

"Paul Karnak? We've met. He can't stop me from talking to you."

Alex looked frightened, as though he might dart back inside at any moment.

"I have my own in-house counsel," I continued. "I'm not a lawyer myself, but I've worked in this industry long enough to tell you how things look on paper. The van Aust family was murdered. Your family were the only ones on the property besides the van Austs, and somehow all of you survived that night."

"My parents weren't there that night, and neither was I. The police questioned us for months, and they never found anything."

"Alex—"

"I can't help you," he said abruptly. I was startled by his change in tone, and I sensed I had touched a nerve. "I don't know anything."

"You know more than you think—" I started, but Alex suddenly cut me off.

"You know what? Fuck that bitch. My parents worked for her for years—years! They gave up everything, man. And she just comes back, out of nowhere, and fires them. Tells them to move out and never come back."

I was taken aback.

"I'm sorry," I said.

"Yeah," he said, his voice heated. "You know what else? She said—she said, if they ever came back, she'd call the police."

Before I could respond, he turned back inside and slammed the door. I glanced up once more toward the upstairs window. A pale face stared down at me, mouth open. As I stood there, the face vanished, the curtains were snatched over the window, and all movement in the house went still.

TWELVE

⁓⁓⁓

After talking to Alex Endo, I stopped at my apartment and slipped through the lobby, hoping I wouldn't have to see Robbie or Paulina. Before I moved any further along in the investigation, I wanted to check in with Melia. I hadn't spoken to her since she had signed the contract two days before, so I hadn't had the chance to fill her in on the investigation or what had happened with Karnak. After changing into a slip dress and pinning my hair back, I called her.

"Hey," she said, after picking up. "What's up?"

"I wanted to discuss some things with you," I said. "Are you good for me to come over?"

"Sure, I'm free all day."

⁓⁓⁓

Willow Glen Lane was quiet as I pulled up in front of Slant House. The air had a curious, living quality that sometimes accompanied stagnant Los Angeles afternoons: while there were no signs of life, no neighbors strolling down the street or peering through windows, I felt watched. Seen. The power lines crackled overhead. I felt claustrophobic, hot, ready to crawl out of my skin.

And then I saw him. A man standing outside Slant House, peering through the window, back crouched and hands cupped to the glass. He wore a hooded sweater, which hid his face. There was something menacing in the way he stood, and as I watched, he banged a fist on the window.

"Hey!"

I slammed my car door, and the man turned. Not a man, after all, I realized—just a delinquent, overgrown boy. Zac Flack. He seemed startled, and then a look of irritation crossed over his face. He shoved his hands in his pockets and nodded at me.

"Oh, sup."

I advanced up the steps toward the house.

"Do you need something?" I asked pointedly.

"Nah, I'm chill." He rocked on his heels and gave me an insouciant smile. There was something oddly childlike about his features, something guileless: his forehead was slightly too large, giving him the baleful features of a sunfish, while his eyes gave him a dim-witted appearance—unaided, I thought, by his weak chin and habit of leaving his mouth open in an expression of mild surprise.

"So . . . why were you banging on the glass?"

He twitched a little, then rolled his head to the side, cracking the bones in his neck. "I heard Melia was back," he said. "Just wanted to say hi."

"Did you try the front door?"

He laughed. "She didn't answer."

"Maybe she isn't home," I pointed out.

"Then why are *you* here?" His tone was mocking.

"Not your concern."

"Chill." He turned and peered through the window again, then knocked on the glass.

"*Zac.*"

"Yo." This time he didn't even bother to turn around but kept walking along the path next to the window, crouching and staring through the glass. He didn't seem surprised that I knew his name, or else he just didn't care.

"You need to leave," I said, trying to hide the irritation in my voice. I hated that he had gotten under my skin.

"I'm gonna say hi to Melia first." He pressed his face against the glass, cupping his eyes to shield the sun. When he stepped back, there was an oily crescent in the shape of his forehead on the glass. Something about his slouchy, entitled demeanor enraged me, and I fought the urge to grab one of his beanpole arms and yank him back from the window.

"Should I call the police or just your mother?" Even to my own ears I sounded bitchy, pathetic.

Zac laughed, the corners of his eyes crinkling up. He rocked back on his heels and assessed me slowly, his eyes traveling down my body.

"Go ahead," he said. "If it would make you feel safer."

"I'm not scared of you."

"Then invite me inside. Let's have a cup of tea."

My phone pinged. I slipped it out of my pocket and glanced at the screen. A text from Melia.

Melia: DO NOT LET HIM INSIDE.

I looked back at Zac, who was squinting down at my phone.

"Maybe some other time," I said.

Another text came through.

Melia: Come around back entrance. Right side of house.

I put my phone back in my pocket.

"What was that?" Zac asked, scratching his stomach.

"Your mom," I said. "She was wondering what you wanted for dinner."

I walked around to the side of the house, turning occasionally to make sure Zac hadn't followed me. Eventually I saw a sleek metal door, set flush into the wall. Before I could knock, the door flew open and an arm shot out.

"Quick—get inside!"

Melia grabbed my shirt and yanked me in. I stumbled across the threshold and blinked against the dim interior.

"What are you—"

"Shhh." Melia threw the door shut and locked it, then peered through the peephole. "Okay, it's fine. He's not out there."

She turned around and gave me a relieved smile, but I didn't return the smile.

"What?" she asked, frowning.

"You lied to me."

She scoffed. "Lied to you about what?"

"You obviously know him. He was looking through the windows, trying to get in."

"Yeah, he's *sick*."

"Melia, I'm not stupid!" I exclaimed. "Most people who just got out on parole do their best to stay out of trouble. There's a good reason he's trying to get in."

She sulked, examining her fingernails.

"I can't help you if you're not honest with me."

"There's nothing to tell you," she said. "I'm the victim here, Rainey. He's the one harassing me—why am I responsible for his actions?"

"Because you told me you had nothing to do with him," I said, then remembered what Blake had told me. "You were wrong, by the way—he didn't go to some remedial school. It was Berkeley Hall. That's a great school."

"Who cares?" she exclaimed, laughing. "He obviously dropped out or something."

"Zac was kicked out for selling drugs," I said. It was all coming back to me, and I suddenly felt very stupid for not seeing it before. "Was he your dealer?"

Melia stared off into space, and a slow flush crept up her neck. She looked like she was stalling for time.

"Melia," I prompted her.

"Yes," she said, her voice faint. "Yes, okay—he was. But it was a long time ago, and we haven't spoken since I moved away."

"What does he want from you?"

"I don't know." Her voice was so quiet that I had trouble hearing her. "I imagine he wants to sell to me again, but I put all that behind me a long time ago."

"I'm going to call the police," I said. "If he's harassing you—or trying to sell you drugs—he's out on parole, for God's sake."

"*No!*" Melia grabbed my arm and held it so tightly that I almost gasped from the pain. "No, Rainey, you can't. If you call the police, Karnak will find out—he has so many connections. If he gets even the slightest indication that I might be doing drugs again, he could have me thrown back in rehab. I'll never get control of my own estate. Rainey, you can't!"

"Okay," I said, finally putting my phone away. "Okay. It's okay."

Her cheeks were burning, and she looked so ashamed of herself that I suddenly felt wrong-footed for accusing her of lying.

"Melia," I said, reaching out to touch her shoulder. "It's okay, really—you don't have to be ashamed of your past. Considering all the things you went through—that's totally normal. You experienced traumas, and sometimes people use drugs to cope."

"Yeah." Her voice was thick. "I guess."

"Why didn't you tell me?"

"You have such a perfect image," she said. "You seem so put together—I just . . . I just wanted you to like me."

"You do?" I was surprised.

"Of course I do. I was so starstruck when I met you . . . I've rewatched all your videos since then. God, I'm so embarrassed."

"Don't be," I said, then laughed.

"You going to drop me as a client now?" She was having trouble making eye contact with me, and my heart went out to her.

"No, I'm not." I took out my phone and started typing.

Melia looked alarmed. "What are you doing?"

"I'm sending you the number of a security company," I said. "They're called Domicile, and my team thinks they're the best one out there. I want you to call them, *today*, because if Zac tries to break in, you're going to need a better security system."

When I glanced up from my phone, Melia was standing right beside me. I could smell her perfume—something fresh and musky, like lime peel and sandalwood. Standing this close to her, I could see how long her eyelashes were. There was a slight imperfection in one of her irises, a little star. I blinked, then forced myself to take a step back.

"Do you want to stay with me?"

She no longer seemed as shy as she had been before. I laughed, unsure if I understood what she was asking.

"Stay—the afternoon?"

"Stay the night."

Her gaze was calm, and she held my eye contact. I suddenly felt myself blushing furiously, and Melia put her hand on my arm.

"You're beautiful," she said. "But you're not just a pretty face. I feel so safe with you, Rainey. Don't you want to make sure I'm safe, that Zac doesn't come back?"

For a full five seconds I imagined leaning in and kissing her, framing her chin with my fingers and breathing in *her*—everything about her, from the clean, soapy smell of her shampoo to the musky smell of her perfume. I wondered what it would be like to hold her, to be able to drop our pretenses.

Walk away, Rainey.

"Do I make you uncomfortable?" Melia asked, and once again there was something frail about her.

"No," I said, squeezing her arm. "No, you don't. Call the security company—really. I think you'll feel safer. Call me if anything else happens."

It took every ounce of self-restraint I had to walk away, leaving Melia behind me.

THIRTEEN

———◦◦◦———

I got home at the magic hour, that illusory time of evening in Los Angeles when one could believe dreams really can come true, when the light was hazy but not polluted, pollen floated through the air, and everything smelled like star jasmine. The sky was still pink as I parked behind El Palacio, and my mind was so occupied with thinking about all the things Melia was going through—her lawyer, her neighbors, not to mention the threats—that I didn't see someone crouched behind a car next to the back entrance of the building.

"Rainey."

I startled as I heard my name. It took me a moment to recognize Calvin—his shaggy hair had been trimmed back, and his skin was pale. He looked like he might have lost forty pounds, and as he raised himself up off the ground, I noted a haunted look in his eyes.

"Jesus," I hissed. I backed away from him, almost without realizing I was doing it. "Calvin, this—you can't be here. You have to go."

He held up both hands, palms facing me. "Just hear me out."

"If you want to talk, send me an email."

"You blocked my email address," he said with a slow smile.

"Did I?" I dug in my bag for my keys, my heart beating wildly. "That doesn't—I mean, it was so long ago—you could write me a letter, or call me—"

"What's your phone number?" He cocked his head to the side, giving me a playful look.

"You know what? I'll call you."

I jammed the key in the lock, my hands shaking. *Stupid El, with its antique locks and nonexistent security protocols.* Calvin materialized behind me and placed a hand over mine, steadying my wrist and turning the key.

"Don't touch me!" My voice was shrill, and my hands flew up to protect myself.

Calvin held up his hands again in mock protest, standing in front of the door so I couldn't get past him.

"I love you, Rainey," he said. "I *love* you. Even after everything—you have to believe that."

Shivers of disgust went down my spine. Still, I tried to keep my voice neutral as I asked the next question.

"How did you find me?"

He looked wounded. "I'm not some sort of criminal, Rainey," he said.

"No?" I hoped he didn't hear the tremor of fear in my voice. "Okay, you're not a criminal. But let me ask you something, Calvin—is this normal behavior? Would a normal person hide and wait for me? I saw you the other day. In Hollywood. You've been following me for a while."

He stared at the sky somewhere above my head. "Let me take you to dinner. When was the last time you ate at Mars—a year ago? More?"

"I haven't—what? Wait, how did you know that?" I stared.

He was quiet. "I do still have friends in this town, Rainey."

Shit.

A curtain on the first floor flapped open. Paulina's face appeared behind the glass, stony and impassive. I stared at her, willing her to open the window or call the police, but she didn't blink or look away.

"You have to leave," I said, turning back to Calvin. "Let me go, Calvin, really. You're holding onto something that doesn't exist."

Calvin grabbed my arm. His fingertips dug into the flesh above my wrist.

"I came all this way," he said, anger rising in his voice. "I'm a different person than I used to be. I've changed, Rainey."

My wrist was starting to hurt. I glanced up at Paulina's window. She was smirking.

"Now, you are going to give me five goddamned minutes to explain myself," Calvin continued.

"Let me go," I said, trying to keep my voice calm.

"Yeah? Or what?"

"I'm going to give you three seconds to let go of my wrist, and then I'm going to hurt you."

"*You're* going to hurt *me*?" His voice had gone ugly. This was the Calvin I remembered: behind the smooth voice and sweet gestures, this darker man had always been there, even if it had taken me a few months to see it.

The self-defense class I had taken with my team had been useful more than a few times. The three of us had gone to a big, airy studio space filled with women of all shapes and sizes: tiny women with wrists like bird bones, thick-limbed women who lumbered across the floor, tall and muscular women who looked untouchable, models and actresses alongside women who might have been plumbers or mechanics. It had been one of the most fun weekends of the summer, spending time bonding not only with my friends but also with other women who had walked through the city and felt a sense of unease.

The workshop had emphasized the most common moves and showed us Krav Maga techniques for how to defeat attackers. One of the most likely attacks an assailant might pull was to grab your wrist, which was what Calvin had done. The natural reaction for a victim was to pull backward, but that only engaged the strength in your bicep. Instead, the proper technique was to aim your elbow at your assailant while also retracting your arm into yourself.

After the workshop, I had made my colleagues practice with me—again, and again, and again.

I quickly slipped my wrist out of Calvin's grasp, then backed up into a tactical stance. He looked surprised, then pissed.

"You cunt."

There was another move that I had rehearsed. When Calvin moved to slap me, I grabbed his hand and elbow simultaneously, then jerked the arm up and sideways, pressing his hand forward and down.

"I'm going to ask one more time," I said. "Are you going to leave me alone?"

"Fuck . . . you," he managed.

I dropped my hold on his hand and laced fingers with him, then jerked the hand sideways. There was a loud crack and ripping sound, and Calvin's eyes went wide. A small whistle emitted from his lips, and he gasped.

"Stop *following me*, Calvin," I said. I released him and stepped away, quickly unlocking the back door and running inside. My whole body shook, and I wiped a tear away. I wasn't upset about hurting Calvin, not by a long shot, but the adrenaline surging through my veins made me feel extremely emotional.

"*Hall*. Get into my office, *right now*."

I froze at the sound of Robbie's voice, then melted against the wall and hoped he couldn't see me.

"Hall! I'm not going to fucking repeat myself."

I groaned and stepped away from the wall, then slouched toward Robbie's office. He appeared in the doorway, apoplectic.

"What did I tell you," he said, "about causing a nuisance in public areas?"

"A nuisance!"

"I heard you! I fucking heard you!" He stood so close I could feel his spit on my face. "You were out there in the parking lot, screaming at your boyfriend about God knows what. You frightened my wife, *yet again*."

"Your wife—your wife! Jesus, she was watching the whole thing unfold like it was nude wrestling on pay-per-view!"

"Hey!"

"She could have called the police, Robbie," I said, knowing even as I spoke that the words were pointless. "She could have opened the window and yelled down at him to leave me alone. She was *enjoying* what she saw."

"You are on thin fucking ice, my friend."

I laughed in his face.

"This is your last warning, Rainey." He rubbed his chin. "If this happens again, you're out of here."

"You know what, Robbie? It's not even worth my time trying to defend myself to you. Go on and try to evict me. I'd love to see how it holds up in court."

I could hear his derisive laughter all the way up to the third floor.

Once I got to my apartment, however, I was in for another surprise. Ever since I had discovered that Robbie was sneaking into my room while I wasn't there, I had started leaving tiny items in precarious places that would be disturbed if anyone broke in. I had cycled through a variety of things—hair didn't work as well as it looked in the movies, while tape under the door was an okay alternative—but the most effective method for detecting an intruder was a ping-pong ball. I would close my door almost all the way, then reach back inside and place a ping-pong ball just behind the door. It was small enough that someone breaking in wouldn't necessarily feel or notice it, but it would be completely obvious to me if someone had managed to break in.

When I stepped inside my door, the ball was gone. Not just misplaced, kicked across the room, but *gone.* I stood there for a full minute, paranoid and exhausted, trying to piece together the events of that morning. I couldn't remember if I had actually put the ball in place; I had been so distracted with Melia's case and everything else going on that there was a slim chance I had forgotten it.

Then again, seeing Calvin outside El Palacio didn't bode well. There was nothing to say he hadn't already been inside my building, somehow managed to break into my apartment, and found that I wasn't there. A wave of panic rose over me. If someone had broken in, and it *wasn't* Calvin, I didn't even want to think about it.

I also didn't want to linger there for another moment. I started throwing things into an overnight bag, and less than five minutes after I had set foot in my apartment, I turned around and left again.

FOURTEEN

⸕⸕⸕⸕

After I left my apartment, I headed straight toward Little Armenia. There was a cheap electronics store ten minutes from my apartment that was open until midnight. I stopped by the store about six times a year, because in addition to picking up old parts that nobody else carried in Los Angeles—parts Blake insisted she needed—you could get an unlocked cell phone for about thirty dollars. It was the type of cell phone with no frills, a barely functional camera and no Wi-Fi capabilities, but it was still a cell phone.

The young man behind the counter nodded and closed a textbook when I came in.

"What's up, Rai."

"Hey, Salim," I said. "I need a really shitty phone and a prepaid SIM."

He opened a drawer and rooted around inside until he found an old flip phone.

"God, I miss those," I said.

He passed the phone and the charger across the counter, then turned around and slipped a cardboard sleeve containing a SIM card off a dusty rack.

"Thirty-five all up," he said. "You'll probably need an hour of juice on that thing before you can make any calls."

⸕⸕⸕

Twenty minutes later I sat outside Slant House, weighing the moral and ethical implications of what I was about to do. I thought about calling Lola, knowing she would stop me from making a bad decision, but I didn't want to talk about Calvin, whoever might have broken into my apartment, or the fact that I was going to have to look for a new place to live. I could have called Marcus or Diego, too, but I didn't feel like explaining to them why I was sitting outside Slant House or what had happened at El Palacio. I just wanted a single night to forget about all the drama swirling around me. I wanted to prove to them that I was doing better, and sitting outside a client's house without a firm plan was not the way to do that.

I held my phone, Lola's number pulled up on the screen. A text came through.

Melia: Creep.

My heart rate sped up. I glanced up at Slant House, but there was no sign of Melia. I wondered where she was hiding, and whether I should call her. Before I could think up some excuse about why I was sitting in front of her house, however, my phone rang.

"Hi," I said.

"I thought you were off duty." Melia's voice was playful. "Did you come back to secretly keep an eye on me?"

"No," I said, then laughed. "I was thinking about your request, actually, and wondering if it was a good idea."

"If what was a good idea?"

"I've never done this before. I mean—I've never spent the night at a client's house." *Except for Calvin*, I added mentally, but Calvin had never exactly been my client.

"Thanks for clarifying. I might have gotten confused." Her tone was decidedly flirtatious.

Turn around, Rainey.

"Come up," she said. "Don't stay out there too long either. I saw someone suspicious walking around out there earlier."

I climbed out of my car and walked toward Slant House. The house glowed above me like a Japanese lantern, a paper box all lit up from within. Behind the house, the hills and brush were invisible in the night, and once again I was reminded how very vulnerable Slant House—and by extension, Melia—really was.

I hesitated at the front door, then knocked. Melia opened the door and smiled when she saw me. She wore a heavy robe made of dark gold silk and a slip underneath.

"Don't you ever walk around the house in sweatpants?" I asked.

"I don't own sweatpants. Come in."

I followed her into the living room, suddenly nervous. I felt like I was crossing a boundary by being there after dark, even if it was under the guise of protecting her.

"Are you here to stay the night?" Melia asked. She tucked a strand of hair behind her ear, then sat on the living room couch, folding her legs beneath her.

"Well—"

"You've got your pick of the bedrooms," she said, cutting me off. "They all come with their own morbid slice of history, but there are no leftover bloodstains—promise."

I stared at her.

"I'm sorry," she said. "I've always had this thing where I make dumb jokes when I'm nervous."

"You're nervous?" I was surprised to hear it—Melia looked at ease, stretched out on the couch.

"Of course I'm nervous. I don't have any friends, and I can't remember the last time I spent the night with someone who wasn't my aunt." She shuddered at the mention of her aunt.

"There's no need to be nervous," I said softly. "I'm happy to be here."

She blushed.

"You said something on the phone about seeing someone outside," I said. "When was this?"

"Just after dark. Seven or so? I like to walk around the yard as the sun's setting."

I had a quick mental image of Janine's son.

"Not Zac?" I suggested. "You'd recognize him, wouldn't you?"

She rolled her eyes. "I said this person was *walking*," she said. "Zac doesn't walk—he does a sort of shuffle-stagger." She jumped up and did a grotesque imitation. "*Meat . . . give me . . . meat . . .*"

I couldn't help laughing. "Did you get a look at his face? You're sure the person was male?"

"I know what a dude looks like." She sat down again and threw a cushion at me. "Can't you just be a friend for five minutes? Drop the detective act?"

"Describe him to me." I took a seat on the couch opposite Melia. Her dark eyes flashed at me.

"Tall. Slender. Wearing a hoodie and dark slacks. Furtive, you know? His hands in his pockets. And I think he had a beanie on."

"And where was he?"

"Outside the Flack Observatory." She raised an eyebrow. "I call it that because Madam Flack is always watching."

"You don't sound concerned."

"I have a baseball bat in the coat closet," she said. Then, with a sly smile, "And I had a feeling you might change your mind and come over."

"Don't assume next time." I was concerned by her laissez-faire attitude toward the whole thing.

"I'm sorry," she said. "Hey. Let me make you dinner, okay? It's the least I can do. I bought groceries today for the first time in months. I never had to do it when I was living with Belinda."

"I'm not hungry, but thanks," I lied.

"I don't make anything fancy," she said, rising to her feet and stretching. "I have a real white trash attitude toward food. I love mac 'n' cheese. With olives and frozen broccoli. You game?"

"Fine," I said, relenting. "Hold on a moment though. There's another reason I'm here."

She turned and raised an eyebrow.

"Regarding what you said," I started. "About your lawyer. You said you don't trust him."

I saw something like fear flash across her eyes, and then, just as suddenly, it was gone.

"I trust you," I said. "I'm not saying you're right or wrong, but I can understand why you'd be suspicious of him. I have good reason to suspect that he might have this whole house under surveillance. That includes the phone lines."

She was quiet for a long moment. "Why didn't you mention this to me last time?"

"I had to think about what you said," I replied. "And I didn't want to frighten you when you were already stressed out."

She blew out an impatient sigh. "I can take care of myself, Rainey."

I produced the cheap phone and the charger I had bought in Little Armenia. "That was never in question," I said quietly. "But just in case—I bought you a phone. It takes prepaid SIM cards, so you don't have to sign up for a contract. Karnak will never be able to trace this back to you. We can communicate safely through this. I've already programmed my number into it."

She crossed the room and accepted the phone. "Did you rob a museum? I can't remember the last time I saw a phone this old."

"Old is good," I assured her. "You wouldn't believe how easy it is to track and hack modern phones."

I had a surprisingly good sleep in a room overlooking the canyon. The walls were gold wood, and the floor was the same with a pale rug. Eucalyptus leaves gently prattled against the window. A thin haze of mist and smoke rested in the trees outside the window when I woke, and for a moment I lay there, not remembering, feeling the relaxation in my bones.

The sound of humming from another room brought me back to my senses. I sat up and rubbed my eyes, then ran a hand through my hair until it tumbled around my shoulders. I wrapped it in a loose bun and pinned it at the back of my head, then pulled my jeans on and wandered out into the house.

Melia sat at the kitchen table, wearing the same slip from the night before, her scar visible against her skin. She hadn't heard me approach.

"Melia," I said softly.

She jumped and whirled, then smiled when she saw me. "God, you scared me. I guess I'm a little jumpy with everything going on. Did you sleep okay?"

"I slept great."

"Can I make you breakfast, or did the macaroni from last night scare you off?"

"It was great. I should get going though. I have to go to the office."

She leaped up from her seat and put a mock serious expression on her face, then pretended to fuss over my shirt and hair.

"You go earn lots of money, my darling husband," she said. "I'll be here with a martini when you come home."

"Listen," I said. "I'm still not sure there's a need for me to stay here. I'll head back to my place tonight, but if anything happens, or if you see anyone suspicious, give me a call. Okay?"

She looked disappointed, but finally nodded. "Sure," she said. "I understand."

"You sure you'll be okay?"

Melia swallowed. "It's fine."

"Melia."

"You asked me not to lie to you," she said. "So I won't. I'm lonely as hell, Rainey. I don't have any friends."

"Oh, Melia."

Her face trembled as though she might start to cry, but she turned away and coughed instead. "Um, yeah, I'm not great with people. It's so much worse when everyone knows your name too—you become this idol, this thing behind glass. I guess I'm lonely, that's it. That's all I'm trying to say."

I already knew I had crossed a line by sleeping at Slant House—my only excuse, should I need one for Lola, was that I was concerned about Melia's well-being. Having Calvin back in my life was punishment enough; I didn't need another albatross hanging around my neck to remind me of how poor my judgment could be.

"I'll come by this afternoon," I said, relenting.

Her face brightened, and she looked hopeful. "Will you?"

"Sure. Of course. I'll check in with my team, see what's going on, and I'll come back and see how you're doing. I promise."

FIFTEEN

⸺

It was a peaceful summer morning. It felt like the beginning of a very hot day, where leaves would shrivel on the branch, the water in the Los Angeles River would dwindle down to damp stains on the concrete, and cars would bake on the freeways, caught in beach-going traffic. "Murders happen on the hottest days," Lola always said. It was hard to imagine that now, though, from this neighborhood: Willow Glen Lane seemed somehow exempt from the chaos and clutter of other parts of the city.

I winced against hot leather as I climbed into my car. The air itself felt singed, roasted from the beating sunlight. Light glanced through the windshield, and it was so bright that I almost didn't see a lone figure standing in front of the Flack house. *Zac.*

Everything in me said to turn on my car and drive away, but there was a lingering feeling about him I needed to quash. I sighed, hesitated, and then climbed out of my car.

Zac watched me as I walked down the sidewalk. He was smoking a cigarette and shielding his eyes against the sun.

"Hot morning," I said.

He grunted his assent.

"I think we got off on the wrong foot," I said. "Yesterday."

He sucked on his cigarette, giving me a wary look.

"When you were banging on Melia's windows?" I prompted.

"Yeah," he said. "You made a joke about my mom."

"Easy pickings," I said, and to my surprise, he laughed.

"Oh, fuck off."

"Look," I said. "You live in this neighborhood, and you deserve to feel safe and respected in your own home."

Zac looked suspicious. "What do you want?"

"I'm hoping we can try again," I said. "We don't have to be friends, but I'm hoping we can aim for some kind of mutual respect."

He finished the cigarette and dropped it on the ground, then crushed it. To my surprise, he picked it up and wrapped it in a leaf, then gently tucked it in his pocket.

"I'm not an asshole," he said, off my look. "And I'm not about to start California's next fire."

"What did you want from Melia?" I asked.

"What's it to you?"

"I'm trying to keep her safe," I said after a momentary pause.

He let out a surprised laugh. "You're trying to keep Melia safe? Right."

"Why does that surprise you?"

"Have you *met* Melia?" He gave me a steady look. "Melia doesn't need anyone's protection."

His words caught me off guard, and he must have noticed, because he pressed on.

"She's real good at playing dumb," he said. "Melia uses people. Stone-cold psychopath."

I took his words with a grain of salt; it wouldn't be the first time a man dismissed a former acquaintance as crazy. His words didn't necessarily mean anything, not without context. "A psychopath? Don't you think that's a bit dramatic?"

"I don't, no."

"Statistically speaking, only two percent of the population actually qualifies as psychopathic—"

"I know how to read," he snapped. "I'm not as dumb as I look. And yeah, I've seen those figures too. I'd still say Melia qualifies."

His words gave me chills, but I did my best to hide it. "What did she do to you then?"

"Nah. Nuh-huh."

"Go on. What are you scared of?"

His dark eyes revealed nothing. "Janine said you're some kind of spy or something?"

I laughed. "No, nothing like that. I work in security, that's all."

"Uh-huh. You back because of Jasper?" He looked interested, genuinely curious.

I kept my face neutral. "What makes you ask that?"

"Because the house has been empty and all that. And they haven't caught Jasper."

"Were you friends with him?" I asked, sidestepping his question.

"Nah," Zac said, leaning down to scratch his leg. "That kid was weird. I *was* friends with Melia, but obviously she ain't trying to reach out."

"Do you want me to pass on a message?"

He gave me a long, hard look. "I'm not about to bring someone new into this," he said. "But yeah. Tell her this. She took something that belongs to me."

"Can you be more specific?" I asked after a pause. I wasn't inclined to believe anything Zac said—he had the nervous, scoping look of someone who knows he doesn't have long before he goes back to prison—but Melia obviously hadn't told me the truth when she said they had no relationship.

"No," he said. "I won't. But she knows what she did, and I haven't forgotten. I want my money."

He didn't wait for a response, but turned around and walked back to his house, closing the door quietly behind him.

I was going to have the office to myself that morning, and I was looking forward to getting a lot of work done. Left City had been in operation for almost three years, and it had taken us that long to hone our business model and balance our income, expenditure, and future projections. We each had our specialties: Lola was in charge of legal matters and contracts, Blake was responsible for tech problems and tracking down hard-to-find information online, and I was responsible for hitting the pavement and asking questions.

When we first started out, we had tried to tackle one case at a time, but not only did that leave us with a serious cash deficit, it also wasted our resources. Now we had one big case (whichever paid the most and took the most energy), as well as any number of smaller client problems that sometimes only took a day or two to solve. These items ranged from infidelity investigations to unfair dismissals to insurance cases. Blake and Lola usually handled the latter two, and since we had just been contracted to help a woman who had slept with her boss and then been fired unjustly, I knew both Blake and Lola would be out of the office, taking care of different things.

I let myself into the office and headed straight for the small kitchen, intending to make a pot of coffee. But I stopped when I realized I wasn't alone.

"How's it going?"

Blake leaned back in her chair, thumb and pointer finger framing her face. The light on her glasses blocked me from seeing her eyes.

"Jesus, you scared me," I said, recovering my breath.

"Apologies."

"I thought you were out today. Did that . . . do I have the calendar wrong?"

"No," Blake sighed. "I finished most of my work at home, then realized I had the VPN configuration nicely set up here and didn't want to change all the settings on my computer."

"This for the Macintyre case?"

"Yeah," Blake said, rubbing her eyes. "I've spent the last two hours reading through the filthiest text messages you can imagine—and I do mean *filthy*. I'm on the verge of going celibate."

"Thank god I don't have to be involved."

"How are you though?"

"I'm fine," I said.

"Really." Her eyes were fixed on my face. While Lola knew me better than anyone, Blake always had a way of deciphering my body language and reading my emotions. I wondered what she would say if I told her about Calvin's surprise visit and my decision to stay at Slant House. I trusted my team implicitly, but I didn't want them to worry about my situation—I could handle things myself—or tell me my judgment had been skewed by spending the night at Slant House.

"It's just a weird case, that's all," I said, occupying myself with my bag and sunglasses so she would stop looking at my face. "Melia's, I mean. This social tier of Los Angeles. It reminds me of high school in all the worst ways."

To my surprise, she laughed. "Tell me about it. I'm not going to say I told you so, but I did warn you about taking this case."

As far as childhood trauma and memories of a gilded cage went, Blake was one of the only people in my life who really understood where I was coming from. We had an unspoken bond—that of people who had survived the kind of privileged neglect that ends in beautiful injury. We had both buried friends who had overdosed before they were twenty, people who grew up with vacation homes and two nannies and saw their parents twice a year.

Blake was from San Marino, a tiny enclave in Pasadena with yawning driveways leading up to sleepy mansions. Her parents were both lawyers, and she had gone to an ultracompetitive girls' school where students were clever with their in-school hazing and malicious forms of social castigation. Her entire future had been mapped out, she told me later, since she was five. There was never room for a free moment, a lazy summer, an afternoon that wasn't spent studying, rehearsing music, training to perform. Always preparing for what was next. Her father was a high-powered attorney who didn't think much of musicians as a whole but used his connections to get her an audition with the Los Angeles Philharmonic.

Instead, Blake was in a car accident that killed two of her friends, put another in a monthlong coma, and landed Blake in a wheelchair.

In the aftermath of the accident, a number of uncomfortable truths came to light. Four months before the accident, Blake's school had experienced a minor crisis when someone had managed to hack into the school's mainframe, find the entire catalog of upcoming exams *with* answers, and then email it out to every registered student.

Blake might not have been caught for this other infraction if her father hadn't confiscated her technology in the wake of the accident. I couldn't presume to imagine his justifications for doing so, but since Blake was a whiz with technology, perhaps he considered it a just punishment for nearly winding up dead. Blake's father hired a technician to go through her computer, and that was when he discovered that rather than studying, playing cello, or preparing for her future, Blake had been hacking into her school's database for over a year, reading teachers' emails, and occasionally sharing them around campus.

"Hypocrites, all my teachers were fucking hypocrites," Blake later told me.

After these discoveries, Blake's parents went into crisis mode. Her older brother was already safely ensconced in his third year at Yale, and they could focus all their energy on Blake. They saw a bored, spoiled girl who had been given too many privileges instead of what was actually there: a brilliant student who had turned her energy away from music and instead was hell-bent on destroying herself methodically, one piece at a time.

She had known her friend was too drunk to drive that night—they were all too drunk to drive—but later, she told me that some small part of her didn't care if they crashed; a part of her wanted to die. It hadn't been her first attempt at self-destruction, but oddly enough the incident that would confine her to a wheelchair for the rest of her life was also something that would finally set her free.

She spent three months in a physical rehab facility, where she also turned eighteen. When she was finally released, she calmly told her family that she had found her own place, that she didn't need their money, and that she would be in touch when she was ready. She spent six months feeling sorry for herself before starting work as an underpaid computer technician and volunteering with homeless youth in Downtown Los Angeles.

"It was the only place where nobody looked at me like I was wasted potential," she told me. "Nobody knew where I came from. Nobody cared about me, and it was liberating."

At the encouragement of her physical therapist, she started taking drum lessons, and the rest was history.

"I'm not saying Melia's a perfect victim or anything like that," Blake said, leaning back in her chair. "But I can empathize with her a bit after reading more about her. I know what it's like having people telling you what to do your whole life."

"You're right," I said, a little surprised to hear Blake say it.

"We've all experienced that to a degree."

"Yeah."

If there was a time to tell Blake about spending the night at Slant House, this was it.

"Then again, I'm not saying I'd want to get involved with Melia on a personal level," Blake said. "People like that, victims or not, have a way of manipulating the people around them. It's a special kind of skill."

The moment was gone.

Blake took off her glasses and looked at me again. "You sure you're okay?"

"Fine."

"Sorry, were you going to say something?"

"Actually, yes," I said, remembering something I had wanted to mention. "I keep meaning to tell you guys about this, but it's slipped my mind a few times. I think someone might be following me."

"Calvin?"

Tell her.

"I'm not worried about Calvin anymore," I lied. "It's someone I don't recognize. Six feet one or thereabouts, two hundred pounds, probably used to be fit but looks a bit out of shape now. I'd say he's somewhere in his fifties, pale skin and freckles, thinning red hair."

Blake frowned. "Where was this?"

"The first time I saw him was outside Catalina's house," I said. "I thought he was watching me but discounted that to paranoia. Then I saw him later that night, at your show."

"Oh!"

"Yeah. I don't have any more details than that, but later that night, Robbie said someone had showed up to my place asking questions."

"Robbie," Blake said, rolling her eyes.

"Yeah, he wasn't helpful."

"Keep an eye out for him," Blake said. "If you get a license plate or anything else, I'll see if I can track him."

"I'm guessing it's someone Karnak sent to spy on me," I said. "I'm not too worried for my safety. It's more of a nuisance than anything else."

When I went over to my desk, I saw a rectangular package with my name scrawled across the front. I picked it up, wondering if it was another warning from Karnak.

"Oh, someone dropped that off for you," Blake said.

"Melia's lawyer?"

"Uh, no. An annoying woman wearing way too much bronzer. I think her name was McKenna?"

"Mackenzie." I slid a finger under one of the flaps on the box, then opened it. I pulled out a pale pink book. The cover image was Catalina von Faber, sitting on a throne, holding a finger to her lips. A sticker read: ADVANCED READER COPY: NOT FOR SALE.

"What is it?" Blake asked.

"*Shhh*," I said.

Blake looked confused.

"It's Catalina von Faber's memoir," I said. "That's the title: *Shhh*."

Blake smacked her forehead and closed her eyes.

"I actually can't wait to read this," I said, opening the cover. Catalina had scrawled a message on the inside:

> *Don't let the fuckers get you down, Rainey!*
> *XOXO, Catalina*

SIXTEEN

— ∞ —

I planned to head back to my apartment and have a quick look through Catalina's book to see if I could gather any new information about Wilhelm and Abigail's social life. There were a lot of unknowns to explore around Melia's case, all possibilities for who might want to threaten or harm her.

Something occurred to me as I drove back toward my apartment that afternoon. Maybe the goal of Melia's anonymous pen pal was just to frighten her away from the house. Could something of value have been hidden in the walls? It would make sense, I reasoned, and might have even been motivation for the original murders.

I arrived back at my apartment and was relieved to see that there was no sign of Robbie or Paulina in the lobby. I was so excited about my new line of conjecture about Slant House that I didn't immediately notice the ping-pong ball had been knocked away from its hiding place behind my door.

I dropped my bag onto my desk, and there was a moment of stillness before I detected something was wrong—a smell I didn't recognize, papers strewn across the floor. Then I registered movement out of the corner of my eye. I whirled around and caught a glimpse of pale skin, wide eyes, and dark hair before my assailant was upon me, shoving me against the wall.

The wind was knocked out of my lungs. My desk lamp shattered on the floor. I struggled against the pair of arms pinning me to the wall, but it was hard to get a good grip, and I still hadn't caught my breath.

We struggled in an uncomfortable standstill until I finally grabbed a pen from my desk and jammed it into my attacker's leg. With a loud hiss of pain, he released me. I stumbled across the room, toward the door of the apartment. I was desperate to put as much space between me and the stranger as possible. I hesitated by the door, wondering if I should flee and find help or see if I could identify who had attacked me.

He was bent over, hands probing where I had stabbed him. I couldn't see his face, just a hank of dark, unruly hair.

"What are you doing here?" I hissed, out of breath. "Who the fuck are you?"

"You stabbed me," came his voice, but he didn't look up. "You *stabbed* me!"

"Who are you!"

He slowly raised his eyes to meet mine. There was a moment of confusion, and then it all came back to me—the wide, unblinking eyes, the pale face, the features that looked almost too delicate to belong to a man. He was older than in the photographs I had seen, but his face was too unusual for me not to recognize him.

I was looking at Jasper van Aust.

"Oh my god," I whispered.

He glowered at me.

"How—when did you . . . what are you *doing* here?" I was aware I sounded like an idiot, but my thoughts were spiraling so quickly I didn't have time to grab on to a single one. Without fully realizing what I was doing, I had blocked the door with my body. I couldn't let him escape, not now: I had too many questions. There was another thought too—this one much more selfish: the possibility of handing Jasper van Aust in to the police was almost too glorious to consider.

Jasper reached into his pocket and produced a notebook. *My* notebook.

"What is this?" he asked.

"That's nothing," I said quickly.

He glanced down at it and started flipping through the pages. "You spent the night with my sister," he said. "I saw you there."

I needed to keep him talking so I could figure out a way to signal for help. I could try to tackle him, maybe restrain him somehow, but based on our earlier struggle, there was a chance he might overpower me.

"You were at Slant House last night?"

A sneer. "What are these notes? Who are you?"

"A friend of Melia's. Just a friend."

"Friends don't take notes like this!" His eyes had gone wild again. I hadn't been afraid of him at first, but then I remembered what Alex Endo had said about him. Jasper had been sent away. Catalina had mentioned something about a brutal boarding school for boys.

"I'll tell you anything you want to know," I lied. "Ask me anything."

He looked wary, caged. "What did you tell her?"

"Tell her . . . tell her about what?"

"About me," he hissed. "You've done something to her. I know you have, there's no use denying it!"

"Jasper," I said, trying to keep my voice calm. He had somehow broken into my apartment, in a city where people knew his face from newspapers and magazine articles and warnings on the television. There was no telling how disconnected from reality he was. "Jasper, you have to be more specific."

"She won't talk to me," he muttered, almost to himself. "You've done something, you witch, you witch. You've done something to my sister."

I tried to keep my face neutral while I processed the meaning behind his remarks. Melia had told me she hadn't seen or spoken to Jasper since before her parents were murdered, more than four years previous. Jasper's words, however, indicated something else was at play.

"When did she stop speaking to you?"

He jerked toward the window, responding to some external stimulus I couldn't see.

"Jasper."

He jerked back to me.

"What are you doing with her?" he snarled again, holding up the note-book. "What is this?"

"I told you, I'm just a friend."

"Lies." He flipped the notebook open. "I had time to read this while you were gone. I see your game, I know what you've been doing."

There was a pounding on my door, and we both jerked toward the sound.

"Rainey! Rainey Hall!" It was Robbie. *Damn it, Robbie, of all the worst times to interrupt—*

"Give me the notebook," I told Jasper, desperate. Most of my notes from the case so far were contained in the pages. "It's got nothing to do with you."

Jasper's wide eyes flicked to the door. He held my notebook in both hands, considering, then tucked it into his pocket.

"Jasper!" I hissed.

The pounding recommenced. "Hall, I can hear you in there! You open this door right now!"

I glanced over my shoulder, and Jasper took advantage of my distraction. He leaped toward the balcony and smashed through the glass. I gasped at the unexpected violence, and the pounding on the front door of my apart-ment got even louder.

"I swear to god, Rainey, if you *don't open this door right now—*"

Without thinking, I ran after Jasper. He had disentangled himself from the shards of glass and was climbing down the fire escape. I grabbed at his sweatshirt, and for one dizzy moment I thought I might have caught him. With the finesse of a reptile, he slithered out of the sweatshirt and dropped down to the balcony below.

"Fuck!"

I watched as he disappeared down the road, darting between cars and then running down a side street. I'd almost had him. In the apartment behind me, I heard the door being unlocked.

I whirled to see Paulina and Robbie entering my apartment.

"You have no right," I cried, desperate and furious. "No right! What are you doing in my apartment! You can't just . . . just . . . barge in here!"

"I am the landlord of this building, and I will do whatever it takes to keep my tenants safe!" Robbie roared, his face a mottled red.

"I don't need your protection!" I yelled. "It's none of your business!"

"I'm not protecting *you*," he snarled. "The other tenants! Nobody feels safe around you! Always coming in at all times of the night, inviting strange visitors . . . There's something wrong with you!"

I was so incensed that I didn't know how to respond. If Robbie hadn't interrupted just then, I could have cornered Jasper, I could have caught him. Paulina wandered into my apartment and began looking around, a tiny smirk on her face. Robbie sat down on my bed, exhausted from his tirade.

"Get off my bed," I snapped.

"I've had enough of your problems, Hall," he said. "I came up here to let you know you're being evicted."

I was so focused on how I had narrowly missed Jasper that his words didn't register.

"This," Robbie said, gesturing around at the broken window, the shattered table lamp. "It's too much."

"You can't evict me," I said, slowly catching on. "This is my apartment. I haven't done anything wrong."

Paulina snorted.

"Every day is a different disaster with you," Robbie said. "Strange men always dropping by and making threats. You can read the apartment rules, if you like, but I'm well within my rights to evict you after all this damage."

I could only stare at him in disbelief.

"I'll give you two days," Robbie said. "You have to be out in two days, or we'll have the police help you pack."

He stood and wiped the sweat off his forehead, then left the apartment, trailed by a very happy-looking Paulina.

SEVENTEEN

—∞∞∞—

Lola didn't speak for a very long time after I told her what had happened.

"Here," she said, handing me a handkerchief. "Your nose is bleeding again."

"Thanks." I gently wiped my nose and then stuck the handkerchief in my pocket. We were in Lola's kitchen at her Echo Park bungalow. After making sure nobody was following me, I headed straight to her house without telling her I was coming. It was rare for Lola to withhold her opinion, and the longer she stayed quiet, the more uncomfortable I felt.

"Just tell me."

She sighed and leaned against the kitchen counter. The room was full of color: lemon-yellow tiles and peach-colored walls. Lime-green curtains hung from the window above the sink.

"I think Melia's hiding something," she said.

The thought had crossed my mind, but I hadn't wanted to admit it to Lola. Clients lied to us on ninety percent of our cases, but most of the lies were innocuous: for example, sometimes when we were hired to track down a cheating partner, we didn't know our client had been unfaithful as well. None of those lies mattered though. This one did.

"The only way Jasper could have stayed hidden this whole time is if he stayed with family," Lola went on. "The only living family they have is in Georgia: Aunt Belinda. I'm guessing that, until recently, Melia was in contact with him. And then something happened, so she decided to come back here. But why?"

"No idea," I said. "None of it makes sense."

"Maybe there's a good reason she's protecting him."

"Then why hire us to find him?" I asked.

Lola shrugged. "Remember that this is all hypothetical; we don't know for certain that Melia *has* been hiding Jasper."

My head was spinning. I suddenly remembered that I had promised to stop by Slant House in the afternoon, but it was early evening, and I couldn't stomach the thought of seeing Melia. Not now, not with the possibility that she had been hiding Jasper from me.

"I wonder how he found me," I said.

Lola nodded thoughtfully.

"You know, Robbie mentioned that someone had come by the apartment looking for me," I said. "He said the guy seemed dodgy."

"If *Robbie* thought he was dodgy, that's a bad sign."

"It could have been Jasper," I said. "That never occurred to me. I just assumed it was someone Karnak had sent to keep tabs on me."

"Where are you going to stay?"

"I'll start looking tomorrow."

Lola glanced over her shoulder. "I have a guest room."

"You mean your closet?" I smiled.

Lola scoffed. "I could set up a bed in there."

"I'll stay for tonight," I said. "But you know that we'd drive each other crazy after two or three days."

"What are we going to do about Jasper?" Lola asked, her face serious.

"I'll see if Blake can find a way to trace him. See if he has a phone or anything like that."

"That's not what I meant," Lola said. "Do you think we should go to the police with this?"

I thought about it for a long moment. "No," I said. "For one thing, I want the chance to figure out what's going on with Melia. If the police get involved, we won't be allowed near her or Jasper, and the whole thing will be out of our hands. They bungled the case last time. The same thing might happen this time around."

Lola looked uneasy.

"What?"

"This isn't just a stalker case anymore. It now involves a fugitive," she said. "We could be in serious trouble if it gets out that we haven't turned him in. We could be accessories after the fact."

"According to whom?" I said. "Lo, nobody else saw him. He looks completely different—unhealthy and wild. Nobody could even prove that I knew it was Jasper. I could say it was just a break-in."

She mulled this over. "What about Robbie and his creepy wife? Don't they have security cameras? Jasper might be on one of them."

I thought about this.

"Okay, I'll get the footage," I said.

Lo gave me an incredulous look. "They hate you, Rainey. They just evicted you. How do you plan on doing that?"

"Relax, Lo. I still have a few tricks up my sleeve."

<hr />

I waited until the next morning to return to El Palacio. In some ways I was nervous about the upcoming confrontation, but at the same time, I had nothing to lose: I had already been evicted. Besides, I had never had the chance to give Robbie or Paulina a piece of my mind, and it was sorely overdue.

Paulina didn't hear me approach the office, and her back was to the door. She had her feet up on Robbie's desk, one hand in a bag of Cheetos. I could see why she was distracted: a trashy reality show was playing on one of the computer monitors in front of her. I stood in the door of the office, watching Paulina chew and snicker at a catfight between two of the women on the show.

Another woman entered the screen, and I was surprised to see it was Catalina von Faber. *Paulina must be watching Three L,* I realized.

"No subtitles," I finally remarked.

Paulina snapped backward, startled. Cheetos flew everywhere.

"It must be difficult to understand the complex interplay of all these underhanded interactions if you don't speak English," I went on. "Is that still true?"

Paulina wiped her fingers on her pants without taking her eyes from my face.

"Robbie?" she called. "Robbie!"

We continued to stare at each other until I heard footsteps from an adjacent room. Robbie's apartment was in the space behind his office, and I sincerely hoped he would emerge fully clothed.

"What is it, my dumpling?" he called.

A moment later, his grinning face popped through the doorway. When he saw me, the smile vanished.

"You," he growled. His face had gone dark. "You here to drop off the keys?"

"Not yet," I said, my voice calmer than I felt. "I'm here to make a deal."

He scoffed. "A deal!" He slouched forward and scratched his belly. "You're still evicted, Hall. I'm not letting you stay."

"I don't want to stay," I replied. "Just listen."

Robbie folded his arms across his chest. "Well?"

I felt a wave of revulsion thinking of all the times he had cornered me when I was trying to get to my apartment, confronting me about nonexistent issues and making me feel powerless in my own home. I should have confronted him years before.

"I'll pay to have the window fixed," I said, reminding myself to stay civil. Robbie was an explosive person who couldn't control his emotions, and it would be easy for things to go south if I didn't stay calm. "I know someone reliable who can have it done by the weekend."

Robbie scowled, picking at something in his ear. "I don't need your help."

"Let's make a deal—I won't take you to court for your repeated failures to secure my safety in this building," I continued, ignoring his interruption. "I'll forget all the times you broke into my apartment and went through my things. Yes," I said in response to the shocked look on his face. "I know. Most importantly, though, I won't tell the police that your wife let someone into my apartment last night."

"You can't—" Robbie started, but I cut him off.

"She could go to jail for that. He *attacked* me, Robbie." Even though I had promised myself I would stay calm, I could feel hysteria creeping into my voice as I described what Jasper had done. There was an element of insanity about the whole situation, and every time I thought about how I had to fight to protect myself in a place where safety should have been guaranteed, I got angry all over again. *Calm, Rainey,* I reminded myself. *Stay calm. You never have to see these lunatics again after this.*

"You can't prove anything," Robbie said, but he sounded uncertain.

"Sure I can." The anger was fading, and I was starting to feel triumphant. I had another trick up my sleeve. "You've met Lola."

Robbie's face was impassive. He glanced down at Paulina, who looked frightened. "What do you want?" he finally asked, his voice quiet.

"The full deposit, for starters," I said. "I'd like until this weekend to move out because I'm working, and the additional time constraints will be a strain on my resources."

"Oh, is that all?" Robbie said sarcastically.

"No," I said evenly. "I'll need all the security footage from the last week. Not just copies either—I want you to destroy the files on your computer. I'll have my lawyer draw up a contract that stipulates these conditions."

"Ooh, your lawyer, your lawyer!" Robbie squealed, throwing his hands up and dancing around. Paulina burst into laughter, and Robbie did a little twirl. "I'm Rainey, and I have a lawyer!"

"For fuck's sake," I muttered. "Can't you just be an adult for once?"

Robbie rubbed a hand over his face. "What if I say no to all of this? What are you gonna do then?"

"You do know what I do for a living, right, Robbie?"

"Something about snooping on unsuspecting people and going through their garbage."

"That's exactly right. I find things people want to stay hidden. I look under rocks. Nothing can stay secret forever." I leaned against the doorway. "Is there anything in your past you don't want me to find?"

He stared at me, but his eyes flickered away from mine.

"No," he said.

"Of course there is," I said. "And I'm going to find it. I already know what Paulina's trying to hide."

There was a protracted silence. Neither of them looked at me for a very long time. Finally, Robbie cleared his throat and nodded at Paulina.

"Do it."

Paulina hesitated, then started typing. A bank of files appeared on the screen. She took out a hard drive, and I watched the progress on the screen as she started copying them over.

"I have your word," Robbie growled. "Your word that this is the last we'll hear from you?"

"You have my word," I said. "That still counts for something with me."

The progress bar finally completed, and Paulina removed the hard drive. There was no malice or contempt as she handed it to me, still not meeting my eyes.

"Delete everything from your computer," I said. "While I'm here."

She followed my orders, breathing heavily. After she finished, I nodded.

"I'll call my contact and have the window replaced as soon as possible."

For the first time since I had moved to El Palacio, my exit from Robbie's office was accompanied by a dumbfounded silence.

EIGHTEEN

———⊶⊷———

After leaving El Palacio, I went straight to the Left City offices. Blake and Lola were already there, sitting at their respective desks. Blake was chewing mindlessly on a chocolate bar, while Lola's chin rested on her hands. They both looked tired.

"Any luck?" Lola asked, looking up.

I held up the hard drive in response.

"You're a wizard," she said, shaking her head in disbelief. "What small animal did you sacrifice to get that footage?"

"I told Robbie and Paulina that I knew what they were hiding," I said, rolling my eyes.

Lola raised a quizzical eyebrow. "And what's that?"

"No idea." I sat down at my desk and connected the hard drive to my computer, then laughed. "The important thing is that they *think* I know. Besides, I'm sure it wouldn't take too much digging to find something in their past."

The hard drive appeared on my computer screen.

"Did I miss something?" Blake asked. She looked between me and Lola, frowning.

Lola quickly filled her in on what had happened with Robbie and Paulina as I scrolled through the footage from El Palacio. I scanned the footage until I came to the four P.M. mark, which was shortly before I returned home. When there was no sign of Jasper, I went back about an hour.

"There!" I exclaimed, tapping the screen. "That's him. That's the sweatshirt he was wearing."

Lola and Blake came around to look over my shoulder. We all watched the grainy footage as Jasper entered the front of El Palacio, slipping past a tenant who was leaving. He moved toward Paulina's office and spoke to her for a few minutes.

"Is there an audio track?" Blake asked.

"I don't think so," I said, frowning.

We all watched as Jasper handed something that looked like money to Paulina. She retrieved a key from her desk, and then the pair of them walked up the stairs to my floor.

"I *knew* she was letting people into my room!" I exclaimed. "That little Russian cow."

"Wow," Lola said, disbelieving. "That's . . . that's not even remotely legal."

"Tell me about it," I muttered. In other circumstances I might have felt irate at the obvious violation of my privacy, but now, the only thing I felt was vindication.

Blake toggled over to a different file, and the camera angle changed to show the hallway outside my apartment. My team and I watched in silence as the video showed Paulina letting Jasper into my apartment. I glanced at the time on the footage: more than an hour before I was due to arrive home.

"He was in my apartment for over an hour," I said slowly, watching the scene unfold. A wave of revulsion washed over me. "Waiting for me. Going through my things."

We were all quiet, letting the meaning sink in.

"We could take the Grundles to small claims court," Lola offered, clearing her throat. "Or we could make this a police matter."

"We can't," I pointed out. "It's been almost twenty-four hours since Jasper attacked me, and we haven't told the police he's back in the city."

"Damn," Lola muttered. "Good point."

I closed the video and then went back to the files Paulina had given me.

"What now?" Lola was watching me.

"Someone came to my apartment when we were at Blake's show too," I said. "Remember, the guy Robbie described as dodgy? I want to see who it was."

Robbie hadn't told me what time the man had come looking for me, so I sped up the footage. We all watched in silence as people speed-walked down my hall, faces blurry and hands jittery.

"There," Blake said. "Stop there. That guy's checking out your apartment."

I paused the footage, then rewound it until the man first appeared outside my door, scanning the hallways for activity. He wore a baseball cap and a nylon bomber jacket.

"Calvin?" Lola suggested.

"Calvin's smaller than that."

I still couldn't make out the man's face.

"Try a different camera," Blake said. "They gave you all the footage, right?"

"Good thought." I found the footage from the lobby camera, then scanned through it until the man in the bomber jacket first appeared. "There!"

He glanced up just once, but it was enough. His face was perfectly visible under the brim of his hat.

"Are you sure that's him?" Lola asked. "He was outside your door, but that doesn't mean anything. He didn't try to break in or anything."

"That's him," I said, my voice grim.

"How do you know?"

The footage was grayscale, but I didn't need to see the man's red hair to know who he was.

"Because he's the man I told you about," I said. "The one who followed me to Calabasas and then showed up at Blake's show."

Blake looked alarmed. "That guy? He knows where you live too?"

"Not for long. I'm moving out soon."

"Thank god for that," Blake muttered darkly.

Something had just occurred to me. "Hold on a second."

I toggled through the security camera folder until I found footage of the parking lot. I watched the video with bated breath—and only a little hope—until the man in the bomber jacket appeared, climbing into the car he had been parked in when I saw him outside Catalina's house.

The license plate was blurry, and part of it was cut off, but five numbers and letters were something to start with.

I turned to Blake. "Can you look into this? See if you can get an ID?"

She narrowed her eyes at the screen, then typed the numbers into her phone.

"I might not get a match on the plate, especially if the car isn't registered to his name," she said. "But we have footage of his face, so the combination should turn up something. Give me a few days."

NINETEEN

───※───

Most of the prevailing stereotypes about Los Angeles were true: on any given day you could bump into movie stars while dropping off your dry-cleaning; towering palm trees lined many of the boulevards; most of the city's residents were trying to make it in the film industry; and nearly everyone was unnaturally good-looking.

Part of the American dream was believing everyone was talented and anyone could be famous—which was all true. Anyone *could* be famous if they were willing to suffer long hours of mind-numbing, underpaid labor while struggling to make a name for themselves. Most of the would-be superstars who trekked out from Anywhere, USA, with big dreams and too much self-esteem, however, didn't like washing dishes. They didn't like working for idiot bosses—bosses who were once aspiring actors before they aged out of the industry and settled down. They didn't like attending cattle call auditions with no prospect of a callback, and most of all, they didn't like feeling invisible. Everyone in Los Angeles has felt invisible at some point.

The upside of all this, of course, was an abundance of available housing. Aspiring actors arrived and departed in the space of six months, vacating apartments with high ceilings, advanced security systems, and original floor tiles.

"And just wait 'til you see the pool!"

I nodded and followed the leasing agent outside. It was my third apartment inspection of the day. All of them were within my price range, all beautiful and spacious. This one had been built in the twenties, but the owner had gutted the space and gotten rid of a lot of the charming old details. I always had a bit of trouble finding a place because I liked stodgy old buildings with sinister histories. I couldn't comfortably settle down somewhere unless I knew there were at least three ghosts in residence, preferably 1920s-era starlets with tuberculosis eyes and slender limbs. I couldn't stomach modern apartments with sleek kitchenettes and newly tiled bathrooms, regardless of how splendid the water pressure was. I needed creaky floorboards and curved archways, artful touches and termites.

My phone rang as I followed the woman down the path between the apartments. It was another stinking hot day, and my hair was stuck to my neck.

Melia. She was calling from the burner phone.

"It's a communal pool, of course, but most of the people who live here are workaholics," the agent went on. "You'd have it to yourself most of the year."

I nodded and then glanced at my phone.

"You can take that, I'll wait!"

I hesitated, then accepted Melia's call.

"Hi, Melia."

"Hi," she said, her voice cautious. "Are you okay?"

"Sure, why do you ask?"

"Lola called me and told me what happened." She lowered her voice. "With *Jasper.*"

I held up a finger to the leasing agent, then gave her an apologetic look. She responded with an enthusiastic smile, waving me off.

"Rainey," Melia said, her voice breaking. "Rainey, I feel terrible. I can't even *begin* to apologize, I just feel rotten to the core—"

"It's not your fault," I said quickly. "You hired us to find him; there was always a chance we'd come into contact with him."

"Where are you?" she asked, her voice fragile.

"I'm looking at apartments."

Melia was quiet, then gasped. "You're moving out? Because of what happened with—because of what happened?"

"It was time."

"I think you should drop my case," Melia said after a pause. She sniffled again. "It's not worth it."

I was surprised. "Why?"

"You'd never be in this situation if it weren't for me. I'm nobody to you, Rainey. I'm just a client."

"Slow down for a minute."

"I'll get Lola to send me the number of another good agency. Thanks for everything though—I'll still pay you for what you've done so far."

I glanced back at the pool, where the leasing agent was humming to herself and smiling. She stroked the leaves of a lemon tree, then dusted off some pollen.

"We're not dropping your case," I said. "This isn't the first time I've had someone threaten me."

Melia was quiet. "Are you sure?"

"Of course. I'm not the type to back down at the first sign of a challenge. Besides," I added, "it's a good idea to move every few years in my profession. Sometimes past clients discover where you live."

She was quiet for a minute. "Move in with me."

I laughed. "Melia, I can't."

"You can," she pressed. "You *should*. It's the least I can do."

I thought of the white sheets and spare furnishings of Slant House, the clean angles and geometric beauty. I thought of Melia's gray eyes, her smile, the food she had cooked for me. I couldn't remember the last time someone had cooked dinner for me.

"It would be temporary," I cautioned, knowing even as I spoke that it was a mistake, a concession. "If I stayed with you, I mean. A few days at the most. I'll keep looking for my own apartment this weekend."

"Of course. Plus," she said, "you'll be doing me a favor by moving in with me. I mean, if half your energy is consumed with finding a place to live, you won't have much left over for my case."

I rubbed my eyes. She made a fair point.

"Who knows?" she mused. "Maybe this will all be over before we know it."

TWENTY

—⁂—

Marcus and Diego came over the next day to help me pack up my apartment at El Palacio. As much as I disliked Robbie and Paulina, leaving was bittersweet. I loved living in Los Feliz, with its tree-lined streets and bustling little village, but my apartment had become too unsafe. I half-expected Jasper to make an appearance at any moment.

Diego returned after making a coffee run. He handed me an Americano and rolled his eyes.

"Your landlord's a riot," he said. "He interrogated me for twenty minutes downstairs."

I took a sip of my coffee. "This is cold."

"Blame your landlord." Diego drank his coffee and started rummaging through my closet. He held up a holey Slayer shirt. "Is this mine?"

"Probably not." I avoided his eyes.

"This *is* my shirt," he said. "Dad, back me up here."

"You never even wear that thing," I countered.

"Yeah, because I couldn't find it! I'm taking this back." He rolled it up and shoved it in his back pocket.

"You know I'm going to take it back next time I'm at your house."

Diego pounced on me.

"Ouch! *Ouch!*"

"Diego, enough!" Marcus rumbled. "I have to be at the studio in a few hours. Let's start taking things to the car."

The Loew household had always felt more like home to me than the house I actually grew up in. For one thing, it was always full of life. When I went over there as a kid, Diego and his siblings were always running around, causing mischief and chaos. Even as the kids grew older and moved out, the evidence of them hung around the house: drawings and school commendations on the fridge, weird artwork sprinkled about (tucked between books and on side tables or hanging from the ceiling). Their rooms were left mostly intact, with the exception of newer bedspreads and better lighting for when guests came to stay.

The house was a rambling California Spanish mansion, three stories of balconies, alcoves, and stairways leading up to various rooms. The grounds were huge too; just like all good mansions in Hollywood, this one had belonged to a wealthy family that went broke and sold it down the line until Marcus bought it in the seventies. Bougainvillea dripped over the entrance to the house, and as we sat down to eat dinner that evening, everything felt just as though I had never moved out. I missed nights sitting around with Marcus and Jac, all the windows in the house open to the night air.

Jacqueline had gone to the market that morning and bought enough vegetables to make gallons of soup. I lingered in the kitchen, listening to them interact. Jac was from Spain and was the same height as Marcus. I had never seen a woman who was so tall.

"My father was an ogre," she told me the first time we met, making a fist with her long, tapered fingers. "That's why I'm so *big*."

She had black hair with streaks of gray. Her dark eyes were captivating. I watched her scowl at vegetables and boss Marcus around, wishing desperately that I had a mother like Jac, someone who would make plans and arrangements, someone to rely on. They were so different from every other married couple I had seen: Marcus was always lost in his thoughts, interrupting conversations with sudden brilliant tangents on a completely unrelated topic. Jac was highly emotional and yet gracefully composed; she was a union of contrasts.

Jac and Marcus had been friends with my parents since before I was born, but there was an unspoken agreement at the Loew household not to discuss my family. Jac never asked if I had heard anything from my mother, and I felt safe in knowing they would never put me on the spot. Jac must have already known that I had been evicted from my apartment, because when we showed up with my things in boxes and bags, she didn't ask why I was there, how long I was staying, or even what I had been up to. She just came over and wrapped me in a very long hug.

As Jac prepared dinner, Marcus beckoned me aside.

"I want to talk to you about something," he said. "Step into my office."

Marcus's office was filled with movie props from various projects he had worked on. There were old-fashioned pipes and magnifying glasses on the shelves, peeling globes and ancient shipping trunks in the corners of the room.

A rifle sat in the middle of his desk, surrounded by musical scores.

"That's not real, obviously," Marcus said, gesturing to the gun. "Just a convincing prop. We're going to Colombia at the end of next month to work on an adventure film."

As much as I loved working as a PI, I often missed working for Marcus. As his assistant, I had been invited on several trips to movie sets around the world. Although the bulk of Marcus's work was done at a recording studio, he liked to observe production so he could get a proper feel for the kind of score he would need to write.

"You could come, you know," Marcus offered. "To Colombia."

"Alas, work calls."

"Don't you miss it? The sense of adventure and foreboding of film shoots?"

"I get plenty of adventure and foreboding in my job, thanks, Marcus."

He sat down behind his desk. It looked like something was weighing on him.

"What is it?"

"I talked to your dad," he said, his voice quiet.

"Okay."

"He mentioned he doesn't have your current phone number."

There was a faint ringing in my ears, and dark spots appeared in my vision. I vaguely wondered if I was going to faint, if Marcus could see that I had suddenly faded from the room. My chest felt constricted, and I realized that I hadn't taken a breath for a while, I was going to pass out—*oh god*—

"Rainey." Marcus's deep voice brought me back to the room.

"Sorry, did you hear something from the kitchen? Maybe Jac's ready for us to go in there. We should check—"

"You don't have to pretend with me." His eyes were on my face. "I know you don't speak to him. I don't blame you."

I was having trouble meeting his eyes.

"I blame him for everything, if you want to know the truth." Marcus leaned back in his chair and sighed. "You're still just a kid."

"I'm not a kid, Marcus."

"We watched it all happen and did nothing. We should have done so much more for you, Rainey. I hope you forgive me for that."

"Marcus, stop."

"You were just a *kid*. To have Matilda vanish like that . . . I can't imagine. And then it happened all over again, when your father just . . . well, when he vanished too."

My throat was tight. There was a reason why I never talked about my family, why I never thought about them.

"I don't want to talk about this."

He tapped his fingers on his desk. "You should know," he said quietly, "he's going on tour in Europe for three months. Leaving next week. I only mention it because you said you were looking for a place. If you wanted to stay at Dune House, he wouldn't even know."

I picked at a fingernail, not trusting myself to respond.

"He wanted to call and let you know, but—"

"He doesn't have my number."

Marcus gave me a little smile. "You're right," he said. "I think I *did* hear something from the kitchen. We should go check."

As I followed Marcus out of his office, my cell phone pinged. I glanced down to see a text message.

> BLAKE: *Where are you?*

I quickly wrote back.

> *Loew house. Everything okay?*

The reply was just as fast.

> BLAKE: *I'm coming over.*

⁂

Even though Blake was coming over, I drifted off to sleep in the living room after dinner. I had been lulled into comfortable security by the sound of Jac and Diego bantering, the dogs running around and biting at each other's tails, and the Django Reinhardt record Marcus put on in the background. There was no pressure to participate, but there was still a sense of community: while I had been left alone at my parents' house, whiling away my hours doing whatever I wanted, the solitude had been limned by isolation. At the Loews', I had the option to be alone, but there was always some activity going on that I could easily join if I wanted to.

I woke to a gentle hand on my shoulder. Jac was kneeling over me, concern in her eyes.

"Rainey," she said softly. "Blake's here to see you. She said it's important."

I stumbled into the kitchen, rubbing my eyes. Blake was sitting at the table. She didn't look happy to see me; she almost looked scared.

"Hi," I said. "What's up?"

"I found out who's been following you," she said. "That redheaded guy who was at the show? It's why I came straight over here instead of calling."

I felt a tug of anxiety in my stomach. "What is it?"

Blake passed something across the table, and I picked it up. It was a photograph. The man in the photo was younger than the man I recognized, more fit-looking, but it was unmistakably the same man who had shown up at my apartment.

He was wearing a police uniform.

"Who is he?" I finally asked, looking up at Blake.

"Dane Bradley," she said. "Former detective with the LAPD. He was fired three years ago after a disciplinary hearing, but the files were redacted, so I couldn't find out why."

"Why is he following me?" I asked, hardly wanting to hear the answer.

"I don't know," Blake said. "But there's something else you should know."

I waited.

"He was one of the cops who investigated the van Aust murders," Blake said. "Rainey . . . it was his last case."

TWENTY-ONE

———

I drove over to Slant House early the next morning. I no longer had any qualms about staying with Melia, at least not until we had tied up all the loose ends surrounding her case. The dead coyote thrown through her window, Zac's proximity to her, and the fact that Jasper was definitely back in Los Angeles had all made me think she needed real protection. Hearing that one of the cops who had bungled the original case was lurking around only strengthened my resolve to close ranks around Melia.

As I parked down the street from Melia's gate, an idea occurred to me. Keeping an eye on the Flack property for any signs of movement, I took out my phone and called Maya.

She picked up after a few rings. "Morning, Rainey."

"Hi," I said. "Everything go smoothly with Brendan?"

"Locked up and awaiting trial on charges of solicitation of a minor." A pause. "Thanks."

"I've never asked you for anything, have I?"

I could almost hear Maya rolling her eyes. "Careful."

"I just need information," I said. "Whatever you can give me."

"Let's hear it."

"Dane Bradley," I said. "I know he worked on the investigation around the van Aust murders."

"I know Bradley," she said after a beat. "Why do you want to know about him?"

"Melia van Aust is back in Los Angeles."

"I heard something about that."

"Someone's been writing to her," I said. "She hired Left City to look into it."

"And where does Bradley figure into this?"

I hesitated. I had known Maya for a few years, but we weren't exactly friends. I also knew that cops and detectives tended to protect each other, regardless of personal feelings.

"Do you have any idea where things stand on the original van Aust case? It's not ongoing, is it?"

"Technically any unsolved murder case remains open until we catch someone," Maya said. "But as far as I've heard, there hasn't been any activity on it for at least two years."

"I heard Bradley was fired from the police force. Do you have any idea why?"

There was a long silence on the other end of the phone. "I've heard rumors, but unfortunately that information is sealed," she said. "I'm sorry, Rainey, I wish I could help you."

I was disappointed, but not too surprised.

"Is there anything else I can help you with?" Maya sounded impatient to get off the phone.

"No," I said. "That's it. Thanks, Maya."

⁘

As soon as I knocked, Melia threw open the door. She grinned at the sight of me.

"You came," she said, tucking a strand of dark hair behind her ear. "I thought you might have changed your mind."

"No," I said. "I thought about it for a while, and I realized it's actually not a terrible idea for me to stay."

Melia threw her arms around me, catching me by surprise.

"Thank you, Rainey," she murmured into my hair. The embrace lasted a moment too long, and for an instant I was caught up in the smell of her, a blend of grapefruit, soap, something musky, a bit of cigarettes, and a faint element of sweat. Then she was off, turning away and running through the house, laughing and beckoning me to follow her.

"Come on, come on, come on!" she called, disappearing through the living room and down the hall that led toward the bedrooms.

I followed the sound of her voice to the room where I had slept a few days ago. It had been cleaned in a clumsy fashion: a wrinkled bedspread lay stretched across the mattress, and I could see swipes of cleaning solution across the enormous window, which, like other windows in the house, stretched from floor to ceiling. This one afforded a view of the canyon ridges beyond Willow Glen Lane.

Melia sat on the bed, feet tucked beneath her. A small bouquet of wildflowers sat in a jam jar on the bedside table. She followed my line of sight to the flowers.

"Oh," she said. "I picked those this morning. The garden's become an overgrown mess without the Endos, but it's full of pretty weeds."

I bit back a laugh.

"What?" Melia asked, turning back. "What is it?"

"Nothing," I said, setting my things down. "This is lovely. I'm touched, really. Thank you."

The yard and the canyon beyond the window looked wild, overgrown, peaceful.

"Hey," I said, turning. "Were you able to sort everything out with Domicile? Have they come to install a new security system?"

Melia perked up. "They're coming by today," she said. "They told me they should be able to install most of it today, and the rest tomorrow. You hungry? Do you want something to eat—some coffee, maybe?"

"Coffee would be great."

Melia swung her legs off the bed and walked out of the room, humming. I followed her down the hall, through the living room, and into the kitchen. She paused at the counter, frowning at some wide sheaths of paper that were spread across the surface. Blueprints, I realized.

I went to go stand next to her.

"The woman from Domicile said it would be helpful if I could get the blueprints for Slant House," Melia said.

"Good idea."

"I found these upstairs in my father's office." She shivered. "I was never supposed to go in there as a kid, and it still feels like I'm breaking some sort of rule when I do."

There was something fragile about Melia, something that tragedy and a stolen youth hadn't managed to extinguish. I deliberated about whether I should share the new revelation about Dane Bradley with Melia. She had agreed that we didn't have to tell her everything when she had first signed her contract, and I didn't think it would be in her best interest to know about him—not yet—not until we figured out what he wanted and what he might do to get it. Since Melia was about to have a new security system installed, on top of having me move in, Dane's presence potentially didn't matter yet.

"I wanted to ask you something," I began carefully. "It's about Zac Flack."

Melia rolled her eyes. "What now?"

I had been mulling over my conversation with Zac, trying to reframe it in my head. He clearly had a different impression of Melia than I did, and I still couldn't fit the two images together: Melia as victim, Melia as psychopath. Standing in front of her now, his words seemed like the irate ramblings of a spoiled boy, all too easy to forget.

"He said you have something that belongs to him," I said. "He said you owe him money."

"I don't know what that means." Melia's face was blank.

"No?"

She laughed, wide-eyed. "Search the house! Really! Do you know—when I went to Aggie—they took everything I had with me. *Everything*. They're supposed to lock it away and give it to you when you leave, but they stole every last thing."

She began ticking off her fingers.

"I was wearing this emerald ring from my great-grandmother," she said. "*Gone*. Worth a fortune too. I had an Hermès scarf—super old, too, with moth holes—gone. I don't know what they'd want with that anyway. It was just sentimental. My earrings from Paris—I saw one of the nurses wearing them, too, but of course that bitch denied it. My Chanel bag . . . well, I'm not sure what Zac is implying, but whatever he thinks I have, he's wrong."

"He seemed like he might try to get it back," I said, trying to deliver the news gently. "Are you sure you don't want me to call the police?"

"The security company is coming today, right?" Melia said. "Hold on—when did you talk to him?"

"When I was leaving your house the other day," I said, almost feeling guilty, though I didn't know why.

"There's nothing here," Melia said. "He could search the entire house and find nothing."

We both jumped as a phone began to ring on the counter beside the stove. Melia looked at me.

"Let's see who it is," she said.

Two cell phones sat side by side: one was the cheap burner phone I had given her, and the other phone was ringing. She made a face when she saw who was calling, then held up the phone so I could see the name.

Paul Karnak.

"I'd better get this," she said. "Do you mind waiting?"

"Not at all."

"Hi, Mr. Karnak," Melia said, answering the phone. She trailed her fingers along the wall as she walked out of the room, her face bent in concentration. "No, not at all. That's fine. Yes, yes, I understand."

There was a long moment of silence as Melia listened to Karnak speak. I heard the couch wheeze as she dropped into it.

"Today? Does it have to be today?"

There was another pause.

"Of course. I remember where it is."

Melia reappeared at the edge of the dining room. She looked dismayed.

"I have to cancel the appointment with Domicile," she said.

"Why?"

"Karnak needs to see me," she said. "I've been trying to meet up with him since I got back, and it's the first time he's been able to make time for me. Jesus Christ, of all the days. Where did I put that number?"

"Don't cancel," I said. "I'll stay here."

Melia looked at me, confused. "Don't you have to work?"

"I have my laptop. It's not a problem."

Dismay turned to relief. "Oh, Rainey, that would be such a big help," she said. "You have no idea. I'm so stressed about this whole thing—thank you, thank you!"

She threw her arms around me in a clumsy hug.

"You won't have to do anything other than let them in and show them around," she said. "They're going to install new locks and put a proper keypad on the front gate so it's harder for people to get in. What else do you need . . . oh, spare keys. You might as well keep these since you'll be staying here now." She fished in her pocket and took out her key ring, then slipped a pair of keys off. "Front door and the front gate."

"Thanks."

She blushed. "Thank you. Look, there are plenty of groceries in the fridge—I had some delivered yesterday because I was so excited to have you. The internet password and everything are written on the fridge. I don't think you'll need to use the landline, but you can, of course . . ."

"I'm sure I'll be fine."

"Anyway, I should go," she said. "I won't be more than a few hours. Wish me luck, hey?"

And then she was gone.

———

As soon as Melia left, I called Lola. I had told Blake about my plans to stay at Slant House the night before, when she brought me the information about Dane Bradley. Blake was a lot more circumspect than Lola, but she seemed to be refraining from comment when I explained the situation. I dreaded to hear what Lola would say, and I had asked Blake not to say anything until I had a chance to speak to her myself.

"Hey, Lo," I said when she answered the phone.

"Morning. You coming in to the office today?"

"Change of plans," I said, looking out the window.

"What's up?" Lola asked.

"Have you talked to Blake yet?"

"Yeah, she said she got an ID on the guy who's been following you. A former cop? I'm going to look into that today. Have you called Maya yet?"

"Yeah, she wasn't able to give me much. Said that information was sealed to the public."

"I'll file a petition with the records division today," Lola said. "It might be sealed to the public, but as representatives of the victim, we should be able to access those files."

"I love it when you talk legal to me."

"Yeah, yeah. Do we have any theories about why this cop might be following you?"

"Blake said he worked on the van Aust case," I said. "That it was his last case."

"Well, that's ominous."

"It could just be a coincidence," I countered.

202

"Here at Left City, we don't believe in coincidences. Rainey, be serious."

"Not a coincidence then," I said. "But maybe not as bad as it looks."

"Here's what it looks like to me," Lola said. "Something nefarious happened, maybe there was a payoff to the police, a cover-up, and your cop got in over his head. Maybe his bosses found out. The fact that he's following you—and that he's no longer bound by police protocol—well, that's a cause for concern."

I took a deep breath before I responded because I didn't want Lola to hear anxiety in my voice. "Let's see what the petition with the records department turns up, yeah? And then we can circle back as a team and come up with some more substantial theories."

"Fine."

"There's something I have to tell you," I said, more seriously. "I'm at Slant House right now."

"Everything okay?" Lola sounded concerned.

I hesitated. "I'm going to stay here for a few days. Melia's having a security system installed today, but with the new information about Bradley coming to light . . . I don't feel safe leaving her alone."

There was a long silence.

"Lola?"

"She can't afford to hire a proper security guard?" Lola scoffed.

"Apparently she has to go to Karnak every time she wants to pay her cell phone bill. I think hiring security is out of the question."

A pause on the other end of the line. "Can you explain Melia's financial situation to me? Because I'm confused. She's the heiress to this massive fortune, but she can't get a dime unless she goes crawling on her hands and knees to daddy's lawyer, or her rich aunt. Then again, hiring us wasn't an issue—so she does have money. Or does she? Does she have money, Rainey?"

"I'm not completely sure what's going on with her finances," I admitted. "But I don't think she's completely sure either. I'm guessing Karnak agreed to the cost of the new security system after someone threw a coyote through the window. I know he wasn't on board with Melia hiring us, but having someone else in the house will probably reassure him on some level."

"Jesus," Lola muttered. "Why is this your responsibility?"

"It's not," I countered. "But I don't have a place to stay anyway, so it kind of worked out."

There was another long silence on the other end of the line, and I could only imagine what Lola must have been thinking.

"What? *What?*"

"I didn't say anything," she said. I could hear the shrug in her voice.

"It's so much worse when you give me that tone."

"I'm not going to tell you what to do, Rai. Just remember what happened last time you got involved with a client. *His name was Calvin,*" she added, in a mock whisper. "Calvin, that dude who rocked up to your apartment and scared the shit out of you—"

"Got it, thanks so much," I said, then hung up before she could say anything else.

———

The Domicile technicians arrived shortly past eleven that morning. They wore dark blue uniforms, and the woman in charge introduced herself as Taylor.

"Melia's not here, but I'll be around all day if I can help with anything," I said. "And she left these blueprints for you to reference."

"Great, thanks for that," Taylor said, accepting the rolled-up blueprints. "I noticed a guesthouse out back—is that on the original house plan?"

"I haven't taken a look, sorry," I said. "I think it might have been added after the original house was built though."

"All good. I shouldn't need too much from you. Just stick around in case we give you a yell."

"Can I ask what you're installing today?"

"We'll see how much we can get done right now," Taylor said. "It looks like the previous security company was Green Haven—that right?"

"Sorry, I actually don't know. I haven't known Melia for very long."

"I saw a badge out front. It makes sense—Green Haven's great for apartments and smaller houses, but if you're worried about threats or break-ins, Domicile's a better bet."

"Sure."

"Anyway, we're going to install cameras around the house," Taylor said. "We'll update the doorbell so you can hear it throughout the house, because it looks like this one's got limited range. I'm definitely going to take a look at that front gate, make sure you need to punch in a code to gain entry. There'll be a buzzer on the gate that rings up to the house too."

"Sounds good."

"And we'll hook it up to our main grid, so if you get any intruders, we'll be alerted."

I sat at the dining room table for the next few hours as Taylor's team moved around the house, silently testing and measuring and occasionally drilling into the walls. They moved so quietly and efficiently that I was able to do a lot of menial administration work for Left City despite their constant presence. At one point I watched a pair of technicians go outside and start measuring the front gate. I half-expected the Flacks to make an appearance, but there was no sign of life from within their house.

When I had finished the bulk of my work for the day, I pulled out Catalina's memoir and a pen. I hadn't even flipped past the first page yet, because I half-doubted there would be anything of value within its pages.

With a sigh, I started reading. The first two chapters were full of salacious celebrity fare: Catalina hinted at a few affairs with married men, including a disgraced Oscar-winning actor twenty years her senior. The man's pseudonym was so blindingly transparent that I suspected Catalina might have another lawsuit on her hands, on top of the one Karnak had already threatened. I was about to set the book aside when Wilhelm van Aust's name caught my eye.

Anton had been friends with Wilhelm for a very long time. They had a special bond, the kind that goes beyond normal friendship. If you know what I mean.

"Here we go," I muttered.

I knew there was something wrong with Abigail. She was a cold, heartless bitch. I admired her in a way—she always went for what she wanted. Always. Even when it came at a great cost.

I dog-eared the page and kept reading.

Both of them were blind. Blind to their children. Those poor, lonely children—rich and yet poor, in every sense of the word. I don't know why we agreed to go on vacation with them—maybe it was because Lem had a humongous yacht, and we would all have our own bedrooms.

One day, after taking a long swim, I returned to the yacht and found Melia and Jasper in bed together.

I turned the page so quickly I almost tore it out of the book.

"Good read?"

I gasped and flung the book down, as if I'd been caught rifling through someone's underwear drawer. Taylor stood in the doorway of the dining room, a little smile on her face. I was aware my own face was bright red.

"It's not what you think," I said.

"I don't think anything."

"I wasn't—I mean, I wasn't reading anything dirty," I said. "It's not like a dirty romance or anything like that."

Taylor held her hands up in mock defense. "It's none of my business."

I was flustered, aware that the more I protested, the guiltier I seemed.

I set the book aside. "Um, can I help you with something?"

"I hope so," she said. "I'm going to need the code to get past the door in the pantry."

"Sorry, what?"

"There's a door in the pantry," she repeated. "Next to the kitchen."

I frowned. "I don't know anything about that," I said. "*Inside* the pantry, you said?"

"Yeah, at the very back. You wouldn't know it was there unless you were looking for it."

"Wow, I had no idea. I don't have the code. Can you show me?"

She took me through the house, into the kitchen, and then opened the pantry door. It was a spacious, L-shaped space, and behind shelves of canned and dried goods I was stunned to see a large metal door. A gleaming pad of numbers sat above the handle. An eerie feeling came over me, and I felt the hair on my arms stand up. *Bizarre.* I couldn't exactly name the feeling I was experiencing—unease, maybe?—but there was something off about the door. It was like reading a biography about a beloved figure and learning they had done something gruesome halfway through the book.

"I didn't even know this was here," I said.

"It's not on the blueprints," Taylor said. "We had a little walk around the house, and it looks like a basement was added after the original house was built. It happens a lot with these old houses. People want more features, or possibly a heightened level of security."

"I'll call Melia," I said finally. "She can sort this out right now."

I dialed and waited. The phone rang all the way through to voicemail. I shook my head and hung up.

"My guess is that it's either a basement or a panic room," Taylor went on. "I'd like to get the entire house on the same security system, but I can't do that unless I have access to this room."

I waited until the security team was gone to pick up *Shhh* and continue reading.

> *Melia and Jasper claimed that nothing had happened. I didn't believe them. For the rest of the trip, I had my eye on them.*
>
> *And then, several months later, Jasper was sent away to a special school. A school for troubled boys. Draw your own conclusions.*

There was nothing else about Jasper and Melia. I frantically flipped through the next few chapters, looking for something—anything that elaborated on what Catalina had alleged in the chapter about the yacht. Nothing.

"For fuck's sake!"

When I had calmed down, I called Blake.

"Ahoy hoy."

"Hi," I said.

"Everything okay? You sound . . . kind of pissed off."

"Disappointing literature. Look, I need your help. I'm at Slant House, and Melia finally arranged to have the security system updated."

"Which company?"

"Domicile, of course. On your recommendation."

Blake made an assenting murmur. "Good choice."

"Melia's not here right now," I went on. "But there's a locked door at the back of the pantry. The technicians said it probably leads to either a panic room or a basement, but it has a coded entry and I can't get hold of Melia to ask her what it is."

"Do you have the blueprints?" Blake asked.

"Old blueprints," I said. "Whatever's behind the door was added after the original construction."

"Hmm," Blake said. "It does raise some odd questions."

I could feel my heart beating faster. I had sensed something odd about the door and whatever lay behind it, but I almost felt disloyal to Melia for even entertaining those thoughts.

"I'm sure the police have already looked into this," Blake said. "But the main question I have is this: If they've had this locked door the whole time, why didn't Melia at least try to hide behind it when her parents were being attacked? Don't you think she would have heard something and known where she would be safe?"

TWENTY-TWO

———◦◦◦———

Melia came home in the early evening. Her hair was flat and she looked completely exhausted. She came in carrying bags of takeaway food, which she deposited in the kitchen before coming into the living room and sinking onto the couch. She draped her arm across her eyes and groaned.

I came into the living room and sat opposite her.

"Hey," I said softly.

She moved her arm just enough to look at me. "Hi."

I wanted to be cautious. I didn't know whether I should mention Catalina's book to Melia, or what she had alleged about Melia and Jasper. My rational mind knew the allegations were insane—and that Catalina was even more insane for being bold enough to print them.

Melia glanced at me. "What? What is it?"

"It's nothing."

"You're lying," she said, sitting up. "Tell me."

"It's just . . . well, Catalina von Faber gave me a copy of her book." I felt tense, cagey; the book was trash of the highest order, but there were still enough insinuations about the van Aust family that it might do some damage.

To my surprise, however, Melia chuckled. "Might be time to put the fireplace to good use."

"Right," I said, relieved. "So—just to be clear—you're not concerned about what she might have written? You don't think she's a threat?"

"You read it?" She slipped off her shoes and started massaging her feet. "Go on. Spill."

"There's a part about a trip to Greece," I started. I could feel myself blushing, uncomfortable in my own skin. All of a sudden I was furious at Catalina for writing the book, then mad at myself for reading it when I should have just chucked it in the bin.

"Uh-huh." Melia's eyes were on my face.

"And a yacht." I was having trouble maintaining eye contact with her.

Melia groaned, leaning back on the couch. She draped her hands over her eyes. "Yes," she said. "I know what you're talking about. Jasper and I were jet-lagged, and we fell asleep in the same bed. Am I on the right track?"

"Yes," I said, then cleared my throat. "She . . . well . . . she broadly hints that you and Jasper might . . . might have had sex."

Melia was quiet for a very long time. I couldn't read her expression because her arm was covering her eyes. Finally, she cleared her throat and sighed. "I wish I could summon the energy to care." She dropped her arm and glanced at me. "It's not *true*, you know. You don't have to wonder."

"No, of course," I said quickly. I was still having trouble meeting her eyes, because whether or not the rumor was true, the fact that Catalina was willing to write about it in a highly publicized memoir felt akin to some sort of assault.

"Forget it, Rainey," Melia warned. "I don't want to dwell on that trash. It's not true—we move on."

"Got it," I said, nodding. "I understand."

"What a day," she said, glancing at the ceiling.

"Do you want to talk about it?"

She sat up and rubbed her eyes, then leaned forward. "I've always been treated like a child," she said slowly. "Everything has always been taken care of for me. Bills, food, safety, my future, everything I had to do—but now it's all on my shoulders."

I nodded, listening.

"I thought I could do this," she said. "I really thought that if I got all my paperwork organized, I could petition some powerful old white men to let me have control of my own life for once."

"What happened today?"

"Karnak," she said bitterly. "Apparently I don't have any control over my inheritance until I turn twenty-five."

"That's not very far away," I said. "Three years, right?"

"That's not the point, Rainey," she said. "The inheritance was set up when my parents were still alive. Those rules were established so I wouldn't blow a hundred million dollars on a trip to Europe or get married without a prenup to some moneygrubbing cling-on."

"A hundred million?" I was shocked at the figure.

She waved a hand. "I'm exaggerating. My point is that everything has changed. I'm a lot more responsible than he gives me credit for, and besides, who *cares* if I get the money early? My whole family's dead."

"Except for Jasper."

"Except for Jasper." She looked at me. "Right."

"Does he . . ." I cut myself off. "Never mind. It doesn't matter."

"No, what?"

"It's none of my business."

"I think we're past that," she pointed out.

"What's Jasper's stake in this? If he goes to jail, does he still get half the money?"

She blinked. "I hadn't thought about that. I should ask Karnak."

A chilly feeling settled over me. I wanted to change the topic of conversation. "Do you want my advice?"

She blinked, shrugged. "Why not?"

"Have you thought about the future? I mean, what do you want to do with your life?"

"I'm not very good at anything, Rainey."

"I don't know very much about estate law," I said. "Lola would know more. If your money's in a trust, there might not be anything you can do to change things."

"I could get a new lawyer."

I shrugged. "You could definitely try. I'm not sure that would change things regarding your inheritance though."

"Maybe."

"Does Karnak give you any money? You said he pays all the bills, but anything else?"

She gave a bitter laugh. "A thousand dollars a month. It barely covers groceries."

"I'm sorry."

She sat up and shook her head as though to clear it. "I got Thai food," she said. "Come on, let's eat before it gets cold."

Melia lit candles and brought out bowls and chopsticks.

"Sorry, I didn't know what you liked," she said. "You're not a vegan or anything, are you?"

"I eat pretty much everything."

"Well, good, because I got a little bit of everything."

She spooned noodles onto her plate and then dug into a salad. I remembered the locked door in the pantry and the conversation I had with Blake.

"I tried to call you earlier," I said. "There was a minor problem with the Domicile installation."

"Oh?" She frowned. "Sorry, I had my phone on silent when I was meeting with Karnak. What's the problem?"

"There's a locked door in the pantry," I said. "It has a keypad, and since I didn't know the code, they weren't able to finish installing all the security around the house."

Melia hesitated. It was only for a second, but I caught a faint look of concern cross her face.

"Of course," she said. "That door leads down to the basement. I guess I didn't mention it."

"No."

"I haven't been down there in years," she said, passing me the salad bowl. "For all I know, it's full of dusty old junk and broken furniture."

"It wasn't on the blueprints you gave me."

She was looking at her plate. "Right," she said. "I must have given you the old ones. I'll see if I can find the updated plans for the house, but I'm not sure where they would be."

"Do you know the code?"

A thin line appeared between her eyebrows. "No, I don't," she said. "Even when I lived here, there was no reason for me to go down there. Caroline used it as dry storage, and sometimes, when we had parties, she would do all the food preparation down there. There's a kitchen and a rumpus room down there."

I waited a moment before asking my next question. "So I'm guessing you haven't changed the code since the Endos were here."

"What are you getting at, Rainey?" She sounded tired, annoyed.

"There's a second door that leads into the basement, outside the house," I said. "Taylor showed me earlier today. It looks like it has the same code as the door in the pantry. What I'm trying to say is . . . anyone who knows the code could get into the house through the basement."

There was a long, eerie silence as Melia contemplated my meaning.

"Someone could be in the house right now."

Melia blanched. In that moment, Slant House seemed cavernous, much too large, every angle and shadow a potential hiding spot. Her hand slowly closed over the knife beside her plate.

"There's a way to lock it," she said, rising to her feet. Her hands were trembling. "From this side, on the keypad, even without knowing the code.

I used to get in trouble all the time because Jas and I would be messing around and I'd lock him in there."

She jumped up and went into the pantry, the knife clutched in her trembling hand. I followed behind her.

There was a red button on the bottom of the keypad. It read: OVERRIDE—LOCK. Melia pressed it, and there was a mechanical slotting noise.

"There," she said. "Even if there is someone down there, they're not getting up here. Not tonight."

<hr />

Even after Melia and I had gone to our separate bedrooms, I couldn't sleep. The hours had slipped past without me realizing it, and now it was late. After dinner I had insisted Melia lock herself in her room while I searched every room in the house, just to make sure no one was there, that nobody had broken in. We were safe: all the rooms were empty. We were alone in the house.

I lay in my bed, watching lights along the walls of the canyon. Houses weren't visible from here, but I could see their outlines illuminated, showing up as nothing more than pinpricks, tiny stars. I didn't want to think about what might be hiding in the basement at that very moment, waiting to be found, waiting for the right moment to make its appearance.

I lay there for at least another thirty minutes, wide-awake, before finally admitting to myself that sleep would not come. Keeping half an ear out for noises in the house—specifically movement from Melia's room—I threw back my covers and swung my legs over the side of the bed. The house was silent. I padded to the door of Jasper's room, still listening for sounds. There was nothing.

The light under Melia's door was off, and the house was plunged in darkness as I made my way down the corridor toward the living room. Once

I emerged on the other side, I saw that everything—the living room, the dining room, the entryway—was steeped in moonlight. It was so bright I didn't need any other light.

After a moment's hesitation, I turned and made my way toward the library. I hadn't spent much time in that room, partly because there had been no need, but also because something about it gave me the creeps. I couldn't even glance into the library without remembering the dark swath of coyote blood on the wooden floor.

I turned on the floor lamp, and the room was suffused with yolky light. Walking around the bookcases, I trailed my fingers along the spines of books, seeing what caught my interest. Just like everything else in Slant House, the library had been flawlessly appointed, yet subtle enough to appear informal. The bookshelves displayed old classics—Joyce, Faulkner, du Maurier—alongside cult Los Angeles fableists like Joan Didion, John Fante, James Ellroy, and Francesca Lia Block. Rough-hewn marble bookends rested against thick sheets of notepaper, scrawled with careless disregard. I glanced at the first sentence, which read: "Melia—85; Jasper—68 (trip. word score!!)." An old Scrabble score sheet, by the looks of it.

Wooden animals lingered on a lower shelf, next to a folded piece of old map. A framed pair of brilliant blue butterflies leaned against a copy of *The Awakening*. I stopped when I reached a tall set of books with leather spines. Photo albums.

My heart started pounding as I pulled the first album off the shelf. Something about what I was doing felt illicit, wrong somehow, although I could well have argued that I had been brought to Slant House to do something much more personal than flip through a few old photographs. Still, I stood still for a moment and listened to the house, waiting to hear footsteps from the direction of Melia's bedroom. When I was sure I was the only one awake, I took the album over to a green leather chair and sat down, then opened the cover.

On the first page was an image of Melia, dressed in a vintage ball gown and diamonds. She was sitting on the hood of a vintage Thunderbird, which was parked beneath a huge tree with leafy, spreading branches. In the background I could see what looked like an old Southern plantation house with white pillars and a wide porch. Melia was throwing back her head and laughing . . . but no, there was something wrong. It *wasn't* Melia in the photo.

ABIGAIL BEFORE WAKELY HALL PROM, a legend beneath the photo read. A second hand had added, beneath this, WORE MAMA'S DIAMOND NECKLACE—AND A DRESS MADE SPECIAL IN CHARLESTON.

I flipped through the next dozen or so pages, feeling an eerie parallel between Melia and the images of a young Abigail. Abigail as a young girl looked so much like Melia that it would have been very easy to mistake one for the other; indeed, I already had.

It was clear that Abigail had penned all the descriptions under the photographs, and at times, I almost felt like I was peering over her shoulder as she wrote. There was something so intimate about watching from afar, reading about her hopes and petty observations about friends and the handsome men who stood next to her in these photographs. She had saved pressed flowers; ticket stubs to concerts, plays, and movies; pages torn out of books; and old love letters.

The photo album gave me more insight into Abigail's life than any forensic psychologist ever could: she had been rich, pretty, spoiled, and popular, but there was a wistfulness, too, a longing for something that existed beyond the confines of her charmed life. The photos and their captions hinted at something else too: either a latent intelligence, dormant and unexplored, or else a knack for ferreting out weakness in others. A casual cruelty. My mind conjured an image of Abigail's lifeless body sprawled across her bed, the sheets soaked with blood.

I sat there for a moment, horrified by that mental image contrasted against the bewitching young woman in all the photographs. Shaking the image from my mind, I got up and replaced the first photo album, then pulled down the second one.

The photos in this album started in Los Angeles. Here was an image of Abigail in tennis whites, lacing up her sneakers. Abigail, running toward the surf near the Santa Monica Pier. Abigail, sipping a cocktail against the drifting palm leaf wallpaper of the Polo Lounge at the Beverly Hills Hotel.

After this, the tidy considerations and pithy captions ceased altogether. The next few pages were blank, and as I continued to flip through the album, a mess of photographs fell out onto my lap. The first image I picked up was Abigail, lying in a hospital bed, looking ill and almost unrecognizable. A second image showed her holding an infant swaddled in bunting, but there was no joy in Abigail's face. I turned the photo over and saw that someone had scrawled: ABIGAIL AND BABY MELIA—CEDARS-SINAI.

As I continued to pick up photographs from the pile in my lap, I saw they were nearly all of Melia. She had been an adorable, gawky young thing—in most of the photos, her smile was nearly too big for her face. A shock of dark hair contrasted against her pale skin. Abigail was nowhere to be seen in these photos; Melia was always alone. Melia, playing with a toy giraffe, sitting on the floor in a massive bedroom. Melia, climbing a tree, her face red with the exertion.

I set the album aside and went to pick up the third photo album, already feeling a sense of trepidation as I did so.

Here, the pattern of affixing photographs and annotating events continued, and I recognized Abigail's ghostly scrawl beneath the images. The first image was of a young Melia holding baby Jasper. The images advanced rapidly through the years; apparently Abigail hadn't taken too many photos of her children, so a page might jump from Melia at six to one of her at nine years old.

MAMA SAYS THE BEAUTY SKIPPED MELIA, Abigail wrote beneath an image of Melia in a dress. I felt a sudden pang reading this—the image of Melia was stunning, almost jarringly so; it was odd to see such adult beauty in a young girl. As I continued flipping through the images of Melia—Melia with a pet dog, Melia bent over a book—I could see what was abundantly obvious, even if Abigail couldn't admit it to herself. Melia had been gorgeous, even as an awkward child. Perhaps *too* beautiful for her own good. Here and there were images of Abigail, growing older in the pages, and in each one there was an element of wariness, holding the viewer at a distance.

As much as Abigail seemed to resent Melia, though, it was clear she adored Jasper. Each photograph of Jasper was accompanied by a glowing caption—JAS ALREADY SHOWS MUSICAL TALENT! or CLEARLY HIS MOTHER'S SON—LOOK HOW CHEEKY. In many of the photos of Jasper, Abigail hovered in the background, glowing with pleasure.

As the photographs of Melia continued, the light in her eyes seemed to gradually dim, then fade away. The last photograph in the album was of Melia, and when I looked at the date in the caption, I realized—with a chill—that it would have been only a month before her parents were brutally slain.

In the photo, Melia sat on the bench by the tennis court behind Slant House. She held a book in her lap, her head bent over the pages, deep in concentration. She hadn't been aware of someone taking her picture, it seemed.

As I looked closer, though, I felt goose bumps all over my body. Melia's face was bent down, but I could see her peering up at the person behind the camera through the curtain of her hair. Her jaw was clenched, her eyes dark slits. There was only one way to interpret the look on her face: it was loathing.

I closed the album, then put everything back where I had found it. The house was silent as I made my way back to my bedroom, then climbed back under the covers. I couldn't shake the image of Melia, or the sad progression of Abigail's life, from a hopeful young woman to the victim of a violent crime. Just when I thought I would stay awake all night, sleep finally came, falling upon me like death, like the lid of a coffin.

TWENTY-THREE

———

I left Slant House early the next morning before Melia woke up. The neighborhood surrounding the house was quiet, and I was relieved to see no interference or activity from the Flack house. Maybe they would finally leave us alone.

When I got to the office, I was surprised to see Blake and Lola were already there.

"Morning," Lola said. She was leaning against Blake's desk, arms folded across her chest. It looked like I had interrupted their conversation. "Coffee's on."

"Thanks." I went over to the fish tank and opened the top, then sprinkled some flakes over the surface. Dart hid behind a plant at the bottom of the tank, but when I knelt to look through the glass, he swam out and came over to me. "Look! He finally recognizes me!"

"Can frogs recognize people?" Lola frowned.

I picked up one of the books on tropical aquariums and waved it at her. "Better minds seem to think so."

"Don't you think he might get lonely?" Blake asked. She ran a hand through her hair. "Maybe you should get a second frog to put in there with him."

"Thought of that," I said, peering through the glass. "But African dwarf frogs are solitary creatures. They get along with fish, but if you put another frog in there, one will kill the other."

"How are things going with Melia?" Lola asked. "Any more letters?"

"No, there haven't been," I said. I went over and sat at my desk. "I'm starting to get concerned about the lawyer though. Paul Karnak. We already knew he was condescending, but I'm starting to wonder if he's not a little power-hungry too."

Lola moved to her desk. "How so?"

"He talks to Melia like she's a child, for one," I said. "And he only gives her a thousand dollars a month. It's her money, after everything."

Lola sighed. "Afraid not," she said. "Inheritance clauses are basically iron-clad. If the will stipulated that Melia wouldn't have access to her inheritance until she reached a certain age, there's nothing anyone can do about it."

"Even if her parents got murdered?" I drummed my fingers on my desk. "Hold on—that's her inheritance. Wouldn't she have access to her parents' money before that? Surely that's separate from the inheritance."

"I can look into it," Lola said, scratching her neck. "But intestate law isn't my forte, and Karnak seems like one powerful motherfucker."

Blake cleared her throat, then said quietly, "What if Melia was in on it?"

Lola and I glanced at each other.

"In on . . . what?"

Blake shrugged. "I'm just playing devil's advocate, so hear me out. What if Melia killed her parents?"

I let out an involuntary exclamation, and Blake raised her eyebrows at me.

"Sorry," I said. "I wasn't expecting you to say that."

Lola gestured at Blake. "I'm listening."

"There's this huge inheritance," Blake said. "We haven't found out quite how *much* money, but we know it's big. Melia was eighteen when the murders happened, which meant seven years until the inheritance kicked in. Maybe she wanted it early. Then again, she probably thought she'd be legally entitled to it, since she was an adult."

"But she nearly died that night," I pointed out. For some reason I couldn't articulate to Blake or Lola, hearing these theories about Melia felt like a form of betrayal.

"True," Blake said. "But the police determined that Melia and her parents were attacked with different weapons, right? Maybe Melia was in the process of killing her parents when Jasper came home and stabbed her."

"So . . ." Lola frowned. "Why would Jasper disappear afterward? It only makes him look guilty."

Blake adjusted her glasses. "It would be hard to claim self-defense if Melia wasn't attacking *him*. A good lawyer could get him off, probably, but if he came home and found Melia killing their parents, then went ballistic . . . he was only sixteen. Maybe he freaked out."

"Or!" Lola said. "What if they were in on it together?"

"I think you guys are running away with this theory," I said.

"You're not being objective," Lola said. "See, I knew it was a bad idea for you to move into Slant House. You're getting invested. It's tainting your perspective."

"Don't you talk to me about taints."

"Grow up."

"There's another possibility at play here," Blake said. "It's pretty far-fetched, but I think we should keep our options open."

"Tell me," Lola said.

"What if Jasper wasn't involved at all? What if someone else was helping Melia kill the parents, and Jasper wasn't even there that night? Nobody ever proved he was in the house. He was supposed to be at boarding school, right? What if there's another party the police never found?"

There was a profound, uneasy silence. I had to admit that all these theories were possible, no matter how uncomfortable they made me.

"Then again, maybe they *were* in on it together. Maybe Jasper got cold feet, which is why he attacked Melia, then ran. He *was* guilty of conspiring to kill his parents, which is why he couldn't claim innocence . . . especially since Melia survived and could tell them what really happened! *Boom!*"

"Well done." Lola yawned. "You've solved the most beguiling true crime of the century."

"Which means Rainey will be spending the night with a murderer." Blake winked at me. "Lock your door tonight, Rai Rai."

"Thanks for that."

"Moving on," Blake said, shifting gears. She reached into her bag. "I downloaded a more recent copy of the blueprints from an architectural firm that consulted on the house. This version has the basement addition."

She spread the blueprints out onto the table, and we all peered at them. Laid out in blue and white, Slant House seemed so innocuous, so neutral. It was hard to believe anything bad could have happened within its walls, or that the inhabitant might still be in danger.

"You can take these," Blake said, rolling them up and passing them to me. "In all seriousness, though, be careful. Don't lose sight of the fact that you could both be in danger."

⁓

When I returned to Willow Glen Lane, I was distracted thinking about everything Blake had said. So distracted, in fact, that I didn't see someone run up behind me, didn't see them until it was too late, until there were hands on me, grabbing, yanking—

"I know what you did! I *know* what you did!"

I ducked, throwing my arms up over my face to protect myself from the blows.

"Ouch—stop! Stop it!" I stumbled backward and fell to the ground—*hard.* I looked up and saw Janine Flack standing over me, crouched as if ready to attack me again.

"Wait—please stop—stop *hitting* me!"

She advanced, fists raised.

"I could kill you right now," she said, her voice a low hiss. "I could fucking kill you. Tell me why I shouldn't do it!"

"Janine," I said, still using my arms to protect my head. "Mrs. Flack. I'm going to stand up now. Let's talk about this *calmly*. I think there's been some kind of mistake."

I started to rise to my knees, but Janine lunged forward and grabbed my hair.

"Ouch! What the hell!"

"He's *gone* because of you! He's fucking gone, and he's never coming back!" She yanked my hair so hard that I jerked sideways, saw stars. "I have nothing left now—you took it all!"

"Please, Mrs. Flack—I don't know what you're talking about!"

"My *fucking son*! You took him away from me!" Her voice was a hoarse scream, and all of a sudden, she burst into tears. She backed away from me, her face contorted in a wobbly howl.

I climbed to my feet, afraid she might attack again, but she remained at a distance. "Your son," I echoed. "Zac? What happened to him?"

"Oh, as if you don't know." She collapsed into soft sobs. "They took him away this morning. The police. I'll probably never see him again."

I was at a loss for words. "I'm sorry to hear that," I said, my voice cautious. I tried to stay calm, hoping it would prevent her from freaking out. "I'm not sure what happened or why you think I had something to do with it."

"I know Zac isn't perfect," Janine said. She sounded raw, exhausted. "I know he had problems with drugs, and why he got kicked out of school."

"So . . ."

"Someone called the police this morning. They said Zac was selling again."

"But . . . I'm sorry, I still don't see why you think I was involved—"

"The tipster told the police that Zac left drugs in the mailbox for someone to collect, and if the police looked in there, they'd find a bag of pills." Janine gave an awful, hollow laugh. "Well, what do you think they found? A little Ziploc baggie full of pills. Only, Zac doesn't have *access* to that kind of drug anymore. He's been with me day and night ever since he got out. I don't have a job anymore, and the only thing I do is protect my goddamned son."

Her eyes went wild, and I saw some of the original fury return to her face.

"I didn't frame your son," I said, my voice firm. "You have the wrong idea about me."

"If it wasn't you, then who was it?"

"I'm sorry," I said. "I really don't know anything about this."

She jerked her head toward Slant House. "I know about them," she said. "I know all about Melia. Little Miss Perfect, wasn't she? Always had her whole life ahead of her. Zac used to sell to her too. I might have reported her to the police if I didn't think it would take Zac down with her."

I felt cold all over. If Zac had been telling the truth about his connection to Melia—and she had something that belonged to him—it would make sense that Melia might want to frame him, to send him away. And it might also make sense that Zac hadn't been lying after all. Maybe Melia really was a psychopath.

Janine stepped forward, jabbing a finger in my face. "You stay *away* from my family! Both of you!"

She whirled around, then marched back toward her house.

⚬⚬⚬

Melia wasn't home when I let myself into Slant House. I found a note scrawled on a piece of paper on my bed.

> *Going back to meet with Karnak again. See if Daddy Warbucks will up my allowance. Just kidding—but may mention the possibility of finding another lawyer. See if that lights a fire under his ass.*

If I'm still gone when you get back, please DON'T LET ANYONE INSIDE.

See you this evening. Hope you like sushi.

M

I still felt numb and dazed from my conversation with Janine. The idea that Zac had been telling the truth about Melia—and that Janine might be right about her too—was almost too much for me to comprehend. A part of me was tempted to leave right then, to get in my car and drive somewhere else, anywhere else.

A better mind prevailed, though, and I decided to give Melia the chance to explain her side of things.

I went into the kitchen and made a cup of coffee. When it was ready, I pulled out a pen and my copy of *Shhh*.

The count and I had an understanding, like many other couples with our social stature. No matter how many conversations we had about our "arrangement," however, Anton was always jealous when I returned from a night away with a new plaything.

I rolled my eyes at the stilted writing and purple prose. After making mention of the van Aust family, Catalina had moved onto topics that no longer pertained to the case at hand. I flipped through the next few chapters, curious about whether they would come up again, but the upcoming pages only promised more anonymous orgies in penthouses and four-star resorts. I set the book aside and took out my computer, determined to see what I could find about Dane Bradley.

The first few images that popped up were of Bradley in uniform. He was clean-shaven and quite a few pounds lighter, but it was unmistakably him. I recognized the thinning red hair and dark eyes. I clicked through a few articles until I found one on the *LA Lens*.

*Staff Sergeant Bradley ended his contract with the Los Angeles Police
Department after serving on the force for seventeen years. The LAPD
did not clarify why Bradley ended his tenure at the department three
years before retirement, rendering himself ineligible for a pension.*

I scrolled further, but a series of bells jolted me out of my thoughts.

Ding-dong, ding-dong, ding.

It sounded like a generic cell phone ring, but the sound seemed to be
coming from everywhere at once. I glanced up at the ceiling and saw a
tiny speaker.

Ding-dong, ding-dong, ding.

I closed my computer and went to the window overlooking the front of
the house. The technicians had updated the security on the gate, which had
been broken since a few years before the murders. Through the bars of the
gate, I could see a figure, but from this distance, I couldn't make out a face.

Ding-dong, ding-dong, ding.

I hastily put my shoes on, opened the front door, and then cautiously
made my way down toward the gate. As I got closer, I could see the visitor
was a slender man with dark hair and glasses. His hair was combed back
in a tidy cropped style, and it was patterned with gray. He looked vaguely
familiar.

"Hi," I said, cautious. "Can I help you?"

"My name is Katsumi Endo," the man said.

"Oh, Mr. Endo—of course! I recognized you from an old photo," I said,
and for some reason I felt relieved. "My name is Rainey. I came to your
house the other day and spoke to your son."

He inclined his head in a slight nod. "Alex mentioned that to me. That's
why I'm here."

His voice was different than I had expected. He had the remnants of
an accent.

"Are you . . . are you a Kiwi?" I ventured.

He gave me a surprised smile. "Very good," he said. "Most people assume British or Aussie."

"I worked on a film with some musicians from New Zealand," I said, smiling at the memory. "Is there something I can help you with?"

"I was hoping to speak to Melia," Katsumi said, adjusting his glasses.

"I'm afraid she's not here," I said. Even though we had just met, and I had little background information on him, Katsumi didn't seem to be a threat—or at least, he didn't seem dangerous, and I doubted he was violent. There was something very calming about his presence, something almost trustworthy. I could never quantify feelings like this, but over the last few years I had learned to trust my gut instincts about people.

"I don't mind waiting," he replied. His face bore an inscrutable expression.

I was about to open the gate for him when I remembered Melia's note about not letting anyone inside.

"She's going to be quite a while," I said evasively. "I'm actually not sure what time she'll be back. It could be late at night."

He sighed. "Please don't take this the wrong way, Rainey," he said. "But do you mind if I ask how you know Melia?"

"I can't get too specific, but my team and I have been contracted to work for her."

"Is it security related?"

"Again, I'm not sure I should say." For some reason I almost felt guilty turning him away, especially when I remembered that up until a few months ago, the Endos had lived here. Katsumi could have railed against me, could have insisted that he come inside, but he remained calm, and I was incredibly grateful for that.

"Look," he said sternly. "I'm only going to ask you this once. Is she still sober?"

"Oh—yes—yes, I think so." A few hours before, I would have been able to answer the question without any hesitation. Now, though, I had my doubts. Was Melia doing drugs? Had she started buying from Zac again?

"You're not camped out up there, doing drugs?" Katsumi pressed. There was a hard edge in his voice. "Is she bankrolling all of this?"

"I'm here for Melia's protection," I said softly. "And I'm afraid that's all I can say."

"People have taken advantage," he said, his voice still stern. "She's a gentle person, and people have taken advantage of her before. I've seen it too many times."

"I understand."

He glanced around, then looked back at me. When he spoke again, his voice was softer. "Is she okay? You can tell me."

"She's . . . well, she's been a bit on edge lately," I said. "But for the most part, she seems okay. She's really trying to strike out on her own."

"I can understand why she had to ask me and my family to leave, as hard as it was for us to break ties with her. She doesn't trust people very easily, Rainey. I don't think anyone in her position would."

"Of course."

"People have taken advantage in the past," he repeated. "She doesn't know how tough the world can be. What people are like."

"I'm not too worried about her," I said honestly. "I thought she was really naïve when I first met her, but she's stronger than you'd think."

I saw movement on the Flack property. A window had opened slightly, and a face appeared behind the glass. *Janine.*

"I think everything's going to be okay," I said. "Really. Can I ask—when was the last time you saw Melia?"

"Two weeks ago," he said. "Nearly three, I think. It was right when she got back. And she seemed spooked, that's all. Like she kept looking over her shoulder."

"Over her . . . sorry, what do you mean?"

He shifted slightly, glanced over his own shoulder. Janine's face disappeared, and a curtain was snatched across the window. Katsumi looked at me again, and his face was grave.

"The neighbors?" I asked. "Are you worried about the neighbors?"

"No, no," he said. "I shouldn't have said—forget that."

"You can tell me," I said. "Please—the only reason I'm here is to keep Melia safe. Anything you can share might help."

He hesitated. "There was something wrong with that family," he said. "The aunt from Georgia came out a few times before . . . before the deaths happened. I knew it was a bad idea for Melia to go live with her, but of course, I'm not family, so I didn't have a say."

"You think Melia's worried about her aunt?" I pressed.

"I don't know. I'm not sure what she was scared of." He shook his head, thinking. "But she looked like someone was chasing her."

TWENTY-FOUR

—— ◦◦◦◦ ——

Melia returned just after five. She was wearing black tights and a man's formal shirt, which covered her wrists and rode over her thin frame like a sail. Her hair was pinned back from her face. She looked casual but elegant.

"Hey!" she said, smiling as she came through the door. She carried a large paper sack in one hand, and a thick canvas tote was slung over her shoulder. "How was your day? Not too eventful, I hope?"

"You had a visitor," I said, rising from my seat at the kitchen table.

"Oh?" Her voice was light.

I cleared my throat. I had been nervous about breaking the news to Melia all day, but I couldn't prolong it forever. "It was Katsumi Endo."

Her face was unreadable. She went into the kitchen and set the paper bag on the counter, then began removing boxes from within. When the bag was empty, she carefully set the canvas tote on the counter and turned.

"What did he want?" Her voice was abrupt.

"I don't think he wanted anything," I said, slightly taken aback. "He said he just wanted to make sure you were okay. I think . . . well, I think he's worried about you."

She huffed and sat down on a chair, clearly annoyed.

"He's not worried," she grumbled. "He's angry because I *fired* them."

"He really didn't seem angry," I countered. "He wanted to make sure I wasn't taking advantage of you."

"Great. So glad he still cares about me." She sounded sarcastic.

"I'm going to ask you something," I said. "And I need you to be honest with me."

Melia turned to look at me. "Well?"

"Zac Flack was arrested this morning," I said. "Apparently the police got an anonymous tip about him selling drugs. That would violate his parole conditions, obviously, so he might be going back to jail."

She looked genuinely surprised. "Shit. Poor Janine. I mean, I've never liked her, but still. That can't be easy."

"You had nothing to do with it?"

"Yeah," she joked. "I planted a bunch of drugs in his car and then told the police where to find them."

I stared at her. "The drugs were in his mailbox."

"Oh, shit!" She laughed, then frowned. "Wait, you don't think I actually had anything to do with this, do you?"

"I'm asking you." I gave her a pointed look.

"I had nothing to do with it, Rainey."

Melia hopped up again and began pulling plates and cups out of a cabinet. She grabbed the takeaway boxes and set everything on the table before opening a container of miso soup and pouring it into cups.

"I know it's early for dinner, but I skipped lunch. I'm starving."

I lingered by the door for a minute before coming over to join her at the table.

"You haven't exactly answered my question."

"Yes, I did," she said, irritation gilding her tone. "Zac is trouble, always has been. I've changed a *lot* in the last few years, even if he hasn't. I wish you'd give me more credit for that."

"Fine," I said, softening.

"Think of everything I've been through," she pleaded. "Zac going away is a good thing. One less thing for us to worry about."

"Okay. I'm sorry."

"Good. I'm starving."

"You don't have to buy me dinner every night," I said, changing the topic. "I'd actually prefer you didn't."

"Why?" she snapped. "Can't I be generous toward you?"

My face burned. "That's not . . . it's not what I meant. I just feel like . . . if I'm going to stay for more than a few days, I should help out. We can go get groceries together."

"I'm too tired to cook." She stabbed a few pieces of sushi with a fork and flung them onto a plate, which she thrust toward me. "I can afford this, you know. Or at least I will be able to once Karnak signs everything over."

"I thought—"

"What?" she snapped. "What did you think?"

Her sudden change of tone was shocking. I closed my eyes and forced myself to take two calming breaths before I answered.

"I don't want to take advantage of your generosity," I said. "And I think that until you get some more control over your situation—from Karnak, I mean—maybe you should be careful about how much you spend."

She dropped the fork onto the table and stood up, then went over to the window. *This is it,* I thought. *She's going to kick me out.*

I watched her stand there for a minute, breathing very quickly. She finally turned, and I could see something in her begin to yield.

"I'm sorry," she said, to my surprise. "I don't mean to take all this out on you."

I nodded, still holding my breath.

"I used to care about the Endos a lot too," she went on. "They were my family. I mean that in the most literal sense possible—they lived here my whole life. Caroline cooked all our meals, which is probably why I never thought that being an adult meant cooking for yourself. I spent my whole childhood being friends with Alex, but now, I don't think I'll ever see him again."

"Why not?"

She took a deep breath. Even across the room I could see she was trembling. "You can't tell anyone about this," she said. "Not even your team. It's not related to my case."

"Okay."

"Do I have your word?"

"Of course."

"It was before my parents were killed," she said softly. "I heard my parents arguing, and the next day, Caroline confronted my dad. She had discovered something. Something bad."

"What was it?"

"I don't know," Melia said. "I was supposed to be at school that week, but I had stayed home sick. My parents knew I was there, of course, but Caroline must not have. I was in the living room when she came up through the door in the pantry. She was yelling at him, saying something like, 'What would you do if everyone found out?' They screamed at each other for a few minutes, and then my mom came in and saw me. That was the last I ever heard of it."

"When did that happen?"

She shrugged. "Maybe a month before they were killed," she said quietly. "It was at the end of my school term, just before summer."

We were both quiet for a very long time.

"What did she want from him?"

"Money," Melia said bitterly. "A lot of money. He must have paid them, too, because eventually things went back to normal. I never found out what it was."

I rubbed my arm. "Why didn't you tell me this until now?" I asked, trying to keep the irritation out of my voice.

"I know what you're thinking," Melia said. "It wasn't them. They didn't kill my parents, Rainey. Their alibis were solid."

"And the letter?"

"No." Melia was having trouble meeting my eyes. "I really don't think so."

It occurred to me yet again how alone in the world Melia truly was. Her parents were dead, but she had also lost her brother in a tragedy that had made her famous, very much against her will. For the last four years she had been a walking target for paparazzi and anyone with a half-decent camera, and even before that, she had been susceptible to the whims and decisions of others.

She suddenly smiled. "I have a surprise for you," she said.

"Oh?"

"There is something Karnak can't keep from me," she said. "My parents didn't trust him with *everything*, after all."

Melia went over to the canvas bag she had deposited on the counter. From within this bag, she produced a slender rectangular box. The box was coated in black velvet.

"Can you guess?"

"It looks like a jewelry container, but that seems too obvious."

"I've never been one for subterfuge."

Melia approached me and set the box down on the dining room table. "Open it."

I used both hands to slowly open the box. When the lid sprang open on its hinges, I gasped. Sitting on a little cushion inside the box was an elaborate necklace entwined with emeralds, diamonds, and sapphires.

"It's beautiful, isn't it?"

"I . . . wow," I said. "It's . . . well, it's incredible."

Melia sat down next to me. "It belonged to my mother," she said. "It was a gift on her sixteenth birthday, can you believe it? I used to beg her to tell me the story . . . It was the middle of summer, so hot you wouldn't believe. They had arranged a big party, with all the most important people in Savannah set to come. My mother wore a silk chiffon gown made by the finest tailor in Georgia. Just before the party started, her father gave her this."

Melia touched the necklace with her index finger.

"I used to ask her if I could wear it. *Please, Mama, just ten minutes!* She'd never let me. Said I ruined everything I touched."

She blinked and looked away, then ran a hand through her hair.

"She can't stop me now though."

The story had given me chills. I imagined Abigail as a young woman, spoiled and haughty, given everything she had ever wanted. Such a beautiful young girl was bound to catch the eye of a wealthy young man, an affluent heir himself. *Slings and arrows of outrageous fortune,* I thought, remembering a line from a play in high school.

"Where did you get it?"

"I emptied the safety deposit box," she said, taking more and more boxes out of the bag. "This is something like four million dollars' worth of jewelry."

"Are you sure you want to keep it here? Now? Maybe it's safer at the bank."

"Why?" she said, shrugging. "Domicile installed the new security system. It's not like anyone can break in without the police arriving in seconds."

"Melia, I think it's a bad idea."

She opened another box and produced a silver necklace with a large sapphire pendant. She winked at me and then fastened it around her neck.

"What do you think?"

"I think you look like royalty."

It was true: with her dark hair pinned back and the sapphire glinting against her pale skin, I could picture Melia sweeping down the staircase of some wicked castle tucked high up in the mountains, or else leaning against a balcony and contemplating a wide ocean beneath her.

"Here," she said, opening another box. This one contained ornate ruby earrings. The main stones were framed with tiny diamond clusters. She removed them from the box and then came around the table, kneeling before me.

"Come here," she said softly. "Lean toward me."

Melia very gently fastened the earrings onto my earlobes. I didn't move or breathe, altogether too aware of her proximity. She smelled like jasmine and soap, with the slightest tang of sweat.

"Melia, what are you doing? I can't—"

"It's okay, you don't have to keep them. I just want to see how they look on you."

"Just—"

"Just relax," she said. "Shhh."

I finally gave in, relaxing. When the earrings had been attached, Melia leaned back slightly, appraising me. She nodded approvingly and then leaned against me, settling her weight against my lap.

I stiffened, cautious.

"Is this okay?" she whispered. "I'm exhausted, all of a sudden."

"It's okay," I said quietly. "Melia, you know I'm not going to keep these earrings."

"Why not?"

"Don't be ridiculous." I laughed, moving to take them off.

"Leave them on," Melia said, reaching up. She put her hands over mine. Her face was very close then, and my heart beat faster, but I didn't move. We held each other like that for a moment, reveling in the dizzy stillness, and then—and then—Melia leaned up and kissed me.

The moment stretched on forever, yet it seemed to be over altogether too quickly. I was standing at the edge of a precipice. I wanted to dive, but I wasn't sure what awaited me down below, or if I would survive the fall.

"Rainey," Melia whispered. I framed her face with my fingers, then rubbed away a bead of sweat with the ball of my thumb.

"What are you doing?"

"I have no idea," she said. "It just feels right."

I leaned in and kissed her again, and then she pulled away, laughing.

"It's ridiculous," she said. "I've wanted to kiss you since you first walked in the door. I mean, I'm not gay or anything—nothing like that. Being around you makes me feel so safe."

"Me too," I said after a moment of hesitation.

She tucked a piece of hair behind my ear.

"Do you still want me to stay the night?" I asked.

"Of course I do," she whispered. "Don't sleep in Jasper's room though. Spend the night with me."

I had only been with one girl before, back in high school. We became friends in the English class of our exclusive private school—Edendale Academy—and started spending all our time together. We'd band together in the hallways or at lunchtime, and spend our weekends doing drugs at the Hollywood Forever Cemetery or Venice Beach. Emily had a sweet face, with wide brown eyes framed by long lashes. She only washed her hair once a month, and the rest of the time, she wore her dirty tresses in braids or a Gretel twist. She accented her eyes with thin sweeps of black eyeliner, smudged where her hands shook. She wore long flannel shirts and leather skirts over stockings, regardless of the weather.

We'd lie side by side on her bed, working on homework and listening to Sonic Youth, the Pixies, or the Smiths. We started sharing clothing, getting used to smelling like each other. We swam naked in Emily's pool when her parents were away, usually at night.

I didn't know what a normal friendship between two young women looked like. I assumed it was normal to fall asleep naked together, skin still wet from the swimming pool. It felt natural when we kissed, never anything more than a chaste conjoining of lips, quick exchanges that always left me wanting more. Emily had wide hips, but she was slender, and her rosebud breasts were so small she never bothered with bras. Her skin was creamy, but the same crop of zits popped up above her eyebrows, in the center of her forehead. At times Emily had seemed so innocent that I was scared of breaking her, scared she might wake up the next day and regret our intimacy.

With Melia, though, I didn't find myself second-guessing where to put my hands, whether it was okay to lift her up when she rocked her hips against me and then pin her down again. I didn't feel self-conscious at all, the way I sometimes had with Emily. Part of the reason I had never been with another girl—another woman—after Emily was because I didn't want to crush someone with my intentions, to overwhelm a delicate lover with how much I wanted it, to fear someone might allow it to happen and then express regret afterward.

Not so with Melia. She was surprisingly dominant in bed, and although she had struck me as someone small, someone who needed to be protected, I found myself following her lead as the evening slipped into night, as we soaked through the sheets, as we lost track of the boundary line between us, as we breathed all the air in the room and I finally, finally found myself feeling like I wasn't scared anymore.

That night, I dreamed that I was back in Copenhagen. The city floated on the edge of the water, and all the buildings bloomed in chalky colors: indigo, lilac, neroli orange, Indian paintbrush. Our hotel was on the water, and my father let me stay up late, watching the boats glide down the river, slicing through the water without a sound. At night the city was enchanting, strands of light twinkling throughout the streets, tall narrow buildings with too many windows. I was content to sit at the window for hours, watching the reflections of the boats and windows in water, dripping with light.

It was before my mother had disappeared, back when I was still per-forming music, before the documentary about my grandmother had come out. It was the last time I had felt safe, the last time I had felt like everything was okay, and anything was possible.

TWENTY-FIVE

———⊸⊶———

Light slanted in through the windows of Melia's room. The morning was still and peaceful, and for the first time in I couldn't remember how long, I didn't feel the urge to jump straight out of bed and start my day. Melia was still asleep, curled up beside me. She was so quiet and unmoving that if I had walked in and found her like that, I might have thought she was dead.

"Melia," I whispered. When she didn't stir, I put a hand on her shoulder. She groaned and rolled away from me, still deeply asleep. As she moved away, her shirt rode up, exposing the skin on her lower back. My heart hammered inside my chest at the sight: a filigree of scars laced together, so thin and fine it looked like the work of some insane spider.

This was years of scars, by the looks of it, repeated again and again, the skin allowed to heal only to be opened up again. How had I failed to notice it all the night before?

I must have startled physically because Melia groaned and rolled over, tousled hair in her eyes.

"What is it?" she mumbled, half-awake.

"Nothing," I said quickly. "Nothing, I—it's okay. Go back to sleep."

She continued to stare at me with one unblinking eye. The moment held for so long that it was almost eerie. She finally sat up and squinted.

"You okay?"

"Your back. I just . . . I'm sorry, I didn't mean to say anything—it caught me by surprise."

Melia nodded and rested her head against her knees. "Yeah. Not really first date material."

"You don't have to explain," I said quickly.

She was quiet for a minute. "Are you . . . are you going to leave now?"

It took me a moment to grasp her meaning. "I'm not going anywhere."

"Right," she snapped.

"Don't put words in my mouth. I'm not scared of your history, Melia, or whatever caused those scars. I only meant that you don't have to tell me anything you're not comfortable sharing."

She gave me a wary look.

"I have scars too," I said. "Just not where you can see them."

Melia's scars had caught me off guard, had reminded me that she wasn't just some helpless heiress whose family had died tragically. The tragedy in Melia's life had started long before her parents died.

"That's cliché." She withdrew into herself. It was like watching someone pull down the shutters inside a house, one by one. The house was still visible, still the same from the outside, but there was no indication of what was going on inside.

"Melia," I said softly. "You don't need to pull away like this."

She was quiet for a long moment, pinching the inside of her leg as she looked out the window.

"I've never been with a girl before," she said. "I've always been attracted to girls, and boys—just people, you know? I thought I wouldn't know what to do"—she gestured toward my body—"but it was pretty intuitive."

I was quiet, watching her.

"My parents would be sick about this." She gave a nervous laugh. "I've kissed girls, plenty. At school that was kind of the only option. It wasn't weird or anything."

"None of this is weird." I suddenly felt defensive, and more naked than I wanted to be. I wondered if this had all been an experiment, if Melia's barbs about my making excuses to leave were a mask for her own discomfort and desire to be away from me.

"That's not what I meant," she said. "Sorry. I just—I'm not really sure what to talk about."

"We don't have to talk."

She turned to look at me. "Do you ever have something in your life that seems so completely normal for years, and then someone looks at it from an outside perspective and you realize it wasn't normal at all?"

"I think everyone does."

"So what's yours?"

I smiled. "Why do you think I only have one?"

"Tell me all of them, if you like."

I traced a line down her knee with my pointer finger. "I have no idea where my mom is," I said.

She sat up and looked at me. "Estranged?"

"That's an elegant way of putting it," I said. "She just . . . disappeared one day."

Melia frowned. "How?"

"I've been asking myself that question for almost ten years."

"But what do you mean? Like, you just came home and she was gone?"

"Kind of."

"And were all of her things gone too?"

"Nothing." I shook my head and looked out the window. "She didn't take anything with her. I mean, we opened a police investigation and everything, but there were no signs of foul play. No body, nothing."

"What about her credit cards? Her phone? Did you think to check those?"

I gave her an ironic smile. She smacked her forehead with her palm. "Durrrr. This is your job, sorry."

"We did all the right things. Nothing. It's like . . . it's like she just vanished into thin air."

Melia looked thoughtful. "Is that the worst thing that ever happened to you?"

"The worst things that ever happened to me are the things I did to myself after she left."

She was quiet for a long moment. "She was having an affair."

"It's a distinct possibility."

"No—I mean, *my* mom was having an affair. Probably more than one. I only know about the guy she was fucking right before they got killed."

A few years ago, a late admission like this would probably have angered me. My relationship with Melia aside, I was still there to do a job, which was to find Jasper and hopefully determine whether or not he had anything to do with the recent threatening activity toward Melia. Nowadays, however, my reaction was much more circumspect. My first thought was not about the client withholding information—therefore wasting both my time and theirs—but about the client's ignorance regarding the value of the information. Most people couldn't see their lives clearly because they were way too close to the important things. They couldn't see the full picture.

Melia must have seen the look on my face, though, because she shook her head. "He didn't do it," she said. "I mean, he didn't kill my parents."

"How do you know?"

"He had an alibi," she said. "The police looked into it."

"If the police knew, why wasn't it in the news?" The police were notoriously awful at keeping secrets, especially when gossip rags and television hosts paid well for information.

Melia shrugged. "Karnak took care of it," she said. "He is actually good at some things."

"So why are you mentioning this now?"

She lowered her shorts and turned to show me a shiny welt on her hip. It looked like a perfect burn mark that had turned into thick scar tissue.

"I was going to tell my dad when I found out about the affair," she said. Her voice was calm and emotionless. "But my mother caught me first. This was from a bronze teakettle. She was in the kitchen when I told her what I knew, and she didn't even say anything. Just pressed it against my skin."

I was careful not to react, just to listen. "Your mom did that to you?"

"Oh, yes."

"Did you go to the hospital?"

"What do you think?" Her face was emotionless. "That would have immediately destroyed the illusion. The van Austs were this perfect, untouchable family. You're from a rich family, aren't you? Nobody keeps secrets like the rich."

"So, what happened? A burn like that can get infected, you could have gone into shock . . ."

"We had a private physician," Melia explained, waving away my comment with a hand. "He was very well paid, and he never would have reported my parents. Report my mother, actually—my dad never did anything to hurt me. The worst thing anyone could say about him was that he was a fucking coward." She said the words without malice.

"The first duty of a doctor is to take care of people, especially children," I said, indignant. "I can't believe a doctor would continue to work for your parents after he saw this."

"Well, he didn't actually see this one," Melia said, tracing the circular burn with the tip of a finger. "My mother took care of this one herself. I was out of school for three days though. I slept on the kitchen table with a bag of ice on my skin at all times. She didn't even flinch when she wiped away layers of dead skin."

I was at a loss for words. I didn't know if Melia wanted me to say anything at all, or if she just wanted me to sit there and listen. She looked up into my eyes and laughed.

"That bad, huh?"

"Melia, I . . . I don't know what to say. I'm so sorry, that's just awful."

"Awful," she echoed. "You're so sweet to me. Nobody's ever been so sweet before."

She pounced on me then, catching me by surprise. I felt the wind go out of my lungs as I landed on my back, and she was kissing my neck, catching my lower lip in her teeth. I pulled away.

"Wait just a moment," I said, disentangling myself.

She recoiled. "Here we go."

"I'm not running away," I said, keeping my voice even. "It's not like that. I just want to be here for you for a moment without turning this into something else."

She sat across the bed, hair a slash across her face, wounded.

"You can be vulnerable with me," I said softly. "It's okay—really."

"Fuck this." She stood and began dressing.

"Melia."

"I've never felt so naked in my entire life." She wrapped herself in a silk robe, tugging the belt around her waist with an angry *zoooot*. I could hear the tilt of a Southern drawl in her vowels, the lazy dip of Georgia diphthongs.

"You're a bit more Southern when you're angry."

She whirled. "Don't you dare make fun of me."

"Oh, darling. I would *nevah*."

Her mouth twitched. She picked up a pillow from the bed and threw it at me as hard as she could. I deflected the pillow and drew my knees up to my chest.

"You must really hate your mother," she said. "For leaving you."

I felt my stomach twist. "I don't *know* that she left. Not for sure. Nobody ever found out anything about her."

"No? Do you still think she was kidnapped?"

I was quiet for a long time. "No," I said finally. "Not really, when I'm honest with myself."

She came over and sat on the edge of the bed. "I hated my mother," she said. "In some ways I think I always have."

I had never imagined Melia's childhood to be perfect, but I had always imagined that her father was the disciplinarian, the cold Germanic figure of authority.

"Everyone hates their mom sometimes."

"No, I *really* hated her," she said. "Usually that's the kind of thing you regret after your parents die, because you feel like you wasted so much time focusing on dumb shit. I don't blame my younger self though. Believe me."

I didn't know what to say. I had the feeling that Melia hadn't been this vulnerable with anyone for a very long time.

"I couldn't sleep when I was little," Melia went on. "I had these horrible nightmares. I'd wake up screaming. The Endos could sometimes hear me all the way across the yard, it was that bad."

"Do you remember what the nightmares were about?"

She shrugged. "I don't know. I was always anxious about dumb stuff. The one thing my mom was really good at was telling me stories. She could always twist words out of the air. So she told me stories to fall asleep. When I was seven, she started telling me about the girl in the wall."

A faint chill ran down my spine. The name alone spooked me, but I couldn't say whether I had heard the story before.

"It started off like a fairytale," Melia said. "But it wasn't, not at all, and it wasn't the kind of story that little girls should be told just before bedtime. It was a story about a little girl with a perfect family. They all lived together happily until the mother had a new baby, and all of a sudden, they didn't want their little girl anymore. So they left her in the woods.

"They took her so deep into the woods that she couldn't find her way out again. It took her years and years and years—and when she finally returned home, her family didn't live there anymore. But all that time in the woods had confused her. It must have been a magical wood, too, because the girl didn't get any bigger or older. That whole time she only ate insects and rodents, and the woods were so dark she didn't get any sunlight.

"She didn't have anywhere else to go, so she hid in the walls of her old house. When a new family moved in, and they had a little girl of their own, the girl in the wall would come out to play with her things, wear her clothes. Eventually she grew so bold that she killed the new little girl and dragged her into the wall, then switched places with her."

Melia fell quiet, and I stared at her in horror.

"Your mom told you that story to help you fall asleep?"

"No," Melia said. "She told me that story so I would keep quiet, stay in my place, learn good manners. I don't think I actually slept through the night for the next two years. I kept thinking about Tule Windsor going mad as she designed our house, and the families that had lived here before my parents bought it."

"What kind of lesson does that story impart?"

"The wrong lesson," Melia said, smiling. "She meant to scare me, but instead, I learned that nobody stays a victim forever."

Taylor and her team of Domicile technicians came back the following day to have another crack at the door leading down into the basement. This time Taylor brought a computer technician who had a few ideas about how to get past the unknown passcode.

"Green Haven uses an outdated mode of technology," she explained to me and Melia. "They were at the forefront of the game for a while, but they haven't kept up with bugs and hacks, which works to our benefit. See this?"

She pointed to a symbol at the top of the keypad.

"Most wireless keypads, especially Green Haven ones, connect to Wi-Fi. This lock is only as strong as your Wi-Fi network, and since you already control the network, we should be able to get right in."

"Wow," Melia murmured.

"Sometimes we can break into these Geiger locks manually, but they can get a little funny. It shouldn't take too long to bypass it through the network."

Melia went into the kitchen to make coffee.

"You okay?" I asked.

"Yeah," she said, her voice distant. "The only time I went down there was when my mother locked me up for being bad."

"Nobody deserves that."

"You didn't know me as a kid," she said, her voice light.

I was about to respond when the computer tech reappeared. "Easier than I thought," she said. "Got the door open, and we'll replace the old lock with something better. It's a good thing you're switching to Domicile—you guys would have been sitting ducks if you'd kept that Green Haven lock for much longer."

The woman didn't seem to recognize her faux pas, or maybe enough time had passed that not everyone knew about what had happened to the van Austs. I glanced at Melia, but her face registered nothing. Eager to put the moment behind us, I rubbed my hands together.

"Come on," I said to Melia. "Let's have a look. Don't you want to see what's down there?"

Melia lingered in the door of the pantry as I stepped through the locked door. The light switch was to the right of the door; I flicked it on and saw that the steps leading down into the basement were not the creaky, nightmarish wooden slats I had imagined, but rather modern beams of dark wood. The lights all appeared to be working, and everything was well-illuminated.

Melia hesitated at the threshold.

"You coming?"

"I've been down there before, Rainey," Melia reminded me. "Just not since I've been back."

"Suit yourself," I said. "I think I'll feel safer if I know what's down there."

And without waiting for her to follow me, I headed down into the basement. I shouldn't have been surprised to see that it was spacious and clean. It was the size of the entire first floor, but there were no partitions down there.

Along the right side of the room was a professional working kitchen, with a huge fridge, a double oven, and a stove with six burners. There were cupboards and what looked to be the door to another pantry. Next to the pantry was the enormous steel door of a walk-in cooler. All the fixtures were modern, and all the metal was a uniform pale gold.

I heard a creak as Melia began to descend the steps behind me. She looked around cautiously, like a dog sniffing the air for danger.

"You must have thrown some really big parties," I said. "I've never seen a house with a walk-in fridge before."

"It's a freezer," Melia said. "And it's broken. I don't think we've ever used it for anything. I wouldn't be surprised if a rat had gone in there and died—probably smells awful after all this time."

The left side of the room was decorated like a sort of rumpus room. There was a pool table and bookshelves lined with probably a thousand books. Various comfortable-looking leather chairs were clustered in the corner, and Japanese artwork hung from the walls.

"The Endos kept this place in great working order."

"Yeah, whatever." She shivered, wrapping her arms around herself. "It's so cold down here."

"I think it's because it's underground," I said.

"Are you satisfied?" she asked, turning around. "I'm going back upstairs."

TWENTY-SIX

———

Late summer felt like an admonition, and the air smelled like copper, spilled blood. Summer nights were cool, the city lingering beneath a web of pollution and stars. During the day, everything burned. The city couldn't breathe.

In some ways, living at Slant House made me feel like the preceding weeks had never happened. It was almost too easy to tuck away the past, to forget about the predators and lying attorneys who lived down beyond the canyon, in the crevices and more hellish parts of the city. I didn't want to think about work or all the unsolved cases and missing children who still waited to come home. Living at Slant House afforded an unusual sort of privacy, one where I could shut out my thoughts about the rest of the world.

"No one can get us here," Melia said. "You have no idea how dangerous it is out there."

"I do know," I reminded her.

"Well, good," she said, wrapping her arms around me. "There's no excuse to leave then. We don't have to leave, not for anything."

Every time I thought about leaving, even just for the day, Melia pulled me back in. "This is what everyone wants," she would say. "We can live how we want, do what we want, and we never have to see anyone else."

We had created our own world; we were the curators of a modern fantasy.

———

For the first week, Melia ordered all our food to be delivered to the house. She didn't want to cook anything, not even something as simple and quotidian as oatmeal, but I finally put my foot down, and we came to a compromise: I would make breakfasts and lunches, and she was allowed to order anything she wanted for dinner.

I consented to borrowing Melia's clothing as well, discarding the black jeans and silk camisoles that I favored and dressing instead in simple dark and light linens, silk robes from Japan and Norway that must have cost hundreds of dollars. My hair, uncombed and tangled, fell down around my face. My eyebrows had come in thicker than before, and neither Melia nor I wore makeup. In the evenings I would wear simple cotton dresses that buttoned all the way up to the base of my neck and out to the edges of my wrists. I felt fiercely beautiful. I wasn't afraid of anything.

The yard, too, had started to go wild without anyone to rein it in. Vines climbed over the guest cottage, where, until recently, the Endos had lived. A stalwart fig tree spread its generous umbrella over the clay tennis court, where Melia and I sometimes took books and pitchers of tea, content to read in silence. A wall of wild plums had gone up against the right side of the property, affording Slant House even more privacy from the neighbors.

There were some days when I felt like we might recede from the world altogether, the plants taking hold and claiming Slant House for good.

———

Melia started telling me more about her time in Savannah. She had done a semester of community college during one of the breaks from rehab. She had wanted to study medicine, she told me, but had dropped out after one semester.

"I would have made a terrible doctor," was the excuse she gave me. "I could never keep my hands steady enough to hold a knife straight."

Without a rigorous school schedule, she finally had time to explore a wide range of hobbies. She tried the clarinet, but her mouth was the wrong shape, so she taught herself mediocre piano pieces by Beethoven. After music came dance, and an obsession with Martha Graham, then Marina Abramović. Melia studied ballet until her bones telescoped out of her and she towered over the dance instructor. ("Too tall," Melia sighed. "I've always been too *something*.") Her ballet slippers still hung on a bedpost in her bedroom, like the broken feet of some flightless bird.

Melia picked up hobbies and new skills as quickly as she discarded them. Unable to sit still, she started smoking cigarettes. Never one to do anything half-heartedly, she bought a dozen different brands to see which ones she liked best, then settled on Fantasias. She obsessed, ruminated, memorized. Nothing was ever enough; Melia always needed to be something more. She was obsessed with death, and she collected deaths the way some people might track baseball scores. She wasn't content with modern fables and stories in the newspapers; she wanted to see something bleed. She clipped stories of train wrecks in China, collapsed bridges in the Midwest, Swiss salt mines that crumbled with men still inside them.

"I feel like I've spent most of my life trying on different personalities," Melia admitted to me. "Trying to figure out who I am. It's like pulling on a new costume every few months."

"You can put your costumes away now," I told her. "You don't need one when you're with me."

She screwed up her face, thinking. "It's on the tip of my tongue," she said. "Those pictures—you know, where you can see two things at once?"

"Optical illusions?"

"No, more like two overlapping pictures. Where it looks like a mistake, almost."

I thought. "Juxtaposition? Or . . . double exposure?"

"That's it!" she said, snapping her fingers. "Double exposure. A broken piece of film. Damaged imagery, you know? Where do I fit in? Sometimes I think I'll never know."

The more time I spent with Melia, the more I noticed that what I had once interpreted as innocence or naïveté was something more like calculated disregard. She didn't want to hear bad news, even when the unknowing could harm her. After spending three sleepless nights together, during which I overanalyzed every clank and groan in the house, I finally broke down and shared my suspicions about Dane Bradley and his involvement in her family's investigation. She waved them away.

"I have the best security money can buy," she insisted. "I'm not scared of him."

But I *was* scared, and the more Melia insisted on sweeping ignorance, the more out of my depth I felt.

"You spend too much time on your phone," she remarked one afternoon at the house. "Weren't you the one who told me that phones could be hacked? That someone could be listening in?"

I knew where all of this was coming from, of course. Every time Melia went to see Karnak, she would return deflated, or worse, invigorated with a sense of righteous anger.

"I'm going to kill him," she muttered, pacing through the living room. "It's *my* money. He can't keep it from me!"

Some mornings she was too depressed to get out of bed. Other days, though, she woke with purpose, then sat down at the dining room table and began making lists. Lists and plans, strategies and agendas for ways she could regain control of her life. One particularly bad afternoon, she accused me of working for Karnak.

"How do I *know* you weren't sent by him?" she asked, her face pale.

"You found *me*, remember?"

She stared at me for a long moment, then collapsed into tears. I went over and rubbed her back, murmuring consoling words, wondering what on earth I had brought upon myself. Melia didn't like it when I took phone calls in another room, insisting that she found it hard to trust people.

"You don't understand what they put me through at Aggie," she said. "I didn't have any privacy there."

I had trouble checking in with my team, with Melia always looking at me askance, questioning who I was calling. Already, there were three unanswered texts sitting on my phone:

> Lola: *Can you check in, please?*

> Lola: *Any more letters? What's going on with the case—does Melia still want us to keep going on this?*

> Lola: *R. Seriously? If you don't respond I'm going to come over there myself!!*

I finally picked up the phone and texted Lola back.

> *I'll talk to her about it tonight. You don't need to worry about any-thing. I'm fine, really. I'm happy here.*

"Who was that?" Melia asked, glancing at my phone.

"Lola," I said.

Melia scowled. "Turn off the phone," she said. "*They* could be listening in."

"Who, Melia?" I said, exasperated.

"Anyone."

———

We went for walks off Mulholland, or else strayed from the paths near the Hollywood Reservoir. Charlie Chaplin had strolled along these high bluffs, toeing the foreign desert earth with each step. He nearly drowned in his Olympic-sized swimming pool, twisting and writhing beneath a Technicolor sky. *You do not belong here.* I tried to picture the world of Old Hollywood that Marcus had once described to me: Charlie Chaplin and Douglas Fairbanks riding horses to the distant mountaintops, early residents falling asleep to the sound of coyote calls. It wasn't there anymore, not even a distant murmur. It had been replaced by taco stands and neon lights, a new world cinema and parking lots.

Even though Melia had her bad days, I could sympathize with where she was coming from. No wonder she didn't trust anyone, I reasoned to myself; her entire family had been taken away from her, and nobody had been convicted of the crime. Even now, four years later, she didn't feel completely safe, completely in control of her life.

Some days, too, I felt like I had failed her, that I had neglected to fulfill my one professional obligation to Melia, which was to track down her brother and make her feel safe. Sometimes I woke up in the middle of the night with these thoughts pressing in on me, and it was enough for me to feel like I couldn't draw breath. Then Melia would roll over in bed and pull me close to her, and I would let myself sink back into the fantasy, closing my eyes against the truth, against what was staring me in the face.

Los Angeles was meant to exist in a half-light anyway.

In the evenings, after we had gone for a walk, it was easier to set the rest of the world aside. My favorite part of the day was the magic hour, the stillness before dark, when the sky held indigo before tilting into gray, then black. Sometimes we would end the day by walking up the path behind the Hollywood Reservoir, where a strip of eucalyptus trees stood sentry over the city. Everything was hazy and pink at sunset, and you could almost ignore the pollution and noise. Even the bugs hovering over the clumps of witch hazel seemed entranced, watching the sun vanish over the crest of mountains. There was a blue glow over the chaparral and coral sage in the valley down below, and the winking neon of Hollywood was nothing but a rumor.

At times we went out during the day and people recognized Melia. Sometimes their glances were innocuous, easy to ignore. Other times people would openly stare as though they recognized her but couldn't quite remember how they knew her face. It was difficult for Melia to hide her scar under layers of clothing because it was so hot, and her scar drew attention.

I had always existed on the fringes of celebrity, even after I had stepped away from fame, even after my family suffered wide scrutiny after the documentary about my grandmother was released. I had never before experienced anything like this though: people stared at Melia as though she were a phantom, someone they considered dead, because the van Aust murders were so famous that the story was sometimes butchered or misconstrued. Melia existed only as caricature, a collection of famous features that people recognized a mile away: her inky black hair, pale skin, thin limbs, and the scar bisecting her collarbone. Features, nothing more.

Once, a woman came up to Melia as we were sitting on a bench along the Runyon Canyon track.

"I thought you were dead!" she exclaimed. "I heard the stories about your family, and I thought you died along with them!"

"You have the wrong person," Melia stammered.

"No, it was you! You were dead, I was sure you were dead!"

After that, Melia stopped going out during the day, and nothing I said could convince her otherwise. Sometimes when the neighborhood fell silent and night stretched across the canyon, I could coax her to sit in my car while we drove in silence. We took trips late at night, safe from prying eyes and a ravenous public who felt entitled to press in, asking questions with no easy answers.

There was no need to speak as we drove; we were each content to sit with our thoughts. Instead of sleeping we would drive through the quiet streets of midnight suburbia, luxuriating in insomniac privilege. She was curious about all the people in the houses we passed, safe in their anonymous lives, their blank little nooks of existence. "Fascinating," she would say, and I could never tell if it was irony.

—

I couldn't deny the darkness in Melia, something that lingered beneath the surface and showed itself in quiet flashes. She grew irritated without warning, then cooled down just as quickly. I wondered what a psychiatrist would make of Melia's behavior, her willful indecision, her inability to be alone. Against my better intentions, the house fell into a state of lush decay. Melia had never lived without maids, and I refused to slip into the vacancy. If she chose to leave cups and bowls around the house, that was her prerogative.

I was starting to chafe at Melia's arbitrary rules, and one day, when she was in the shower, I called Lola. It was early evening, and outside, the shadows were sliding into dusk.

Lola answered after two rings.

"This should be good," she said.

"What?"

"Nothing," she replied. "I just mean it's been a few weeks of silence, a week of ignoring my calls, and now you reach out."

Her words stung me. "That's not fair," I said.

"You're right, it's not fair," she said. "You only call me when you need something, but I guess that's what our relationship becomes when you're involved with someone new. So what is it, Rainey—what do you need this time?"

"Nothing," I shot back, keeping half an ear out for Melia. "I'm calling to see how you're doing, that's all."

There was a long silence, and then Lola laughed. "Oh, me? Yeah, I'm great! How are *you*, though, Rainey?"

"There's no need for sarcasm."

Lola was silent.

"Lo?"

"What, Rainey."

"I'm sorry I haven't been calling," I said. "Really. Melia's paranoid about phones, and I think that's fair. She has a hard time trusting people."

"Fine."

"I think the security system is working," I went on. "We haven't gotten any more letters from Melia's stalker."

"That's good," Lola said, softening. "We've been keeping an eye out for Jasper, but nothing's come up."

"I don't want to say that I'm impressed with how long he's stayed hidden," I said. "But I'm impressed."

"Yeah," Lola admitted. "Me too."

There was a silence.

"Do you feel safe, Rainey?" Her voice was soft, concerned, with a tenderness that I didn't often hear Lola use.

I was startled by the question.

"What do you mean?"

"Just that . . . if Melia's monitoring your phone calls—"

"She's not," I said, cutting her off. "I'm happy here. It's the first time I've been happy in a really long time."

"Are you sleeping with her?" Lola asked quietly.

"That's none of your business," I said quickly, immediately regretting it.

When Lola spoke again, she sounded hurt. "If you're no longer sharing details of your personal life with me, that's one thing," she said. "We can talk about that later. But since this relates to the business—*our* business, Left City—it does concern me."

"I really wish I could be open with you, Lo," I said. "I wish you'd give me the grace to explain how this is different from before."

There was a pause, then a sharp laugh. "Different from Calvin, you mean? Different from the last time you got involved with a client?"

"Calvin was *never* our client," I snapped. "It was his family."

"We're splitting hairs," Lola said. "My point is that your objectivity has been . . . how should I say this . . . *questionable* in the past. You can be a little too trusting sometimes, Rainey."

"Well, trust this," I said. "I can handle myself."

I hung up without waiting to hear her response.

That night, Melia was in one of her odd moods, and I didn't object when she asked for privacy. She had gone to see Karnak that afternoon, and even without asking, I could tell things hadn't gone well.

She needed space to think, Melia told me. If Karnak wasn't going to allow her to access her money early, she had to make other plans.

I went into Jasper's room without another word. I hadn't wanted to admit it to myself, but something was unnatural and almost claustrophobic about our arrangement. I didn't want to stay away from Melia for too long, and I realized that in itself was probably a bad sign: it bore similarities to my relationship with Calvin, only a year before.

Once I was in Jasper's room, though, I couldn't sleep. I clipped my hair back, away from my face, then opened the door to Jasper's room and went into the kitchen to find cleaning supplies.

When I walked back through the house, toward the bedrooms, I heard a noise coming from Melia's room.

"No," she was saying, her voice low. "Everything's *fine*. Don't even think about it."

I froze, wondering who she was talking to. I didn't want to eavesdrop—we didn't have that kind of relationship, and I wasn't that kind of person—but the anger in her voice was something new to me. I couldn't resist listening in.

"I swear to god, if you do, you'll regret it."

There was a long silence. I knew Melia must be on the phone since nobody had come into the house since we had last spoken. If she was on the phone, then a silence this long could only indicate that she had ended the call, or that the person on the other end was making a long, impassioned argument.

When Melia finally spoke again, her voice was almost too low for me to hear anything. It seemed sweeter.

"You can *trust* me," she whispered. "I've already shown you that you can." Another silence.

"Just be patient," she finally said. "Not long to go. I know," she added after a pause. "I miss you too."

I heard her bed squeak and then a soft thump as her feet landed on the floor. My heart was in my chest as I lunged back toward the door to Jasper's room. I turned the handle with sweaty palms, determined to get through the door before Melia entered the hallway and saw me standing there. I had just crossed the threshold and managed to shut the door again—silently, *silently*—when I heard the door to her room open.

"Rainey?" she called.

I fervently began cleaning, sweeping up piles of clothing into my arms. I stumbled toward Jasper's closet and stepped inside, then opened the drawers to his built-in dresser and dropped to my knees, folding the clothes.

I heard the door to Jasper's room open behind me. "Rainey?"

"In here!" I called. I closed my eyes and took a deep breath, trying to force my heartbeat back to normal. After a moment, I scooted around and then stuck my head out of the door. Melia turned toward me, bemused.

"Hi," she said. "What are you doing?"

"I couldn't sleep," I said, avoiding her eyes. "I thought I'd do some cleaning."

She nodded, glancing around the closet. "Something about this room always gave me the creeps."

I nodded, hoping my face looked neutral. I tried not to look like I had just been spying on her, listening in on a conversation. Who had been on the other end of the phone? Surely it couldn't have been Belinda, a relative Melia had only mentioned with passing disdain.

Fortunately enough for me, Melia seemed lost in her thoughts.

"You're not mad?" she asked, finally turning to look at me.

My heart started hammering again. "Mad—why?"

"That I want space tonight?" Her eyes sought mine. "It's nothing personal."

I laughed—a startled, genuine laugh. For a minute I thought she knew I had overheard the conversation. "Of course not," I said. "Nights apart are normal. Take your space. I'll see you in the morning."

When she was finally out of the room, and I heard her footsteps recede down the hall and disappear into her bedroom, I leaned against the wall of the closet. The sudden spike in adrenaline made my limbs weak and numb. I could still feel my heart beating a crazy, jagged rhythm in my chest, and I forced myself to sit there and count down from ten—a technique a former therapist had taught me for enduring a panic attack.

I miss you.

Sensation returned to my limbs, and I started to stand up. As I did, something out of the corner of my eye caught my attention. There was handwriting on the inside wall of the closet, hidden from view unless someone was in my position, fully inside the small room.

The handwriting was so small and cramped it could have been dismissed as strangely patterned wallpaper. It extended from the left interior wall, across the door to the right. In certain lines it flared up and looked swollen, angry, determined. I flicked on the light and moved closer to read what it said.

It was not sentences, not a complete story, nothing but one word repeated again and again, hundreds of times, thousands, written in the same tight, angry script with different pens. I stood there for so long, reading the manic, furious writing that eventually, the letters ceased to make any kind of sense to me.

Melia melia melia melia MELIA MELIA Melia Melia MELIA MELIA Melia melia melia melia MELIA Melia.

TWENTY-SEVEN

—ɷ—

"We need to talk."

It was early the next morning. I had crept out of the house when I saw the screen of my phone illuminating with Lola's name, hoping to answer the call before the ringing woke Melia. I was still furious with Lola about what she had said, but I knew better than to have a drawn-out argument with her over the phone.

"What do you want to talk about?"

"A few things," she said, her voice short. "Come to the office."

I picked at a seam on my pajamas. "Tell me now."

"Not over the phone," she said. "We need to meet as a team. Blake's coming in too. I'll be there by nine."

And with that, she hung up.

—ɷ—

I hadn't forgotten about the crazed writing I had found in Jasper's closet. I wanted to ask Melia about it, but she was still asleep when I went back into the house. Whatever Lola wanted to talk about sounded serious, and there was no point in putting it off. If I showed up late, she would only have more time to stew, and by the time I finally arrived, things would likely escalate into a full-on brawl.

I got dressed quickly, then slipped out of the house, scrawling a quick note to let Melia know where I was going. I wrote that I might be gone all day, just in case the meeting went longer than expected.

Traffic was light, so I made good time to Culver City. It wasn't even nine yet, so I thought I might even get there before Blake and Lola. To my surprise, though, they were both already there—Blake sat before her computer, hands folded in her lap, and Lola leaned against Blake's desk. They looked up abruptly at my entrance, as though I had walked in on an intimate conversation.

"Hi," I said. "Should I make coffee?"

"Don't bother," Lola said.

"Okay." I walked over to the fish tank and looked in. Dart looked lethargic, tired. I dropped some flakes into the tank, but when he didn't swim up to eat with the other fish, I grew concerned.

"How long has he been like this?" I asked, turning around. "Blake?"

"It's not Blake's job to feed your fish," Lola snapped.

I was stunned, and recoiled as if Lola had slapped me. "Wow, sorry. I've been gone for a few days, that's all."

"I'm going to make this quick," Lola said, her voice brisk. "No need to draw it out. Blake and I have decided to drop Melia as a client."

It took me a moment to process what she was saying.

"You can't make that decision," I said, taken aback. I was still sore from her earlier comment. "What I mean is—you can't make that decision independently; it has to be unanimous."

"It's done. We voted." Lola's voice was firm, cold.

I laughed, surprised. "Come on—what do you mean, you voted? There was no meeting. I wasn't ever informed that this was up for discussion."

"You haven't been answering your phone," Blake said with some reluctance. "We had no way to inform you."

Hearing this from Blake made the whole thing worse somehow. Blake never took sides.

"Do I need to remind you that *you're* the one who pushed to take Melia as a client?" I pointed at Lola. "I had reservations, remember? You insisted."

"I was wrong," Lola said with a shrug.

"I feel like you guys are ganging up on me," I said, growing defensive. "This is bullshit."

"Nobody's ganging up on you, Rainey," Blake said quietly. "It just doesn't make sense to keep Melia as a client. She's not in any danger, she installed a new security system, and she hasn't had any threats since the coyote incident."

"What about Dane Bradley?" My voice sounded shrill, even to my own ears. "The connection to the old case?"

Blake nodded. "Fair," she said, considering. "Have you seen him since he showed up at your apartment?"

I had backed myself into a corner. "No."

"Maybe he's moved on," Blake pointed out.

"We have other clients," Lola cut in. "You haven't been coming into work as much. You spend all your time at Slant House—sometimes I think you don't even care anymore."

"This is the first time I've been *happy*—"

"Jesus, give it a rest!" Lola exploded. "Nobody cares how happy you are!"

The stunned silence was absolute. Blake even looked offended.

"That's not what I meant," Lola quickly amended.

I stood up. "It's exactly what you meant," I said. "Thanks for finally being honest with me."

"Rainey, wait," Lola said, standing and moving toward me. "That came out wrong."

"Did it?" I looked at her. "What *did* you mean then?"

For the first time in a very long time, Lola looked flustered. She ran a hand through her hair, then shook her head. "I think we're all a bit stressed, that's all."

"Sometimes," I said slowly, "I think you're more comfortable with me being your fucked-up friend. You don't recognize me when I get my life together."

Lola looked wounded.

"Rainey," Blake started, clearing her throat.

"I have to go." I turned to leave, then stopped and glanced toward Dart's tank. While Blake and Lola watched in stunned silence, I hastily transferred Dart to a smaller tank, one I used when I needed to clean out his home. I didn't know when I would be coming back to the office, and since Dart seemed to need special attention, I wanted to take him with me. The other fish were easy; Blake and Lola could toss them a few flakes every now and then to keep them thriving.

Carrying Dart's tank beneath one arm, I walked out of the office without waiting for my colleagues to say anything else.

After parking in the driveway of Slant House, I climbed up the stairs and walked through the door, carrying Dart's tank with me. Melia sat in the living room but rose from her seat when she saw me, startled. Her face was pale.

"Rainey," she said. "I got your note. You're home early—"

"I had a fight with my team," I said. "They can be *such* assholes."

"I'm so sorry . . ."

"Yeah. Don't be. This is a good thing, believe me."

Melia glanced at the tank, then frowned. "What's that?"

"It's my frog. He was a gift from a client." I held the tank up so Melia could see. "Animals are so much better than people, aren't they? They never betray you. You never have to wonder if they're talking about you behind your back . . . I swear to god, if I weren't so angry I might actually start crying."

"Rainey, wait," Melia said. "I have to tell you something."

There was a creak in the next room, then footsteps.

"Hold it right there," came a voice, silky and charming. "I need some tissues. Y'all are making me tear up."

I spun around to face the voice. A young man with a head of dark hair stood in the doorway holding a half-eaten apple. He looked amused, and his eyes flicked between me and Melia.

I turned back to Melia.

"I was trying to tell you," she said, apologetic. "I didn't have time to explain—"

"Who is he?"

"He's Chet," the young man replied. He sauntered into the room and stooped to peer into my fish tank. Something about him—the way he stood too close, his sordid familiarity—repulsed me, and I stepped back, feeling protective of my frog.

If Chet noticed my revulsion, however, he didn't seem to mind. Dark curly hair tumbled around his face, and his features—cheeks, nose, and chin—looked like they had almost been sculpted. He possessed the kind of delicate looks that tended toward beautiful when cultivated, but the gaunt shape of his face indicated hunger, or perhaps desperation. His eyes were sharp, and they didn't leave my face.

"Oh, don't stop now," he said. "Let's talk about how everybody leaves."

I felt vulnerable and angry, in equal measures. How much of our conversation had Chet overheard?

"I am possessed of a certain gift," Chet went on. He had a deep, Southern drawl, but I couldn't tell if it was affected or genuine. "People tell me I have the third sight."

"Right."

He held up a hand and narrowed his eyes at me. "I see great betrayal in your past," he said quietly. "Something about . . . a woman . . . with dark hair. She looks just like you. A relative, perhaps? Did you have a relative go missing?"

I stared at Chet. He held my gaze for a long moment, then burst into laughter.

"You're *such* an asshole," Melia growled.

I turned back toward Melia, dread filling my body. "You told him."

"Oh, yes," Chet said, picking a piece of apple from his teeth. He wiped his hand on the couch. "That and much, *much* more. You're some kind of prodigy, aren't you? Piano? No, violin. Classical shit." Chet raised an eyebrow. "Will you play something for us?"

"No," I replied, trying to keep my voice cool. "I imagine your tastes veer closer to something along the lines of a drunk person banging mindlessly on a trash can lid."

Melia snorted behind me, and Chet blinked. He glanced between us, a slow smile growing on his face.

"You'd be surprised," he said. "I've watched your videos. I get it. I really liked the one that went, *DUM DUM DUM, dum dum DUM DUM DUM!*"

He started to dance, miming the actions of someone thumping wildly on a keyboard. His eyes were closed, and there was something almost rhapsodic in his movements. I took advantage of the moment to glance at Melia. She, however, was watching him warily, as if a wild animal had come crashing into the house.

When Chet finally stopped, he dropped into a crouch on the floor, then sat down. Melia still wasn't quite meeting my eyes.

"So," I said. "How do you two know each other?"

"Oh, that's a lovely story," Chet said. "Melia, you go ahead."

She picked at a seam on her pants.

"Melia, I said, tell *the goddamn story.*"

"We know each other from the hospital," she mumbled.

"From the hospital. That's right, sweetheart. I took real good care of you. Isn't that right?"

"The best." Melia's voice was faint.

"You might say I know Melia better than anyone in the world," Chet went on, finally looking up at me. "Did you know that Melia likes classical music? She just loves that old piano."

She glared at him. "Fuck you, Chet."

"Oh, she's modest," he said. "She probably didn't tell you that she took ten years of piano lessons. Ten years! Surely there's something you remember from all that time, darling girl."

Her face had gone pale.

"You used to talk about it all the time," he went on. "You know, Chopin . . . Mozart . . . what's the other one?"

"The other one?" Melia mimicked. "Because there's only *one* other classical composer?"

"Come on, Melia, don't hold out on us. Play us a song. I know there's a piano in the library."

I wondered how long he had been there, if he had already seen the whole house. There was something very odd about this whole setup, and as my sense of unease grew, so did my anger.

"You've made your point," Melia said softly.

"I'll stop asking once you play us something," he replied. "Just one little song for this heartbroken Southern boy. Come on, Rainey. Don't you want to hear a song?"

"Leave her alone, Chet."

Chet's eyes flickered toward me, then he smiled. The smile didn't meet his eyes.

"Do you like jokes?"

"I'm not in the mood."

"Everybody likes jokes," he said. "Go on. Let's share a joke. When is a door *not* a door?"

"When it's ajar."

"Very good!" He leaped to his feet and clapped in real delight. "You know your popsicle sticks. Let's have another. Man goes to a bar. Next morning he wakes up in a hospital, missing his liver. What happened?"

I glanced at Melia. She looked catatonic.

"I don't know."

"Overnight de-liver-y."

It took me a moment to parse the joke. "Funny."

"Oh, I got all kinds of hospital jokes," he said. "We nurses have a *real* dark sense of humor."

I didn't bother to hide my disbelief. "You were a nurse?"

"Sure was," he said. "One last joke. What gets smaller the more you feed it?"

Melia whimpered.

"A vacancy," I said after a moment. I knew I shouldn't play his game, but there was some small satisfaction in beating him too.

He looked startled. "That's good," he said. "Oh, that's real good. There's a better answer though. Melia knows this one. Go on, sweetheart."

She remained silent.

"Just tell me," I said, impatient.

"A bulimic," Chet said. His eyes glinted. "Get it?"

Melia suddenly bolted from the room. Chet stood and stretched his arms over his head, displaying an ease and familiarity that made me furious.

"Well," he said. "I'm gonna go unpack. Melia hasn't told me which room is mine. I assume you guys are sleeping together?"

I willed myself not to react, but it didn't matter: Chet already knew. She had told him everything. With a little smile, Chet slapped his knees and jumped up from the couch, before sauntering out of the room.

TWENTY-EIGHT

———— ∞ ————

I backtracked down the hall before I even knew where I was going. I stumbled into my room—into Jasper's room, I mentally corrected myself—and stood there for a moment, trying to catch my breath. A thought came to me then, unbidden: *How could you be so fucking stupid?*

I was standing by the window when Melia slipped through the door and crossed the room, then put her arms around me. I startled at her touch, then pulled away.

"Rainey, please."

"Don't."

"Are you . . . are you mad at me?"

I considered my response. "When were you going to tell me that he was coming?"

"I didn't think he would actually come," Melia said. "Chet says a lot of things he doesn't mean."

Something occurred to me, then, and I felt like a massive idiot for not seeing it sooner.

"He called you," I said. "Last night. He called and said he was coming, and you told him not to."

I miss you.

A small crease appeared on her brow, and she looked confused, then angry. "You've been listening in on my phone calls?"

"It's the way the house is designed, Melia," I said, exasperated. "Sound gets trapped in here."

"You have *no right* to eavesdrop."

"Like I said, nothing stays secret in this house," I snapped. "You can hear everything. I can't *believe* you told him about my mother." I went to the closet and started packing. Lola had been right, I realized, and I hated myself for not seeing it sooner. "This was a mistake."

When Melia finally spoke, I was surprised to hear tears in her voice. "Don't say that. You don't *get to say that.*"

I turned. Her face was blotchy, streaked with tears.

"I haven't made the best choices in my past," she said, her voice tight. "Chet was there for me during a very rough time. You don't know what it was like at Aggie. He was kind to me."

"Kind? You think he's *kind*? What was that joke he just made about bulimia?"

"It's . . . he can be coarse. He's just nervous. You have to give him a chance."

"I don't think so."

She was quiet for a moment. "Sometimes you don't realize how much you've changed until your past shows up at your front door."

My anger had dissipated, but I wasn't ready to let my guard down completely. My warning bells had gone off in a very bad way around Chet, and I knew he was hiding something.

"So what is he doing here?" I asked. "What does he want?"

"He's trying to start a new life," she said, sitting on the edge of the bed. "He wants to change. He made some bad choices in Georgia, and he's determined to start over."

"He wants to start over here in Los Angeles."

"In California," she amended. "I told him he could stay through the weekend, and *that's it*. I still want my life with you. We'll get out of here."

"What?"

"You were right," she said. "You were right all along, Rainey. Coming back here was a mistake. I can't start over when I'm still living in this house. We'll leave, together. Go up to San Francisco, or maybe somewhere like Portland."

After being humiliated by Lola and Blake, the idea of a new city was definitely tempting. I had never lived outside Los Angeles.

"When?"

"By the end of the week," she said. "I *promise*. I just need a few days to get things together. I have a plan."

"Okay," I said finally, even though I still had my doubts. "I'll stay."

Melia smiled and came over, then slipped her arms around me again. "You don't need to worry about Chet," she said softly. "He's harmless. I do owe him a lot, you know."

"What do you owe him?"

"I got her out of the mental hospital once," Chet said from behind me. Melia and I both jumped, then turned around. "Yeah, it was a real hoot. We drove all the way up to Virginia and lived in a cabin by a lake. Lost my job and all because staff weren't meant to interfere with patients. In the end, it was worth it."

Melia was silent.

"Oh, she didn't tell you that?" Chet said, feigning surprise. "Well, now. I'm guessing there's a lot Melia hasn't told you about me."

TWENTY-NINE

I tried not to think about what Lola would have said about Chet and the new situation at Slant House. *Lola's opinion doesn't matter now*, I reminded myself. *Lola's not here, and she wouldn't understand any of this.*

In the end it was agreed that Chet would sleep on the couch in the basement, and Melia and I privately agreed to stay in separate rooms. I didn't want to sleep with Melia, not with Chet there; I had an idea of what he might say about a relationship between us, and thinking about it made me sick.

"If he starts to piss us off, we'll lock the basement door," Melia murmured to me.

"Why wait?"

In the evening I begged off dinner, opting instead to lock myself away in my room. The stress of the day—the confrontation with Lola and Blake, then coming home to Chet—weighed heavily on me, and without meaning to, I drifted off to a deep, dreamless sleep.

Something jarred me awake in the middle of the night. My heart thudded against the walls of my chest, and I felt like I couldn't breathe. It was the same sensation I'd had hundreds of times before, back when I was still drinking: I would wake in the night, adrenaline shuddering through my bloodstream from the alcohol. I would lie there for hours, panicked and full of self-hatred, thinking over every single thing I had said or done during the day, how I fucked up my life again and again, how my world was spiraling out of control. Those nights always ended the same way: I would eventually drift back into something approximating sleep, then wake the next morning exhausted from a lack of real rest.

This was different though. I sat up in bed, trying to determine what had woken me up. Moonlight sifted in through the window, and for the moment, everything was peaceful. Then I heard it again: something sliding across the floor in another room, cloth on wood, and then a squeak.

I swung my legs over the side of the bed and quickly got dressed in the dark. The noise was coming from the living room. It was the sound of drawers being opened and rifled through, furniture being moved, rugs being peeled back from the floor. I hesitated, then walked into the living room.

Everything was in disarray. The furniture was shoved to the side of the room, and the rug sat in a heap on the couch like a layer of dead skin. Chet was on the floor, running his hands along the floorboards.

"What are you *doing*?"

He jerked backward in surprise, then looked up and saw me. He quickly composed himself and sat back on his heels, then smiled.

"Ahh," he said. "You're still here."

I narrowed my eyes. "Why does that surprise you?"

He heaved a sigh and shrugged. "Everyone leaves Melia eventually. She has a way of driving people crazy."

It was hard for me to determine his angle. A smile danced at the corner of his mouth, but it was the kind of smile that intended to wound. I knew it was dangerous for me to take anything he said literally, or to divulge any real information to him.

"You haven't answered my question," I said.

"What question is that?"

I gestured at the crooked furniture, the rumpled rug. "What are you doing?"

He glanced around at the bedlam he had created. "Oh," he said. "This. I was just . . . cleaning."

"Cleaning. At midnight."

"Shh-*hhhh*!" He tapped a finger to his lips and rose in a slow, dramatic move. "Melia . . . is . . . sleeping! Wouldn't want to wake the little princess, now, would we?"

"*My . . . point . . . exactly.*"

We were fighting in whispers now. With Melia now a shadow of her former self, I felt like a ballast, the measure of calm in a house that already bore a dangerous legend of insanity. Chet's arrival had tipped the balance in favor of the inmates. I was increasingly aware that I had no control at all, that I was outnumbered. Reason would not override.

"Go back to bed," I hissed. "Whatever you're doing, it can wait until morning."

"Can't sleep. I'm on Georgia time." He pretended to pout.

"Which is even later than California time," I pointed out. "Shouldn't you be more exhausted than the rest of us?"

"I don't sleep well in strange houses."

"There's no sense in waking up the rest of the house because *you* can't sleep."

Chet mimed slapping his own hand in punishment. "Bad Chet. Bad!"

I caught myself, aware I was being dragged down a diversion. I knew Chet must be looking for something—the jewelry collection, in all likelihood, if he knew about it.

"She hasn't told you about the neighbors, has she?" I leaned against the doorway. "They're very light sleepers, and it wouldn't be the first time they called the police because they heard strange noises at Slant House."

He gave me a dull look.

"Go back to sleep."

He blinked, then folded his arms across his chest in a stance of casual disregard. "Do you know why you're here, Rainey?"

"Oh, I'd love for you to tell me."

"You're here to babysit. Melia's never been alone in her life, and she can't sleep when she hears things go bump in the night."

"Good to know." I turned to go.

"I know about the letter," he said. "Oh, I know all about the letter."

I stopped walking but didn't turn around.

"You know who wrote to her, don't you?"

I willed myself to keep walking, already knew what he was going to say, and I didn't want to hear it.

"She wrote to herself, Rainey."

Don't turn around, don't do it, do not engage—

"Fuck off," I hissed, turning around. "Why don't you go back to Georgia?"

"Cain't."

"Then go somewhere else. She's extending her hospitality to you, and this is how you repay her?" I swept my hand through the air, indicating the mess in the living room. "What will you do when you find the jewelry, huh? Sell it? Don't you think her lawyer will find you, send you away?"

At the mention of the lawyer, he gave a slow, loopy laugh. "Melia's lawyer treats her like a twelve-year-old back from boarding school. He's not going to hand over a cent unless I'm here to supervise."

"Supervise?" I held back a laugh, but he must have seen the derision in my face. "Oh, thank god you're here to save the day, Chet. How would she survive without you?"

He smiled, but I could see I had pissed him off.

"You know who killed the family?" he asked finally. "Have you figured it out yet? It's pretty obvious if you have half a brain. And that person knew exactly where someone might hide the money. All I have to do is find it, and then Melia and I can start over, fresh, somewhere far away from this shitty city."

He turned his back on me and continued running his hands along the floorboards, searching, I imagined, for a seam that would reveal a trapdoor.

"She's not leaving with you," I said, but my voice was faint. I was still stuck on what he had said about the origin of the letter. It couldn't be true; it couldn't. Chet was doing his best to rile me up. The thing was, it was working.

"Sugar," he said. "Let me guess. She told you all manner of lies about how good life was going to be once she got her hands on that money. Right? Am I close? She'll say whatever it takes to get what she needs from you." He stretched luxuriously. "Thing is, I'm the only one who knows Melia. *Really* knows her. And I'm the only one who can control her."

"She's changed," I said. "You don't know her as well as you think."

I finally managed to tear myself away and go back down the hall.

"Let me give you a piece of advice," he called after me. "See people the way they really are. Don't get caught up in the romance of an idea, because the world isn't a fairytale. It's a cold, dark, awful place. Melia will destroy you without a second thought."

THIRTY

Slats of sunlight falling across my bed woke me up. I rolled over and squinted at the clock on my bedside table. It was half past nine. I felt so groggy that I leaned back and closed my eyes, hoping to fall back asleep. The sound of voices in the living room prevented that, though, and finally, I sat up and rubbed my eyes.

I strained to hear Chet and Melia, but neither of them sounded confrontational or agitated. I wondered how Melia reacted when she saw the furniture torn apart, the rugs thrown asunder. I quickly got dressed, then tiptoed down the hall and emerged into the living room.

To my surprise—to my complete shock—the living room had been completely reassembled. I was still so groggy that I wondered if I had completely imagined or even dreamed the events of the night before. None of the furniture was out of place, and the rug was straight. As I blinked away my exhaustion, I realized everything had been cleaned as well. Even the surfaces gleamed.

"Good morning, Rainey," Chet said. He looked quiet, circumspect. His hair had been washed, and he wore fresh clothing. "Will you come sit with us for a moment?"

I glanced at Melia, and she gave me a weary smile. I descended into the living room and sat down on the couch across from them, waiting for them to speak. I already knew what this was going to be about before either of them spoke. Chet had worn Melia down, and now they would tell me to move out. In some ways the idea of leaving was almost a relief, after everything I had seen from Chet.

"I wanted to apologize," Chet said. "For the way I behaved yesterday, when you arrived, and again last night."

I glanced at Melia, and she nodded.

"What?"

"I'm sorry," Chet said. "I know that I can be . . . well, abrupt sometimes. I have an uncouth manner and I make bad jokes. Tasteless jokes. You've been so helpful to Melia, and I don't take that for granted."

I was so surprised that I didn't know what to say.

"Melia talked some sense into me this morning," Chet said. He looked almost abashed.

"It's okay," I said, uncomfortable. I was still on the fence about whether I wanted to stay in Slant House while all this drama was going on. "Let's just put it behind us, yeah?"

"That sounds good," Chet said. "I'm hoping we can all live in perfect harmony."

Outside, a bird sang.

"I could use a coffee," Chet said. "Melia, would you do the honors?"

She gave him a sheepish smile. "Rainey's the only one who knows how to make coffee in this household," she said.

Chet turned to me. "Rainey, sweetheart, would you mind fixing us a coffee? I'd offer to help, but you know me. I'm completely useless."

"It's fine," I said. "I'll make it."

I rose and made my way into the kitchen. Behind me, Chet and Melia resumed their conversation, and the sounds of their voices knit together in a rhythmic sort of unison. I was so tired from days of interrupted sleep, on top of the conflict with Lola and Blake, that I didn't notice what was in the kitchen in front of me.

It took my mind a moment to catch up with my eyes. The first thing I noticed was the smaller fish tank I had used to carry Dart from the office to Slant House. It was empty, turned on its side. The fake plant and toy were scattered across the table. *No water,* I thought idly, caught there for a moment in numb misunderstanding. I thought Dart might have knocked the tank over—a silly thought—or that Chet or Melia had spilled the tank and moved him to a different container.

And that's when I saw him. The first thing I saw was the knife, standing upright on the counter on a chopping block. There was something underneath it—something archaic about the tableau before me—and something in my mind prevented me from understanding what I was looking at. Then: *No no no NO NO NO NONONONONONONO—*

Dart lay on the chopping block, held in place by the knife. As I stood there staring in strangled horror at what I was seeing, Dart's back leg gave one final kick, then he lay still.

THIRTY-ONE

—◆◆◆—

I managed to throw my things into my bag in under three minutes, not bothering to separate my tangled clothing from the items Melia had given me. I would do all of that later; for now, I just needed to focus on getting out, getting away, leaving as fast as possible. I grabbed pants and camisoles from the back of a chair, then emptied the contents of the single occupied dresser drawer into my bag.

My skin crawled, and I knew that if I stayed for even *one minute longer* I would start screaming. I couldn't stop seeing my dead frog, impaled on a knife. *It was an accident,* one part of my brain pleaded, while another voice screamed: *not an accident, not an accident at all, get out, GET OUT.*

Melia had stood up from the couch when I'd fled the kitchen. She'd called after me, but I hadn't bothered to respond or even look at her. Now I heard her footsteps coming down the hallway, and she was calling my name again, but I didn't stop throwing things into my bag.

I slung my bag over my shoulder, then slipped past her and hurried down the hallway. I stumbled out of the house and blinked against the sunlight. Black stars danced in the corners of my eyesight. The heat was absolute, penetrating, a dizzy call to arms. I realized I hadn't had any food or water since yesterday afternoon.

"Rainey! What the hell—where are you *going*?"

My car was parked beneath the house. Sweat gathered under my armpits as I hurried down the stairs, cursing and hoping I could get out before either of them could stop me. Across the street, Janine was washing her car, making listless circles with a bright yellow sponge. She turned toward me and watched as I fumbled for my keys, my hands shaking as I managed to unlock the car door and slide into the car seat.

A flash of color appeared in the corner of my vision, and before I could turn on the engine, Melia was standing in front of my car. Her eyes locked with mine, then she slowly rested her hands on the hood of my car. Her jaw was clenched.

"Move," I said.

"Rainey, please. Come on, be reasonable! He apologized!"

"I'm not going to argue with you, Melia," I said. "Move. You can't prevent me from leaving!"

I was acutely aware that Janine had abandoned her pretense of washing the car and was now standing in the street, watching us with interest. She took her phone out and it looked like she might actually be filming the argument.

"We have history," Melia said. "I've known Chet for a very long time—I don't expect you to understand. At least let me explain."

"There's nothing to explain," I said. "You don't owe me anything. Just let me leave."

When I could see that she still wasn't going to move, I got out of my car and closed the door. I gently took her into my arms and tried to move her away from the car.

"I love you," Melia said.

"It's too late for that. Did you see—oh my god. Chet killed my frog. And you brought him here!" I could hear the nervous strain in my voice, the high note that threatened to turn into hysterical tears.

Her face was creased with confusion. "Your frog?"

"In the kitchen. He *killed my frog!*"

283

"Shh-*hhhh*," Melia said, backing me up against the car door. She glanced at Janine, then back at me. "What the hell is wrong with you?"

I pushed her away from me. "You seriously don't believe me?"

"Chet wouldn't *do* that. I know him, and he wouldn't do that. There's been a mistake."

"It wasn't a mistake—"

"I've known Chet for a really long time," she went on. "Years. *Years.* He's the only one who's always been there for me."

"Congratulations. I hope you're very happy together."

Melia stared at me for a long moment. Across the street, Janine was still watching the unfolding spectacle. Melia stroked her palm with one long finger, then glanced up at me.

"Fine, go," she said. "Since you don't seem to trust me."

"I'm going."

She stepped aside in dramatic slow motion. "Good riddance."

I got back in my car and started the engine. Melia watched me glide down the drive, and the gate slowly clicked open to allow me to leave. Right before I drove through the gate and out onto the street, Melia came running down the drive, her hair wild.

"Don't you ever come back here, Rainey Hall! I'll never forgive you for this—never!"

Before I turned off Willow Glen Lane, I took one last glance at Slant House, which seemed to deflate in the light of day. As I drove away, I could feel the house sigh, swallow, close its eyes. It wasn't waiting to pounce, after all; it had just been holding its breath for years and years and years.

THIRTY-TWO

⎯⎯ ⎯⎯

Leaving Slant House felt like coming out of a dream. There were very few places in Los Angeles to find true solace; even in private homes, the city pressed in at the edges, reminding you of its presence. Emerging back into the real world was, in some ways, an unwelcome exile. Slant House had always felt like a time capsule, where technology and the outside world were muted.

My car was saturated with baked heat. It smelled like dust and worn leather, sunshine on the dashboard. I had forgotten a cup of gas station coffee in the cup holder, which had been reduced to an oily black stain on the bottom of the cup.

I pulled up at a red light and glanced at my phone. I frowned at what I saw.

BLAKE: *We care about you. There's something else—didn't get the chance to tell you yesterday. You left so quickly.*

I was so angry at Lola and Blake that I had half a mind not to respond, to just drive into the mountains and disappear, to cut off contact with absolutely everyone, to ignore them altogether. My better mind prevailed, however, and I glanced at my phone again.

What is it? I wrote back.

BLAKE: *Domenica and Javier want to see you.*

My head was so clouded with thoughts of Melia that it took me a moment to place the names. Javier. Domenica. *Of course.*

I texted Blake back.

Everything okay?

She responded immediately.

BLAKE: *They've been calling the office, but you haven't been here. They're so grateful, R—want to thank you in person.*

The sun lapped at the edge of the sky, and heat washed the mountains in gold and pink. I wondered what it was like to maintain the same routine for years on end, always knowing how you would spend your weekends and holidays. How nice it must be to belong to your life in that way, to owe your hours and days to the people around you. I felt a sudden sweep of longing for that simple life, for the joy of knowing that I belonged, that I was needed.

⁂

There was only one place left for me to go, and in some ways, it felt like going back to rock bottom. I still kept the key on my keychain, although I hadn't used it in nearly three years. Maybe it could be compared to how kids who grew up with landlines still had their home numbers memorized ten years after the lines were disconnected. I pressed the key into my palm as I sat in my car at the base of Mulholland Drive, wishing desperately that I had other options.

I had nowhere else to go, though, so I finally turned my car and headed up the long, winding road back to my parents' house.

The air was different along Mulholland Drive: more fecund, overgrown, with the hint of something decaying in it. These were the houses of musicians and artists once, but now the canyon was full of abandoned homes or properties that had tripled in their initial value and yet sat vacant for most of the year, owned by anonymous billionaires in other parts of the world. The canyon was too steep and winding for any kind of neighborhood to exist; flat surfaces were rare, even in backyards. If you played any kind of ball game it was only a matter of time before the ball went rolling down the hill and got lost in some patch of oleander or wild blackberry.

Slats of jade light sliced through the canopy of leaves, and a light breeze sifted through the aspen trees. The golden leaves hung like slim coins. Marcus had said something once about Los Angeles being nothing more than a stage. I wondered now if, as soon as I turned my back, the cast and crew would materialize out of nowhere and begin disassembling the houses around me.

⁂

My dad had never bothered to change the security code on the gate circling our property. He wouldn't listen to reason, even though it would have been so easy to change it. "Just something new for me to memorize," he had told me. "I can't see the use in it."

I punched in the code and waited as the gate yawned open, then drove my car up and parked beneath the house. As I made my way up the steps leading to the front door, it all started to come back to me.

It felt like there was something dark and wicked hiding behind the hedges; I could almost see it pacing. Standing outside the door of my childhood home, I remembered the childhood incantations I had muttered under my breath, willing myself to grow older, willing myself to leave.

Here was a life I had abandoned long ago. The stage upon which a dozen childhood tragedies had played out was winking in the sunlight, proving once and for all that I was no more in control of my destiny than the clients I thought I was helping. I was a product of those years through and through, so much so that stepping through the gate brought it all back to me. I hadn't fooled anyone by moving away, by trying to reinvent myself, and the landscape that grinned back at me with bloody teeth was sterling evidence of that.

All the painful memories I had tried to forget were still there, behind a series of terraced gardens that ended in a sweeping emerald lawn, framed by lurid blue hydrangeas. To anyone else it might have looked idyllic: a childhood romanticized by someone who had never seen my timid aunts fading into twilight while their husbands got drunk and abused the household staff. It all came back to me then, the garden parties and croquet mallets sinking into the grass, my tall pretty cousins lingering beside the pool, unable to make conversation.

For the first time since I moved away, I was able to see the truth of what my life had always been, the ornaments and high walls, the excess and futility of it all, how out of touch I had always been with the real world.

I wasn't prepared for the smell of the house, however, which washed over me as soon as I stepped through the door. It smelled like home, not something preserved or faded but *home*, the same insistent greeting that didn't understand the passage of time or the concept of loss. I closed my eyes against the sudden rush of emotion as I walked through the house.

The things I had taken with me to Slant House now seemed like childish implements of a life tucked away in shadow: torn linen and silk camisoles untouched since my arrival. I had been wearing Melia's things for days, having cast aside my own worn clothing.

Lola was right, I thought. Lola had been right about Melia all along.

THIRTY-THREE

The next morning I drove toward Echo Park, where I planned on meeting Blake. I no longer saw the city as a dense jungle paradise, drunk on the smell of blooming flowers. It was a dirty backyard filled with discarded toys. Summer had killed nearly everything, and as I slowed against traffic, I caught glimpses of fractured lawns, the same color as peeling skin. Los Angeles was heady with trapped heat.

Moving back home had been a wake-up call. In some ways, it was the end of an era: we had been living on borrowed time at Slant House, our days filled with extravagant food and moonlight soirees, completely separate from reality. Gone were the days of living like ruined aristocracy in a mansion tucked away from the rest of the neighborhood, a secret world we had filled with what we longed to see, somehow managing to ignore the world around us.

I got off the freeway and dropped down into Echo Park. It was a beautiful late summer day, and the sky looked like baked ceramic tile. It seemed like only yesterday that the beauty of the lake had been marred by scaffolding, bulldozers, and chain-link fences, but almost ten years had passed since the renovations had finished, and the lake was more beautiful than ever. A restored boat shed rented out paddleboats to happy couples, and picnickers lounged on the grass along the shore. I could never come here without thinking of Jake Gittes and his detectives rowing around, blowing each other kisses and snapping photographs.

Blake sat outside the boat shed, hidden behind a pair of very dark sunglasses. She wore an oversized vintage Def Leppard shirt and skinny black jeans, and a book sat in her lap. She glanced up when she saw me coming and smiled.

"Ay, Lazarus!"

One of Blake's most endearing traits was that she could acknowledge the elephant in the room without making anyone feel like shit, then deftly segue into something else.

"Hi, Blake."

"Wasn't sure you were coming," she said.

I scowled. "Don't make me out to be the asshole here."

"Nobody said you were an asshole," she said, raising her hands to placate me. "Except maybe Lola, once or twice. Five times?"

I laughed in spite of myself.

"You're not doing yourself any favors when you get sucked under," she reminded me. "Think of us as a safety net."

"Yeah, yeah."

"I feel like such a tourist every time I come here," she said, wheeling forward to give me a hug. I leaned into her and inhaled her smell of lemons and rosemary.

"One of the worst things about living in Los Angeles is that you never visit the most beautiful places," I said.

"Agreed. The tourists get all the best bits." Blake slipped her phone out of her pocket. "Domenica works here now. She should be getting off any minute."

"Anyone else coming?" I asked casually.

Blake raised an eyebrow. "You mean Lola?"

"Oh, I don't know."

"She's still upset with you."

"*She's* upset with *me*? I don't even know where to start with that one."

"So don't start," Blake said, putting her hand up. "Here they come."

I saw Javier crossing the grass in front of the boathouse, an enormous grin on his face. He was radiant with joy and looked a lot more robust than the last time I saw him.

"Where's Domenica?" I asked as Javier got closer.

"She's right there," Blake said, giving me a funny look. "With Javier."

I had to do a double take because I didn't recognize the young woman. Her hair had been chopped in a chin-length bob with bangs, and her body had filled out in a healthy way. She wore a dark blouse and slacks. She gave me a shy smile.

"Rainey," Javier said, coming over and wrapping me in a hug. "We can never thank you enough. You saved our family."

He held me for a long time, and I let myself soak in the feeling of safety and comfort.

"Thank you," I mumbled. "I didn't do it alone, though, not by a long shot. Blake and Lola were mostly responsible for finding the house."

Blake and Javier exchanged a look I couldn't decipher. They were quiet for a long moment, and finally Domenica broke the silence herself.

"Hi, Rainey," she said shyly, stepping forward and offering her hand. "I couldn't thank you properly at the time, but I feel like I have a second chance, thanks to you."

She glanced at Blake. "And your team."

"It was mostly my team," I repeated. "But I'm glad you're safe."

"She's being modest," Blake said. "Lola and I had a lot of other work on our plates. Rainey's the one who didn't give up. She sat up night after night reading through notes and police tip-offs about pedophiles."

Domenica blinked and looked away. I was starting to feel vaguely uncomfortable about Blake's lack of recognition in this whole thing.

"Javier, have you met Blake?" I prompted. "She's our technical supervisor—well, the whole department, really—"

"Rai, it's okay." Blake cut me off.

"No, it's not," I said. "You deserve most of the recognition."

"Rainey."

"What?" I was tired from lack of sleep and knew I sounded irritated, but I was having trouble being pleasant.

"Rainey," Blake said quietly. "Javier and I have already met. Four days ago. He and his wife threw a big party for Domenica, and . . . and . . ."

"Your colleagues were our guests of honor," Javier said. "We wanted to invite you too, but your colleagues said you couldn't make it."

He was still smiling, but the smile had started to waver. Domenica put her hand on his arm and whispered something into his ear.

"Rainey," Javier said. "I'm so grateful for what you have done for me and my family. We can never repay you. And I know you didn't ask for any money, which tells me you have a good heart."

He seemed hesitant to continue.

"If you need any help . . . any help at all . . . it would be an honor for my family to provide that." He and Domenica were studying my face.

Blake glanced between us, then put a hand on my wrist. "That's lovely, Javier, thank you," she said. "Rainey and I have some business to attend to in Venice, though, and I'm starting to get worried about traffic. We should go."

Before I could say anything, Blake cut me a look. I nodded.

"It was nice to see both of you," I told them. "Thank you for coming to see me." After Javier and Domenica had turned back toward the boat shed and we were alone again, I glanced at Blake. "What's going on? We don't have anything in Venice."

She met my gaze and held it. "You haven't exactly been yourself for the last few weeks."

"Myself? Blake, what are you talking about?" I laughed, uncomfortable. "Come on."

"This month hasn't exactly been a picnic. I mean, first my ex-boyfriend showed up, and then I started getting threatening visits from people connected to this case, which—guess what? It looks like I failed to solve."

Blake's eyes were on my face, but I couldn't read her expression.

"This month has been hard for me," I said. "I admit it. It's been rough. But just because I'm struggling with something doesn't mean I'm a different person."

There was still no response from Blake. I was angry and ashamed, but I also felt completely alone.

"For god's sake," I said. "Is this meant to be some kind of intervention?"

"Rainey, please," Blake said quietly. "I don't know exactly what you're going through, but I love you, and I care about you. Don't do this alone."

I felt my throat constrict with tears, but I wasn't going to let myself break down.

"I'm sorry," I said, in a hoarse voice.

"It's okay," Blake said quietly. "It's okay to be emotional about these things."

I blinked back some tears and then turned away, back toward the lake. I didn't know what had made me so emotional, whether it was because Domenica *was*, in fact, okay—or because I had, once again, fucked up so colossally that I was probably going to have to rebuild again. I had been cruel to Blake and Lola, pushing them away. I had lost track of what was going on with Melia, had wasted the entire last month in indolence and self-indulgence.

Blake put a hand on my back.

"Hey," she said. "Not everything's lost, you know. Let's get together, as a team."

"A team?"

"Yes," she said. "We are still a team, you know. We always have been."

THIRTY-FOUR

If I thought going back to my childhood home would be hard, there was something even harder still ahead of me: I was going to have to face Lola and acknowledge that she had been right. So Blake arranged a face-to-face meeting with the three of us.

The hardest part was knowing I deserved everything they were going to say about me: that I had lost track of myself, that I had lost track of what we were doing, that I had put my own needs above those of the team. There was no way they could hate me more than I already hated myself, but the idea of seeing disappointment reflected in their eyes—in Lola's eyes, especially—was anxiety-inducing.

We had agreed to meet somewhere neutral, outdoors, both to take advantage of the nice weather and to prevent things from getting too heated. Blake had suggested the park next to the Silver Lake Reservoir. She had been the intermediary for the whole thing, arranging the time and the place so Lola and I wouldn't have to be in contact until we were all sitting down together.

I arrived early and parked behind the Green Grove Market. The Green Grove always reminded me of my mother—she would take me there after stopping at the farmers' market. We'd stock up on frozen mangoes, white wine, avocados, bags of organic sugar, and coffee beans, then go home and realize we hadn't bought a single ingredient for dinner. Those afternoons always ended with us eating yogurt straight from the carton and watching grainy documentaries on cable.

I was half an hour early, which is why I was surprised to arrive at the appointed spot and see Lola already there. I lingered at a safe distance, hesitant to approach, nervous about what I was going to say. I stayed there a minute too long, though, because Lola finally glanced around and saw me.

We stared at each other for a moment, and finally she cocked her head, inviting me closer.

"I knew you'd be early. You always are," she said. "I wanted to get here first."

"Why?"

"Because I think I know how you feel," Lola said quietly. "And I know what you do after conflict. You retreat into your shell and self-destruct there."

I had known Lola for years, but I was always surprised by how intuitive she could be.

"I *am* mad at you, but I don't hate you," she went on. "And I don't want you to hate yourself either."

I sat on the table next to her. "I always find myself back here," I said. "I just don't know how I keep fucking up the same way, over and over."

She put a hand on my back. "You trust people," she said. "You still have faith in humanity, I guess. Unlike the rest of us cynical Los Angeles bastards."

"I'm sorry, Lo."

She was quiet.

"I'm sorry I ignored your calls," I went on. "And that I didn't tell you what was going on sooner."

She nodded. "You're allowed to have your own life," she said. "You *need* to have your own life. Just don't throw everything else away when you do."

"You're right. I know, you're right."

"I've seen you get like this before," she said. "It's as if nothing in the world can get through to you. You have this spectacular way of self-sabotaging . . . like there's this deep pit inside of you, and every once in a while, you climb inside and pull the lid over your head. Nobody can reach you."

"Well, it might comfort you to know that everything's over with Melia," I said. "You were right."

"I'm always right."

"And you were right about that other thing," I said. "When you asked if I'd gotten involved."

"I know."

I frowned at her. "*How* do you know?"

"Because you've got really rotten taste in partners."

"You are *such* an asshole. I can't believe you!" I hit her arm.

Lola burst out laughing, an almost evil cackle.

"She was never a partner though," I muttered. "It was just a fling."

"Really?"

"I wanted it to be more," I admitted. "It seemed like we were on the same page before Chet showed up."

"Chet?" Lola looked like she was trying not to laugh again. "His name is Chet?"

"He's from Georgia."

"Sounds like proper white trash. Melia's got good taste too."

I sank my face into my hands. "Don't, Lo," I groaned. "I think I still care about her."

Blake arrived and saw us sitting together. She glanced between us.

"Am I late?"

"You're right on time," Lola said.

"Have you started airing grievances without me?"

"You can have your turn," I sighed. "But please know that I already feel like a total piece of shit, a terrible friend, and I wouldn't blame you if you wanted to kick me out of Left City."

Blake looked conflicted.

"I was half-joking," I said, slightly alarmed.

"We're not kicking you out," she said. "But you can't get lost like that. Not again. Our team needs you. We don't function as well without you."

Lola nodded. "No more being a self-involved asshole."

I made a Girl Scout cross across my heart. "I promise."

"I know this isn't a work meeting, but I thought it might be a good time to discuss moving forward," Lola said. "We can go to Mars for milkshakes afterward."

She reached into her bag and pulled out her iPad. "It's a good month for infidelity," she said. "We can knock off a few cases in the next week and increase our cash flow. I have about ten potential clients who want to hire us. I know how you feel about this stuff, Rainey, but we're honestly behind on bills."

Blake looked like she was deep in thought.

"It's fine with me," I told Lola, then turned to Blake. "What is it?"

"It's not really relevant anymore," she said. "Because we dropped Melia's case."

Lola put her tablet back in her bag. "What's up?"

"I found something about her parents."

"And?"

"Well, I've been looking into their finances since we took the case," Blake started. "It's the most obvious place to start, after all. From everything I've read about them, it sounds like they might have been killed because there were all these rumors about the money, the insane fortune. If someone could get to it through one of the family members, they'd all be sitting ducks."

Blake was brilliant, and I knew she wouldn't have brought it up unless she had found something.

"I can't hack into the bank accounts," Blake continued. "I mean, they're in Switzerland and the Cayman Islands, from what I was able to find through documents online. I may be good, but that's virtually impossible."

"Sure. So, what *did* you find?"

"There are other ways to track investments," Blake said, taking out her iPad. "I went through the last twenty years and looked at what Wilhelm did with his money. And from all my research, that's all I could find in terms of financial activity. He didn't seem to have an actual job; he just managed the family wealth and invested it accordingly."

I waited as Blake opened a program on her iPad.

"I made a graph," she said. "He seemed to be doing well for a while, but then he made some very bad calls. In one of them, he lost something like three hundred million dollars."

"Three *hundred* million?"

Blake slowly nodded. "At one point this family was worth billions, so maybe he felt like he could risk it," she said. "But look, these fortunes weren't made for modern times. At least, the way they were traditionally maintained isn't viable anymore. Four hundred years ago a nobleman could live off the tithes of peasants and landowners, but obviously laws and countries have changed. Wealthy heirs can't just sit on their asses and live the good life. The money will disappear eventually."

"I know you can't get into the bank accounts," I said. "But do you have any idea what the van Austs are worth today? Or what they were worth before they were killed?"

Blake looked hesitant to speculate. "It's bad," she said. "I've been going through all the articles I was able to dig up, all the lawsuits from people Wilhelm went into business with . . . I mean, I keep coming up with the same number."

"Which is?"

She tapped away on her iPad, annoyed. "It's just speculation," she said. "I made an algorithm to weigh net losses against income streams and debt, so again, a *lot* of speculation."

"Tell me," I pressed. "We're just brainstorming."

"Somewhere around thirty grand."

I was so stunned I couldn't even formulate a response. "And that's . . . what?"

"All they have left. That doesn't include the sale value of the house, but Wilhelm took out a mortgage on it about five years ago to cover the debts of a lost investment, so . . . that's not worth as much as you'd think either."

"Thirty grand," I echoed. The number didn't even register with me. "I thought—I mean, I thought they were insanely wealthy."

"They were," Blake said. "But you'd be surprised how easy it is to lose money when you make bad decisions."

"Damn," Lola said quietly.

"I wonder if Melia knows," I said.

"It's hard to tell," Blake agreed. "I mean, I don't know what her lawyer is obligated to tell her, if anything—if the will stipulates that she's not allowed to access funds until she's twenty-five, then he might not have to tell her anything. Then again, depending on how corrupt he is, he might just be trying to run out the clock with billable hours so he can funnel as much money into his pockets as possible."

We ended the meeting by dividing up the list of new clients and assigning some of them to each of the team. I wasn't normally a fan of infidelity cases, because more often than not our findings led to the end of relationships, but it was easy money. Plus, it was unlikely that I would get emotionally involved with anyone we were investigating.

Lola and Blake asked me if I wanted to go out for dinner in Silver Lake, but I felt reclusive and begged off, saying I needed to spend a night alone after so much time with Melia.

I had been heartbroken and hurt before, and I knew the best way for me to get over it was to submerge myself in work. The first thing I did when I got home was to brew a pot of English breakfast tea and then clear off the kitchen table.

Dune House was huge, with lots of empty rooms and long hallways; there were plenty of desks and tables throughout the house, but the kitchen table was where everyone had always gravitated toward when they needed to get work done. The table was tall, a giant slab of wood hewn from the heart of some enormous tree. Although Marcus had told me my father had recently departed on a European tour for three months, the house had the air of nonoccupation. I had the feeling that he had been gone from the house for much longer. There were thin reams of newspaper cast across the table, a cluster of teacups, and the stalks of dead flowers in a vase. I wet a dish towel in the sink and cleaned off one corner of the table before setting up my laptop and opening my email.

Evening had fallen outside, and the panes of glass in the kitchen window were dusky blue. My phone pinged. It was across the room in my bag, so I ignored it. I could see from the addresses on the list of clients Lola had sent me that they were wealthy: residents of Pasadena, Holmby Hills, and even one as far as Montecito. Although we mostly dealt with local clients, we had taken cases based as far away as Manhattan. With Blake's talents, we could take cases anywhere, even if we preferred not to.

There was another ping from my phone. A moment later, it started to ring. I hesitated for a moment, then jumped off my seat and went across the room.

When I glanced at the screen, my heart fell. *Melia van Aust.*

I wanted to reject the call, return to my computer, and forget the last month altogether. I had always wanted to be the person who walked away, who disentangled myself so casually that I could disappear with blithe disregard, as though an abrupt separation had no more effect on me than a minor illness.

I had never been that person, though, and with regrets, I accepted the call.

"You have to help me, Rainey," Melia whispered, before I could ask why she was calling. "Oh, god, Rainey. He's going to kill me."

She sounded petrified.

"What's going on? Melia? Where are you?"

"It's Chet," she said. Her voice was so quiet that I struggled to hear her. "I asked him to leave. I realized as soon as you left that I had made a mistake."

My heart skipped a beat. I didn't trust myself to respond right away.

"He has a gun." Her voice sounded strangled, hoarse. My heart leaped into my throat. "Rainey, he has a gun!"

"Call the police. I'm on my way right now, but just in case I don't get there in time—"

"I need you, Rainey," Melia whispered. "I've always been so scared of Chet. That's why I couldn't ask him to leave when he came."

"Where are you?" I felt suddenly resolute.

"I'm at the house. He wouldn't let me leave."

"Call the police," I repeated. "I'm on my way."

"I did," she said. "But just in case anything happens—oh, god, I can hear him coming—no! *No!* Leave me alone!"

There was a loud banging on the other end of the phone, then the sound of something shattering. The phone cut off, and I was left in silence.

THIRTY-FIVE

———◦◦◦◦———

I called Lola as I left the house.

"You change your mind about joining us for dinner?" She was shouting to be heard. I could hear music and laughter in the background. They must have gone to a busy spot, full of people happy to be out on a summer night.

"It's an emergency!" I said, raising my voice so she could hear me over the din. "Lo? Can you hear me?"

"Hold on," she said. After a wait that dragged on for too long, the sound of voices fell to a dull murmur.

"I stepped outside," she said. "Rainey? What's going on?"

"It's Melia," I said. "Before you say anything, just listen. She called me because Chet has a gun. I think he might kill her."

She didn't hesitate to respond. "Did she call the police?"

"Yeah, but I'm heading over anyway, just in case."

"Pick me up, I'll go with you."

"No time," I said. "I'm about five minutes from the house. I have a plan."

"Rainey, this could be very dangerous," she said.

"It's too late for that. I can't let him kill her."

She was quiet for a long time. "I know I'm not going to change your mind," she said finally. "Will you call me as soon as you can? I'll call the police right now and make sure they're on their way."

I didn't want to drive my car all the way to Slant House. If Melia was in real danger, then Chet would probably be keeping an eye on the road for anyone coming to interfere. One of the downsides of my car was that, in addition to being recognizable, it was loud. Chet would hear me coming from a mile away.

So I parked on a street a few blocks away and then ran toward Slant House.

I reached the edge of Willow Glen Lane. Slant House was visible from the end of the street, and the lights in the living room were on. The house glowed like a blocky paper lantern. Evening had fallen upon the neighborhood, and though it was still light enough for me to see where I was going, there was enough cover of darkness for me to creep among the cars and trees without being observed. Hulking shadows lurched across the street, cast by cars and houses. My heartbeat was near deafening, and every sound felt like Chet, sneaking up on me.

There was no sign of life from the Flack house. I moved down the street, reaching the edge of the van Aust property line, then slipped behind a Chinese elm.

There was a slight chance that Melia had changed the code to the front gate since I had left, but given her aversion to all things technological, I doubted she had. I held my breath as I punched in the eight-digit code, then breathed out a sigh of relief when the light on the keypad went green and the lock snicked open.

The weeds in the overgrown yard worked to my advantage, but just to be safe, I crawled on my hands and knees through the long grass. It was dark enough by now that movement outside was unlikely to be seen from one of the windows, especially with all the lights on inside.

It felt like it took forever to crawl all the way around to the back of the house. The windows of the dining room were opaque, the tall glass panes reflecting the navy dusk. Beyond the large dining table, I could see the faint glow of the living room. The back of the kitchen was obscured, and when I finally made my way to the far side of the swimming pool, I was afforded a view into part of the living room, and from another angle, into the library.

For a long time, there was no movement inside Slant House. I had shut off my phone completely, not wanting the slightest possibility of the phone making an unwelcome noise and alerting Melia or Chet to my presence behind the house.

Then I saw her. Melia passed in front of the window in the living room. She looked agitated, gesticulating with her hands. I only caught a glimpse of her before she was gone.

My heart hammered in my chest. I was uncomfortable, crouched there in the dying grass beside the swimming pool, watching and waiting for some opening. I didn't know exactly what I was looking for, or what possible opening I was hoping to find.

And then it came to me.

I waited until I saw Melia pass in front of the window once more, then ran around the pool and down toward the basement. The basement door opened onto the garden beneath the living room, facing the back of the property. My hands shook as I entered the same eight-digit passcode that had released the gate.

The light above the keypad went green, and I let myself into the basement, holding my breath and making as little noise as possible. My heart was beating so loudly that I irrationally thought it might be audible to Chet and Melia upstairs. I glanced around the basement, surprised to see all the lights on. Closing the door behind me as quietly as possible, I quickly glanced around the room, praying Chet wasn't already downstairs.

My plan hadn't extended much further than getting inside the house. I knew it was important to have the element of surprise; my only chance of getting the upper hand was to catch Chet unawares.

Footsteps pounded overhead, followed by shouting. Chet's voice.

"You're lying to me," he said. "I know you're lying to me!"

I moved closer, surprised I could hear everything. Light spilled down the stairs, and I could see the door to the pantry was open.

"She's not coming." It was Melia's voice. She sounded calm, detached.

"You're a fucking liar!"

"I'm telling you, she's not coming. She would have gotten here by now."

I glanced around the basement. It was spare, minimalistic, with very few places to hide. This could present a problem, I realized with dread, if Chet came downstairs. *Why are the lights on? Why is the door open?*

I pressed myself against the wall in the kitchen. If Chet were to come downstairs, I'd need a place to hide. I might not be able to move quickly enough to make it across the room and get out the door into the garden, and besides, he would be able to see me leave, then chase after me with a gun. I needed to hide—*now.*

"We're leaving in *five minutes,*" Chet said.

"That's fine." Melia's voice still held no emotion. I wondered if she was muting her emotions so she would appear docile. Where was Chet taking her?

"When did you call her?"

Melia's voice was quiet. "Twenty minutes ago. Give it another five."

Something wasn't adding up. I turned around, realizing I might have to arm myself. A knife, a rolling pin, something—but the kitchen was bare. I opened the top three drawers and found nothing but stacks of napkins and takeaway chopsticks. The cupboards were empty, save a few cans of beans.

There was some luggage on the floor, luggage that hadn't been there a few days ago. *They must belong to Chet,* I realized. A thought came to me then: there was a chance that he had something in his luggage, something I could use to arm myself. Glancing up at the stairs, I moved across the room and knelt by his duffel bag, opening it as quietly as I could.

The bag was packed with nonperishable food items: beans, microwave popcorn, beef jerky, canned tuna. Brand-new packs of underwear and socks,

T-shirts and sweatpants with the tags still on them. No signs of weapons. I opened up the side pouch on the duffel and reached inside.

Passports. Two of them.

My first thought was that Chet had taken Melia's passport so she couldn't go anywhere without him. It was the only logical explanation. I quickly pocketed both passports. If he attacked her and then vanished, I needed something to give to the police.

"It's been five minutes," Chet whined. "Get the car. I'll get the bags. We gotta go."

Melia murmured something I couldn't hear, and then there were footsteps above me. I raced across the room, glancing around for a place to hide.

The walk-in freezer.

Chet's heavy footsteps came pounding through the pantry as I opened the freezer door.

"Yeah, I know, I'll be right there!" he called angrily.

I slipped into the freezer and closed the door, praying beyond hope that he wouldn't hear me. The freezer light kicked on when I stepped inside, and once the door was closed, I could hear nothing but the steady hum of the generator around me. The walls were lined with thick ice, and even though it had been a hot day and I was full of adrenaline, I started to shiver. It was partly nerves and partly the cold. I traced a finger along the wall and then glanced around, taking in my surroundings. It was a spacious freezer, the type you might find in a restaurant kitchen. Two large metal shelving units lined the sides of the freezer, each one stocked with tubs and bags of frozen goods.

The faintest thump and creak outside the freezer told me Chet was still moving around in the basement. I prayed he wouldn't open the door, that he wouldn't come find me. There was nothing to stop him shooting me now, especially here, where it was unlikely that anyone would be able to hear the gunshot. By the time someone found me, I would be long frozen and dead from the gunshot wound. Lola alone knew I had come to Slant House; I could only hope the police were on their way.

More thumps beyond the door told me Chet was making his way up the stairs. I was about to leave the freezer and emerge into the basement when something occurred to me. Melia had told me the freezer was broken, but it was clearly in good working order. The shelves were neatly lined with frozen goods, and there wasn't so much as a spill on the floor to indicate that it might have been broken at some point.

I cautiously opened the freezer door and peered out. Chet was gone, as were his bags. The lights were off, and the house was silent.

I stepped out into the room and shuddered, then reached into my pocket and produced the passports.

They were crisp, brand-new, without so much as a crimp in the covers. My hands shook as I opened the first one; CHET LENNARD DAWES. Chet's unsmiling face stared up at me from the identification page. I put it back in my pocket and opened the second one, knowing there would be something inside that I didn't want to see.

She looked changed, diminished somehow, but I still recognized Melia's face. The name was the thing that I couldn't move past: HANNAH MARIE ROTHCHILD. My thumb traced the letters, willing the document to be fake, willing some clue or explanation to make itself known. Her hair was different too; in the photo it looked lighter, almost brown.

Hannah.

The pale skin, the wide eyes and elfin features. All of it was the same. Behind me, the freezer let out a draft of cold air. I hadn't closed the door. I moved toward the freezer door, my eyes adjusting to the moonlit gloom that filtered in from the windows.

My rational mind knew they would return, that it was only a matter of minutes perhaps before Chet or Melia realized their passports were missing. They had a reason for calling me back here, a reason for fresh passports, a reason why Melia was traveling under a different name. They were leaving the country. There was a reason, too, why Melia had lied to me about the broken freezer. Something was in there.

It hadn't occurred to me until then that Chet already knew the layout of the house—a house he had never visited. There was a reason, too, why he had set up camp downstairs instead of choosing the master bedroom, when I doubted the master bedroom's macabre history would have deterred him from sleeping upstairs with us.

The freezer yawned open, emitting a slice of cold air and chilly white light. I hadn't seen it before, when I had taken a quick glance around. At the back of the fridge was a large box covered in a white sheet. It was big enough to hold—*a body, a frozen body, it's a tangle of bones and blood*—something large, human-sized. *Jasper,* I thought. With fresh terror, the image of Jasper's cold face burst into my mind.

It had been there all along, but I hadn't wanted to see it. Melia had killed her family, and Jasper had taken the fall for the whole miserable affair because Jasper was tormented and Melia was smart. I had fallen into her trap, fully, completely, because she had lured me in with praise and feigned helplessness.

Thoughts tumbled through my head as I stood there, looking at the box. When had they found time to kill Jasper? Were the police still on their way—and if so, how close were they? Chet had given me the biggest clue of all, but I had written him off: *Have you figured it out yet? It's pretty obvious if you have half a brain.* And now I was going to be framed for Jasper's murder. All the evidence was there, and Robbie and Paulina would hasten to give their own evidence—proof that Jasper had broken into my house that one night. Melia's last words came echoing back to me, words Janine had heard her scream at me: *I'll never forgive you for this—never!*

I tugged away the sheet and then pulled open the lid. A layer of frost obscured the dark hair, the frozen blood. My heart was pounding so loudly in my ears that I couldn't hear anything else. I knelt down and pushed back the hair, frozen stiff, trying to get a better look at the face.

I was working against borrowed time. It was probably only a matter of minutes before the police arrived, before they caught me in the freezer, in flagrante delicto. I knelt down, ignoring the chill that shot through my knees, and tore away the rest of the box. Fingers—there were fingers—it was indeed a body. The hands were clawed together across the chest, and the knees were drawn up. The face was quite pretty, distorted though it was by fear and agony.

And then I saw it. The corpse wore a torn white T-shirt, thoroughly saturated with frozen blood. The torso bore evidence of repeated stab marks, and then, above the top of the neck of the T-shirt, I saw something that made my blood run cold.

It was a thick, flagging scar in the shape of a backward J. I was staring at the body of Melia van Aust.

THIRTY-SIX

⚬⚬⚬

The first time I saw her was in Venice. It had started like any other day: Marcus was writing music for a film from New Zealand and was collaborating with some Kiwi artists who lived near Abbot Kinney.

Later, I would remember how everything about that day was so very normal: it was a Tuesday, late April, and traffic had been light because it was three P.M. and most people were stuck at work. It was impossible to find a parking spot within three blocks of Abbot Kinney, so I circled the neighborhood for ten minutes, unwilling to pay for parking even though Marcus always reimbursed me.

My job varied from one day to the next, which was one of the things I loved about working for Marcus. Sometimes I holed up at the library for hours on end, reading about ancient Mayan civilization, while other days I waited at the airport to pick up visiting composers from other countries. It was three years after my mother's disappearance, and for the most part, my life was back on track. I had stopped drinking a few months before and was starting to feel like my normal self again.

And then I saw her. She was crossing the street, casually glancing both ways as she sauntered from one side to another. Her hair was down around her shoulders, dark and silky. She was smiling.

My mother.

I nearly lost sight of her because it all happened so quickly. I had braked suddenly to let a car merge ahead of me out of a parking lot, and that's the only reason I saw her. For the next month, and for years after that, I would wonder what might have happened if I hadn't seen her at all, knowing without a doubt that my life would have turned out different. Left City probably wouldn't exist at all if not for that one, casual sighting. Just a flash of dark hair, her heart-shaped face, those long graceful limbs, and she was gone.

I pulled into the parking lot and threw coins at the automated ticket machine, barely registering how much time I had bought. For most of the three years she had been gone, I had spent almost every day obsessing about her, wondering what happened to her, why she had disappeared.

She was walking down Abbot Kinney when I caught sight of her again. It was too warm to wear layers, but I tucked my long hair under a hat and wrapped a scarf around me, hoping she wouldn't see me walking a block behind her. A year before, I might have run up to her and thrown my arms around her, weeping with gratitude that she was still alive. Too much time had passed though; I was no longer so naïve. She was here, *in Los Angeles*, and perhaps she had been all along. What's more, she was by herself, not captive to some fiendish criminal. She hadn't been maimed or tortured, at least not from what I could see.

I followed her for two blocks before she stepped into a smart-looking clinic fronted with tall, glass windows. I watched from afar as the receptionist greeted her warmly and ushered her through another door, where she disappeared from view. I made note of the name on the door of the clinic—DR. MONASH—and then hurried to go meet the Kiwi musicians.

⸻

I didn't tell Marcus that I had seen my mother. I got back to the office an hour late, but Marcus either didn't notice or he didn't care. I was so keyed up that if he had questioned me, or even given me a look of concern, I might have broken down and told him everything. That was the day everything changed for me, even if I didn't realize it at the time. To the outside world I carried on as normal, but inside I carried around a feverish little secret that sustained me and threatened to destroy me in equal measure.

As soon as I got back to my room that evening, I opened my computer and looked up Dr. Monash.

Dr. Eliza Monash studied gynecology at Oxford University and has been serving the Los Angeles community for over twenty years.

The website offered me no insight or clarity until I visited the SERVICES OFFERED tab.

Dr. Monash and her skilled team of clinicians specialize in fertility treatments . . .

I couldn't read any further, because somehow, I already knew. I shut down the browser and then scrubbed my computer's search history, convinced I could talk myself out of what I was about to do, as if there was any choice for me at all in the matter.

All that week, I became an expert in diversions and excuses. I volunteered to run errands and pick up minor grocery items like creamer and organic kale chips. Marcus raised an eyebrow when I offered to take someone's car for detailing, an errand that would cost me three hours, but he didn't question me. I had earned Marcus's trust a long time before, and although the guilt of lying weighed heavily, I couldn't seem to stop myself.

I found a café down the street from Dr. Monash's clinic, and for days after I spotted my mother on Abbot Kinney, I camped out at a hidden table at the café until at last—at last!—she made another appearance. This time, however, she was with someone.

He was handsome, with a close-shaven head and dark skin. He was so young that I thought he must just be my mother's friend, perhaps even an assistant. When they reached the clinic, however, he leaned in to kiss her. My heart stopped when I saw him place a hand on her stomach, and they both smiled.

I should have stopped then. There was a new feeling, something I had never experienced before but felt many times since, sometimes when meeting new clients and sometimes just when doing research. *Don't interfere. This is not for you.* I didn't always listen to that feeling, but usually my willful ignorance came at a cost.

I waited outside the café until my mother emerged again, but this time I followed her back to her car. I watched her unlock a Porsche SUV, the kind of gauche and ostentatious wealth she had once ridiculed. The swell of her stomach was clearly visible as she climbed into the enormous car. I watched her drive away, writing down the license plate even though I had already memorized it.

For the next month I lived a double life. I knew I was neglecting some of my duties to Marcus, and that I was pulling away from my friends, but I didn't care. The illicit thrill I got from shadowing my mother around and learning everything I could about her new life was too much for me to abandon.

I waited outside Dr. Monash's clinic again until she made an appearance, but this time, I followed her home.

We never would have looked for her in the Pacific Palisades, which is where she was living. The house was beautiful, new, and sturdy-looking. It was uniform enough to blend in with the rest of the neighborhood, impossible to pick out from the houses surrounding it. One day, when my mother and her new partner were away at work, I opened their mailbox and went through their mail.

She had changed her name to Isabel Munro and was an architect. The bulk of the mail was invitations and bills, but it contained all I needed to know. For one thing, she worked at an architecture firm called Starkley Partners, and for another, she took a number of classes around town. Trying on different personalities, testing things out to see which attributes fit.

She had stopped drinking coffee, but I didn't know if that was a long-standing feature of her new life or if she had temporarily forsaken it in favor of the new baby. She was only thirty-nine, not too old to have a new child, but I wondered how much her new husband knew about her former life and the family she had left behind. I got up early to sit in my car down the street from her house, watching and waiting for her morning routine to begin.

First, she went to a yoga studio that specialized in prenatal stretching routines. The class lasted an hour, and afterward she went out for breakfast with a group of women from her class, some sporting baby bumps of their own. I knew what I was doing was sick, but I also felt entitled to it. Some days I fantasized about strolling into the studio midclass and announcing the truth, just to see the look of shock on her face. Other days I longed to be incorporated into her new routine, the new rhythm of her life. Was this life so much better than the one she had? Was I so easy to cast aside?

After she had smoothies and health food with the women from her class, she went straight to work. Sometimes she would emerge and head to a nearby restaurant for lunch with her colleagues, but most days she stayed inside her office, and I didn't see her again until the workday was over. I couldn't follow her like this every day, of course; I had to work for Marcus. Even on those days, however, I was frequently able to find excuses to slip away and watch a small segment of her day.

Her husband's name was Lucien DuPont. She must have changed her name before she met him, I realized, because she hadn't adopted his name. Lucien ran an industrial design business. He was only thirty-five. Once I followed them to a restaurant in Brentwood and heard them speaking

French together. Her accent and rhythm of speech was flawless, as though she had been gone for a decade, not three years. How could I have ever been foolish enough to believe I had known anything about her?

~

The offices for Starkley Partners were in Santa Monica, just off the Third Street Promenade. Over the next week I switched from surveying Dr. Monash's office to visiting the Starkley offices. The building was all glass and clean metal lines, an airy simplicity that led to a feeling of deep calm. Astonished at my own boldness, I walked up to the reception desk one afternoon and asked if I could speak to someone about design plans.

The man behind the counter didn't seem suspicious of how young I was. I imagined he spoke to a lot of assistants who worked for high-profile people, too busy themselves to drop by.

"What sort of design are you looking for?"

"My boss is doing a home office renovation," I explained, the lie dropping smoothly off my tongue. "Sort of a cross-purpose building to be built behind the house. Not too commercial, obviously, but professional enough for clients to visit."

"Of course," he said. "Let me give you our catalog. You can get an idea of our team and what each of them represents."

~

There were days when I thought it might go on forever. Living a double life wasn't too much trouble; in some ways I had more energy than ever. I left the Loew house at dawn, driving all the way across Los Angeles to sit outside my mother's new house in the Palisades. Her routine was like clockwork: rise, short walk around the neighborhood, yoga, breakfast with friends, work. In all my life I had never known her to have such a reliable existence. The woman I lived with had been erratic, an artist, ricocheting from one extreme to the next.

No matter how much time I spent following my mother around, though, I could never envision what an encounter might look like. It would have to be by accident, I reasoned; I couldn't exactly walk up to her front door and announce that I had been following her for weeks on end. Nor could I allow her to catch me unawares, as she very nearly did one morning when I fell asleep in the early dawn outside her house, the light in the sky like milky tea. The longer I followed her, the more I allowed myself to detach from reality, and the less my chances were of experiencing an impromptu reunion.

And then, all at once, everything ended.

It was six weeks after I had first seen Matilda walking to the fertility clinic in Venice. By this point I had an entire dossier of her whereabouts and activities stashed under the passenger seat of my car. It had become a sick sort of obsession, and on some level I think Marcus must have known, but I hadn't built up the courage to talk to him about it. I knew my mother's architecture firm was throwing a big summer party that evening, and all the partners and their families were invited, as well as some big clients they had represented. I knew about all of this from the receptionist. I had popped by the office so many times that we had become friendly, if not exactly friends, though he was still under the illusion that I worked nearby and my boss was considering hiring their firm to build an office.

"You should stop by," he told me. "We don't have a guest list or anything. It's going to be pretty casual. There'll be music, dancing, food . . ."

That night, I told Marcus I wouldn't be home; I was going out with some friends. He nodded and sighed, then motioned for me to follow him into his office.

"Tell me."

"What?"

"You're hiding something." He looked at me over the top of his glasses. "I'm not interrogating you, I just need to know—should I be worried?"

"No," I said, not meeting his eye.

"You were in a bad place when you first came here," he said softly. "We've watched you grow, change, shed that part of your past. I just . . . I don't want to see you go back there."

"It's not going to happen."

"You've been keeping to yourself lately," he continued, then raised his hands. "I'm not saying it's any of my business, I just need to know if I need to worry."

"You don't."

"You know," he added, almost as an aside. "If you're sneaking out to meet someone, you don't have to. You can bring them here."

I was confused for a moment, then realized he thought I was dating someone and keeping it secret. "It's not what you think, Marcus."

"Fair enough," he said. "Just can't remember the last time I saw you look so happy, that's all."

———

That night I parked in one of the big structures off the Third Street Promenade. I had rehearsed all the possibilities for how things might go. I would bump into her, perhaps, then feign a double take. While I struggled for words, she would take me aside and explain everything to me. *I never forgot you,* she would say. *I've been trying to contact you all these years, but the letters must have gotten lost in the mail. How did you find yourself here?*

Oh, I would say. *My date used one of the architects here to design his summer house a few years ago.*

The party was in full swing by the time I arrived. I lingered outside the building, watching couples enter, laughing, chattering, talking amongst themselves. I had worn a dress from high school because it was still the nicest thing I owned: a dark silk slip that flowed down around my ankles, sleeveless . . .

I was so caught up in the fantasy that I didn't hear the rapid footsteps behind me. Then there was a hand on my shoulder. I turned around and found myself face-to-face with my mother.

She looked young and very pretty, with her dark hair cut in a sleek pixie cut. She must have just had it done; it had been longer a few days before. She wore a light blue asymmetrical dress that looked very expensive, and when I looked at her face, I realized she was furious.

She gripped my arm and pulled me away from the firm.

"You can't be here," she growled. "Come now, quickly, before anyone sees you."

I stumbled after her, caught off guard. When we were a safe distance from the architectural firm, she turned to face me. Her features were hard.

"You need to stop following me," she said.

I could only stare at her. There was nothing in her features that I recognized, no love or sympathy. I wondered if she had amnesia, if she somehow didn't recognize who I was.

"Do you hear me? Rainey?"

I swallowed hard and blinked away tears. In addition to what she was saying, I had to stomach the humiliation of knowing she had been wise to my presence. I wondered how long she had known.

"But—where have you been?" I whispered. "Why did you leave?"

She let out an impatient sigh and glanced toward the party. "I can't stay out here too long," she said. "They expect me inside."

"I've been looking for you for years," I said. "Years!"

"I never *asked* you to do that."

"You can't mean that." Tears were streaming down my face. "I love you."

"Well, don't." She reached into her purse and produced a packet of tissues. "Here. Your face is a mess."

"Can't we go somewhere?" I begged. "Just talk?"

"There's nothing to talk about. This is my choice. You need to respect that."

"I could tell him, you know," I said, wiping roughly at my face. "Your husband. Lucien."

She raised an eyebrow. "You think he doesn't know?"

I forced myself to hold her gaze, a tissue clenched in my hands.

"I was dying," she said. "That life—what we had was a cage. I didn't want any of it. The fame, the fans, the clout. I was dying, Rainey. I didn't see any other way out."

I looked past her, at the party spilling out of the architecture firm.

"I didn't want to hurt you," she went on. "I just want you to forget about me. Forget you ever saw me. Live your own life."

Lucien stepped outside to smoke a cigarette. He was talking to friends and hadn't seen us.

"What did you tell him?"

"I didn't have to tell him anything," my mother said finally. "He's the one who helped me leave."

I could feel myself tearing up again.

"I haven't told him that you've been following me," she said. "But it has to stop. This has gone on long enough, Rainey. Don't contact me again, don't follow me anymore. You need to forget me."

And without a backward glance, she turned and joined her friends at the party.

———

As I drove back to the Loew household that night, something in me changed. For years I had been lost, trying to find myself in alcohol and then searching for comfort in the knowledge that someday I might track my mother down, confront her.

I knew I could never tell anyone about this. It was bad enough to be cast aside once and forgotten. If anyone knew she had rejected me twice,

I wouldn't be able to bear it. The only scrap of dignity I had left was that everyone thought she might have been taken, dragged away from our house against her will. In death there was no betrayal, no humiliation.

By the time I reached the Loew household, I had decided two things: One, that I was never going to tell anyone what had happened, or that I had spent so much time trying to track down a woman who didn't want to be found. And two, that I would never be a victim again.

THIRTY-SEVEN

———⋘⋙———

Even though I hadn't been in the basement freezer for too long, I shivered from the cold and shock. I was having trouble wrapping my mind around what had happened, and what I'd found at the back of the freezer. The rational part of my brain, however, knew I had very little time to figure out what was going on and how to sort out an escape plan.

I glanced at my phone. It was eight P.M. Without hesitating for another moment, I called Blake.

"Blake," I said, doing everything in my power to remain calm. "It's me. I checked the movie times, and I don't think we'll have time for dinner."

There was a long pause on the other end of the phone, and I prayed Blake remembered the protocol.

"I'll pick something up on the way," she said, without a trace of confusion in her voice. *Thank god for Blake.* "What kind of food do you feel like?"

"Thai food. Whatever you want. See you at the theater."

After hanging up, I opened the back of my phone, then removed the SIM card and snapped it in half. I went into the bathroom and flushed the plastic chips down the toilet, knowing this was a superficial measure that would only buy me time. Then I tucked the powered-down phone into my pocket and left the house through the back door, the sound of police sirens staining the otherwise idyllic afternoon.

———

There was an old firebreak trail that led up to Griffith Observatory at the edge of Los Feliz. At a leisurely stroll, someone could get there from Melia's street in less than half an hour. I made it there in fifteen minutes.

The movie theater ploy was something I had come up with after an extremely paranoid client had started bugging our phones and surveilling my team. There were no disastrous consequences from that particular case, but that level of scrutiny had been more than a little alarming, and it had made me realize we needed a way to communicate the need for an emergency meeting without anyone else knowing what we were talking about.

I had spent a month going around the city, compiling a list of locations that would be safe from anyone overhearing our conversation. They ranged from abandoned buildings to defunct cinemas to nature reserves. The ploy was simple: one of us would call another member of the team and deliver the line about going to a movie, and the type of food we specified was linked to a specific location.

Thai food was Griffith Park.

———

As densely populated and overrun as Los Angeles was, there were still wild parts of the city, including Griffith Park. The sprawling expanse of brush and desert soil felt like an anomaly compared to the sections of Los Angeles that bordered it: while Los Feliz was densely forested, with sweeping tree-lined avenues and shady enclaves, Griffith Park was a rolling, mountainous expanse of dusty trails, scrubby canyons, and sparse trees, home to coyotes, deer, and the occasional fox.

The early pioneers must have encountered something similar when they took trains out West from their cities and dead-end towns in the Midwest, traveling out to the dust and the desert with nothing more than hope and crazy, desperate dreams.

I hid in the bushes at the edge of the firebreak until I saw Lola's car pull up and park. I emerged and gave her a faint wave before going over to the car and grabbing Blake's wheelchair from the back. Lola opened the passenger door and lifted Blake out, then lowered her into the chair.

"Okay," Lola said. "Rainey, please explain what the fuck is going on."

I took a deep breath. "Just listen, okay? This is going to sound crazy—it is *completely* crazy—but you have to listen because we don't have much time."

Blake nodded.

"Melia's dead," I said.

"*What?* When—what happened—how?" It was rare for Lola to panic, but she rushed forward and grabbed my shoulders.

"I just need you to listen, *listen* to me, Lo, because it's only a matter of time before the cops find the body." I was numb, and I knew I would panic later, but for now, I felt nothing, blessed nothing. "I've been framed."

Blake and Lola watched me in disbelief as I rushed through what had happened. They both looked stunned and uncomprehending when I finished, though, and I was starting to feel desperate.

"Melia was in the freezer," Lola said slowly. "So . . . who killed her? And when?"

"She's been dead this whole time, Lola," I said, trying to keep the strain from my voice. "That's what I've been trying to tell you."

I took another deep breath.

"The person I met—the person I thought was Melia—was actually someone named Hannah Rothchild." I took out the passports and showed them. "I'm not sure when they killed Melia, or which one actually did the killing. The only thing that matters is that right now, the police are at Slant House, looking for a body, and it's only a matter of time before they come looking for me in connection to the murder."

Understanding dawned on Blake's face. "Holy shit," she said. "Shit. That's . . . I've never heard of anything like that."

"So . . . who's Hannah?" Lola said. "And where is she?"

"Chet was one of the nurses on the rehab ward at St. Agnes," I said. "He freely admitted it. After the murders, Melia was walking around with this huge target on her back. I'm guessing he seduced Melia so she would open up to him. And maybe Hannah, possibly another nurse, had enough of a passing resemblance to Melia to impersonate her."

"But—the scar . . ." Blake looked dazed.

"What would you be willing to do for millions of dollars?" I asked. "Hannah must have done it to herself."

"We're going back to Slant House," Lola said. "If the cops aren't there yet, we'll call them. This can all be explained."

"No, Lo, it *can't*," I said. "Nobody else has seen Hannah this entire time, not close up. She looks almost exactly like Melia, especially from a distance."

"I'm your lawyer. I'll explain everything—"

"You've never met her!" I almost yelled. It was becoming impossible to keep the panic from my voice. "They planned this perfectly. Hannah's gone—*poof!*—just like a ghost, a fucking phantom, and I'm the only one who can prove any of this."

Blake and Lola were both silent. I had never seen them speechless before, and I realized, for the first time, that I was completely alone.

"You have to turn yourself in," Lola said. "It's not too late, Rainey. If you run, you'll look guilty, and we won't be able to help you."

"Listen to yourself," I begged. "It can take up to a year for a case to go to trial, even for an *innocent* person. I can't take that risk, Lo. Hannah will be long gone, and nobody will ever find her. I have to catch her."

Lola finally nodded. Her eyes were glistening with tears. "What are you going to do?" she whispered.

"I'm going to Savannah," I said. "She's not going to stay in Los Angeles, not with the cops everywhere. As soon as they see her, and the scar, I'm halfway free. I have Chet and Hannah's passports, so they can't leave the country. I'm not sure what I need, not yet, but I'll try to find employment records, or something at Melia's aunt's house that connects her to Hannah."

Lola was mulling something over. "How are you going to get to Savannah? You can't fly, obviously."

I had already thought this out and knew of only one option available. "I need you to call Javier for me."

When Lola's car pulled up again, it sat in the darkness for a minute before the engine turned off. It was hard to know how much time had passed, whether it had been ten minutes or three hours. I was starting to feel spooked. Another car slowly rolled up behind Lola's, and I felt my panic shift into overdrive. Anyone could be in the second car. I was on the verge of making a run for it when Lola's door opened.

"It's okay," Lola called softly. "You there? Rai?"

My heart was pounding so fast I felt dizzy. I grabbed my knees, then stood up and slowly peered out from behind a tree to see Lola.

"It's okay," she said, holding her hands up. "It's okay, Rai. It's just us."

"You and Blake?"

"No," she said. "Blake and I decided it would be best for Blake to stay at the office and hold down the fort. It's just me and Javier."

The door of the second car opened, and I squinted to focus on the shadowy form that emerged from behind the headlights. There were heavy footfalls, and I couldn't see anything, but then Javier emerged into the circle of light. His face was creased with concern, and I felt a stab of guilt. If I failed, I was risking Javier's safety as well.

"Javier," I said, stepping forward. "Thank you so much for coming. I—I debated calling you, but I think you're the only one who can help me."

"Of course, Rainey," Javier said, his voice quiet. "We owe you everything we have."

"Let's turn off the lights," Lola said, glancing around her. "We don't want to draw attention to ourselves. Actually, Javier—I think it's best you wait in your car and don't listen to anything I tell Rainey. For your own protection, that is—just in case the police question you."

He looked nervous but took a deep breath and nodded. "Okay, Lola."

Lola waited until Javier had climbed back in his car and killed the headlights.

"Blake's been listening to chatter," Lola said quietly. "There's . . . there's a massive manhunt around the city."

None of this felt real. I was riding high on panic and adrenaline, and my thoughts were cloudy. "That was to be expected," I said, my voice hoarse.

Lola's face was tense. "I explained the situation to Javier—just as much as he needed to know, of course," she added. "That you wanted him to take you to the Los Angeles truck depot and get you on a truck heading toward Atlanta."

"Thanks." I was having trouble keeping up with my thoughts.

"There's some bad news," Lola said, picking at her fingernails. "There was no mention of Chet in any of this. Apparently none of the neighbors saw him come or go—they thought it was just you and Melia. So, for the moment, you're the only suspect."

I swallowed hard and nodded.

"They don't know about Hannah, obviously," Lola went on. "That's good news, in a way, because it means you've got a head start. It won't even occur to the police that you'll be going to hunt them down. They won't be looking for you in Georgia, not yet."

"That's a start." It was hard to feel anything like hope.

"Here's a burner phone," Lola said, placing it in my hand. As I took the phone, she drew me into a bone-crushing hug. "I love you so much,

Rainey. You know that no matter what happens—*no matter what*—I am going to be by your side."

"Thanks, Lo." My voice was muffled, and she finally let me go.

"The phone's turned off to save battery. Get a SIM card when you land in Atlanta, then call me. I'll arrange everything for when you arrive."

"They're going to start monitoring everything," I said. "They'll be watching both of you. Everyone I know."

Lola winked, but the gesture didn't quite work. "You think I don't know how to hide things from the police? Just use the protocol. We'll be fine."

I walked over to Javier's car, and he immediately got out and opened the trunk.

"So?"

"You still have a chance to say no to all this," I told him.

"No, I don't." He gave me a worried smile, then ran a hand through his hair. "You saved our daughter. And now you need help. There is no question that we will help you."

<hr />

It felt like we drove forever. Javier had blankets in the trunk of his car, but I still felt every bump, turn, and stop like I was hanging off the bottom of his car instead of riding inside it. He finally stopped the car and turned off the engine. I heard the sound of his door opening and the dull thud as it snicked back shut. I braced myself, waiting for his footsteps to come around and open the trunk. It sounded, however, like he was moving away from the car. For a very long time after that—five minutes, maybe ten—I heard nothing but the muted sounds of cars in the distance and muffled commotion.

Fear crept in. I didn't know Javier very well, I realized—actually, I didn't know him at all. One of the first things I told all my clients was that it's never possible to fully know anyone, even yourself. People are often shocked at their own capabilities, what they're willing to do for money. Sometimes killers aren't aware of their own psychological deviancy until the body is lying on the floor and the knife is in their hands.

I had been stupid enough to climb in the trunk of a stranger, right when I was the most wanted person in California. What was I worth to the police? Would Javier turn me over right away, or would he lock me away somewhere for a few days, watching the reward money tick up into the hundreds of thousands of dollars?

My heart thumped so hard that I knew I was dipping into the edge of a panic attack. The contours of the trunk seemed suddenly smaller. I couldn't breathe. I couldn't—

There was a soft tapping on the lid of the trunk, and then a whisper. "Rainey," came Javier's soft voice. "I'm back."

The trunk opened a crack, and I could see Javier silhouetted in the sodium glare of a streetlight. He knelt to eye level.

"Hi," he whispered. "I'm sorry I took so long. I just had to set up a ride."

"Javier!" I couldn't seem to catch my breath.

His face creased with concern. "Rainey, what's going on? Are you all right?"

I squeezed my eyes shut. "I'm sorry," I whispered. "I'm sorry, I'm sorry—"

"Are you okay? Are you hurt?"

I couldn't stop myself from crying, then buried my face in my hands. "I didn't know where you were. You were gone for so long, and I thought . . . I don't know what I thought. I'm not sure who I can trust right now."

He took a clean handkerchief from his pocket and pressed it into my hands, then squeezed my shoulder. "Rainey, I'm so sorry," he said. "It was less than ten minutes—I didn't want to leave you here without saying anything, but I needed to make sure nobody was watching."

I wiped my eyes with the handkerchief, which smelled like laundry soap. "I understand."

He smiled, and then looked like he was trying not to laugh. "It's going to be hard to ask you to do this," he said. "But I need you to trust me one more time."

"I trust you."

He shook his head and chuckled. "I know how this looks, believe me," he said, then produced a duffel bag. "At least it's clean."

Climbing into the bag within the confines of the trunk was nearly impossible, but every time I felt like I couldn't bend my legs any further, I reminded myself what was at stake. Javier stood guard over the trunk as I finally got inside, and then he zipped me into the bag and gently lifted me out of the trunk.

Javier had managed to find a friend who was heading out to Jacksonville that night, and after a little convincing, she had agreed to take a bundle through Atlanta first. Javier filled me in on the details as I squirmed into the bag: although a lot of truckers were simply hard-working blue-collar workers, the economy had been hard on many of the contracted employees, and even with union protection, their salaries had been gouged. The workforce was inundated with overeducated people and workers who had been edged out of their own industries, so there were enough drivers around for the bosses to slash salaries. As such, even the most honest drivers were occasionally prone to taking the less-than-legal deal on the side. The periodic delivery of stolen goods or illegal merchandise—and drugs—was a much-needed influx of cash for many of these drivers.

Plausible deniability was a big deal, though, especially with the more illegal deliveries. These were called bundles, Javier explained, and it was an unspoken rule that a driver who agreed to deliver one of these bundles would not ask questions or look inside.

I didn't ask Javier whether I could trust his friend. His answer was irrelevant at that point, and I had no other options.

"She will make one overnight stop to get rest," he said. "With occasional stops for breaks and gasoline. When she leaves, the back door will be left unlocked . . . if you need some air, or . . ."

"A restroom," I provided, and he looked relieved that I had understood the inference.

"When you are in Atlanta, she will leave the truck to get breakfast," he explained. "The cab will be left unlocked for you to leave. Do so carefully, when no one is watching."

Once he had helped me get situated in the compartment behind the driver's side, he unzipped the top of the bag and handed me a soft canvas bag.

"Food," he said. "For the journey. Lola put an envelope of cash in there too."

"Javier . . . I can never thank you enough for this," I said, suddenly feeling that words were completely inadequate.

"Take care of yourself, Rainey," he said, putting a hand on my shoulder. "We will all be praying for you."

THIRTY-EIGHT

⠶⠶⠶

The trip from Los Angeles to Atlanta was more than forty hours, including breaks. I didn't feel like I slept at all, but there were moments when pictures and faces surfaced or lingered on the periphery of my imagination—words, thoughts, and events that hadn't occurred—and I realized they were fragments of dreams. Then I would shake myself awake. I had unzipped the top of the duffel bag to get some air and could see fractured bits of scenery: cities that yielded to plains, mountains that collapsed into rivers and suburban sprawl. Darkness expired into daylight, unrelenting white light that filtered into the cabin. I lost track of time, and since my burner phone was turned off, I didn't have a way to orient myself.

At long last the truck stopped in Atlanta. I woke after a nap to see that we were surrounded by trucks at an enormous depot, with warehouses and a long fueling station visible from the window. There was no sign of the driver. I sat up and looked around—no other truck drivers were nearby. I gathered my things and pulled my hair up under the hood of my sweatshirt, then climbed down from the cab.

Nobody stopped me as I left the depot and made my way to a cheap electronics store, where I bought a SIM card. I had memorized Blake's and Lola's phone numbers a long time ago, and as soon as I had inserted the SIM into my phone, I called Blake's unlisted burner phone, watching my surroundings as I waited for her to pick up.

"Yes."

"I'll be home soon," I said. "You need me to pick up any groceries?"

There was a pause, then: "Hey, Mom."

"Hey," I said. "Got in safe."

"Great," Blake said. "I booked a car for you in the first city. There's a room waiting for you in the final city. I'll send the information through when I can."

I knew Blake always operated with an abundance of caution, so that even if nobody was listening in (and the police almost assuredly *were* listening in, in some capacity), she would disguise the specifics of Atlanta and Savannah.

When I found an open Wi-Fi network, I checked my hidden email account and found an encrypted message from Blake.

> *Car booked for you at rental in first city—address attached. Remote pickup possible—scan the code in the parking lot and the key will be released from a lockbox.*
>
> *Likewise with room in final city—remote check-in guaranteed. Address below; key code to enter home is 42562.*
>
> *Call when possible.*

I felt nervous as I took a bus across town, toward the address of the car rental facility. I was able to follow Blake's instructions and pick up the car without interacting with anyone, and soon I was on the highway heading southeast, toward Savannah.

The townhouse Blake had rented for me was in the historic district. A small plaque next to the front door explained the place had once been the home of Jacques Lapin, an eighteenth-century rumrunner from France who had been accepted into Savannah's aristocratic society. The townhouse was spacious with brick walls, dark wooden floorboards, and a claw-footed bathtub. I didn't have time to enjoy any of it though. After taking a shower and getting dressed, I tucked my hair up under a hat and pulled on some sunglasses, then headed to the library.

I knew Belinda Harris, Melia's aunt, lived in a historic plantation house, but I didn't know the name of it. After a few futile searches on my phone, I had realized that a better resource might be the historic section of the library. Blake would have been able to help me within about five minutes, but I didn't want to risk contacting her; there was too great a chance she was being surveilled.

The library had a wealth of information on old plantations around the area, and after taking a stack of books into a quiet corner of an unoccupied room, I began to flip through them.

It didn't take long to find what I was looking for. The Harris family, it turned out, was almost as old as the van Austs, and the estate in question was a sprawling property about thirty minutes outside Savannah.

Tallowood. I ran my finger along the iron letters in the photo of the front gate, and a chill went down my spine. The Harris family, I read, had lived in Savannah since the 1700s, owning slaves and fighting on the side of the Confederate Army during the Civil War. The property was stunning, all jewel greens and verdant undergrowth. The house itself sat at the end of a long, pebbled driveway lined with live oak and Spanish moss.

Unlike other former plantations, Tallowood was still a private family home, and they had no visiting hours. The address, however, was printed in the book, and I copied it down in my notes.

I should have left the library then, headed out to Taliowood and whatever fate awaited me at the old plantation. Instead, I lingered to do something very stupid. After glancing around to make sure nobody was watching me, I went to a computer and opened the internet, then went to the *New York Times*.

It was so much worse than I had expected. A picture of me was on the homepage of the news site, under the banner: FORMER VIOLIN PRODIGY WANTED IN CONNECTION WITH VAN AUST MURDER.

It had been foolish of me—*so foolish*—to forget that my former fame would catch up with me, and to forget that my connection with the van Aust tragedy would make inevitable front-page news. In spite of my better instincts, I clicked on the article and began reading.

In the span of a day and a half, they had found everything I wanted to keep hidden. The article went into a quick backstory on how I had founded Left City with Blake and Lola, then divulged my past failures, including my romantic relationship with Calvin. The woman who wrote the article had found out about the restraining order I had against him, about his legions of rabid fans online, and about all the money he had stolen from his family.

Sickened, I read on. There was mention of my missing mother, my father's retreat from fame following the death of his mother, and my own struggles with substance abuse.

Thinking it couldn't possibly get worse, I read on. The journalist had spoken to Janine, who described me as a "raging, vengeful lesbian" who interfered with the peace and sense of neighborhood community.

"I knew Rainey was wicked and full of hate when I laid eyes on her," Janine was quoted as saying, "but I didn't know she was *that* evil."

The article ended with a quote from Katsumi Endo. His words were more restrained, but I still read animosity between the lines.

"I've known Melia since she was born," he said. "I'll never forgive myself for failing to protect her from this. I'll never stop wondering why I didn't do more."

THIRTY-NINE

I didn't head back to my lodgings before going to visit Tallowood. As the stately old buildings of the city slowly gave way to tenement housing and then countryside, I rolled down my windows and let the summer air wash through the car. Everything seemed more alive here, more sinister. It seemed like you could fall asleep in the weeds on the side of the road and slowly the ground would grow over you in the form of creeper vines and marsh sedge.

It was twilight, shortly past seven o'clock, but the sun didn't seem to be descending any further in the sky: if anything, the ambient light seemed static, like it was trapped in a thick honey sap that filtered the sky. Gradually the buildings disappeared altogether, and my map indicated I was near the edge of the plantation.

Tallowood was five hundred acres of untouched Georgia land. I had read that many of the trees were older than the defeated South; they had survived the musket balls and hiding soldiers during the Civil War. Tallowood had its own private cemetery too—a detail that had given me chills. The dead here were almost as old as the city of Savannah, and they included buccaneers and priests among their lot. A high brick wall appeared on the road ahead of me, and as I followed it along, it gradually revealed an enormous wrought-iron gate.

From the outside, it didn't look like Tallowood had changed much in the last two hundred years. There were no modern security advancements, no locked gate or keypad to buzz the main house, no cameras trained on the drive. After considering my options for a minute, I drove past the estate and parked down a little rural road designated only with a state census sign.

The day's heat had melted into something milder; I only started to sweat a little bit as I walked back along the main road toward the old estate. I hadn't seen or heard any cars or other signs of life since I had departed the edge of Savannah, a fact for which I was grateful. Fewer prying eyes meant a smaller chance of someone seeing me walk up to the estate, but also a smaller chance that Belinda had friends who might drop in at a moment's notice.

The walls outside the old plantation were crumbling under layers of ivy, and the property was dotted with old-growth trees dripping with Spanish moss. Sweat trickled down my neck as I skirted the long road leading into the heart of the property, which was lined with a regiment of old trees. The evening light filtered in through the dense canopy formed above.

Four cars were parked next to the house. One of them was scarcely more than a rusted hull of a thing, missing two tires. Next to that was a stately old Mercedes, then two modest sedans. I wrote down the license plates of the three functional cars, then skirted around the back of the house.

A long, low living room stretched the length of the house. French doors offered me a good view of what was going on inside: old couches with floral upholstery squatted in front of a small, old-fashioned television, which looked like it was tuned to a news station. I ducked behind a low brick wall on the terrace as a tired-looking woman in nurses' scrubs entered the room and walked over to the couch, picked up a purse, and started rooting around in it.

I sat there watching her for five minutes before she exited the French doors and stepped onto the patio, only a few feet from where I hid. The nurse took a pack of cigarettes out of her pocket and put one in her mouth, lit it, and leaned back against the wall, inhaling. I could smell the sweet scent of burning tobacco.

The woman had been out there for less than a minute before the door banged open behind her.

"*Hssst!* You, Debra! I told you already—no smoking!" The second woman's voice was angry. She sounded French.

"I'm on break," the nurse protested.

"You will not smoke anywhere near the windows!" the French woman snapped. "I have told you the smoke irritates Belinda."

There was a moment of silence, and then the nurse—Debra, I could only assume—spoke again.

"Yeah, whatever." I could hear the sound of a cigarette being ground out on the bricks.

"Pick it up. You do not leave rubbish here."

Debra sighed, and the French woman must have left again, because I heard the doors opening and closing.

"Bitch," Debra muttered.

I waited until I heard Debra sigh once more and return through the French doors. Then I peered over the low wall. I could see her through the living room window. She had her back to me and appeared to be craning her head around, listening for something.

She remained like this for another minute, and then she moved over to a large sideboard that stretched along one wall. She glanced around again and removed something from the top of the sideboard—I couldn't make it out, only that it was small and looked to be made of gold—then stashed it in her purse and walked out of the room.

—⊷⊶—

I didn't need to run the license plates on the cars to find out which one belonged to the nurse. After slipping out of the backyard and making my way out by the cars, I peered into both sedans. The first one, a white Honda, was immaculate on the interior. The second one, an old maroon Buick that looked like it might be from the nineties, bore all the detritus of an owner who spent most of their life on the road. There were about a dozen old takeaway coffee cups from McDonald's, scrunchies and long strands of hair around the gear shift, coins scattered haphazardly around the seat wells, a couple magazines and crumpled romance novels, and a beach towel on the backseat. A lanyard with an ID badge hung around the rearview mirror, and I could just make out a photo of the beleaguered nurse on the plastic. *Bingo.*

I returned to my car and waited over an hour for the Buick to make an appearance. Just as I was starting to blink back sleep from all the hours on the road, my patience finally paid off. The nurse's car shot past me, heading back toward Savannah, going well over the speed limit. I waited until her headlights winked around the corner before I did a hasty U-turn and followed her into town.

The swampy backroads gradually transformed into wide, tree-lined boulevards as I followed the nurse into downtown Savannah. The little shacks and sparse neighborhoods around the edge of the city were replaced by stately mansions, cobbled streets, fountains, and old hotels dripping with light. The nurse finally screeched to a halt on a street near the waterfront, which was lined with hotels and busy restaurants. I wasn't concerned that she had noticed me following her—I had never seen anyone drive so erratically, occupied as she was with her cell phone—but just to be safe, I parked a few spots ahead of her and then waited for her to leave her car.

I watched in my rearview mirror as the nurse shimmied out of the top of her scrubs, snapping a sleeveless dress over her shoulders as she did so. Glancing around to see if anyone was watching, she unscrewed a small bottle of vodka and chugged half of it. She grabbed a can of aerosol deodorant, gave herself a quick once-over before checking her makeup, and then climbed out of the car.

She chucked her work shoes into the back seat, then produced a pair of high heels and leaned against the hood of the car as she strapped them on. Giving her hair one final bounce, she stalked toward one of the bars and disappeared inside.

I didn't have a plan yet, but the skeleton of one was appearing in my mind.

Five minutes after Debra had gone into the bar, I left my car and slipped inside after her. The bar was packed, and for a moment I worried about losing Debra. In one corner, a lively blues trio played a piece that had the crowd in a frenzy. I watched the trumpet player stand up and take a solo, a glaze of sweat illuminating her brow. The people near the stage swayed and snapped their fingers to the beat. Patrons at the bar were three deep, shouting out orders to a staff of three bartenders.

I caught sight of Debra coming out of the bathroom. The purse I had seen her rifling through at Tallowood was slung over her shoulder. She grinned as she made her way toward a booth of women. They screamed in excitement and started dancing in their seats as she got closer. By the look of things, they were already a few drinks in. As soon as Debra got near, two of them leaped up and gave her sloppy hugs, sloshing their drinks against her. She slid into the booth next to them, tucking her purse at her feet.

I didn't even have to feign subtlety to get close to them, the room was that packed. I leaned against the edge of their booth and listened into their conversation while pretending to nod my head along to the music of the band.

"Girl, you're late! We were about to send out a search party!" one of Debra's friends exclaimed.

"Don't get me started," Debra replied, raising her voice over the music. "Belinda thought someone was in the house and wouldn't let me leave the kitchen! I swear to god, sometimes I'm tempted to mix a little Pramipexole in with her orange juice."

They all laughed, and the chatter turned pharmaceutical. I guessed they were all in the medical profession in some capacity, which was probably how they knew each other.

"When are you gonna quit working for that dumbass bitch?" one of the women asked. "You know Helping Hands doesn't pay you enough to put up with those long hours."

"The market's oversaturated," Debra replied. "I swear to god, though, she's canceled my shifts like, three times this month. She's got this bitchy maid, right? Laura? Treats her like a nurse. They're so codependent they basically sleep in the same bed."

"Doesn't she have to pay you if she cancels the shift last minute?"

"Good luck prying a quarter from that woman's cold, dead hands!" Debra laughed. "Whatever, ladies—my shift starts at six P.M. tomorrow, so right now I'm getting drunk."

It never ceased to amaze me how invisible most people felt, to the point where they would openly discuss details of their lives out in the open without ever once considering the possibility that someone nearby could be taking mental notes. Everything they had said so far was fairly innocuous taken out of context, but I was close to getting enough information for what I needed. Close, but not quite there yet.

"I'm gonna get us some more drinks!" Debra said, standing up.

"No, no," one of her friends protested. "It's my turn."

"It's okay," Debra said in a mock conspiratorial tone. "I can afford it."

"You get a raise recently?"

"Why do you think I've stayed working for that pickled bitch for so long?" Debra leaned on the table. "It's not like she notices when one or two of those dusty old antiques goes missing."

There was a hushed silence, and then a loud burst of laughter.

"Do . . . not . . . tell me," one of the women said. "Have you been taking things from her house?"

"Benefits of having a big purse," Debra said. "I've started locking it because I swear I caught that French bitch going through my bag once."

I waited until Debra was near the bar before I started following her. The excess caution was probably unnecessary; the alcohol had already gone to her head. She leaned on the bar and ordered four Aperol spritzes.

"Put it on my tab!" she told the bartender.

"Name?" he asked.

"Debra Heller. Add a nice tip for yourself."

Instead of following her back to the table, I stepped outside, pulled out my phone, and looked up the number for Helping Hands. The main offices were closed, but there was a late-night number. I dialed it and waited.

"Helping Hands, how may I assist you?" came a sweet drawl.

"Hi there," I said. "I work for Belinda Harris, and unfortunately she's going to have to go out of town tomorrow. I know we had Debra Heller scheduled to come in tomorrow, but I can't seem to find her phone number."

I listened as the woman typed something in.

"That's right, I have her down for tomorrow," she said. "Would you like me to call her and cancel?"

"No, please, I'd like to do it," I said. "Belinda feels so bad because she's already canceled three times this month. We'd also like to work out a better schedule so there aren't so many last-minute cancelations."

"Of course, honey," the woman said. "I'll give you her number."

I wrote the number down and thanked the woman. I felt a twinge of guilt and hesitated when I thought about what I was about to do, but if Debra was stealing things from Tallowood to fund her nightlife, it probably wasn't too unethical for me to lie.

FORTY

———

I waited until the next morning to carry out my plan. I didn't want to contact Debra that night while she was still drunk, because that could backfire in a major way. Instead, I went back to my rented townhouse and tried to get some rest. I couldn't keep my eyes closed for longer than an hour at a time, so my night was full of tossing, turning, and fractured slumber.

The air was hot, resentful, and I glanced out the window to see an infected sky. Deep gray veins throbbed against the belly of clouds that hung over the horizon, and the sun bore an unhealthy, yellow tinge. I hadn't really slept since before leaving Los Angeles. I was too wired to be exhausted, and when I remembered what the day ahead held, I felt a knot of anxiety in the pit of my stomach.

A part of me dreaded contacting Debra, but I reminded myself that she wasn't exactly a stellar employee. I found her number and entered it into my phone, then composed a quick text. I hoped she might be hungover enough to ignore any small warning signs that I wasn't who I was pretending to be.

> *Hi Debra, I'm a legal consultant for Belinda Harris. Our team is here to do a cursory disbursement assessment, and we have noticed that some of her more valuable antiques are missing. A member of staff indicated that you may have some knowledge of their whereabouts.*

I sent the text and waited. Three dots appeared on the left of the screen, indicating that Debra was composing a reply. It was shortly past seven in the morning, and I knew from my own personal experience of abusing alcohol that she was probably not in any kind of mental space to deal with this kind of accusation.

A text came through a moment later.

DEBRA: *No idea what your talking abt.*

A moment later—

DEBRA: **youre.*

I sat down, thinking of how to respond. It was only natural that she would deny knowledge; I would have been caught off guard if she had offered to come in and turn the items over.

> *Maybe I wasn't clear. One of Belinda's most trusted staff said she saw you snooping through rooms where you didn't belong. That you carried a large black purse around and were in the habit of locking it. We suspect you might have stolen the missing items.*

The response came through immediately.

DEBRA: *It was Laura wasn't it? Laura told you? Caught her going through my bag that's why I lock it I have every right to privacy.*

I mused over what to say.

> *Your right to privacy was never in question. Disclosure of the identity of the staff member in question will not be possible. We will come to*

your house either today or tomorrow to have a frank discussion about
the missing items.

Debra's text came through almost immediately.

DEBRA: *I quit, so.*

I smiled and slipped my phone back into my bag. *Almost too easy.* The oblique timeline would give me enough room to get in, get out, and move on. If Debra had caught on to my ruse by tomorrow and decided to resume her job at Tallowood, it wouldn't matter; I would already be gone.

The only things I needed were cheap scrubs and a name badge.

As it turned out, I was able to find both at the Walmart at the edge of town. I couldn't remember the last time I had been in a Walmart: I couldn't even be sure we had them in Los Angeles, even though it was a big city. It was the type of place I tended to avoid at all costs, because fluorescent lights and frantic crowds gave me anxiety.

I was surprised, therefore, when I walked through the door of Walmart and felt something akin to excitement. Everything was so *cheap*. And there was so *much* of it. I grabbed a shopping cart and headed toward the uniform aisle, where I tossed in a pair of mint-colored scrubs for a whopping total of ten dollars. I grabbed some sensible shoes for another five dollars, then meandered over to the snack aisle and tossed in a bucket of Red Vines, a turbo-sized bag of pretzel chips, chocolate-covered almonds, watermelon Sour Patch Kids, and a jumbo bag of fun-sized Snickers. I had to stop myself from wandering into the center of the store and stocking up on all kinds of shit I didn't need, like candles and fuzzy socks.

The photo center was run by a bored-looking teenage boy who was messing around on his phone.

"Morning," I said, edging up to the counter. I glanced at the laminated menu of options on the counter, then tapped on the name badge. "I need one of those with my photo on it. The clip-on kind that can be pinned to a shirt."

"No problem," he said. "Name?"

"Sarah Matthews." I had rehearsed saying the fake name all day.

"I have to inform you that Walmart isn't authorized to make official modes of identification like you might need for flights and gun licenses and all that," he droned. "This is not an official license printing location."

"Understood," I said.

He typed something into the computer and showed me. "That's what your badge'll look like," he said. "Spelled your name right?"

"That's right."

He nodded. "Stand against that white wall and face the camera."

I found the number for Tallowood listed online and hoped the landline was still connected. Based on what I had seen the day before, I felt pretty confident it would be.

The phone rang three times before it was snatched off the hook.

"You've reached Tallowood," came the irritated French accent. "Yes?"

I nearly fumbled, having forgotten the name of the home care company that Debra worked for.

"*Yes?*"

"Hello," I said, startled. The name had just come back to me. "I work at Helping Hands, and unfortunately, Debra Heller has called in sick."

"Ah, *putain. Mais bien sur.*"

I cleared my throat. "We've arranged a highly skilled replacement, someone who has worked with us for years. We'll send her over, if that's all right."

"Yes, send her immediately. Belinda will need someone to look after her as soon as possible."

She hung up without saying anything else.

FORTY-ONE

My heart was in my chest as I left Savannah, winding down the backroads toward Tallowood. I had already broken the law in so many ways that even if I did manage to track down Hannah—and then catch her, and then prove that *she* had killed Melia—my life was probably ruined. I would never be able to work as a private investigator again; that much was guaranteed. My career was fucked, and if I didn't get caught soon, I was going to end up dragging other people into my mess.

Tallowood was almost lovely in the early evening light. Fireflies bopped around the garden, illuminating the path of trees to the house. I parked where I had seen Debra's car the day before, immensely grateful that my convoluted lie had worked and her car was not there.

The front door flew open before I could even ring the bell, and a young woman with limp hair and bad skin stood scowling at me. Her eyes were almost too big for her face.

"You're late!" she hissed, and I realized I was looking at Laura, the French woman I had spoken to on the phone. If Debra had been telling the truth about Laura going through her bag, then she was probably someone I would have to keep my eye on. I started to protest as Laura yanked me inside, then gave me a quick appraisal.

"You leave your bag in there," Laura said, indicating a hall closet. "Do you have a cell phone?"

"No," I said.

Laura stared at me in disbelief. "You don't have a *cell* phone? Everyone has a cell phone."

"Mine broke."

"Well. No cell phones allowed during your shift. If I catch you using a phone, I will remove it from you."

I cleared my throat. "They didn't tell me what kind of care Belinda needs," I said. "What do you want me to do?"

"She has digestion problems, and her doctor has her on supplements. Every night at nine, she gets a vitamin injection. I assume they informed you about her opioid dependency?"

I blinked.

Laura gave a loud, annoyed sigh. *"Qu'est-ce qu'il veux, ces cretins? Merde. Alors,"* she said, turning back to me. "She takes pills to combat a prior dependency, which she has been cured of for a long time. Understand? Is that a problem?"

"No, of course not."

I followed Laura down the dim hallway, through the dining room, toward the back of the house. We emerged into the living room.

A woman with wispy blond hair and bad posture was hunched before the television I had noticed the day before. The woman wore a quilted robe over pajamas. Her body listed forward, as though she were about to fall asleep, but her face was transfixed on the screen. One hand gripped the wooden armrest, while the other made periodic dips into a bowl of nuts beside her.

I hovered at the edge of the room.

"Candice?" Belinda warbled. "Candice, come here."

I glanced at Laura.

"That's you," Laura snapped. "Go on, see what she needs."

"My name is Sarah."

"You think anyone cares what your name is? She needs help."

"But—"

Laura pinched my arm—hard. "Ow!"

"Get in there," she said through gritted teeth. "Or you're not getting paid for tonight."

I crossed the room and lingered behind the couch.

"Candice, don't make me wait!" Belinda looked up at me with frightened, childish eyes. "I need my medicine."

"Certainly, ma'am."

I crossed to the back counter and scanned the list of medicines. Once again, Laura appeared at my elbow.

"Are you stupid? How long have you been working at Helping Hands? She doesn't want actual medicine, she wants this."

She removed a bottle of whiskey from a high shelf and plopped it down next to me. "Water it down and stay there to make sure she doesn't drop it."

"You're giving *alcohol* to a drug addict?"

She sneered at me. "Have you ever seen a drug addict go through withdrawal symptoms?"

When she could finally see that I wasn't going to pour the alcohol, she sighed impatiently and snatched the bottle, then splashed some into a glass. She topped it up with water and pressed it into my hand.

"You seem capable of doing all this," I muttered. "So why do you need me?"

"I'm asking myself the same question," she hissed.

I finally took the glass over to Belinda. Before I could lean down and hand it to her, she latched onto my wrist with more strength than I would have thought possible. With the other hand, she took the glass and emptied it in one gulp.

"Oh, Candice, that was all water! You're not fooling me with that again—give me more! Right now!"

Laura stood against the counter, arms folded across her chest. She smirked as I came over and poured another glass of watered-down whiskey.

Once more, Belinda snatched it out of my hands and drank it in one long draft.

"That's better. Stay and watch the show with me, Candice. It's our favorite—look!"

I turned my attention to the television. It looked like a rerun of some campy old soap opera. A woman in frills and eighties hair stood by a window, watching a limousine pull up the drive.

"Just like the old days," Belinda said, leaning back into her chair.

I waited until Belinda had fallen asleep before I stood from the couch, taking care not to make too much noise. Laura had disappeared into the house, and there was no way of telling where she had gone. I stood in the living room for a minute, listening for any errant sounds, then made my way back to the front of the house, where I had seen a staircase to the second floor.

Time was running out, and I knew it might be only a matter of hours before all hope was lost. Still, I wasn't ready to throw in the towel yet, and I hoped to find something at Tallowood that could give me some indication of who Hannah really was, and where I could find her.

The first two bedrooms upstairs were filled with junk: broken fans, piles of linen, moldy boxes of books and magazines. There was a spacious bathroom, then another set of doors. I held my breath, hoping Laura wasn't inside, then opened the door in front of me.

Slats of moonlight fell onto the hardwood floor. This bedroom was tidier than the others, and I could see at once that its inhabitant was female. A cream-colored quilt decorated with tiny flowers covered the bed, and stuffed animals were perched among the pillows. There were movie posters pinned up to the walls, alongside brackets holding jewelry.

There were two more rooms at this end of the hall, and the one next to this room was clearly occupied; under the door, a light was on. As I stood there, a shadow passed over the door. Laura was probably inside. I ducked into the room next to Laura's and quietly closed the door behind me.

Something was stale about the bedroom. It smelled of disuse. I moved to the bed and ran my hands around and under the mattress, then tore the sheets off the bed. Nothing out of place. I went to the wall of photographs and saw photos of a younger Melia, pale iterations of the person I thought I had known. The resemblance between Hannah and Melia was remarkable, but once you took away the distinctive features—the scar, the dark hair, the pale skin—they were obviously different people.

There was nothing under the rug, or behind the paintings, or behind the curtains. I even stuck my hand up the fireplace, hoping I might find something. I sat down on the bed and closed my eyes, thinking, screwing up my face in concentration. The thing that came back to me was the image of the handwriting inside Jasper's closet (*Melia melia melia melia MELIA MELIA Melia Melia MELIA MELIA*). I opened my eyes, stood up, and walked to the closet.

A single light bulb hung down, illuminating racks of clothing. I stepped into the closet and turned around, facing the doorway. Taped above the doorframe was a manila envelope, fat and creased. I jumped up and grabbed it.

The envelope had been handled so many times that the paper was soft. Inside were dozens of letters, some in envelopes, some without. I pulled one out and scanned it.

I immediately recognized the handwriting, the same careful scrawl from that first threatening letter I'd seen at Slant House.

> *I will never forget you—nobody knows you the way that I do. I need you, Melia. Nobody else matters.*

I stuffed the letter back, then pulled out a white envelope. It had been addressed to Melia. The return address had no name, but I didn't need a name, just the address. I tucked the envelope into my pocket in case I needed it later.

When I went to retrieve my bag so I could slip out and leave this house of horrors, I found Laura standing over my bag. Her shoulders were hunched around her ears, and she had a furtive, desperate look. Her hands were methodically going through my purse.

At first I was so stunned that I could only stare. She stiffened, then jerked toward me, yanking her hands out of my bag. She tucked a strand of hair behind her ear and faced me with a blank look.

"Were you . . . were you just going through my bag?"

She gave an unconvincing laugh, but her face flushed. "Of course not."

"I . . . I *saw* you. Your hands were *in* my bag." For some reason heat spread through my neck, as though I should be embarrassed for even asking.

"What would I want in *your* bag?" she spat.

"I have no fucking idea," I said. "Let's let Belinda sort this out."

It was a bluff, but it worked.

She grabbed my arm. "I just wanted to check something," she said, then gave an unconvincing laugh. "It's fine. My mistake."

I jerked my arm away and grabbed her wrist hard enough to make her wince. "This is some kind of power game with you," I said. "You probably do it with all the staff—go through their things, make sure they're not stealing anything. If you find anything, you find some way to let Belinda know she can't trust anyone but you. Is that it?"

She stared at me with flat, hateful eyes. I wanted so badly to let her go, grab my things, and leave, but there was a chance she had seen too much. She might have seen my wallet, my ID, which in a very short time would let her know I was a fugitive. She could have also seen Hannah's passport.

I couldn't let her go.

"Come with me," I hissed, jerking her down the hall toward the entrance. She struggled, but I was much stronger. I was also much angrier.

I opened the coat closet and yanked her inside. She stifled a scream, then started to yell. I clapped a hand over her mouth, and she bit me. I used one of my elbows to hit her in the stomach, trying not to hit harder than was necessary. She let out an *oof!* as all the air left her lungs, then she dropped to her knees. I climbed on top of her and grabbed a trench coat from the rack above me. I loosened the belt from its loops and quickly tied her wrists together.

She struggled beneath me, her face going mottled purple.

"Don't make a sound, or I'll hit your face next," I hissed. I didn't want to hurt her, but something about her sycophantic and duplicitous nature made my stomach turn. I wondered how many of Belinda's nurses had endured her tyranny.

After I had tied Laura's wrists, I glanced around the closet for something to gag her with. The coat closet was just as messy and chaotic as the rest of the house—full of coats, scarves, shoes, and odd knickknacks. I grabbed a necktie and wadded it up, then tried to open Laura's mouth. Her jaw was clamped shut.

"Really? *Really?*"

I held her nose shut until her face started going purple. She finally opened her mouth, gasping for breath, and I shoved the tie inside, then used a loose shoelace to tie it around her head.

As much as I disliked Laura, when I saw her face dissolve into panic, I couldn't help but pity her.

"I don't want to hurt you," I said. "You had to stick your nose in. You *had* to get in my way. I can't let you slow me down."

Her eyes bulged and spun in their sockets.

"You're having a panic attack," I said, trying to calm her down. "That's it. It's one of the worst feelings, but that's all it is—I promise. At worst, you'll pass out and your breathing will return to normal. Well, mostly normal. Just think calming thoughts. Someone will be here soon enough to let you out."

I slipped out of the coat closet and down the hall.

"You may remember the tragedy that befell her family a little over four years ago," came a voice from the other room. *"On Monday police discovered the body of Melia van Aust in the basement of her family home. Police are on a nationwide manhunt for this woman. She is believed to be armed and extremely dangerous."*

The words traveled up my spine and settled somewhere at the base of my neck in a low, throbbing pain. I should run—I knew that in every part of my body—but I had to look. I had to know.

I tiptoed back down the hall and stood in the doorway of the kitchen. The static in my brain had become so loud that it all but drowned out the voice of the news anchor whose job it was to read the grim pronouncement. Belinda's back faced the kitchen door, while her front was trained on the small television. It was impossible to tell if she was still asleep or if she had woken up again to see my face, *my face*, blown up on the television with a phone number beneath it that you could call with information.

"A reward of one hundred thousand dollars is being offered for informa-tion leading to an arrest," the anchor went on.

I stayed there for ten more seconds before I had the wherewithal to turn and run down the hall toward the back of the house, through the garden, and out the verandah. I couldn't breathe, couldn't think. It was over.

I stumbled, nearly tripping over a tree root in my quest to reach my car. I was almost there, almost. I dug in my bag, looking for my car keys, hoping against hope that I could get to Hannah's house and find her before I was apprehended.

There were footsteps behind me, and then someone laughed in disbelief.

"Rainey Hall," came a male voice. "I thought I might find you here."

FORTY-TWO

—⊶⊷—

"Turn around—slowly. Hands where I can see them."

Shit, shit, shit.

I put my hands on my head and turned around to see a man pointing a gun at me. He wore a baseball hat and dark clothing. The darkness and distance obscured his features. My first thought was that Calvin had found me, but that thought was quickly dispelled: I would have recognized Calvin's voice, for one, and this man was more heavyset than Calvin. He must be one of Belinda's staff, I realized, with a sinking feeling. Or maybe someone who had seen me at the library, or even the car rental place. I had been discovered. I was going to jail.

He reached into his pocket, still keeping the gun trained on me. A pair of handcuffs glinted in the moonlight. He tossed them to the grass at my feet. As he glanced up, I saw his face.

"Put those on."

"I know you," I said suddenly.

"Slowly," he cautioned. "No sudden moves or I'll shoot you in the leg."

"Dane," I said. "Your name is Dane Bradley."

He looked surprised to hear his name, but he didn't pause for too long. "The cuffs. *Now.*"

I bent down to pick up the handcuffs, not taking my eyes off him. My brain was working rapidly, trying to find which angle I should use.

"I'm impressed," I said. "They said it couldn't be done."

His face was impassive.

"They were wrong about you. Maybe you should still be a cop. You're clearly good at this."

Dane chuckled. "Nice try, sweetheart. You know nothing about me."

"More than you think," I said, fingering the cuffs. "I know why you were kicked off the police force three years before retirement."

I had caught him off guard, but he recovered quickly.

"I said," he growled quietly, glancing back at the house. "Put on the goddamn cuffs."

I slowly closed one half of the handcuffs over my left wrist. "Did you get what you were looking for?"

"What's that?"

"You've been following me for weeks."

"Not bad," he said. "I guess that's why people pay you to track down their cheating husbands."

"Why follow me? What were you hoping to find?"

"The cuffs. I'm not going to tell you again." The gun was still trained on me.

"You're not going to shoot me," I said quickly. "We're too close to the house. They'll hear you right away and call the police. Unless you plan on dragging my body off the property, but that's a long way."

He laughed. My bluff hadn't worked. "The only people in that house are a deaf old lady and a maid. Nobody would even hear me over the racket from that television."

I quickly weighed the pros and cons of making a run for it. The grounds around Tallowood were slightly overgrown, with tall grass waving in the moonlight, which could be either a help or a hindrance. Unkempt meant more places to hide, but also more potential obstacles to trip on.

Dane aimed at the ground near my feet and pulled the trigger. I stumbled backward in shock as a big clump of dirt exploded next to me. The ringing in my ears was compounded by my thumping heart.

"Now!"

I slipped the other cuff over my right wrist and held out my arms, trembling, for his inspection. I could feel myself on the verge of a panic attack. Guns had been aimed at me before; I had heard bullets go off nearby. Never had I felt quite so vulnerable as I did at that moment, however. I was far from home, with federal charges hanging over my head, and a man was pointing a gun at me. I started to shake uncontrollably.

He saw this and scoffed. "I'm not going to kill you," he said. "We're in the same line of work, actually."

"Why are you following me?"

"Your ex hired me to keep tabs."

I blinked at him.

"Calvin Hurley. Ring any bells?"

"For *fuck's* sake," I hissed. "Calvin hired you?"

"Yep. Seems like kind of a creep, if you ask me, but he paid me good money."

"So—so it had nothing to do with the van Aust case?"

"Nope. I'm not a cop anymore, told you that. I became a PI a few years back."

I shook my wrists at him. "What does this have to do with Calvin?"

"Nothing," he said. "But the moment they put the news out about you, I knew there would be a reward."

"And how did you . . . how did you find me?"

He tapped the edge of his nose. "Tricks of the trade."

"You might as well tell me. I'm fucked, aren't I?"

He sighed. "I was at your house, the one on Mulholland," he said.

A chill went down my spine. I must have really been off my game the last few days if I hadn't even suspected him of following me then.

"You left in a big hurry a few nights ago, so I followed you to that house on Willow Glen. Melia's place. Saw a couple of kids leave in a big hurry, then I followed you to Griffith Park. I heard the whole thing. Where you were going and everything. It only took me a day or two to piece together why you'd be going to Georgia. Guess I got lucky."

"If you overheard our meeting at the park," I said, through gritted teeth, "you know I didn't kill Melia. This whole thing is a setup."

"I don't have a horse in this race," he said. "Let's get a move on. I already called the local police and told them I was bringing you in."

As we walked across the overgrown gardens toward the edge of the property, I imagined what Lola and Blake would do once I was in jail. I hoped they would continue the agency without me. It was possible they would have to rename it after everything with this case. And then, as much as I didn't want to, I thought of my mother.

Melia van Aust was big news, and once this story broke in all its complexity, it would be on newspapers all around the world. I didn't know if my mother was still in Los Angeles—in some ways, I hoped she was long gone from California—but regardless of where she had ended up, she was bound to see this story. I wondered if she would feel shame, or if her connection to me had been severed so long ago that she would feel nothing more than benign curiosity at the unfolding scandal.

There were quick steps behind me, then a gasp, and the sound of something wet. *"Huuuurrrrrrrfffff!"*

I whirled and saw Dane fall to his knees, a shocked expression on his face. He still held the gun, but as I watched, his muscles first contracted and then relaxed. The gun fell from his hand. He was still watching me, but his eyes had gone vacant.

"Dane?"

His mouth hung slack, and a rivulet of blood appeared at the corner of his mouth. "What the . . . ?"

There was a moment of silence, and then Dane collapsed face-first into the dirt. I hesitated, but only for a moment. I started toward Dane's prone body, hoping to grab the gun from beneath him.

"Don't move."

I stopped, glancing around me. There was movement from the shadows, and then Jasper van Aust stepped into the moonlight. He was holding a bloody knife.

FORTY-THREE

———

"Jasper."

He looked even more crazed and emaciated than the last time I had seen him. Hair stuck up in clumps on his head, grown wild from a lack of grooming and basic maintenance. His skin was sallow, pale from what I could only assume was a lack of sunlight. He almost seemed to glow under the moonlight, a fragile, wounded creature unshackled from its tethers and uncertain how to behave. Jasper looked thin and malnourished, but there was a wild glint in his eye that told me I might not best him in a physical match. The scariest thing of all was that he didn't even seem to register Dane's body, which lay at his feet.

My mind tumbled through a few scenarios: I could make a break for it, running through the plantation, which was so overgrown I probably wouldn't make it ten feet without tripping over jungle vines. Or, crazier still, I could head into the proverbial briar patch and run back to the house. At the house, at least, there were other people, no matter how malicious or intoxicated. Surely Jasper wouldn't gut me in front of them. In every other direction, there was nothing but swamp, dense forest, and a road to nowhere.

"Jasper," I said. My voice went up as I could feel myself starting to hyperventilate. "Jasper, listen to me."

His voice was eerily calm. "You killed her. You killed Melia."

"No," I said carefully, keeping my eyes on the knife. My voice was high and wild, but I couldn't seem to calm it down. "I didn't kill her."

"I saw it on the news," he said. He spoke slowly, doling his words out one by one. "Everyone's looking for you."

"Her name is Hannah," I said in a rush. "I think she was a nurse at St. Agnes. Hannah killed your sister, Jasper."

"You're *lying!*" His hands tensed around the handle of the knife. Moonlight glinted off the blade. I turned to run, and then he lunged at me.

I didn't have time to do anything but drop to the ground and huddle in a ball. Jasper tripped over me, taken by surprise, and yelled as he went flying. I winced at the sudden impact, but there was no time to hesitate. I climbed awkwardly to my feet—the handcuffs made things difficult—and glanced at Jasper, who had landed on his stomach. The knife lay in the grass a few feet from where he lay. We both lunged toward it at the same time.

Jasper scrabbled through the grass and grabbed the knife, but I was quicker. I jumped and landed on the blade, pinning the knife to the ground with my shackled hands. We were at a standstill. Jasper growled up at me.

"You can kill me," I said. "But then you'll never know who did it. They'll be free for the rest of their lives, and you'll have—what? You'll always wonder."

"Stop talking. *Stop talking! You shut your mouth!*"

"She was a nurse from the rehab center," I said, trying to calm my breaths. I was on the verge of hyperventilating. "Two staff, actually. One of them looked like Melia. I have her passport in my bag—oh, please, Jasper, just look."

His eyes flicked toward my bag.

"I have nothing to gain from this," I said, pleading. "*Nothing.* Take me to her house and we'll find her together. Or kill me now, the choice is yours. They'll go free."

He took rapid breaths.

"It's in my bag. Jasper—"

"Shut up!" Jasper screamed all of a sudden. *"Shut your mouth! Shut your mouth!"*

There was a noise from the house behind us. The front door opened, and Jasper and I both went still, listening.

"Jasper?" Belinda's wavery voice called. "Jazzy, is that you?"

Jasper was quiet for a moment, then he called out.

"It's all right, Aunty Bel," he said. "I'm coming."

The meaning of the quick exchange was not lost on me. Belinda had known where Jasper was this entire time; she had been hiding him at her rotting old plantation while the police in Los Angeles continued to search for him. All these years, he had been holed up with his aunt.

"Don't stay out in the dark," Belinda called back. "There are snakes, you know!"

We both went still again until the front door closed, and silence closed around us. Then Jasper moved very quickly, catching me off guard. He pushed me backward and grabbed the knife. I screamed involuntarily as he jumped on top of me, then reached into my bag, pulling the passports out.

"Shut up!" he hissed. "I told you to be quiet!"

He flipped through the passports, falling silent as he examined the pictures.

"She looks *nothing* like Melia," he said finally.

It was a lie, and I could hear from the hesitation in Jasper's voice that he saw it too: the resemblance between Hannah and Melia, with or without the scar and black hair. They had the same heart-shaped face, elfin features, wide eyes. In the passport photo, Hannah had an edge that Melia lacked, a hunger—a hunger I had mistaken for a childhood of trauma.

"The scar," I said, squeezing my eyes closed again. It would be very dangerous to try to reason with Jasper, to point out their similarities. "She gave herself a scar just like your sister's. That's all that anybody saw when they looked at her. Jasper, please."

We were on a time limit. If Dane really had called the police and told them he was bringing me in, they would expect us to walk through the doors any minute. If we didn't come—and we wouldn't—it was only a matter of time before they came out to Tallowood to look for us. Jasper threw the passports on the ground in disgust.

"Look," I said. "The police may be here any minute. The man you killed called them to let them know I was here. Jasper—the police have been looking for you for *years*. Regardless of what you do with me, they're going to take you in."

His face finally registered some alarm.

"We don't have time to argue," I pressed. "We can go there together. It's only a matter of time before Melia—sorry, before Hannah finds another way to leave the country."

He thought about this for a second, then seemed to oblige. I watched him rifle through his pockets and produce a car key. I felt a faint stir of revulsion looking at Jasper's hands, which were long and pale with filthy fingernails.

"Get the keys to the handcuffs," I told him. "I'll take you there. I'll take you to Hannah's house."

Jasper went over to Dane's body and searched through his pockets until he found the keys. I took advantage of his distraction to snatch the discarded passports, then stash them in my pocket. I was going to need them if I ever planned to dig myself out of this mess. Jasper hesitated, crouched over on the grass, then stood. He now held Dane's gun, which he trained on me.

He was quiet for a long time, then marched over to me and grabbed my elbow. "If you try anything—anything!—I'll shoot you through the back of your head."

FORTY-FOUR

—◦◦◦—

The car keys belonged to the old Mercedes-Benz parked next to the house. I half-expected Belinda or Laura to come barreling out at the sound of the car engine, but nobody materialized. The meaning was perfectly obvious to me: Jasper's presence was well-established at Tallowood, and he was free to come and go as he pleased. I allowed myself one more hateful thought toward Laura before focusing back on the task at hand.

I couldn't be sure Hannah was actually at her house, and in some ways, I thought it unlikely. A small part of me didn't mind though; I was done fighting. I was just too tired. It had been days since I had gotten a proper night of sleep, and my head kept bobbing as I drove, struggling to stay awake. Every once in a while, I would glance in the rearview mirror and see Jasper's crazy eyes trained on me.

"Eyes on the road," he would growl. "Keep driving, you."

At one point the warm night air lulled me into such a comfortable state that I actually started to drift across the center divide. Jasper hit me in the head with the butt of the gun.

"Ow! What the hell?"

"Stay awake!" he snapped. "No funny business."

Hannah's address was at the end of a long rural road that led past an overgrown cemetery. There were no lights anywhere, and the air was filled with the sounds of frogs and cicadas. The moon waded out of the eastern horizon, illuminating everything below. The noise of nature was almost oppressive, and I couldn't even hear myself think.

Then, to my surprise, I saw lights. I didn't know how Hannah and Chet had managed to get back to Georgia, but then again, if the cops weren't looking for them—and why would they be?—there was nothing preventing them from coming home. It might have been the safest place in the world for them; since all the police activity was back in Los Angeles, the best thing to do might've been fleeing back home.

I pulled the car up to the side of the road and parked.

"What are you doing?" Jasper hissed.

"I can't park right out front," I pointed out. "They'll hear us coming."

"So?"

I slowly turned around, and Jasper pointed the gun at my face. His eyes were wide and frightened, his face pale in the moonlight. Jasper was twenty, but in some ways he looked much younger, small and defenseless away from his aunt's house. I wondered how often he had ventured out of the house, and guessed it hadn't been much. His existence for the last four years had probably been a suffocating, claustrophobic one, with only his aunt and Melia for company—and perhaps the staff, since some of them must have known about his presence.

"I'll go in and talk to them," I said, trying to force some kindness into my voice.

"No," Jasper said. His eyes darted toward the house, then back to me. An unacknowledged truth existed between us then: Jasper was out of his depth. The best way for me to defuse the situation was to speak to him calmly, slowly, and escort him toward the exit, so to speak.

There was still a chance that whoever was inside the house would not, in fact, be Hannah or Chet. The only option I had to get away from Jasper and contact the police lay beyond the house; I needed to leave Jasper behind.

"Jasper," I said quietly. "Listen to me. I bet Hannah and Chet both have guns. If *you* go in, they'll kill you on the spot."

The last bit was partly a bluff; I didn't know how many guns they had.

"If I walk in though," I continued, "and if they kill me, then you can go in afterward and catch them by surprise. They won't expect us to show up together."

He was quiet, and I glanced in the rearview mirror. He looked like he might be mulling it over.

"You're working together," he said, finally. "You and that girl. You planned all this out."

I sighed, irritated. "They tried to *frame me* for Melia's murder," I said. "Right now there's a nationwide manhunt for me. We didn't plan any of this, not together. *This* was their idea all along."

"You've got five minutes," he said. "And then I'm coming in after you."

I held up my handcuffs. "Can you uncuff me, at least?"

"Not a chance."

The house was a ramshackle little place with a deep front porch and columns. A couch sat on the porch, and the elements had long ago eaten through most of the fabric and padding. I could hear country music drifting out the open windows, all twangy chords and melancholy voices, and I noted a car parked in the driveway. The car was a beat-up white sedan, ten or fifteen years old.

I had been in some dangerous situations before, but I had never felt so certain that I was about to die. There was almost a peaceful solemnity in that realization, and since my anxiety had peaked long before, I almost felt numb. I crossed the road, my hands cuffed in front of me, then drew a deep breath. Behind me was a deranged young man with a knife and a gun. Ahead of me lay the uncertainty of whatever was behind the door, and probable death if it turned out to be Hannah and Chet.

I knocked.

If I'd been capable of feeling any sort of satisfaction at all, I would have felt it then, when Chet opened the door and stood staring at me in shock and confusion. His jaw actually dropped open, which under any other circumstances might have been comical.

"Who is it?" Hannah called from a room somewhere in the back.

Chet stared at me, unable to summarize me into a quick sentence. I could see past Chet into the room, where Hannah sat at a table. Her attention was focused on a map unfolded on the table.

"I'm coming in," I said in an even voice. "Don't shoot me."

Hannah glanced up from the table and did a double take, then leaped out of her chair. She looked just as shocked as Chet, but she recovered more quickly. She laughed as she picked up a gun from the table.

"Damn, girl," she said finally. "I have to fucking respect you for this."

"Your voice," I said. "It sounds different."

"This *is* my voice, darlin'."

She had changed, and my heart jumped to see the difference. The young woman I had known back in Los Angeles fell asleep in silk gowns, took off heavy diamond earrings, and left them in places she was bound to forget them. The young woman in front of me looked harder somehow. My eyes scanned her, trying to scrutinize exactly what was different. Hannah's skin no longer had a pearly glow; she looked wan and hungry. She wore an oversized blue oxford shirt, the cuffs rolled up to her elbows, and denim shorts. On anyone else the outfit might have seemed too casual, but the woman in front of me retained an air of incidental elegance. She was still beautiful.

Her dark hair floated just above her shoulders, a messy hack job. All that lovely hair that had once tumbled down her back was gone. In spite of everything, Hannah's gray eyes were calm and looked almost wise.

"You're either really brave or really fucking stupid," she said, shaking her head at me. There was something like admiration in her voice. "How did you even get here? The entire country is looking for you. Big reward, I hear."

"Turn me in and you'll get it."

"Ha! Wouldn't you like that." She looked me up and down, sizing me up. "Oh, Rainey. *Rainey.* I underestimated you."

"I'm curious," I said with more confidence than I felt. "How are you going to hide that scar? It's the first thing anyone will notice about you, wherever you go."

Hannah didn't respond, and as her eyes drifted over me, I wondered if she had even heard the question.

"You know," she said slowly, "when I hired a female detective agency, I thought it would be run by a bunch of power-hungry dilettantes trying to prove themselves on an uneven playing field. I'm sorry, Rainey. Truly. I was wrong about you."

"You hired a female detective agency because all the men turned you down," I corrected.

"Nuh-uh. I called you on a recommendation from one of the other agencies, but not because they turned me down. I told them I wanted a more personal experience. Better customer service."

"You thought we'd have fewer resources," I guessed, translating.

"Right again," she said, admiration in her voice. "If I had any sense left in me, I'd shoot you right now before you talk me out of it."

She pointed the gun at my heart.

"You're not going to shoot me," I said.

"Why's that?"

"I have something you want."

"She's got our fucking passports," Chet muttered, just as Hannah held up her hand.

"Be quiet, Chet."

"They sent me here to make a deal with you," I said, raising my hands to show them the cuffed wrists. "The Georgia police and the FBI are waiting outside."

"Bullshit," Hannah said, dropping down into a chair. She seemed perfectly at ease. "You came here by yourself."

I raised an eyebrow, trying to summon an ironic tone. "You think I *walked* all the way *here* from Savannah with my hands cuffed just for fun?"

One of the only good things that alcohol ever did for me was teach me how to lie. You can't drink throughout the day and keep a semblance of a normal life unless you know how to lie.

Hannah thought this over. "There's no one out there," she said, but she didn't sound certain. "Chet, go look."

"Like hell I'm going," he said, alarmed. "They'll shoot me as soon as I open the door!"

"Why would they send *you*?" Hannah asked, cocking her head at me. I was having trouble separating her from the woman I had thought I knew; it was hard for me not to think of her as Melia. I had never known Melia, at least not in life. The real Melia didn't exist for me beyond the edges of a photograph. *She's not real,* I told myself as I watched Hannah, because as much as I fucking hated myself for it, I wanted her to put the gun down and soften.

"I made a deal, that's why," I said, then shrugged. "Didn't take long for them to find me. If I help them bring you in, I might get off with probation."

"Open the door and show me," she said, cocking the gun and pointing it at me. She narrowed her eyes. "Show me all those agents waiting outside."

I didn't raise my hands in the air the way she was probably expecting me to. Instead, I walked over to the couch and dropped onto it.

"I'm exhausted," I said, and it was true. "I could almost fall asleep right now."

Chet and Hannah exchanged a glance. Neither one of them seemed to know how to react.

"This couch is so comfortable," I went on, curling my feet under me. "That's the thing about modern art furniture—it's all angles and wood. Same goes for everything at Slant House, really. Beautiful and unwelcoming."

"We can pay you," Chet said. "Tell them we're not here, and we'll pay you."

Hannah aimed the gun at him and growled. "Didn't I tell you to keep your mouth shut?"

"I don't want money," I said, closing my eyes. "I just want to fall asleep."

I hadn't meant to actually fall asleep, but once I closed my eyes, I couldn't seem to open them again. I was so exhausted from days of no sleep, so strung out from all the adrenaline and confrontation that I had more or less given up. And so, when I closed my eyes, my brain took over and I drifted off.

There's a state between consciousness and sleep when your mind plays tricks on you. Characters and images emerge from the edges of your mind, memories of a day that didn't happen. I always thought of this state as dream skating, when you're still hovering somewhere at the surface, unsure of whether or not you're ready to fall completely asleep. There can be something unsafe about this time, the sense that your body isn't quite ready to release to unconsciousness. It's not restful, not at all, and if you don't manage to plunge into full sleep, you'll wake up more tired than before.

Something in me jerked me back to consciousness, and I blinked my eyes open to see Hannah and Chet staring at me in mute consternation. I almost laughed: my sleepiness was not an act, but it had caught them off guard. Now they were on the back foot more surely than if I had come in with a brilliant bluff.

"Wake up!" Hannah said. Her voice was wild, unsteady. "I have a gun, and I will not hesitate to shoot you."

I sat up. I wasn't sure how much time had passed, how long I had before Jasper came in and started shooting at random.

"I had it backward," I said, nodding to Chet. "I thought you were the mastermind behind this whole thing, and Hannah just went along with it because you scared her. Now I see I had it all wrong. She's got her fist clenched around your balls, nice and tight."

The slap came faster than I anticipated. The back of Chet's hand connected with my right cheek, slamming me back into the couch. Now I was wide-awake. I spat some blood onto the floor. If nothing else, at least I had managed to leave some DNA for the forensics team to find.

"You know, my team didn't think much of you," I said, glancing at Hannah. "They should have given you more credit."

She narrowed her eyes at me. "How's that?"

"It must have taken months of planning," I said. "I mean, how long did it take that scar to heal?"

Her fingers drifted up to her chest. "Nine months."

"You thought ahead, didn't you?" She glanced at Chet, uncertain. "Or was it all Chet's idea?"

"It was my idea," she said sharply.

"I guess that makes sense," I said. "You kept telling me how stupid Chet was, how the only thing he was good for was providing a gun and a getaway car."

Chet's face went dark, and Hannah looked confused, then furious. "I never said that," she said. "Shut your fucking mouth." She aimed the gun at me again. "I'm tired of talking."

"You know as soon as you fire that gun, they'll come in here shooting."

She hesitated long enough for me to know she believed me. She let the gun drop.

"What do you want?" she said finally. "You don't expect us to actually leave with you, do you?"

"What I want to know is," I said, "was it all fake to you? All of it—even the times when you said you were lonely? I mean, I thought there was chemistry between us."

Her gray eyes were fixed on my face. "You were wrong."

"Just one last question, and I'll go without a struggle," I said. "Where'd you put all the jewelry?"

From the look on Hannah's face, I knew it was exactly the right thing to say.

"What jewelry is she talking about?" Chet growled.

"That was the point all along, wasn't it? Ten million dollars' worth of jewelry? Or did I get that figure wrong?"

Hannah smashed the gun against my head so fast I saw stars. I slammed back into the couch, my vision dark and blurry. I could feel my left eye swelling shut.

"You shut your fucking mouth," she hissed.

"Hannah, what is she talking about?" Chet crossed the room and pointed his gun at her. "You said there was no jewelry!"

Hannah's eyes went wild. "She's lying," she said desperately. "There was no jewelry. You and I searched the entire house from top to bottom. There was nothing—"

Chet's eyes flicked between us. He looked wild, apt to start shooting at any moment.

"I'm so sorry," I said, feigning shock. "I just assumed you had told Chet. Why else would he be here? Unless, of course, you were going to kill him as soon as you got out of the country."

Chet cocked his gun.

"I'm telling you, there is no jewelry! You believe her?" Hannah gave an incredulous laugh, but I heard the fear behind her voice. "Listen to me, baby—the family was completely broke. We looked everywhere in the house, and there was nothing. Right? Remember? It doesn't make any sense!"

"The only thing that makes sense," Chet said slowly, "is that you two were planning to run off together. You fell in love with her, Hannah."

Hannah let out a terrified laugh edged with incredulity. "Listen to yourself! Chet, that's crazy!"

"It wouldn't be the first time!" he screamed, aiming the gun at her. "You've slept with other whores before her! You're lying to me! You're fucking lying to me!"

The gunshot took me by surprise, and I screamed and covered my head. When I glanced up again, it was impossible to tell who had shot at whom:

both Hannah and Chet remained standing, guns drawn, looks of shock on both faces. Then Chet glanced down.

"You shot me?" His voice was sweet and baffled. "You really shot me?"

Hannah dropped her gun and crossed the distance between them. "You didn't give me a choice!"

He dropped his gun and put both hands to his abdomen. They came away bloody. He laughed, stunned, and looked at Hannah.

"It's okay," she said. "It's fine. We'll get you to a hospital."

Both guns were on the floor now. I knew I should move to grab one of them, but I was rooted to my seat. I didn't want to draw attention to myself—I was far enough away from both guns that Hannah could still make a quick move and grab one first. I had no doubt whatsoever that if she came to her senses, she would shoot me between the eyes.

Chet started crying. "I don't wanna die," he said. "Oh god, Hanny, don't let me die!"

I saw my chance and lunged toward the gun closest to me. Hannah saw and twisted her head toward me, but she didn't move quickly enough. I swiped the gun from the floor and pointed it at her.

"Don't move," I said. I kicked the other gun across the room so she couldn't pick it up.

She stood slowly, leaving Chet on the floor. He was still clutching his stomach, but his face had gone completely white. I had never seen someone in so much pain.

"I'm leaving," Hannah told me. "You're not going to stop me."

"You sure?"

"Go on and shoot me then," she said, raising her hands in the air. "You only get one chance."

"Sit down," I said. My voice was a lot calmer than I felt—my heart was pounding so wildly that I thought I might have a panic attack. "I'm calling 911. They can still save his life if they get here in time."

A look of understanding passed over her face. "I knew it," she said. "*Goddamn* it. They were never here."

Chet's eyes were closed, and his face had gone gray.

"You can still save his life," I said, nodding at Chet.

"Save *what* life?" She shook her head at me. "What do you think will happen once they fix him up? He'll spend the rest of his days in jail."

"You're probably right," I said. "It's better than bleeding out in this deserted shack though."

I could see her considering her options.

"You didn't even know Melia," she said slowly. "I probably knew her better than anyone. She was sick, Rainey. Sick in ways you couldn't imagine."

"Of course she was," I said. "You can hardly blame her for that. She came from a twisted family, and she must have lost her mind when they were killed."

Hannah was slowly shaking her head, giving me a look of pity. "You really have no idea, do you?" she said.

I hesitated—just for a second, but she caught it.

"She confessed," Hannah said. "Melia told me everything herself. She had a lot of things to be guilty about. That's the reason her lawyer sent her to us, after all—he had a feeling she was going to break the story wide open. St. Agnes has a sort of reputation for setting wayward children straight."

"What did she have to be guilty for?"

"You know why Jasper went to that school in Utah? It was all the things Melia did to him. Catalina von Faber isn't as stupid as she looks, Rainey. She was right about their twisted relationship."

An image flashed through my mind, and I cringed away from it. "You're sick," I said. "I'm calling the police."

"That's the real reason she wanted to kill her parents," Hannah went on. She was edging closer to me. "She didn't like being told what to do. She was always a bad seed, that one, but you could hardly blame her. That was true, that part of it: her mother had always hated her. Remember all those stories I told you about Melia's mother abusing her? They were true, mostly."

"Those were your scars, *your* body. Not hers."

Hannah gave me a pale smile. "I didn't lie about everything, you know. Some of the stories I told you were mine."

I felt cold all over. "You're saying Melia killed her parents? How did she get her scar then?"

"Jasper did that." Her face was calm, unreadable. It was impossible to know if she was telling the truth.

"Bullshit," I said softly.

"No," Hannah said, shaking her head. "Scout's honor. Jasper managed to break out of school. That part was true. He was home on the day his parents died, and I guess there was some big family argument. Melia convinced him the only way for them to be together was if they killed their parents, but I guess partway through, one of them had a change of heart . . . I didn't get the whole story. Jasper was a violent, confused little shit. Then again, I can't exactly blame him for trying to kill Melia. She was really twisted herself, and if you'd ever met her, you'd know she probably deserved to die."

"What would you have done if we had actually found Jasper? Did you think that far ahead?"

"I *wanted* you to find him," Hannah said. Her voice was encouraging, that of a proud parent. "I really thought you could too. It's always pissed me off the way rich white men get away with murder. Do you think it's fair, after everything he did, that he just got to live his life in peace?"

I was aware she was pulling me down a rabbit hole, the type of slippery diversion invented by self-righteous criminals. It was the type of cagey rationale used by fanatics—fanatics who were convinced the means justified the end, regardless of how many innocent lives they dragged down along with them. Hannah didn't think she had done anything wrong.

"What if he had recognized you? He would have seen through your disguise in an instant."

"Oh, Rainey," Hannah said, shaking her head with disappointment. "You were there to protect me. It's not like you would have brought him back to the house. You would have gone straight to the police with your prize. Jasper van Aust? You would have been famous after that."

"I never wanted to be famous," I said softly.

"You're a better person than some."

Something was echoing through my head, a memory that didn't quite want to dislodge itself. I closed my eyes.

"Zac," I said, remembering. "Zac said—oh, god. It was you, wasn't it?"

Hannah looked confused for a moment, frowning.

"You set him up," I said. "You might as well admit it, Hannah."

I saw a look of comprehension spread across her face, and she started laughing. "Oh, right! The neighbor! Fuck, he was annoying. You know he kept coming over, even after we put the security system in? Little shit wouldn't leave me alone. Of course, if he'd ever seen me he would have known I wasn't Melia . . . I couldn't have that. I didn't know why he kept coming back until you said I had something that belonged to him . . . I looked all over the house and found those drugs stitched into her mattress."

"Oh my god," I whispered. "I can't *believe* I ever trusted you."

"There must be some reason for that," she said, her voice kind. "Come on, Rainey. You're not happy. Admit it—there was *something* about me that made you want to give up on everything else. We have a connection."

"Stop talking."

"It's not too late for us," Hannah continued, giving me a wild smile. "They're hunting you, too, Rainey—remember that. We can still get away. There's still time."

I hesitated—not for long, but long enough. Hannah's smile grew even wider.

"You were never happy there," she said, moving closer to me. "Los Angeles has nothing for you. We can leave all of that behind. We could go anywhere. *Anywhere*. Rainey—you have a choice. It all comes down to this."

Chet's hands slid away from his stomach. I took my phone out of my pocket, fumbling to hold onto the gun at the same time, and kept an eye on Hannah as I dialed 911.

"This is an emergency," I said, when the operator answered. I had to pin the phone to my ear; because of the handcuffs, I couldn't train the gun on Hannah and use my phone at the same time. "My name is Rainey Hall, and I'm at the end of Sweetwater Road, just outside Keller. It's a dilapidated little cottage, the only one for about a mile. Someone's been shot, and he needs medical attention. Send the police as well."

Hannah shook her head after I hung up. I kept the gun trained on her.

"What do you think is going to happen when they see you?" she said. "They're not going to listen to you. You're a wanted fugitive. You've got a gun, and you already killed Chet."

"I didn't kill him."

"The bullet came from the gun you're holding."

I could hear sirens. They were faint, but it sounded like they were getting closer.

"We still have time," Hannah urged. "You and I can leave together. I have contacts. I have plenty of money. All that jewelry—we can split it. The connection we had was real, Rainey. *We can disappear.*"

"I don't do that anymore."

"Who are you protecting?" she said, exasperated. "Melia? Jasper? That family was rotten to the core!"

The sirens were louder now, but Hannah almost didn't seem to hear them.

"You're so smart," I said, shaking my head. "You could have been anything—why did you choose this?"

"I don't expect you to understand," she said, shaking her head. "Not every kid gets Paris and Copenhagen."

I was still aiming the gun at her heart.

"You're just like me, you know," she said with a little smile. "No matter what happens, we're the same."

"I would never do what you did."

"Of course you would," she said.

"When did you do it?" I asked. We were running out of time. "When did you actually kill her?"

Hannah didn't respond.

"Tell me," I urged. "You have nothing to lose now."

"We came to Los Angeles together," she said.

"And?"

"A few days before I met you," she said. "I needed her. She had to be the one to fire the Endos, of course, because I never would have fooled them. They'd known her forever."

"What did you say to make her trust you?" I said. "Didn't she notice that you had the same scar?"

"Of course not. I hid it from everyone."

"So what did you tell her?" I pressed.

"She needed someone who would kill Jasper," Hannah said. "They were still sleeping together, even just a few months ago, at the aunt's place. She was done, but she couldn't kill him. I said I would do it for her."

The sirens were right outside the house now, but I didn't think Hannah even heard them. She didn't hear the door open behind her because it all happened too quickly. The only thing I saw was Jasper's face, those wild eyes. The anger and disbelief in them was enough to tell me he had heard everything.

The last thing Hannah saw was my face. There was one brief moment of understanding as the gunshot reverberated around the small house. I rushed forward to catch her body before she fell. She was so much smaller than I had realized, almost weightless in my arms. I didn't look away from her face as the walls seemed to fall around us, as a dozen police officers burst in through the door and surrounded Jasper, who was still holding the gun, who didn't let go or stand down or look away from my face as the gunshots filled the air around us.

FORTY-FIVE

ONE WEEK LATER

Blake was waiting outside when Lola and I emerged from the squat, non-descript building at the edge of Westwood Village.

"Please don't ask," I said when we got closer. "For the love of god, let's get out of here."

"Dinner?" Blake suggested. "Have you guys eaten anything?"

"Trail mix and candy bars from the vending machine," Lola said, putting a hand on my back. "Should we eat around here, or do you want to drive somewhere else?"

"Here," I said, cutting off further discussion. "I don't care where. I'm ready to sit down."

"She's a bit cranky," Lola whispered to Blake, and I pretended not to hear. "It's been a long day."

I let them lead the way toward Westwood, which was crowded with students and people out looking to have a good time. The streets buzzed with neon signs and lingering heat. The last of the daylight drained into the western sky, punctured by the Santa Monica Mountains, a black and blue landscape. Everything smelled like Mexican food and car exhaust.

I dropped out of the conversation as Lola and Blake moved ahead of me on the sidewalk. It had been a long day, that was true, but it had also been one of the longest weeks of my life. It felt like a year since I had returned from Savannah. After the police arrived at Hannah's ramshackle cottage, everything had happened in quick succession.

In some ways I was surprised I had managed to navigate it all: I spent the night at the Savannah police station, where I had the chance to speak to Lola. As my legal representation, Lola wouldn't allow me to speak to anyone else until I was back in Los Angeles, where we reunited at an FBI building, accompanied by about a dozen police officers from both Georgia and Los Angeles.

I would be forever grateful to Lola for shielding me from some of the worst parts of the aftermath. I hadn't been able to get a full night's sleep since I returned to Lola's guest bedroom; every time I drifted off I saw Hannah's face as she collapsed in my arms, again and again and again. On nights when I didn't sleep, though, all I could think about was Jasper.

"Rainey?"

I glanced up and realized Lola and Blake were watching me, concerned.

"Sorry, what happened?"

"Does this place look good? It's Peruvian food. I've been here with my family . . ."

"Whatever you want."

I followed them into the brightly colored restaurant that was about the size of a walk-in closet. We claimed the last table at the back of the restaurant. I let Blake and Lola pick up the menus and pore over the choices. My mind was elsewhere.

"Hey," Lola said, putting a hand on my arm. "It's almost over. Just hang on a little bit longer."

Three days before, we had gotten word from the police in Georgia. Jasper had been on life support after being shot by the police, but sometime in the night, his heart had given out. If anything, that complicated matters even further; he was the last remaining member of the van Aust family, and now that he was gone, there was no one to bear witness to what had really happened that night in Los Angeles all those years ago.

Tell it to me one more time. It had been the theme of the week. I had repeated the sequence of events so many times that I almost felt like I was playing a role, parroting a line reading of a performance I had witnessed years before. *And after that—but what happened before—which day was this?—can you remember, specifically, what Hannah was wearing when you met her?*

Everyone had been questioned, but they had all been given shorter interviews. Janine was hauled in, as were the Endos. Turned out, Hannah had been telling the truth about at least one thing in the end: the real Melia had sent Katsumi and Caroline away, insisting their services were no longer needed. None of the other things were true though; Caroline had never blackmailed the van Aust family or gouged them for money. If anything, the Endos had been better parental figures to the van Aust children than their real parents.

The food arrived on the table, jolting me out of my thoughts.

"I will die on that hill," Blake was saying. "Jimmy Eat World was *not* a one-hit wonder. If anything, 'The Middle' was the least ambitious song on that album. *Bleed American* rocks, man."

"Is that ceviche?" I took a bowl from the middle of the table, and Blake and Lola looked up, startled.

"Yeah, it's really good," Lola said. "That's what I got here last time."

That day had been a turning point in the questioning process. Lola had successfully convinced the police that I had been in no way beholden to Melia or the van Aust family, that if a seasoned professional like Paul Karnak, who had known Melia most of her life, had been fooled into trusting Hannah, then I didn't stand a chance and shouldn't be punished for any part of the affair. The sticking point for the FBI had been the fact that I had fled instead of handing myself in, but Lola quickly pointed out that if I had done that, I would still be in jail awaiting trial while Hannah slipped through the cracks, never to be seen again.

I left the restaurant early, telling Lola and Blake I was exhausted after the long day. When I got into my car to head back to Echo Park, however, I found I was too keyed up to drive back to Lola's place and fall asleep. Instead, I drove back toward Los Feliz. I wasn't going to drive past Slant House; it would be too much. Instead I took one of the wide boulevards into Griffith Park, then eased my car along the narrow road that led up to one of the lookouts.

Something pulled me back to Griffith Park again and again, even though it was one of the biggest tourist draws in the city. It was the lid of Los Angeles, one of the highest points you could reach and see everything below you collapsing into a crinkled map, the skyscrapers just little spires and the suburbs and freeways nothing more than embroidered points on the fabric of the city. Everything seemed small, but more than that, it all felt accessible. Everyone was reduced to pinpricks of light, too small to see from this vantage point.

From this distance, the city could sometimes feel like a dark, glittering cathedral. Close up, the magic wore off a little, and the city no longer felt like a mirage. There were the dark parts, the seedy underbelly and the abandoned buildings, but there was something I liked about how Los Angeles didn't try to hide its dark side or gloss over it. Deep down it was a city without façades, reveling in its own dirty humor.

I sat there until the sun had crawled into the ocean, leaving a smear of orange light around the rim of the sky. The smog and haze above the city still held the dying sunset, and then one by one, lights started to go on all over the city, shrugging off the oncoming darkness.

From this distance, nothing held meaning or nuance, nothing was open to interpretation. From here, dark spaces could indicate the last remaining wild patches of the city, the slowly shrinking spots that hadn't yet been developed, transformed, turned into something else. Strip malls occupied the spaces where pioneer children and their fortune-seeking parents had once strewn seeds, picked oranges, tilled land. The decades overlapped, dwindled down to concrete and westward expansion, one eager thing replacing another. Grand old mansions collapsed and rotted away, got torn down to build condominiums. Old stars were tossed to the side when they could no longer perform.

This vantage point offered one of the best views of the city: flat winding ribbons were roads, which funneled and tapered into poisonous clusters of cancerous light, hubs and highways. As evening turned into night, the city took on a friendly glow, lights winking on one by one. From this distance, none of it seemed real.

Somewhere out there, in all that light and dark, my mother was putting her new child to bed. As I sat there, shivering against the unexpected night chill, I allowed myself to picture that tableau: my mother, tucking her hair behind her ears, kneeling beside a child's bedside to whisper nursery rhymes, lullabies, night fables. An unspoken promise—*I'll love you forever and a day*—the assurance of stability, of permanence. But nothing lasted forever, especially not in Los Angeles, where each decade slipped in to replace the one that came before. The city was a blank canvas, an empty memory, waiting until sunrise to reinvent itself anew. It was a city that encouraged stories, pretty lies, new names, smokescreens, and disguises.

I sat there for another hour in silence, looking up at the night sky, hoping to see a handful of stars. The city lights were too bright though, the haze in the air too heavy. The constellations remained hidden, obscured by what lay beneath them.

I got back into my car and drove down the mountain.